I0743516

Cowboys and Crowns Collection

PART 2

LACY WILLIAMS

Kissing Kelsey

Chapter One

Seated in the economy class on a cross-country flight, the man repeated his name silently, trying to impress it on his mind. His head pounded. The military doctors told him the constant headache was caused by the roadside bombing, but he thought maybe the pain was a result of trying to make anything stick to the whirling blackness inside his brain.

Amnesia.

He stared out the window into the darkness and wished he could see more than occasional lights miles below, something to focus on besides the seat in front of his and the fact that he'd lost his memory, his sense of self. At least the landscape had some flickering lights. Inside his brain, there was hardly that.

The docs hadn't been able to tell him when his memory would return. He got snatches of things. Two young boys laughing wildly atop a huge round hay bale. Himself? Then who was the other boy?

Another time, he'd seen an image of a young girl hugging a kitten, tears standing in her eyes. He had no idea who she was.

The military was sending him home to north Texas. *The Triple H Ranch. HHH. Hale Hale Hale?*

Other than the doctors, there'd been little traffic to his private hospital room. He'd only been visited by one soldier who had seemed to be a friend, a guy in fatigues about his own age. How old was that, anyway? Mid-twenties? Jimmy had told him he had a sister and brother back home, but not much more. The docs had interrupted the meeting, and at the time, Matt hadn't minded a bit. It had been everything he could do to stay awake through the pounding pain.

He should have asked Jimmy more questions.

Home. He didn't know what that felt like, not with the yawning emptiness inside him. Did he have a girlfriend? A house? A dog?

The airplane shuddered and groaned, and the man's anxiety spiked. His stomach was a tight ball of nerves, but did he hate flying? Or was this feeling simply a result of not knowing anything about himself, not knowing where he was going, not knowing what he was walking into?

He made himself look at his reflection in the scratched safety plastic of the oval window. Who was he? The dark hair, cut military-short, the dark eyes, the crags in his face, the scruff at his jaw. None of his features gave any answers. He didn't recognize the guy he saw in the reflection.

His ears popped as the plane descended. Everything happened too fast. He felt unprepared as the plane landed, as they taxied to a terminal, as the other passengers debarked. He didn't mind waiting. He didn't know what he was going to face when he got off the plane.

He was the last one off, nodding his thanks to the tired-looking stewardess waiting near the door.

The terminal was quiet. Many of the storefronts and restaurants had closed for the night. Only the bar had a few patrons. As he passed it, the blaring TVs and fluorescent lights gave his brain a twang like out-of-tune guitar strings. He saw stars in his vision.

Dread pressed in on him until he couldn't breathe. He sidled to the terminal wall and bent, resting his hands on his knees and panting through the pain in his head and the flashing stars.

An eternity.

Finally, it passed.

The man straightened, thankful that there was no one around to witness his mini-breakdown. The people in the bar seemed totally focused on their drinks and whatever game was on the TVs overhead. All the other passengers had gone.

He had no sense of direction, though he must've flown in and out of this airport numerous times before. He watched the signs, followed them toward the baggage claim, though he hadn't shipped any bags. The olive-green duffel over his shoulder was all he'd traveled with. He'd been told that someone would meet him here to take him home. His sister, maybe? He couldn't remember. The information had flitted away in his exhaustion and overwhelm.

He just wanted to sleep. It wouldn't help his memory. He'd discovered that after waking up so many times wishing to know…more. Just more. But at least sleep would help with the physical exhaustion that drained every atom in his body.

He welcomed the escalator that took him down several flights. It was a moment he didn't have to walk. He passed a huge sign that read *Welcome to Texas!* and an ad for some kind of jeans that featured a pretty dark-haired model. He got a flash of memory, a split-second of a brown-haired teen girl with a soft smile.

He blinked, and the vision disappeared.

Just in time, too, because the escalator dumped him off at the bottom, and he almost tripped on the solid ground. He clutched the straps of his duffel to keep it from sliding off his shoulder.

The baggage claim area had a few more people than the terminal upstairs. Folks were clustered in small groups. Some hugged. One woman had her hands on her hips, grousing at her teenaged son. The luggage carousel chugged with a steady hum and carried the occasional bag.

He stood rooted in place, looking for anybody he recognized. Which was crazy because he couldn't even recognize himself. How could he know his sister, or whoever had come for him?

His stomach pitched and dipped as he scanned the room. And then someone rushed through the outside doors, letting in a gust of warm, dusty wind.

Her dark hair had blown into her face and obscured her

features. He could see her frustration in the impatient flick of her hand to clear the locks away.

Her caramel eyes came to rest on him, and it seemed as if his brain seized up. Pain winged through his cranium, and he couldn't help wincing as something inside connected.

Kelsey Whitley.

Kelsey.

His heart pounded, and he felt heat flush up his neck and into his face as he stared at her. Memories slid into place like marbles pouring into a bucket.

His Kelsey.

Finally, one thing in his life made sense.

He strode toward her and, although she'd frozen in place, he had some sense that she was glad to see him.

He reached for her, pulled her into his arms. "Kelsey." Her name was barely a breath. And then he kissed her.

KELSEY WHITLEY MIGHT BE a world traveler, but nothing had prepared her for this trip to the Dallas airport.

She was in Matt's arms again. Nearly a decade after they'd broken up.

Other than a tinge of desperation, his kiss was the same as always. Sweet, tender. He tasted like Red Hots candy.

And it freaked her out. Her heart banged against her sternum, and her feet itched, like she was crouching in the blocks, waiting for the gun to go off.

She contained it. Barely.

She pushed off his chest, gently, because his sister Carrie had stressed the magnitude of his injuries during their brief phone conversation. *Amnesia. He almost died, was lucky to be alive.*

Kelsey didn't believe in luck.

Matt loosened his grip slightly, though one hand stayed clasped on her waist. The way he looked down at her... The intensity of his warm gaze made that itch to run so much worse.

"Kelsey." Her name was reverent on his lips, just like the way he'd whispered her name before he'd lowered his mouth to hers. "I remember you." But his eyebrows remained slightly pinched, as if he were trying to put a puzzle together without success.

Pulse thudding in her temples, all she could think to do was whisper back, "Is that a good thing?"

He smiled a lopsided, almost sad smile. "Considering I don't remember anything else, heck yeah."

He remembered her, but the proprietary hold on her waist meant he didn't remember everything. He obviously didn't remember that she'd left.

She needed some distance. Couldn't hurt him, not with how fragile Carrie said he still was, so she disentangled herself gently. "Do you have any luggage?"

He reached down to the floor where a duffel bag rested at his feet. Had he dropped it just before he pulled her into his arms? She hadn't noticed. "Just this."

She jerked her thumb toward the door. "Then let's get out of here. We've still got a couple hours to get you home."

He followed her out the doors and toward short-term parking. That act alone unnerved her—Matt Hale usually strode through life in the leadership position, confident in his command—but then he clasped her hand in his as they navigated the echoing, quiet parking garage. Her nose crinkled at the scents of oil and tire rubber.

"I'm glad you came, but I was told to expect Carrie. Or I thought maybe Gideon or Uncle Pat would pick me up."

Her heart dropped at the evidence of huge holes in his memory. His uncle had died six years ago. Mama and Katie had both called her in Houston with the news.

How could she tell him that, when he'd just arrived? She couldn't. So she settled for the easier thing.

"Gideon is overseas with his wife, a princess."

He turned to face her as she slowed near her sporty blue coup, one she'd been gifted by a car dealership after her Olympic silver medal. His face crumpled, and he pressed his fingers against the bridge of his nose.

"I knew that. Gideon came to see me in the military hospital. Stayed several days, until I was out of the woods." He dropped his hand, revealing the distress in his expression. "I still can't figure out what happened to the SEALs. He was supposed to be a lifer. And now he's married?"

She and Matt had been dating back in high school when

Gideon had gone into the military. But she'd been gone these last years when the princess had arrived in town, so she didn't know all the circumstances surrounding the marriage. She definitely didn't have an in with the family. The only reason Carrie had asked her to come tonight was because the woman had been desperate when she'd called. She'd been trying to reach Katie, but she was working a late-night shift at the café, so Carrie hadn't had any other options.

Kelsey shrugged helplessly. She tilted her head to the car, and he climbed in.

She sat beside him. "I'm sure Carrie can fill in some of the gaps." She cranked the key and the engine turned over with a quiet purr. "She was planning to come tonight, but Scarlett had a bad asthma attack, and they ended up at the ER."

"Who's Scarlett?"

"Your niece. Carrie's daughter...?" When his silence went on for two beats too long, she glanced at him long enough to get a glimpse of his face. His open-mouthed expression showed his shock.

"Carrie has a daughter," he whispered. Then, "Do we have any kids?"

He was so far off that it should've been comical, but there was nothing funny in the catch in his voice.

"Exactly how much do you remember?" she asked carefully.

He shook his head, rubbed his forehead with long, blunt fingers. "Not enough. When I saw you, some things just sort of... clicked into place."

That was scary.

"I remember a lot of our childhood. Fishing at the pond." With this, he sent her a genuine, sideways smile. Then, "And I remember your senior prom."

The bottom dropped out of her stomach. Matt was a year older, and she'd been proud to be on his arm. A college guy.

He'd kissed her in the moonlight—though he'd been careful not to go too far—and she'd said she loved him for the first time.

She could still remember the strength of his arms around her, the feeling of soaring because *Matt Hale loved her*. He'd said, *"When we get married..."* and her joy had turned to fear.

She'd hidden it then, and hidden it well, though prom night had been the beginning of the end.

"I can't remember your high school graduation, and I can't remember why I don't have a ring on your finger by now, but we were rock solid back then, and I can't imagine that changing."

Oh, Matt.

His calm confidence that they were still together shook her. She tried not to show it, firmed her grip on the steering wheel to stop her hands from trembling.

"You made it to the Olympics, right? Gold medal?"

That confidence in her had been magic when she was eighteen. When no one else in her life, not even her sister Katie, had believed in her.

Somehow, even though it was now undeserved, it still brought a hot knot to her throat. "Silver," she whispered.

In the dark, there was a slight reflection on the windshield and she saw a flash of white—his teeth—as he grinned.

He'd known she could make it to the Olympics, believed she could earn gold.

But he couldn't imagine a scenario where they didn't end up together.

She'd come tonight as a favor for Carrie, but what had she gotten herself into?

CARRIE HALE SAT at her daughter Scarlett's bedside in the quiet hospital room. The antiseptic smell burned her nose, and the quiet hum of machines and muted footsteps from the hallway had her restless.

Scarlett was sleeping, breathing more easily thanks to the oxygen they'd administered in the ER earlier. Her doctor had wanted to hospitalize the girl overnight for observation, just to make sure Scarlett didn't have another episode.

Carrie was glad for it. Maybe it was her imagination, but she was sure she could hear the faintest rattle in her daughter's chest.

Scarlett is all right. Maybe if Carrie repeated the words to herself enough times, she'd believe them.

So far, the awful panic she'd felt when Scarlett had been gasping for breath hadn't abated, even though Scarlett's color had come back, a beautiful peach-pink against the white hospital sheets and bed that dwarfed her tiny frame.

So many days, she knew she wasn't cut out for single parenting.

And then other days, she remembered why she hadn't been cut out for marriage, either.

Tonight, she was just plain exhausted. She'd been coming off an early morning bridal updo, several hours of trims and dyes, and one perm, all while Scarlett was at school. Carrie hadn't been expecting the cold snap, and she'd sent Scarlett to school with only a sweatshirt. And they'd had outside PE. And several of Scarlett's friends had colds. She was always careful to have Scarlett bulk up on vitamin C, but *germs...*

When she'd picked up her daughter from the babysitter, she'd known something was wrong. By the time they'd arrived at home, Scarlett's breathing had been labored, and it had been too late to administer an inhaler—though she'd tried.

Today's had not been her most stellar performance as a parent.

Her phone rang, distracting her from the whirl of awful thoughts. She didn't recognize the number but stepped away from the bed to the corner of the room and answered it anyway.

"Carrie? This is Kelsey. Kelsey Whitley."

As if she wouldn't know which Kelsey would be calling her. She'd been in such a panic earlier, on the way to the hospital with Scarlett, that she'd barely even registered that it had been Kelsey and not her friend Katie, Kelsey's older sister, who'd answered their home phone. If she'd had any choice at all, she never would've sent the girl who'd broken her brother's heart to pick him up from the airport. But she'd been desperate, and Kelsey had been available.

"How is he?" she asked.

"He's sleeping in the front seat of my car." Kelsey's voice wasn't accompanied by road noise. In fact, Carrie though she could make out the low of a cow. Had they already arrived back at the Triple H?

"He looks fine," Kelsey went on. "Fit and tan. He's still got some bruising at his hairline, and...he remembered me. Oh, hold on—"

He remembered. Was that a good thing or a bad thing? Her brother might kill her for sending Kelsey. No, he'd understand. He doted on Scarlett.

She'd been so worried about her brother since Gideon's call ten days ago from the military hospital overseas. It was a blessing that Gideon had been able to be with him, but Gideon had been called back to Glorvaird and wasn't able to fly home with Matt.

She had known that head injuries were dangerous, of course, but hadn't realized how much so until she'd started researching online. It had to be good that Matt remembered some things, right?

"He remembered the high school me. He thinks...well, he's got this wild idea that we're still together. He only seems to remember things up through senior prom. I...didn't have the heart to correct him."

What a nightmare. Poor Matt. "Don't. At least, not until I can get out there." *To pick up the pieces.*

Gideon had been overseas when Kelsey left. At that time, Carrie had been involved with the man who would become Scarlett's father. As star struck as she'd been, she could still remember the hollow look in Matt's eyes, the depression that had followed him around for months. If he had to relive all of that, she'd needed to be on hand.

"The doctors said his emotions might be fragile due to the head trauma, and I don't want anything..." *To hurt him.* Like Kelsey had before.

"Okay, I..." Kelsey's voice trailed off.

Carrie didn't know what to say either. She'd liked the girl when she and Matt had dated back in high school. Katie was still her friend. But she hated that Kelsey had hurt her brother, and she still felt a little *Mama Bear* about it all.

"Do you want me to stay with him tonight?"

No! Somehow, Carrie managed to modulate her voice. "No, thanks. Just grab one of the hands, they can help him inside."

Although, if he didn't remember the cowboys, that might make a bad situation worse. Hopefully Kelsey could smooth things over, because Carrie didn't have any more energy to take care of another human being.

"Thanks for picking him up," she said grudgingly.

She clicked off the line and pocketed her phone, then stood at the end of Scarlett's bed. It was late. She should bunk down on the cot the nurse had brought her, but her mind continued to froth and foam. She knew she wouldn't sleep. She was a bad sleeper when she wasn't at home and in her own bed. And sometimes not even then.

A soft knock at the door sounded. It creaked open.

"Trey?"

Her traitor heart did a little pitter-patter as the Triple H cowboy stuck his head inside.

Scarlett shifted in her bed. The last thing Carrie needed was her daughter waking up and seeing Trey, so Carrie headed him off at the door and nudged him into the hall. She closed the door behind them with a soft click.

She pressed her hands into the cool wood at her back, leaning against them in case she had the urge to reach for him. "What are you doing here?"

He took off his Stetson and tapped it against his thigh, a sign of his agitation. His other hand was behind his back. Maybe he was trying not to reach for her, too.

She hadn't seen him in over a month, and the sight of his broad shoulders and familiar face made her want things she shouldn't. Why hadn't he stuck to their unofficial, unarticulated deal? When she had to visit the Triple H, he kindly disappeared. When he came to town, she made herself scarce. Should they happen to cross paths, they made polite, distant conversation and went their separate ways.

His appearance tonight was definitely not part of the deal.

"I heard about Scarlett and thought she might be missing Oreo." He extended the hidden hand, which held Scarlett's favorite black and white teddy bear, the one Gideon had bought her when she was a baby. Anyone close enough to know Scarlett knew she was attached to the bear. She'd even taken it to the first day of kindergarten with her, two years ago now.

"How'd you get into my house?"

It was an alpha thing to do, him thinking he knew best and acting on it, not asking permission. Actions like those had scared Carrie off in the first place. Her ex, Scarlett's dad, was a controlling, abusive man.

She couldn't cede control to a man, not ever again.

He must've read some of her feelings in her expression, because the frown line between his eyes deepened. He didn't sigh or make any other sign that her reaction bothered him. "Your neighbor let me in."

Wilma was an elderly sweetheart who fed her cat if Carrie ever had a late night away from home. But they would definitely have to have a talk about that key when Carrie got home. She was too irritated to speak, so she stared dumbly at the bear.

"Look, I didn't come up here to upset you," he said. "I just wanted to check on you guys. Maybe I should've left him with the nurse at the desk."

She took the bear, careful not to touch the man's hand. "Scarlett's better now. They stabilized her breathing, and they're sending her home in the morning."

He nodded, some of the lines around his eyes easing slightly. He'd always cared about her daughter.

And that, plus the overwhelming emotions that today had brought, brought a lump to Carrie's throat. She flared her nostrils, holding back everything she could, so he wouldn't see how deeply she was affected.

"I also brought you this. Figured maybe it might make your night better." He picked up plastic trash bag from leaning against the wall. He shoved it at her and she reacted instinctively, taking it from him. It was squishy inside.

He turned and strode away without even saying goodbye, which was fine with her, because her tears were too close to the surface to stem any longer.

She ducked back into Scarlett's room and let them fall, brushing them away with the back of her wrist as she clung to the trash bag and bear.

When the small outburst subsided, she tucked Oreo into the crook of Scarlett's arm and sat on the cot. She untied the garbage bag, pulled out her very own pillow.

Because he knew she wouldn't sleep well here, and that it might give her some comfort. Because that was the kind of man he was.

She hugged the pillow and squeezed her eyes shut as more

tears threatened. She'd been so close to accepting the relationship he offered eighteen months ago.

But in the end, she hadn't been able to trust that he wouldn't hurt her. Nights like tonight just confused things.

She was better off alone.

Even if it didn't feel that way.

Chapter Two

THE MAN WOKE, DISORIENTED AND WITH HIS HEART pounding. Darkness surrounded him, but faint lights shone at eye-level and the pinpoints of light against the night sent his abused head spinning until he thought he would throw up.

"Hey." A soft female voice intruded into the Tilt-a-Whirl of his consciousness. He felt the sensation of a palm pressing against the back of his hand. "Matt?"

It felt like rounding a corner in a clunker with no power steering, but the man turned his head.

Kelsey.

Her car.

He blinked, and the world came into focus. He was still in the passenger seat of her car. He must've fallen asleep beneath the repeating yellow highway lights. That was the last thing he remembered.

He was shaking and drew his hand from beneath hers because he didn't want her to think he was weak. He rubbed his hand down his face, trying to breathe, trying to gain some perspective.

The ranch. They'd been coming to the ranch.

At least *some* things were sticking to this inside of his noggin.

A light went on somewhere outside the car, and he lifted his eyes to see someone step onto the porch. A man, but he was backlit, and Matt couldn't make out his features.

"Are you okay?" Kelsey asked from the driver's seat. Her door was open, as if maybe she'd been out of the car and sat back down.

He wasn't, but he reached for the door handle anyway. "Sure."

The cold air was bracing when he swung his legs out of the compact car and stood. He only had to grip the top of the car for a couple of seconds before the spinning in his head settled.

Someone was coming off the porch now, and Kelsey's high beams illuminated his face. Enough for Matt to recognize Nate O'Malley, though he'd aged since the teenaged Nate in Matt's memories.

Kelsey seemed surprised to see the man who'd been a friend in high school.

"Kelsey Whitley. Didn't expect you." Nate might be hiding his surprise, but Matt clearly heard the cautious tone in the other man's voice. Why?

Nate moved toward Matt, his hand outstretched. "It's so good to see you, boss, we've been worried sick."

Boss? With his head still throbbing, it was everything Matt could do to manage one word. "Nate."

The cowboy looked at him, a genuine smile creasing his face. "You remember me?"

He shook his head. "Just...some things from high school."

Nate's expression dissolved into concern. He nodded slowly. "Well, we'll get you settled, and hopefully you'll get everything back before too long."

"Who's 'we'? You said 'we've been worried,'" Matt said.

"I'm the foreman, and we've got Brian, Trey, and Chase working the place."

Matt didn't recognize those names. Nate clapped him on the shoulder. "I'll introduce you in the morning. You look exhausted. Why don't you come on inside and head to bed?"

Three men he didn't know were bunked down on the Triple H. Maybe it should make the man nervous, but he didn't have room in his head for any more emotion. If Nate trusted them, that would have to be good enough.

"Just let me say goodnight," the man said to Nate.

The concerned lines around Nate's mouth tightened, but the cowboy faded back, moving toward the porch steps. Something was off. Something in his reaction, in Kelsey's... Matt's head continued to throb and he closed his eyes and pressed fingers into one side of the bridge of his nose.

When he opened his eyes, Kelsey was there, in front of him. She hesitated before she settled her hands at his waist. It wasn't an embrace, not really, but her touch calmed him.

He cupped her cheek. When he was about to lower his head to kiss her goodnight, she turned her face into his palm. He buried his nose in her hair instead.

She was trembling, or maybe he was. All he knew was he could get through whatever was going to come, as long as she was by his side.

HOURS LATER, shut up in her room at her sister Katie's house, Kelsey still felt shaken from that final embrace from Matt.

The whole night had shaken her, beginning the moment she'd stepped foot in the airport. She hadn't been prepared to see him, pale beneath his tan, his hair cut short.

Even less prepared to pretend to be one of a pair.

She should've told him the truth immediately, but his kiss had surprised and silenced her. And then, seeing him vulnerable...

She'd worried herself into a state when he'd fallen asleep in the passenger seat of her car. She'd kept sneaking glances at him as they'd passed through the one-stoplight town and streetlights had flashed across the interior of the car.

He couldn't have been comfortable with his small frame folded into her compact car. His face had lost some of the stress lines after he'd drifted off. He was just as handsome as she remembered. Maybe more. When she'd last seen him, he'd still had the lankiness of a teen, but now he was all man.

Matt was the kind of man who never let his guard down. The fact that he'd slept while she drove—instead of scanning the area around them for traffic or other dangers—showed how very vulnerable this injured Matt was.

Seeing him again had brought back everything. How much she'd loved him. The pain she'd felt when she'd walked away. The lonely, late nights when she'd stared at the ceiling, wondering if she'd made the right choice.

A knock at her door startled her. She was wedged in the desk chair. She'd been staring out the window for... She winced when she glanced at the clock. Way too long. At least she didn't have a job to rush off to in the morning.

The door opened and Katie stuck her head inside. "Thought you might be sleeping."

Kelsey shrugged. Her lamp made it obvious she wasn't.

"How was Matt?" It was a loaded question. Katie knew how serious their relationship had been back in high school. Tonight Kelsey had left her a voicemail to let her know where she'd gone.

Kelsey couldn't stop thinking about those moments when she'd woken him. His disorientation, the pain etched into his features.

And the way his expression had eased when he'd caught sight of her. Even now, it was like losing her breath to a bad leg cramp.

She shook the thoughts away. "He's...not well."

Katie crossed her arms. "What happened? I hadn't even heard he was coming home." In a town as small as Taylor Hills, the grapevine usually ran rampant. That hadn't changed.

"I think some kind of roadside bombing. Carrie didn't have long to talk." And she wouldn't have shared with Kelsey anyway. "He's had a head injury and...amnesia."

Katie's eyes widened. "So...?"

"He remembered me from high school." Kelsey sighed, jamming her fingers into her hair, squeezing her scalp. "He apparently started remembering when he saw me at the airport."

"Oh no."

Yeah. "He didn't remember everything."

Katie looked appropriately compassionate. "So when he finds out you abandoned him and broke his heart...?"

She vaulted out of the chair and went to her dresser, turning her back to her sister. "I didn't abandon him."

She'd just broken things off without giving him a real explanation. Avoided him all summer and run off to college.

"Yeah..." Katie drawled from the doorway.

Kelsey pulled a ratty T-shirt—one of her favorites from high school—from the drawer. She'd left so much behind when she'd left town all those years ago. She gripped the dresser drawer.

What was she going to do?

Matt had said some of his memories had returned when he'd first seen her. What if more returned? What if his mind was re-filling with memories right now? What if he woke and knew that she'd abandoned their relationship? That she'd run off and left him?

Just thinking about what would happen when he remembered the truth made her want to put on her running shoes and run far away. Her body was up for it, her feet itching for the pounding of pavement beneath her feet, or perhaps for the sight of home in the rearview mirror. For distance between her present and her past. But she couldn't. Not now.

She turned back to Katie with a lift of her chin, her temper flaring. "You want me to call the garbage company tomorrow and have a dumpster delivered?"

Katie struck right back. "You know I don't want that. We can't just throw away Mama's things."

Mama was gone. It still hadn't settled in for Kelsey, even after almost a week of being home. Mama's life hadn't been easy. She'd worked long hours, always on her feet, but there'd been no hint of any health problems. The heart attack she'd suffered had been a complete shock.

Kelsey had grieved, shutting herself up in her Houston apartment. She'd grieved, but she hadn't wept. Mama had never believed in Kelsey's dreams.

When Katie called and asked for help settling the estate, Kelsey had felt guilty enough to get in her car and come. *Settling the estate* was a kind way to put it. What they were really doing was getting rid of all the junk Mama had accumulated. The word *hoarder* was a fitting description of the single mom who'd raised them.

Since she'd returned, she and Katie lived and ate and watched TV and avoided each other, somehow managing to do that from the confines of the second floor, because the first was floor-to-ceiling junk. Trash, all of it.

Except Katie's jutting jaw said she didn't agree that it was all trash. She thought they'd find a few things of value hidden among the piles. Kelsey just wanted to be done with it all. Once the house was cleaned out, she could leave Katie to run the restaurant Mama had spent her life operating.

Kelsey didn't need an inheritance, not after the endorsements she'd scored because of her silver medal.

What she needed was direction. She'd worked since she was ten years old toward her dream of being an Olympian and winning that medal.

Now she had it, and she didn't know what to do with the fifty or sixty years she had left. She was a retired athlete with an unfinished art degree and no job. Cleaning up the mess mama had left was proving to be a distraction, but in a few weeks, Kelsey would have to make some firm decisions about her future.

Decisions that didn't include Matt Hale.

She didn't need more complications in her life, and Matt was a big one. She should've spoken up the moment he'd first set eyes on her. Told him the truth, that they weren't together and hadn't been in years. Now it was too late, but she couldn't imagine Carrie allowing him to believe it for long.

And then what? Kelsey would spend three or four weeks in Taylor Hills and be gone. She could last that long in town.

She just had to stay away from complications.

Chapter Three

"MORNING, BOSS."

The man dredged up a smile and a nod for the cowhand standing near the sink with a plate of breakfast food in hand. Sunlight streamed through the kitchen window and glared off of the unfamiliar granite countertops and stainless steel appliances. The kitchen had obviously been remodeled sometime between high school and now. At least the landscape outside the window appeared the same as he remembered—a softly rolling slope down to the barn.

Boss.

Words to strike fear into any guy's nineteen-year-old heart.

Except he wasn't nineteen, even though he hadn't recaptured any memories beyond that age.

It was crazy weird. He definitely didn't *feel* nineteen, not with the way his knees had popped when he'd rolled out of bed, but there was a disconnect between his memories and his reality.

He rubbed his aching head.

He didn't recognize the cowboy blocking the coffeepot, but his friend Nate had also called him Boss last night.

Boss. Matt.

Neither one felt quite right. Neither had the moments of soldier-like, deadly precision he'd woken with this morning. One moment, he'd been sleeping soundly, the next he'd been sitting up in the unfamiliar bed, scanning 360 degrees for any sense of danger. As if the actions had been ingrained. What kind of missions had he been on during his tenure as a soldier?

He shook his head against the whirl of his thoughts. The cowhand's smile had faded a little as Matt stared, but now he shored it up again. "Here." He stepped out of the way. "Have some coffee. Brian made it, so it'll wake you up for sure."

Brian. Another name he didn't know.

He smiled, a bit chagrined. "And you are...?"

The man's smile faltered. "Chase."

The coffeepot clinked as Matt took it from the percolator; steam rose as he poured. He hadn't had a huge taste for it back in high school. How did he take it now? Sugar? Cream? Black? Thank God the mugs were in the same spot where Uncle Pat had always kept them, a cabinet overhead.

Matt had been shocked and hit with a wave of grief when he'd learned his uncle wasn't around anymore. Nate had been the one to deliver that news last night when Matt had balked at his bedroom door—that room had been Pat's for Matt's whole life. His head was muddled, but hadn't he mentioned his uncle to Kelsey? Why hadn't she been the one to tell him Pat was dead?

He raised his mug to the cowhand still shoving scrambled eggs into his mouth and left the kitchen. Being *Boss* right now felt like too much to handle. Surely they didn't expect him to run the Triple H, did they?

Thinking about Kelsey was a little like tiptoeing around a land mine. He got the feeling there were things she hadn't told him, couldn't figure out why he didn't have a wedding band on her finger after ten years. Last night, he'd been too exhausted and too emotional when the load of memories had dumped into his head to really put any effort into figuring out what he was missing.

He wandered down the sun-drenched hall toward his bedroom, or Uncle Pat's bedroom, as he still thought of it—that had been another shock last night that he hadn't had mental space to absorb. It was located beneath the staircase toward the back of the house.

What if he didn't want to know what he was missing regarding his relationship with Kelsey? She'd been the only steady presence he'd felt since waking up in the military hospital ten days ago. Gideon had been with him in the hospital, but the black hole in his mind made his brother's presence more agitating than anything else.

Kelsey steadied him. What if filling the blanks in his memories would mess that up?

He closed himself in his room and padded in sock feet to the desk he'd noticed last night. The curtains were closed in here, light only seeping around the edges. He toyed with the idea of opening them up, but if cowboys were moving back and forth between the house and barn, they'd be able to see in here, just like he could see them.

He wanted privacy, for now, even just a window's worth.

He set his coffee on the desk next to a closed, silver laptop. It was covered in a fine layer of dust. He'd hoped that the memory dump last night had meant he was in for a deluge of everything else, but so far the last decade or so was a complete blank. If his own mind wouldn't cough up the memories, maybe he could force it.

He made the decision and sat in the desk chair. He flipped open the laptop and booted it up.

Maybe he could make some sense of his and Kelsey's relationship by reading through the emails they must've exchanged recently.

But he was thwarted when he discovered his email program required a password. He tried several things, including Kelsey's name, his siblings' names, and even Scarlett, the niece he couldn't remember knowing. Even his childhood dog's name resulted in a big fat nothing. He searched the desk drawers, thinking maybe he'd written it down somewhere, but nada.

Finally, he settled back in his chair, knowing it was a bust. He gave it one last try by texting Gideon, asking whether his brother knew the password.

Then another idea hit him. He pulled up a web browser and searched. There were hundreds of hits for Kelsey's name in the national news, thanks to her Olympic showing. Although the distance runners didn't get as much coverage as some of the other events, there was plenty to look through.

He found pictures of her mom and sister in the stands,

cheering her on. Where was he? Had he been unable to get leave? On a top-secret mission? The Internet offered no answers. None of the news articles or interviews with her mentioned a boyfriend or fiancé. There was no definitive question as to the status of her singleness. Had they temporarily broken up? Why?

None of it made sense.

And none of it prompted the return of any of his memories.

His cell phone buzzed from the desktop. Gideon.

SOME WEB BROWSERS SAVE PASSWORDS. Try looking under the settings.

MATT HADN'T CONSIDERED THAT. He texted his brother a thank-you while his brain gave an angry throb. He rubbed two fingers against his forehead.

He needed some answers. Couldn't give up now.

He poked around the browser until he found the right menu and sure enough, it looked like he'd saved his password.

He accessed his emails. There weren't many there, though they dated back several years. Methodically, he searched through all the different mailboxes, looking for anything from Kelsey.

Nothing.

She hadn't emailed him once, at least not that he had record of on his computer. He couldn't imagine deleting anything from her. Did that mean she hadn't emailed him in years?

Why not?

Confusion made his head throb harder.

He clicked back to his inbox. There wasn't much there. A couple of new messages from his soldier buddies checking on him. He could answer those another time.

There was a message, a few months old, from Gideon.

MATT,

Your tour is over in another six months and I need to know if you're going to re-up. We both know that managing the Triple H long-distance isn't working out for me, not when Alessandra needs my help here. Uncle Pat left the ranch to the three of us. When my career in the SEALs ended, you were overseas and Carrie needed help, so it was easy for me to take over running the place. I probably haven't brought you in on the operations as much as I should've—stop laughing, we both know what a control freak I am. But now...

I guess what I'm saying is, it's time for you to take over. If you want to (Alessandra says I have to stop trying to run everything).

Stay safe out there.

Gideon

MATT TAPPED THE MOUSE, and the program brought up "related messages." Apparently, he'd responded, because there was a *Sent* message in the box. He clicked on it.

GID,

I'M GETTING OUT. I'm your man.

-M

GETTING OUT. Staying on at the Triple H. Running the place.

He didn't know what to feel about the discovery. He'd been indifferent about the place during his teen years. The never-ending chores had itched sometimes, but he hadn't exactly hated the place.

Kelsey had always wanted to leave town. Why would he be willing to settle down here if she'd left? But she was back now, right? Because she'd picked him up at the airport.

Except... there'd been moments of hesitation, more than what he might've expected if she'd just been worried about his injury.

He'd gone searching for answers, but he'd just come up with more questions.

Frustrated, he closed the laptop with more force than was strictly necessary.

The change in lighting after looking at the bright computer screen had his eyes playing tricks on him, and the walls started closing in. He started to feel like he couldn't breathe.

He stood up, grabbed his coffee mug, and made his way to the door. He needed outdoor air, that's all.

ONE, two, three. Breathe. And hold. Again.

Kelsey's feet pounded the ground in a rhythm that usually brought comfort.

Not today.

Part of it was the difference in landscape. She usually ran through a jungle of concrete, brick and glass along the city streets in Houston. Sometimes along jogging trails. Today, red dust puffed up to fill her nostrils her as she ran the dirt roads around Taylor Hills.

The cool autumn air held a hint of frost. It wasn't cold enough to freeze her lungs, but she still felt as if she were choking. Maybe it was guilt squeezing the air from her lungs.

Kelsey had wrestled with herself all night about what happened with Matt at the airport, and after.

She'd tossed and turned, thrown off the covers and then pulled them back on.

What could she have done differently? She hated feeling like she was lying to him, but she hadn't had the heart to tell him the truth.

He'd just been so...vulnerable. When she'd woken him in the car, she'd seen his genuine terror as he'd taken in his surroundings. He'd covered well, and thank goodness he'd recognized Nate.

Her legs and lungs burned in a familiar pain, one that was usually able to drive away her demons. She checked her wrist pedometer-slash-watch. Nine and a half miles. Plenty far enough, as she wasn't in training. She'd snuck out of Katie's house before dawn, her sneakers in hand so they wouldn't squeak on the wood floors. Now the morning was slipping away...

She stretched out her stride, seeking the elusive peace she'd hoped to find out here this morning.

She didn't owe Matt anything. Carrie either. If she stayed away, Carrie would surely tell Matt what she knew of their breakup, and that would be the end of her need to pretend anything.

And Matt...well, she might owe him an apology for the way she'd ended things after graduation, but she didn't owe him her support, no matter how vulnerable he was. Or injured.

So why had her feet carried her right to the Triple H this morning?

She could see where the property started, because the fencing changed from a plain old, weathered barbed wire to a well-maintained dark wood slat. The nearest field she passed had been wheat—she guessed—and was already turned, ready for the winter's crop to be planted.

Pat Hale had always kept the property in fine condition, and it looked as if his nephews—maybe mostly Gideon, up until now—had continued with his legacy. She imagined the ranch turned a nice profit. Good for Matt.

She should turn around. What was she going to do, show up sweaty after a ten-mile run and ask to join him for breakfast?

She could see the house from the road, though it was set a quarter mile or so back on the property. There was some movement on the porch. It could've been any one of the hands who helped run the place, but somehow she knew it was Matt.

She turned up the drive, pulse pounding in rhythm with her feet.

She stopped on the lawn, several feet from where he'd braced himself against the porch railing. She paced back and forth at a walk, allowing her body to cool down rather than just stopping cold. His expression was inscrutable, and looking at him in the bright morning sunlight, it was hard to remember why she'd thought he was vulnerable last night.

He looked like the soldier he was. Tough. Rugged. Able to take on anything.

"You in training?" he asked.

She took a few deep breaths, working to settle her body into a resting rate. "Just out for a morning jog."

"All the way from your mom's place?" One corner of his mouth kicked up.

"It's Katie's place now." Maybe the words emerged a little sharper than she'd wanted them to. Everything with Mama... Kelsey tried not to hold onto bitterness, but Mama's overture had been too little, too late.

And she got the feeling that Matt saw too much. "Your mom...?"

"Gone." The word burned her throat.

He didn't reach for her. She was sweaty and with everything so confused, she didn't want a hug from him anyway. But his eyes burned. "I'm sorry."

She nodded.

"Katie's place, then," he said slowly. "Not yours and Katie's?"

"I live in Houston." She swallowed. "I came to help settle Mama's estate, but my home is in Houston."

His eyes narrowed slightly, and she could feel the weight of his curiosity. He'd always wanted to know her, inside and out. When she'd been seventeen, that had made her feel like she was worth something. Now, he wasn't going to just let go of the facts she'd revealed.

But a sound had her turning, and a cloud of dust was following a Toyota sedan up the drive. It crawled nearly to a stop and she saw Carrie through the driver's side window.

And now would be a great time to escape, except how rude would it be to just abandon Matt without a goodbye—like she'd done before. Plus, she'd have to run right by Carrie in her car.

She swallowed the knot of fear in her throat. Carrie would be within her rights to throw Kelsey off the property. She pretended the shaking in her limbs was from the workout she'd just given her muscles. She braced for Matt's sister, whom she hadn't seen in years.

Instead of Carrie, a little girl jumped out of the car almost before it had rolled to a stop. Scarlett.

"Uncle Matt!" she shrieked, brown hair flying behind her like a flag as she bolted for the porch.

Matt barely had time to set his coffee mug on the railing

before the little girl threw herself at him. He caught her, and she clung to his neck tightly.

Kelsey couldn't look away. Which is why she instantly caught the panicked, helpless look he threw her way. His eyes had gone a little shiny, too. The soldier was that emotional over meeting his niece?

A car door closed, and Kelsey jumped and looked over her shoulder to see Carrie approaching. The other woman's face was creased with the same concern Kelsey felt.

"Scarlett, honey?" she called out, making her way toward the porch.

Kelsey edged that way too, unable to ignore Matt when he'd once again shown her this vulnerable side.

MATT HAD no idea what the right protocol was here. Some muscle memory had had him tearing up when the little girl—Scarlett?—had thrown herself into his arms.

He didn't cry. Not ever.

But his throat was hot and thick, and he had no idea what to do with this armful of little girl. She smelled like strawberry kiddie shampoo and was clutching a black-and-white stuffed bear in between their bodies.

He sent Kelsey another *come here and help me* look, and maybe she'd known what he meant the first time, because she was climbing the porch steps. So was his sister, who looked older than she did in his memories. And more stressed, which showed in the lines around her mouth that the bright mid-morning sunshine wouldn't hide.

"Uncle Matt, Mommy said you might not remember me. How could you forget me when I'm your favorite niece? Well, I'm your only niece..."

It seemed that once his niece started talking, she had a hard time stopping. Something he remembered about his sister when they'd been little.

The little girl leaned back in his arms slightly, and he got a good look at her. She had Carrie's elfin features and green eyes, though the chocolate-colored hair must've been from her father. He couldn't force one memory of the guy.

"You held me the first time when I was six weeks old," the little girl said. She placed one tiny palm against his cheek, looking earnestly into his eyes. "I have a picture of it on my dresser in my room. Don'cha remember that?"

He shrugged helplessly, and the girl wiggled, so he set her on her feet.

Kelsey crouched to Scarlett's level. She reached up, clasped his hand, and pulled him down to crouch too. His knees popped embarrassingly, like an old guy's.

"Who're you?" Scarlett asked, demanding and curious as only a six-year old could be.

Kelsey glanced at him, seemed at a loss momentarily. "I'm Kelsey. I'm a...friend of your Uncle Matt."

Scarlett's features scrunched up. "Then how come I've never seen you before?"

Never? That was interesting.

Carrie moved in like she would interrupt but paused when Kelsey started talking.

"Have you ever bumped your head really hard?" she asked Scarlett.

"Once, on the corner of my desk. I was dancing and twirling, and I got a little too twirly and dizzy, and I fell and hit my head. I got a huge"—the girl bit her lip in concentration—"chicken egg." Scarlett looked back at her mom for confirmation.

"Goose egg," both Carrie and Kelsey said at the same time.

"Goose egg on my forehead," Scarlett finished proudly.

Carrie shook her head, a tiny exasperated sigh showing she remembered the moment just fine.

Matt's legs were starting to burn, but he didn't want to look like a wimp in front of Kelsey, so he stayed in the squat.

"Well," Kelsey said, bringing Scarlett's attention back. "Uncle Matt hit his head really hard, even harder than what happened to you. And his goose egg was on the inside of his head. And since he's still getting better, some things are mixed up for him. And some things he doesn't remember yet." She squeezed his hand. He loved the familiar feel of her hand in his, but *Houston*?

Scarlett tilted her head to one side and looked up at him, her little eyes curious and earnest. And maybe a little scared.

"But do you know what?" Kelsey asked. "You can give him

extra hugs to help him feel better. And you can tell him stories about all the things you do together when he's home on leave. That might even help him remember."

Scarlett nodded, seriousness etched in every feature of her face. "I can do that." Her gaze moved to Matt. "You wanna start now? Mom let me stay home from school today cuz of my bad allergy attack yesterday."

Carrie put her hand on the girl's shoulder. "I need to talk to Uncle Matt for a few minutes. Why don't you go see if Nate or Chase is out in the barn? Maybe they'll show you the new kittens."

"Oh yeah!" It seemed as if he was instantly forgotten as Scarlett launched off the porch and landed in the dirt on all fours. "I'm okay!" she chirped as she ran around the side of the house. Maybe not totally forgotten, because she stuck her head back around the building. "I love you, Uncle Matt!"

He lifted his hand in a wave, but she was already gone.

He stood, muscles protesting the extended squat. Eyeballed Kelsey, who bounced up with apparently no such problem with her muscles. She was looking toward where Scarlet had disappeared.

"Is she always like that?" he asked Carrie.

His sister grinned. "She's a little subdued today, tired after yesterday." Then her grin disappeared. "Are you okay? Be honest." She cocked one hand on her hip and looked so much like their mother that he choked on a long-ago memory.

He cleared his throat, found his voice. "I'm guessing sometimes I fudge over combat injuries?"

Carrie narrowed her eyes at him. "Injuries, plural?"

He shrugged. "How am I supposed to know?"

Kelsey looked at him in concern, and maybe he shouldn't have made the joke. *Houston.* She hadn't come out and said it outright, but this morning she seemed to be hinting that they lived separate lives. But did that mean she didn't care?

"The doctors think my memories will come back, but they don't know when," he told his sister. "As you can see, motor functions don't seem to be affected."

She nodded, biting her lip, and he could see the totality of her worry in the tears that she blinked back. "Well, I'm—" She broke off with a sniffle.

Kelsey shoved him in the back. "Hug her," she hissed.

Ah. He put his arms around his sister, and she hiccupped a single sob into his shoulder. He started to freak out, because Carrie wasn't a crier either, at least not that he remembered, but then she seemed to calm quickly. She smelled like a hair salon, like expensive shampoo. The scent made his head throb again.

Finally, she pushed out of his embrace. "I love you, you old lunkhead. But if I ever get another phone call like the one I got from that military doc..." She let the threat hang.

He nodded. "I think I can ease your mind on that. They've put my discharge through." Even with everything muddled those first few days in the hospital, he remembered that.

"Oh, Matt." Carrie sighed.

He shrugged. When they'd told him what was happening, he hadn't known whether to be happy or disappointed, because he couldn't remember why he'd joined up in the first place. It had been Gideon's plan to do so after school, not Matt's. Maybe when he got his memories back, the loss of his career would hurt, but for now it just *was*.

Carrie shot an inscrutable look at Kelsey, but when she spoke, it was to Matt. "I'd better go check on Scarlett."

She headed toward the barn. When she was out of sight, he turned to the woman he remembered loving and said, "We need to talk."

Chapter Four

W E NEED TO TALK.

Kelsey shifted her feet, her eyes skittering away from his perceptive gaze. He was right. She just didn't want to think about—didn't want to relive—graduation day.

But at this point, it seemed like there was no avoiding it.

"You wanna take a walk down to the barn? I'd like to see if Beauty is still around."

She nodded, remembering his horse. Maybe if he had something to distract him, this would be easier to get through.

"You mind following me in here so I can grab my boots?"

She looked down. For the first time since she'd arrived, she realized he was on the porch in sock feet. She grinned.

She followed him inside and down a hallway where sunlight spilled through the picture window in the living room. She couldn't help her curiosity as she gazed around the room while they passed. She remembered it from when Pat had been alive, remembered how sparsely it had been decorated. Now, there were throw pillows on the couches and huge canvas prints of the three siblings, one of Scarlett, and a wedding picture of Gideon and a beautiful blonde woman with a long, elegant train cascading around their feet. The faint scent of coffee carried from the kitchen.

She'd spent countless hours here during her senior year,

mostly doing homework on the coffee table. She shoved those memories away. This place had transformed from a *house* to a *home*. Whose doing had that been?

He hesitated, just slightly, before he stepped into a room. He emerged quickly and bent to put on his boots. Sighed and slapped his thigh as he straightened.

"I keep expecting to see him. Uncle Pat. That was his room."

His hand trembled slightly as he jerked his thumb over his shoulder.

For someone who usually exuded confidence and rarely showed softer emotions, this side of Matt was a shock. It showed her just how shaken up by everything he really was.

She put her hand on his forearm. "I'm sorry," she whispered.

"I just need..."

He didn't finish his sentence but pulled her into his arms. He kissed her again.

She didn't push him away again.

In fact, she leaned into his touch. She'd missed this so much. The tender slant of his lips against hers. The possessive grip of his hand at her hip. The sense of his strength at her fingertips as her hands rested on his shoulders.

She'd loved him so much, and now those old feelings rose up from someplace inside her, rushing to the surface.

It was too much.

She backed away slightly. His hands fell away from her waist.

Her feet shifted with an overwhelming itch to run away. She ducked her head to hide the wildness she knew must be showing in her eyes.

"I didn't mean to do that," he said on an exhale.

When she looked up, his face was drawn, and he rubbed at a spot low on his forehead.

"Headache?" she asked.

"Let's go." He pushed away from the wall and led her through the kitchen and mudroom.

Outside, they walked in silence, her shoes and his boots crunching through the long, late-summer grasses.

He still seemed upset, unsettled, though she didn't know whether it was the kiss or his uncle's death—new all over again—or just everything.

"We're not a couple anymore, are we?" he asked.

She struggled to find the right words. She hated to hurt him now, when things were so hard for him. Finally, when he glanced over at her, she simply said, "No."

"Why not?"

Why are you doing this?

The memory of his angry question graduation day hit powerfully, stealing her breath. He hadn't understood then. How could she make him understand now?

"I couldn't see a way to do it," she said. "Working toward the Olympics and being what you needed me to be."

His expression showed that he was listening, head bowed and cocked a little toward her. That's always how he'd been. Processing things, not making snap judgments. The morning sun gilded his hair, and she realized he'd left his hat behind. Forgotten because of his injury?

"I don't understand how I let you go," he said quietly.

She hadn't given him a choice.

"But maybe this injury is God giving me a second chance," he continued. "Everything feels so difficult right now. I have a niece I don't remember. Gideon's married and Carrie's divorced. Pat's gone. And I don't know the guys I supposedly work with here, except for Nate. You're my one constant."

If only he knew.

She tried to smile, but it felt like her lips had stuck to her teeth.

"I know it's a lot to ask. Well, actually, I don't know how much it is to ask. Maybe it's this head injury that's making things seem unfinished between us. But could we just...?" He gestured between them. "Be together for a while? Until I get my memory back. Or get more settled, if the memories never come back."

She hoped that wasn't the case for him.

"I...don't know." She let her gaze go to the horizon, because it was easier than looking at him. It had been hard enough—almost impossible—to walk away from him once, though she'd known at the time it was the right thing to do.

She was older now. Wiser.

"I'm going back to Houston in a few weeks. My life is there, my apartment..." And her coach's job offer. She could join the team from the other side of things, if she wanted to.

The problem was, she wasn't sure she *did* want to.

"I'm only visiting Taylor Hills. To help Katie clean up Mama's stuff and fix the house."

Being with Matt again... If she got too attached, she would be in for another heartbreak. Not to mention what might happen when his memories returned. When he remembered how cruel she'd been when she'd walked away, he'd hate her all over again.

But she couldn't stop thinking about Matt and his expression last night when he'd woken in the front seat of her car. Or this morning, when Scarlett had vaulted into his arms. Lost.

He didn't push as they neared the barn. Only the flex of his jaw told her that he wasn't happy with her non-answer.

The sound of little girl giggles carried through the open barn door.

His hand rested under her elbow as they passed through the door and into the dim interior. She didn't move away from the touch, though it muddled her thinking.

Scarlett sat cross-legged on the barn floor with two kittens tumbling together in her lap. Matt had said he wanted to see about his horse, but he gravitated naturally toward the little girl, letting go of Kelsey.

She wrinkled her nose against the smell of manure. A horse *whuffed* from somewhere nearby, and she glanced down the line of stalls. Her hand twitched at her side. She'd been out here with Matt when they'd dated, and the big animals always made her nervous.

He sent Kelsey a questioning glance before sitting down next to Scarlett on the hay-strewn ground. She shrugged it off. She'd be fine as long as the horses stayed in their stalls.

"Who're these guys?" Matt asked.

"That one is Tom"—Scarlett pointed to a solid gray kitten who climbed over her leg toward him—"and this one is Jerry." She picked up the orange and white striped kitten and nuzzled him against her cheek.

"Did you name them?" Kelsey asked, crouching at Matt's side.

Scarlett nodded. "Mr. Trey let me name them."

One of the hands waved from where he cleaned out a nearby stall. Curiously, Carrie had disappeared, though she'd claimed to be coming to the barn to check on her daughter. At least the man seemed to be keeping watch over the little girl.

"What about the horses?" Matt asked. "Do you have your own?"

"Yep. Peppermint. She lives right next door to your horse."

He looked up, eyes squinted slightly as he stared at the line of stalls. "Remind me which one is mine?"

Scarlett giggled. "You're silly, Uncle Matt. It's Beauty, remember? Just like my favorite fairytale princess."

From beside him, Kelsey felt it as some of the tension left his body. His mare, Black Beauty, had been several years old when they'd been together. She must be old now, but at least she was still alive.

"You wanna see her?" Scarlett asked, standing and apparently ready to abandon her kitten playmates.

"Sure." Matt stood too, clasping Kelsey's hand as easily as he had all those years ago. His warmth still sent the same thrill all the way through her, straight to her heart.

What was she even doing here? Being with Matt, even as a friend, was a bad idea.

But as Scarlett scampered off and he turned his serious gaze on her, she heard herself say, "I guess it wouldn't hurt if we saw each other a couple of times, while I'm in town."

It wouldn't hurt? Oh, yes it could.

What was she doing?

Chapter Five

MATT RUBBED AT THE ACHE BETWEEN HIS EYES, knocking his Stetson back as he did so. At least today his headache didn't seem to be from his head injury.

It was the ream of papers he held that were doing it to him this morning. He set the ranch's accounting records on the passenger seat of the ranch's work truck and let his gaze rove across the landscape. He picked up the ham sandwich he'd packed in a brown bag this morning. A throwback to his teen years, summers when he'd work the ranch with his uncle.

His gaze strayed...

The fence needed repairing. It sagged in several places across the field that separated Triple H land from the dirt road beyond. Earlier, he'd hiked to the craggy gully and seen that a couple of posts were missing down there as well. The barbed wire was rusted in some places and should probably be replaced completely.

His gaze followed the fence line toward the horizon, where it disappeared before it reached their neighbor's property. Replacing a whole fence line wasn't that costly. The Triple H had the manpower to do it themselves. But it would take time, even with multiple guys working on it.

Nate had scrawled notes on the financial statements he'd

handed over to Matt over coffee that morning and he forced his eyes back to them.

The barn was twenty years old now, and though they'd kept up with repairs, it was becoming obvious that there were issues with the foundation. It should probably be redone before the structure fell down around their ears. The ranch had pulled a nice profit last year, but Gideon had been in charge then.

Now it seemed Matt was supposed to make decisions about operations, and that included where to spend money and what to repair. If they put a new foundation in the barn, could the fence wait until next year? Nate had told Matt that Gideon planned to increase the herd by a hundred head—shouldn't they wait on that expense?

But the cattle would reproduce and create additional income for the ranch, while the barn was a passive asset. It wouldn't create income for the property. But it was necessary to protect mamas and calves in the bitter winter and spring months and to house their horses and equipment.

He didn't know what the right decision was.

A shrill whistle brought his head around, and he saw one of the cowboys riding up on a palomino gelding. Matt squinted, trying to make out who it was.

The cowboy headed straight for him, and Matt stepped out of the open door of the truck. Crisp autumn air swirled around him. He raised his hand in greeting.

Brian reined in his horse and dismounted, holding on to the animal's reins as he approached the last few yards.

"Nate send you?" Matt stuffed another bite of ham sandwich in his mouth as he waited for the other man to answer.

Brian looked slightly sheepish. "He asked me to check in on you. Said your eyes glazed over when he gave you those accounting reports."

Matt chewed his food. "Yours would too."

The other man gave a pretend shudder. "Glad I'm not responsible for any of that."

Matt snorted. Brian had no idea. He wasn't entirely sure he wanted to be responsible for it either. Why had he said yes in that email to Gideon? He wished he knew what he'd been thinking at that time. There were still so many blanks... Other than the few memories from his childhood and teen years that had shaken free that first night, no more had resurfaced. Kelsey had been the catalyst that had started the memory dump.

Kelsey.

They'd spoken on the phone twice in the past two days, but it wasn't enough. He needed to see her. Later.

He could make that happen, surely.

"...fence is getting pretty bad."

Matt shook himself, realizing he hadn't been paying attention while the other man had glanced at the drooping fence line.

"Yeah. I'm not sure that's going to be in the budget for this year, though."

"Aw, man, you sound like the Bear." Brian's face creased with humor, but the expression faded away when he realized Matt wasn't sharing in the joke. "You know...our nickname for Gideon?"

He shook his head slightly.

Brian's brows creased, then his expression smoothed and he cracked another, milder smile this time. "When you and your brother brought that princess home—pretending she was a normal person—she got it in her head that Gideon looked like a bear. Because he had this shaggy beard and hadn't cut his hair in months. The nickname stuck because...well, you know Gideon."

His brother had always been short-tempered and surly. Matt still had trouble believing he'd scored a real princess. But everyone kept saying it was so. And Matt had spent lots of time gazing at the wedding pictures in the living room, especially the ones with him in them. He hardly recognized his mid-twenties self or the serious expression he'd worn.

Had he been happy?

The other cowboy made small talk for another few minutes and then rode back toward the ranch house and barn. The talk left Matt unsettled. There were so many things other people knew about him and his family that he didn't. He wanted those memories back.

Feeling itchy made him want Kelsey. He needed to see her. Tonight.

· · ·

KELSEY ANSWERED the knock at the back door only moments after she'd received Matt's text.

I'm in your driveway. Need to see you.

She'd asked him to come around to the back and then sprinted down the hall and stairs to meet him at the door. She was panting slightly as she wedged her body in as small an opening as she could manage in the door. She didn't want him to see Mama's mess.

His forehead wrinkled. "Something wrong?"

He looked tired, stood close enough that she got a whiff of horse and man. One hand was behind his back. He wore a faded chambray shirt and jeans over his boots.

"No." She closed the door behind her and leaned on the portal.

His eyes went to the door and back to her face. "You got somebody in there you don't want me to know about?"

Her face flushed with heat. Not some*body*. "I wasn't expecting you."

As evidenced by the sweatpants and long-sleeved T-shirt she wore. Lounge clothes. She'd been browsing different employment websites from her laptop, upstairs in her bedroom. She and Katie still hadn't come to an agreement about the junk piles, so she'd barely touched anything.

"Want to go out to dinner?" he asked.

She shrugged helplessly. "You couldn't have called?"

"I hoped that if I came by in person, you wouldn't be able to resist my cowboy charms." He waggled his eyebrows.

He was probably right. If he'd called, she would've tried to put him off. As it was, she wasn't sure spending time together—even just dinner—was a great idea.

"I'm not dressed."

"I thought you might say something like that." He pulled his arm from behind his back and lifted the large brown paper back so she could see it.

"Is that from...?"

"Katie hooked me up."

Scents of fried food wafted from the bag. She'd always loved the food from Mama's café, even if the business itself had strained their relationship.

"So can I come in?"

The fact that he was pushing was unusual enough that she took a long look at his face. There were shadows in his eyes, and the smile grooves around his mouth were a pinch too deep. Had something happened out at the ranch?

"I don't—"

"Please."

His whisper was unexpected and hit her in a soft place inside.

"I won't push for anything else," he said. "I just...I need a friend tonight. A friend I remember."

She sighed.

His smile disappeared.

"It's not you," she said. She took a deep breath. There was a reason she'd never invited him home when they'd dated before. "It's this." She scrunched up her nose so much that her vision was blurred as she pushed open the door, allowing him to see the hallway behind her.

She watched his face as he saw the unobstructed view to the living room and the floor-to-ceiling mishmash of boxes, knick-knacks, trash... And the piles in the kitchen, covering all the counters, table, floor... Stuff had even started to creep up the bottom three stairs.

He let out a low whistle. "That's a lot of...stuff."

"Trash. You can call it trash. I do."

He shook his head slightly, his eyes still focused over her shoulder. "This is what you meant when you said you had to take care of your mom's place. You and Katie have to go through all this stuff."

It wasn't a question, but she nodded. "I keep voting for getting a dumpster parked in the driveway and tossing it all out. Katie has this wild idea that there's something of value buried under all that junk."

"Huh."

"As you can see, I can't invite you in because there's no kitchen table to sit at." Not one that wasn't buried three feet under, anyway. And she wasn't comfortable with taking him up to her bedroom, even if all they were sharing was supper.

He shrugged. "We can sit on the tailgate of my pickup. It's not that cold tonight."

It was mild, the evening sun sending a last wave of warmth before the night chill settled in.

She shouldn't but... she slipped inside to put on her sneakers and joined him out front.

Their shoulders brushed as they sat side-by-side on his tailgate, legs dangling into open space.

She was halfway through her burger, eyes closed at the rich, fatty taste—a rare treat for her, as she'd been in training for years and needed to eat healthy foods—when Matt bumped her shoulder.

"If you have to go through all that stuff, what would it hurt to ask a friend for help?"

He meant himself.

She finished chewing her bite, cleared her throat. "It's my problem. Mine and Katie's. Besides, it's embarrassing."

She felt the movement of his shoulder at his shrug. "Well, now I know. So what's to stop from asking me to help, when you gals are ready to start cleaning out?"

She gave him a side-eye. "You want me to say 'nothing,' right?"

He kicked her sneaker this time. "I want to help. You need the help."

Yes, but she didn't need to spend more time with him. Even this, just a simple conversation over burgers, gave her a confusing mix of warm fuzzies in the pit of her stomach and a strange dread that he was going to suddenly hate her when his memories returned. Warm and cold at the same time.

Spending time with Matt was a recipe for disaster, wasn't it?

Chapter Six

"WHAT ABOUT THIS ONE?"

Two weeks after Matt's offer, Kelsey looked up from the cardboard box of various chipped pieces a china tea set to see Katie holding a large canvas that had one of Kelsey's earlier paintings on it. She must've been...a high school freshman when she'd painted it. She winced at the broad acrylic strokes that revealed two tulips and a daisy. It was pretty bad. Professor Bernard—her last art professor—must've been right about her lack of talent.

"Trash it," she said quickly.

"Aw, no way," Matt piped from across the room. She'd almost forgotten he was there, sitting on the floor and almost buried beneath a cascade of old magazines next to the family piano.

All right, she hadn't forgotten. It would be impossible to forget his presence whenever he was in the same room as her.

"If you don't want it," he said, "I'll hang it in my bedroom."

"Nuh-uh." She couldn't imagine that awful thing hanging above his bed. She shivered with horror even thinking it. "It's trash."

"Your ma kept it," he said, oh so helpfully. "She musta seen something of value in it."

"She kept everything," Kelsey gestured to the clutter-filled room.

"I'll just set it over here while you two argue about it," Katie muttered. She leaned the painting against the far wall, in the roughly two feet of space they'd cleared since they'd started two hours ago.

This was their second official workday, cleaning out the house. Hoarder was a term Kelsey was coming to hate. Earlier, they'd unearthed a stack of used, washed Styrofoam dishes from some of the rare times they'd eaten out. Who would keep those? Trash, trash, trash.

Even with the windows open, the brisk autumn breeze wasn't cutting through the stale air inside.

On Sunday, things with Katie had come to a head. They'd argued for the fiftieth time about the dumpster rental-versus-look through it way of doing this and finally agreed on a compromise. Kelsey had rented the dumpster but agreed to a week of sorting before they trashed whatever was left. She knew her sister could use the money from whatever they found to put into the café—assuming there was anything of value in here. And if they got the house livable again, Katie would have the option to sell it once the probate settled and Kelsey was back in Houston.

Her stomach dropped at the thought of going back to the life she'd left behind, and she ducked her head on the pretense of sifting through the box to see if there was anything salvageable there.

She still didn't know whether she should take the assistant coach job. Running was her life, but did she want to coach? The last two weeks spending time with Matt had only confused things more.

After the surprise hamburger-tailgate date, he'd convinced her to visit him on the Triple H, and they'd spent hours riding the property. Matt claimed he was reacquainting himself with the land and the operations. She figured he just wanted to see her uncomfortable on the back of the horse. He'd grinned the whole time, watching her sit nervously atop the huge beast. He'd given her a gentle mare, and the pace had been plodding.

She'd admitted later—when she'd gotten off—that it had been fun. Kind of.

A couple of days later, he'd talked her into a movie night, and they'd curled up on the couch at his place and watched a late-night marathon of the *Lord of the Rings* movies.

She'd fallen asleep on his shoulder.

They'd attended Sunday morning worship together. Then they'd had a picnic with Scarlett and Carrie, who hadn't spilled the details about their post-graduation breakup. Maybe she'd realized Kelsey's presence seemed to settle Matt somehow.

And when she'd let it slip that she and Katie were going to tackle Mama's junk, he'd shown up yesterday.

It was like being back in high school all over again.

Back then, she'd been so starved for attention... Her dad had abandoned the family when Kelsey had been too small to remember. It'd been Mama and the two girls, with Mama working sometimes two jobs until she'd saved up enough to buy into the small-town café. Mama had put her life into the café and made a decent living for the girls by the time they'd gotten to high school.

But she hadn't encouraged Kelsey's dreams of the Olympics, nor her interest in art. She'd told Kelsey she would be better off putting her efforts into something real. Like small town waitressing. It might not pay much, Mama would explain, but at least it was steady, honest work.

Running had been an escape for Kelsey. In middle school, she'd gone out for the track team. She'd been a natural. In high school, she'd had a coach that had pushed her and arranged for carpools with the other team parents when Mama had refused to cart Kelsey to meets. Thank God for her college coach and the scholarships she'd received.

Mama hadn't believed Kelsey could make it to the Olympics, not up until the international meet where she'd qualified. Having Mama in the stands at the Olympics had been bitter-sweet, a motivator for Kelsey. She'd needed to prove to Mama and to herself that she could medal, and she had.

But back in high school, she'd wanted college *badly*. Knew it was the stepping stone to her bigger dream. Her teachers and school counselor knew what Mama thought about college and had gently tried to temper Kelsey's expectations.

Matt had believed in her with an unshakable confidence. They'd started dating in the middle of her senior year, and he'd rained on her parched heart. He hadn't questioned her ability or her drive one bit.

And he had that same confidence in her now. She'd purposely avoided any mention of what she would do once things were finished with Katie. Or of their past. But he still seemed convinced that she could do whatever she set her mind to.

He still believed in her that much. But was he seeing the real her, the *now* her, or just living with the memories of what she'd been ten years ago?

She didn't know.

She decided the cheap plastic tea set was trash and walked out front to chunk it into the dumpster. That was one more cubit foot of space, at least.

Outside, she stood in the driveway and tried to breathe.

"SHE'S HAVING A HARD TIME," Katie said quietly after Kelsey had disappeared outside.

"I know." Matt was no idiot, even if he didn't have all his memories.

He dug through the box, but it was full of awful Christmas sweaters, nothing hiding beneath. He shoved it across the floor to the pile they were making for Goodwill. Some of those garish sweaters might pull big bucks.

He looked around the room. They hadn't even made a dent. Kelsey was dealing with this mess now. Had dealt with it all during her growing-up years, and he'd had no idea. She'd never invited him home. Had she kept all her girlfriends at arm's length too, embarrassed of her mom's hoarding? It must've been awful.

Over the last week, he'd felt the distance Kelsey was trying to create between them, the walls she wanted up. He still didn't know why, and he wasn't asking, though Katie might be able to give him some answers. She'd been in his graduating class, and though they'd never really been friends, they'd both loved Kelsey. She was their unifying factor.

"She's been drifting since the Olympics ended." Katie glanced at the door and lowered her voice. "She never finished her degree, and now she doesn't have a firm direction."

Except the apartment and job she kept mentioning. In Houston.

He knew she wasn't staying, and that killed him. He aimed to do everything in his power to change her mind.

It would help if he had any idea why they'd broken up. She'd shied away from the subject whenever it came up. He'd spoken to Gideon on the phone and Carrie in person, and both of them told him it'd happened around her high school graduation, but they'd had no further details. They'd both said he'd been pretty upset by it.

Well, yeah.

It didn't surprise him his brother and sister didn't know more. He didn't talk about things that hurt deeply. It wasn't his style. Was that why she'd ended things with him? Because he hadn't shared his feelings enough?

He looked over to Katie, who had her head down, one plastic garbage bag in hand.

"Do you know why we broke things off?"

She shrugged. "You know Kelsey. Back then, she was this lost little girl—"

A noise from the doorway brought both their heads up. Kelsey stood there, and from the thunderclouds gathering on her brow, she'd obviously overheard.

"I was coming back to say maybe it was time for a break, but maybe I should take the break and let you guys keep talking about me behind my back."

He straightened, ready to defend Katie, since he'd brought it up, but Kelsey was already turning away. "I'm going for a run," she called over her shoulder. She slammed out of the house.

Crap. He hadn't wanted to upset her, just to find out what he'd done wrong all those years ago. Or if the decision to go their separate ways had been mutual, though he still couldn't imagine a scenario where he'd want to let her go.

He thought about leaving, but there was a lot of work to be

done here, and he'd promised to help. Kelsey would probably run off her frustration and rejoin them later.

Silence reined, now tense between him and Katie.

He lifted a medium-sized cardboard box from the top of a slanting pile, so he could see into it better. It was surprisingly light.

When he opened it, it was like opening a window into the childhood Kelsey. It was full of canvases of various sizes, all with different paintings. A horse. A castle. An orchard, or...something like that. She had talent, which had showed even when she was young.

He angled the paintings toward Katie. "You think she'll want these?"

"After she was so embarrassed about that one?" She jerked her thumb toward the larger painting they'd been fighting over earlier. "As far as I'm concerned, they're yours."

He grinned his appreciation. "Thanks."

He took the box and the larger painting out to his truck and tucked them in the cab. He looked both ways down the shaded, quiet neighborhood street, but Kelsey was nowhere in sight.

He leaned his hip against the truck. Maybe the pictures were a sign. Maybe he was going about this all wrong. He'd been working so hard to help Kelsey find a reason to stay when maybe what he should do instead was help her find a way forward.

It was obvious she'd loved art since she was a kid. She'd set it aside in her single-minded determination to win an Olympic medal. If art was her passion, then it only made sense that some kind of art-related career, even if that meant going back to school to finish her degree, would kindle her dreams again.

Chapter Seven

"YOUR TRANSCRIPT ISN'T HOLDING YOU BACK."

Kelsey dropped the black trash bag on the ground next to the porch steps and turned to Matt, who was stacking toasters on the recently unearthed kitchen counter. That's right. Multiple toasters, all in working order, all ready to be donated. Beside them were piles of kitchen utensils sorted by use. Spoons, spatulas, tongs. They'd be given away, too, once they attacked the last pile in the far corner of the room.

Past the kitchen, the junk that had previously filled the living room had been reduced to several boxes stacked near the door, ready for delivery to a local charity.

After a week of full-time work, they were making a dent. Maybe there was an end to this.

She dusted her hands and shut the back door.

Matt pulled a piece of paper out of his back pocket. He unfolded it and glanced at it. "Your grades are good. Mostly A's."

"Where'd you get my college transcript?" she demanded. She stalked over to him and snatched it from his clutches. There was no way she wanted him to ask about the D she'd made in Advanced Graphic Design. Professor Bernard's class.

She quickly re-folded it and stuffed it in the front pocket of her jeans.

"Katie found it."

"Katie snooped in my room?"

He shrugged unapologetically. "She didn't say *where* she found it."

"Haven't you two meddled in my life enough?"

He grinned at her, his teeth a white flash against his tan. And made no apology for looking at her transcript *or* for the meddling.

She couldn't find the energy to get angry. He'd spent hours here every day, toting hundreds of trash bags and boxes to the dumpster outside. He'd brought food and made her take a break when she was tempted to keep working. He'd cracked dumb jokes to entertain her and kept silent when the task had felt overwhelming.

It *was* overwhelming. The more floor space and walls they'd uncovered in the living room, the more damage they'd seen, damage that Mama's stuff had been hiding. The carpet was stained and nasty, something a vacuum and cleaning wouldn't fix. The floor bowed ominously, obviously affected by the Texas humidity and no doubt the weight of the junk piled on them. The walls were water-damaged and in desperate need of a coat of paint, and the extensions on the ceiling fan were drooping, making it unusable.

Matt hadn't commented, and Katie had been tight-lipped so far about whether she wanted to sell the house or try and repair it.

Now, Matt headed for last pile of junk in the corner, snatched a new black bag, and held it open.

She reached the pile. It appeared to be a stack of empty, used pizza boxes. She wanted to gag. Instead, she hiked up her gloves and looked away.

A colorful brochure was sticking out of his back pocket. "What's this?" She plucked it out before he could turn or stop her. She glanced at it, then held up the college brochure for him to see. She raised her eyebrows. "State?" The university was only twenty miles away.

He shrugged. "You said you were only a few hours short of your college degree."

She shook her head and stuffed the brochure into his trash bag. She shoved two pizza boxes in after it.

But the thought stuck in her brain and he seemed to know it because his eyes twinkled.

She didn't need an art degree to coach long-distance runners. And if she wanted to go back to school, a degree in sports management might be more helpful.

And she didn't want to think about it, not when they were so close to getting this room emptied.

She picked up the first cardboard pizza box, glad for the leather gloves that protected her hands.

Something small darted out from the pile, across the top of her shoe, and along the wall until it disappeared beneath the kitchen counter.

It happened so fast, she didn't even have time to react. Until she realized what had happened. A mouse.

She shrieked, dropped the pizza box. She grabbed Matt's bicep.

He laughed, and she glared at him.

"It's just a little rodent."

She glared harder.

And he laughed harder. She let go of his muscled arm to cross her arms over her chest.

"We've got extra traps in the tack room at home," he said. "I'll bring some over first thing tomorrow."

Tomorrow would mean she had to sleep in the house with the rodent. Her thoughts must've showed on her face, because he barely stifled another chuckle.

"Tonight?" He grinned at her.

She shivered, imagining little mouse feet running over her bed while she slept. But she couldn't ask him to do that.

"In the morning is fine. I appreciate it."

His lips were still twitching, but his eyes had turned serious. He shooed her toward the living room. "I'll finish up in here."

Gratitude surged. "Are you sure?"

"Why don't you take this, though, think about it in your free time?"

He held out a second brochure, this one pulled out of his front pocket. He pushed it into her hand. "Just think about it."

His eyes shone, showing her how much he believed in her.

She wished she had that much confidence in herself, in anything more than her ability to run a fast half-marathon.

But as she wandered into the other room, his excitement spurred a very slight echo of the same inside her.

Kelsey winced as she walked through Matt's living room and into the ranch house's dining room. Apparently he'd taken more from her mom's house than the one hideous painting she'd known about, because along one wall, he'd lined up a grouping of elementary school paintings she'd done.

Amateur, amateur, amateur. Both the paint mixing and strokes. She'd thought she was so much better than she used to be, but...

"What about graphic design?" Matt asked absently, hauling in two brown grocery bags. He deposited them on the long dining table. He'd promised to grill her a steak for supper tonight, a reward for both of them for delivering all those boxes and bags to the charity donation center.

She shook her head. "The job market is too crowded." She didn't know whether that was true but it sounded about right.

All she could hear was Professor Bernard's echo in the back of her mind. *You have no talent whatsoever.* The dressing down in front of the entire class had humiliated her, and she'd been too embarrassed to go to the last three class sessions or the final, which explained her failing grade.

She couldn't go back to art.

Matt didn't seem to get that.

"Art teacher?" he asked, cocking one hand on his hip.

"I don't like kids."

He leveled a look at her. "You and Scarlett are thick as thieves."

She shrugged. "She doesn't count."

He rolled his eyes but didn't push it.

She and Katie had had another fight last night about what they'd say to the attorney when they met with him in a few days. Kelsey wanted everything left to Katie, both the house and the café.

Katie'd suggested that if Kelsey wanted to stay in Taylor

Hills, they could share the house, take care of the repairs themselves. Staying shouldn't have even been on Kelsey's radar. But being with Matt was making her wonder *what if...?* And that had scared her. Scared her good, so she'd lashed out at her sister, laughing off the idea in a cruel way that Katie hadn't deserved.

She didn't particularly want to coach, but she couldn't stay here. Matt still hadn't realized the truth of their breakup, and she wouldn't be able to face him when he knew.

"What're you thinking about so hard?" He stepped close and tucked some strands of hair behind her ear.

"Nothing."

The way he was looking at her, she could tell he didn't believe her.

"We've been so busy," he said, "and you've been so serious..."

She didn't see it coming.

He tickled her side, just beneath her ribs. She leveled a glare on him. "Don't even think about it, mister."

But judging by the dancing light in his eyes, he was doing more than that.

She backed away, toward the front hall.

But she didn't make it that far. He chased her, and she shrieked, darting just out of his reach.

He followed her through the hall and into the living room. She put the sofa between them.

"You call yourself fast?"

"I am fast!" But maybe she hadn't put her everything into it, because he caught her just as she rounded the plush chair. He grabbed her around the waist and tickled her sensitive side, just beneath her ribs.

She shrieked with laughter.

"Hey!" They both froze at the voice from the door. "What's going on here?" Scarlett darted into the room. "Is it a tickle war?"

The girl was smart enough to go for her uncle's knees, a prime ticklish spot.

"Hey!" Matt tried to dance away, but his feet tangled with Kelsey's, and they both went down in a heap on the couch.

"Um, no hanky-panky in front of my daughter," Carrie said from the doorway, having witnessed all of it.

Kelsey laughed from deep in her belly, and couldn't stop.

Matt watched her, grinning.

"C'mon, kid. You're not mature enough to be watching this." Carrie touched Scarlett's shoulder and motioned her daughter toward the kitchen.

"What's mature?" Scarlett asked, trailing after her mother.

"Not your uncle."

That set Kelsey off in more peals of laughter.

Finally, spent and with an aching stomach, she propped her elbow on Matt's stomach and plopped her chin in her hand.

He grimaced and stuffed a pillow beneath her elbow instead.

"I love your laugh," he said quietly, a smile still playing around the corners of his mouth.

And that statement went right over the invisible line into dangerous territory.

Carrie reluctantly followed Scarlett down to the barn. She was glad to see her brother laughing, but she hoped he knew what he was doing with Kelsey.

She didn't know what had possessed her to come out here today, except she'd had her fill of Scarlett's whining to come see the two kittens.

The familiar place elicited all the old feelings. She didn't belong here. Not really.

She could only hope Trey was out the fields today, not hanging around the barn.

No luck. There he was, brushing down a horse it looked like he'd just unsaddled. He was growing his beard back, though it was neatly trimmed. His blond hair was rumpled and damp from his hat. He needed a cut, but she wasn't offering. Not now.

"Afternoon, ladies." He doffed his hat like he was in a western movie or something.

Scarlett shrieked an excited hello while Carrie's stomach did a slow flip. Why couldn't he have gotten ugly in the months since their breakup? Or developed an unattractive lisp. Or grown a mole on the end of his nose. Anything that might've mitigated her attraction.

He knelt for a hug from Scarlett. He'd always been like that, willing to put aside his own work or needs for her daughter.

"When are you coming back to our house for dinner?" Scarlett asked. "I miss you."

He didn't dismiss the girl or look to Carrie—blame her—for an explanation for a difficult situation.

Carrie stepped forward, alarmed by the hurt in Scarlett's face, but he was already talking.

He spoke to Scarlett as if she were a grown up and could understand. "I can't come to dinner as much anymore." He didn't offer lies or blame Carrie for how their relationship had ended. Just a simple statement. "But I tell you what. When your mom is ready for you to take Tom and Jerry home, I'll bring a bucket of fried chicken with me."

"Yeah, yeah, yeah!"

Scarlett threw her arms around his neck again, and this time, Carrie saw naked emotion on his face. He honestly cared about Scarlett. And she about him.

This was all Carrie's fault. She'd let him in, hoping for something that wasn't for her. And now Scarlett was hurting. Trey was hurting.

And she was...

She refused to be hurting.

"The kitties are in the stall next to Peppermint," he told Scarlett, who promptly ran off to see her babies.

"What was that?" she asked.

He straightened and rubbed the back of his neck, knocking his hat forward slightly on his forehead. "Sorry about that. If you tell me when you'll be out, I'll leave the kittens—"

"I don't remember agreeing to take any kittens."

Now his expression tightened. "You didn't." It wasn't a question. He glanced off to the side.

"Did Scarlett say so?"

He looked back at her and nodded, mouth slipping into a half smile. "That girl. She knows what she wants."

Carrie found herself responding with a nod and smile but then stifled it when she realized what she was doing.

His smile faded too. "I'll talk to her—"

"No."

He waited for her to finish, since she'd interrupted him.

But she shrugged helplessly. "If she wants a kitten so badly, maybe we could take one."

He shook his head. His Stetson shaded his eyes from her, but she caught the lines around his mouth. "Those two are particularly attached to each other. It'd be a shame to split them up."

He let the statement hang there. Like it had a deeper meaning, one she didn't want to hear.

"Then *I'll* talk to her. She's my daughter."

He stared at her for a long moment and then nodded slowly. One major point for him—he'd never interfered with her mothering Scarlett.

She had to stop remembering all the things she liked about him.

"I'm sorry we interrupted your workday." She motioned inanely to the horse. "We shouldn't have come out h—"

"Of course you should've." Trey paused, an inscrutable expression crossing his face. "The Triple H is your home. You're one-third owner, and you've got the right to be here anytime you want."

She had to look away from the intensity of his gaze. She shook her head and kept her gaze focused on the sunlight outside the barn doors. The Triple H hadn't been home in a long time. Not since everything had gone down with Uncle Pat.

"Mo-om, c'mere!"

Thankful for the interruption, Carrie turned to join her daughter.

She felt the weight of Trey's gaze follow her. She was to blame for the uncomfortable whirl in her stomach today. She hadn't adhered to her unspoken rule about avoiding him.

She was so stupid.

Chapter Eight

"THIS WASN'T EXACTLY WHAT I WAS PICTURING WHEN you said 'art teacher,'" Kelsey said.

Matt grinned at her. "I couldn't say no to Mrs. Crane when she wrangled me in to subbing for this class, now could I?"

"No one says no to Mrs. C."

The former sixth grade math teacher was a force to be reckoned with.

"Besides, this is a good look on you," Matt said.

Kelsey made a face at him.

A week after their lunch date, he'd wrangled her into helping at the kids' arts and crafts booth for the local harvest festival, an annual event that brought in vendors, food trucks, and hundreds of tourists over one weekend in October.

He'd given himself the job handing out craft popsicle sticks, while she had an apron over her T-shirt and jeans and was manning the finger-paint table. She had a streak of blue paint in her hair. Adorable. He wasn't making any excuses. He was hiding in the back of their booth, plain and simple, because folks he didn't recognize kept greeting him. His headaches had eased, but he still hadn't gained any more of his memories.

No matter what she said, Kelsey was good with the kids. She'd helped a little girl turn a blob of red paint into a realistic barn with a horse beside it. She'd raced a little boy into making a rainbow for his mom.

Every kid who interacted with her left with a smile.

Something had changed between them over the past week. He'd seen the flare of panic cross her face when he'd said he'd loved her laugh. Maybe it'd been the wrong thing to say, but it had been what he was feeling.

After a phone call with his brother, he'd finally made the decision to do both the fence and the barn repairs for the Triple H and to wait on purchasing more cattle. He and the hands had spent most of the week pushing the cattle to other fields and getting the supplies in place for the fence repair.

Now, it was closing in on twilight, and the last straggler kid waved goodbye and left with his grandma. The booth would be open again tomorrow, so their cleanup was mostly wiping down tables and putting lids on paint and making sure the sticks were all put up in their container.

He moved closer to Kelsey as she stacked up the paper plates they'd used as palettes. He smeared his hands in blue paint and then hugged her from behind, transferring the paint to the middle of her shirt. She was so busy cleaning up that she didn't notice.

He leaned his chin on her shoulder. "Come see the fireworks with me?" The town would put on a small show, and the tailgate of his pickup would be the perfect place to watch from.

"Did you just—?" She broke from his hold, and he couldn't help the laugh that escaped at the sight of the blue handprints on her white shirt. "I can't believe you did that."

She swiped her hand toward him.

He dodged, but she was quick, and he looked down to a streak of red paint across the front of his T-shirt.

He held his hands—blue palms and everything—in front of him. "Okay, truce."

She eyed him doubtfully as she gathered up the last couple of paper plates, then headed to the metal trash barrel at the corner of their booth.

He followed, but not too close. "You did well today."

She glanced his way. "You too. Where'd you learn to corral kids like that? I bet you commanded a fleet of men overseas..."

Her voice trailed off as their eyes met, and they both realized he didn't know whether her teasing statement was true or not.

"A hard day's work deserves a reward, doesn't it?" He sidled closer as she dumped the plates.

Her sideways glance was still wary. "Like what?"

"One little kiss."

She obliged him by turning up her face. He framed her cheeks with both hands, grinning into the kiss. She must've forgotten about the paint on his hands.

But before he could pull back and gloat, she reached up and ran both hands down his face. He could feel the goopy red paint on his cheeks.

He blinked through it, red on the tips of his eyelashes. And grinned.

They washed up, and twenty minutes later, it was dark, and they'd settled on the tailgate of his pickup. A slight breeze had kicked up, and she shivered in her three-quarter-length sweater and jeans.

"I brought a quilt." He jumped off the tailgate and fetched it from the cab.

Bringing the single quilt had been a strategy, one that meant she had to snuggle close to his side. He wrapped his arm and the quilt around her shoulders and cherished it when she leaned her head against him.

Having her this close, surrounded in darkness, made him feel like they were the only two people in the whole world, even though the field-turned-parking lot where they'd parked was full of cars and trucks and folks.

The first firework went off over their heads with a pop. Red sparks glittered in the starry sky.

He gripped the tailgate next to his thigh as his muscles reacted to the boom and explosions—a muscle memory that he had no conscious memory to match up to.

She sighed sweetly, and he worked to relax his tense muscles.

This whole time, she'd been reluctant to talk about their shared past or her future plans, but she wasn't shy about seeking his affection. Holding hands, embracing, kissing. She seemed to gravitate toward him on the physical side, even if she couldn't open up to him emotionally.

It gave him hope.

And he wanted this moment to last forever. "You thought any more about your new career path?"

She tensed, just slightly, but he felt it. "Not really. I've been busy helping Katie with some of the repairs at the café."

Funny. He'd been thinking about it nonstop.

"What about you?" she asked softly. He doubted their conversation would carry to even the closest pickup, not with the loud booms going off overhead.

Two blue-and-white fireworks went off together, and some folks nearby cheered.

"What do you mean?"

Her head tilted slightly. Maybe she wanted was to see the sky better, or maybe she was angling for a better look at his face. "You told Carrie your military career was over. What are you going to do next?"

"The Triple H and I are making peace with each other." Although he still didn't remember the cowboys, they'd brought him into the fold. The blanks in his brain bothered him, more and more every day. Like today, when folks he didn't recognize kept saying hi. When he spoke to Carrie and didn't know what she was talking about from some distant conversation. The breakup with Kelsey. He'd hoped for more of his memory back by now, and the lack of progress frustrated him. He'd had some consultations with a doctor in Dallas, and the man said to keep waiting.

He wanted to be done with the waiting.

He rolled his shoulders. "When I was eighteen, I didn't want anything to do with running the place, but now, it's starting to feel like home."

She didn't relax against him.

He didn't know whether his was the right or wrong answer. If she was determined to leave, the fact that he might be staying could be a strike against him.

"My apartment lease is up at the end of the month."

Her words gave him a moment of shiny hope. Which she instantly doused.

"I'll need to be there to sign a new agreement. And the coaching job starts a few days after that."

The world seemed to still. While he knew she'd be leaving eventually—at least she said so—this was a firm deadline. Less than a month, and she could be gone.

It was late when Matt dropped Kelsey off at Katie's place. She changed into her ratty pajama bottoms and stared at herself in the spotted bathroom mirror.

She used a washrag to scrub the blue paint from her cheeks, residue from the handprints that he'd pressed there earlier when they'd been playing around.

Even now, Kelsey couldn't stop a goofy smile because of it.

Her lips looked bee-stung. She'd sat with Matt for a long time in the cab of his truck in the driveway. Kissing.

His kisses had held almost a sense of desperation. It was as if he wanted to convince her through his touch that she should stay. Maybe she shouldn't have told him about her apartment lease, but it was what it was. She'd have to go back at the end of the month, no matter what. If she decided to leave Houston, she'd have to pack up her things. If she decided to stay, there would be papers to sign. And she needed to make a decision about the coaching job.

Matt's touch always had the power to move her. Maybe that was why she was considering what her life could be like if she stayed in Taylor Hills.

A soft knock on the bathroom door startled her.

"You about done in there?" Katie asked from the other side.

"Yeah." They'd always fought for bathroom time as teens. She sort of missed that when she was alone in her apartment in Houston.

She ducked out and went to her bedroom, though she only sat on the end of the bed, hugging her pillow. It was funny. They'd spent so much time cleaning the downstairs, but she hadn't touched a thing up here. There were two track trophies from middle school—plastic painted gold—resting on the windowsill. She'd grumbled about Matt taking her childish artwork home for himself, but her favorite painting, a landscape she'd painted in high school, still hung above her bed.

The sentimental touches brought back memories, both painful and joyful.

What was she going to do?

A few minutes later, Katie leaned her shoulder on the bedroom doorjamb. She was also in ratty pajamas and an even rattier bathrobe.

"You have fun necking with Matt out in the drive?"

Kelsey's face flushed. She buried her face in the pillow, speaking through the stuffing. "We weren't necking."

"Sure looked like something was going on. Are you sure you know what you're doing with Matt? When he finds out how you walked out on him..."

Kelsey buried her face in the pillow again. "I know."

He was going to hate her.

"You're going to get your heart broken," Katie said.

Kelsey shook her head, face still hidden in the pillow. Not possible. She'd been careful to guard her heart.

Except how could she guard against a man who was so charming, so funny, so confident?

A man who had so much confidence in her. Who thought she hung the moon and could hang a second one if she wanted.

She was falling in love with him all over again.

She raised her head from the pillow, felt her eyes go wide at the realization. Katie was still there in the doorway, waiting.

"Oh no," Kelsey breathed.

"You should tell him before you get in any deeper."

How much deeper was there to go when she was already in love with him?

Chapter Nine

Kelsey rushed out of the attorney's office as if
the soles of her sneakers were on fire. The weather had warmed
over the last week, and the bright autumn sun warmed her head
and shoulders.

She wished for a thunderstorm to match her mood.

"Wait up," Katie called out, exiting the Main Street storefront behind her.

Kelsey hurried to unlock her car and get in. In her desire to
escape, she must've hit the *unlock all* button, because Katie
slipped into the passenger seat before she could crank the engine.

Kelsey leveled a look on her sister.

Katie didn't look one iota apologetic. "What are you so upset
about? We did it. The house is cleaned out. And now the
probate is settled."

Kelsey's look turned into a glare. "I'm upset because no one
in there listened to me."

"It was Mama's will. It's impossible to argue with a dead
woman."

So? Her sister's logic didn't make Kelsey feel any better.

She turned her glare out the windshield, wishing her sister
would get out of the car. "I didn't want anything from her."

"I got that. Anybody who knew the two of you got that.
Maybe it's time to make peace."

Kelsey blew out a sigh. "There's nothing left to settle. She didn't believe I could make it to the Olympics, and I proved her wrong."

"Do you really think Mama didn't believe in you?"

"She didn't. She said it enough." Kelsey flexed her hands on the wheel, remembering all the times Mama had told her to dream smaller.

She was tired of sitting here, tired of Taylor Hills, tired of the memories that clung to her like sweaty clothes at the end of a run. Chafing to the point of pain.

She started the car. If Katie wouldn't get out, she could take a ride back to the house and walk back to get her car later.

"It wasn't that she didn't believe in you. She just knew how hard life is. She of all people, right?"

Kelsey didn't have an answer for that. She knew how many hard knocks her mom had taken. Abandoned by her dad. Husband left. Cheated out of a year of pay by an unscrupulous boss.

It didn't change things.

"She didn't want you to get your heart broken. She wanted to protect you."

Kelsey pulled out during a lull in traffic. "That's not what it felt like."

Katie blasted out a sigh. "Fine. Think what you want. What are you going to do with your half of the estate?"

"Nothing." She didn't want it. She'd been frugal with the money she'd received from her post-Olympic endorsements and had a nice chunk still socked away in her savings account. "I don't need the money. Mama might've tried to buy my forgiveness with it, but I'm not selling. I'll give my share to you."

"I'm not taking your half."

Kelsey pulled into the drive and turned off the car. She could find a way to force Katie to take the money. She could buy new appliances for the café kitchen and have them delivered. Katie wouldn't be able to turn them away.

She tapped her left foot on the floorboards. Man, her feet were itching.

"The only way you'd get me to take the money is if you stay in Taylor Hills and run the café with me."

The bottom dropped out of Kelsey's stomach and she clenched the steering wheel tightly. Slowing for a stoplight pulled even more tension into her shoulders.

How could Katie suggest such a thing? Kelsey hated that place.

"It hasn't been so bad, being here with me, has it?" Katie asked. "I thought we've been getting along pretty well."

"Yeah, but..."

But what? How could she tell her sister she didn't feel at home here?

Even as she thought the words, her mind went to Matt.

Katie knew too much. "And Matt's here. Doesn't seem like he's leaving."

"He might." Even as Kelsey blurted the words, she doubted their truth. He'd settled in at the Triple H. Had she secretly wished he'd say something different? Like that he was leaving?

Katie didn't challenge her, but her tone of voice changed from argumentative to resigned. "You could make your home here. Taylor Hills isn't so bad."

The itch in her feet got worse. She shifted the foot not on the brake pedal, but that small movement didn't alleviate it.

"I can't." She swallowed against the truth of it. "I have to go."

THE WEATHER HAD WARMED, allowing Matt and the cowhands to do some needed repairs to the fence in the far west pasture. It was taking longer than he'd anticipated, thanks to some rotted fence posts in a little gully.

The steepness of the terrain played havoc on the muscles in his legs, as he was constantly balancing on an incline while pulling out old posts and replacing them with new ones.

Down the line, Trey and Nate worked in tandem.

Matt took a break as the slant of the afternoon sun changed. He climbed out of the gully and went to the pickup to grab his water jug. He'd quenched his thirst and wiped his mouth with his wrist when he saw someone headed his way. She was a silhouette on the horizon where the gentle hills rolled.

Kelsey. She wore running leggings and a loose long-sleeved

T-shirt. As she neared, he saw she was drenched in sweat, as if she'd run all the way out here. Again.

He dumped the jug in the truck bed and stated toward her. On second thought... he turned back and got the jug out again.

Her eyes were slightly wild and unfocused as he neared.

He extended the canteen, and she took it with a grateful smile and a short nod.

"What's the matter?" he asked as she drank greedily.

She shook her head, capping the water.

He waited her out. *Something* had sent her all the way out here.

Her eyes flicked his way and then off again. "Mama's probate got settled, finally."

He took the hit silently. The settlement was the only thing that had kept Kelsey tethered to town.

He didn't know if their relationship was strong enough to keep her here.

"I'll bet you're glad to have it done with," he said.

She shrugged, her eyes still focused far off. "Katie and I got into an argument. About Mama."

He knew her mom was one of her hot buttons. "You want to talk about it?"

"Not really. I had something else in mind." Now she shot him a hopeful look. "Things have been...different for us since you came back home."

Yeah, because he couldn't remember breaking things off.

"I was wondering...or hoping maybe..." She stopped to take a deep breath. "Is there any way we can keep this going after I head back to Houston? I mean...maybe commute on the weekends or maybe you eventually decide to move on from the Triple H..."

Oh, wow. All the ways he'd imagined this might go, this hadn't been one of them. She was inviting him to tag along with her.

He was close enough to reach for her and he used one hand to tip her face back. He examined her eyes, the slight wrinkle across her smooth forehead, the tension around her mouth. What had prompted this? He couldn't tell if what he was seeing in her eyes was hope... or fear.

He loved her, but he'd promised Gideon in that email that

he'd run the Triple H. He'd spent the last weeks re-learning the lay of the land, reconnecting with his roots and the family property.

Carrie and Scarlett depended on their share of the income from the Triple H. With Gideon out of the picture, the weight of keeping the place afloat fell to Matt.

He couldn't walk away from it. He was needed here.

But he couldn't walk away from the woman he loved, either.

"It's definitely something to think about," he said carefully, aware that he might be stepping into a minefield.

"Something to think about," she repeated softly. A shadow passed behind her eyes.

"What we've got is—always has been—something special."

Now that shadow deepened. Maybe he shouldn't have mentioned the past. He felt like he'd inched closer to one of those mines.

"Special enough that we shouldn't throw it away." He opened his arms, inviting her in and fully aware that she might pull away. He warmed with an intense flash of gratitude when she stepped into his embrace. He tipped her chin up. "I love you, Kels. I've never stopped."

He felt her quick inhale, saw the vulnerability in her face as her eyes scanned his face.

"You can't know that," she breathed. "Your memory—"

"Maybe I haven't remembered everything yet, but I just *know*. I've always loved you. Always known we were meant to be."

He saw the flare of panic cross her expression at his last words. *Meant to be.* Did that have some deeper meaning for her?

His reaction was too slow as she pushed out of his embrace. "I have to go."

"Kelsey, wait."

The way she ducked her head and wouldn't look at him put a pit of fear in his stomach.

"Kels—!"

But she was already running off, running away.

He whirled in a circle, one hand grabbing the back of his neck as he tried to decide if he should get in the pickup and follow her or let her go. Following would mean leaving Trey and

Nate out in the field with their tools, and the day was almost over.

He blew out a breath. Maybe if she had some time to cool down and think, she'd stop freaking out about whatever it was that he'd said wrong.

He glanced her direction once more, but she was already gone, having flown over the horizon and out of sight.

TREY REACHED the top of the gully and spied his boss. Something had happened. Trey could see it in Matt's face as he approached.

Maybe this wasn't good timing, but he'd gathered his courage, and if he waited much longer, he'd chicken out.

He glanced over his shoulder. Nate was still in the gully, gathering his things.

"You got a minute, Boss?"

Matt's expression tightened. "Sure. What's up?"

Was he really going to do this? He thought about Carrie and the expression that had crossed her face when he'd said the Triple H was her home. She hadn't believed it. And he knew it was because of him.

The words wanted to stick in his throat, but he cleared it. "This might not be the best time, but... I'm giving my two weeks' notice."

Matt jerked. He'd been putting some tools up in the truck bed but now straightened and turned to level his gaze straight at Trey. "Come again?"

"I'm quitting."

For someone like him, someone who'd sworn he'd never give up like his pops had, the words tasted like bitter failure. He wanted to yank them back, but he thought about Carrie. She deserved better.

"You can't."

Trey's mouth twisted in what might have been a smile. He appreciated Matt's argument more than he could say.

"I have to."

"This about Carrie? Gideon mentioned something was going on between you two."

Her name was like a punch, but he took that too.

"Nope," he lied. No way was he going to create a situation where Carrie felt even more unwelcome on her own property. He couldn't shake the memory of the shadows in her eyes. "It's just time for me to move on."

Matt shook his head again. "I can't stop you if you're determined, but I'd appreciate it if you could give me more than two weeks. There's no way the boys and I can do the round-up next month without you."

They'd be shorthanded, especially with Dan gone—he was still in prison after stealing from the ranch—but Matt could hire someone temporarily.

He thought about Carrie again. And Scarlett, the little girl who needed a daddy. He'd wanted to be that.

His throat was scratchy when he spoke. "I can stay on a while, but not indefinitely. After the round-up."

It wouldn't be long. Maybe by Christmas. And then he'd be on his way. To where, he didn't know. He'd loved this job, loved the land. This job was what he'd dreamed of. The income wasn't staggering. He'd never get rich, but for someone like him, someone who loved the open land and working with animals, someone who'd come from nothing, this was a good job.

But he loved Carrie. She deserved better, and if it was him keeping her from having it, well, he couldn't live with that.

She came first, even if it meant he lost out. He'd have to find somewhere else to belong.

He just didn't know where.

Chapter Ten

MATT WOKE IN THE DARK OF NIGHT WITH A PIERCING pain in his head, sweating. He hadn't had an ache this bad since he'd been hospitalized after the roadside bomb.

He panted through the agony, which felt like a hot poker jabbing behind his right eye. Reached for the glass of water he knew he'd left on his bedside table. His knuckles knocked into it, sloshing water over the side of the glass and getting his hand wet before he got hold of it.

The tepid wetness in his throat did nothing to soothe the ache in his head. He had prescription pain meds that he'd never used. They were somewhere around here...in the bathroom?

He tried to stand, but the moment his feet hit the floor, his head spun and his legs buckled. He collapsed back into the bed. His head pounded even harder.

He thought about calling out, but the other guys slept upstairs. Would they be able to hear him? He wasn't sure he could muster the strength to shout.

He focused on each pulse of pain behind his eye. For a long time. Forever.

Until the split-seconds between each pain lengthened into seconds and then moments and then breaths.

And he realized that each pain was dumping memories back into his brain. He could remember laughing with his buddies in

"""

a mess hall in a desert, all of them in their uniforms, hidden tension behind their smiles. Gideon's wedding, where he'd stood up for his brother as best man. Getting a video of Scarlett's birth and that moment she'd described for him where he'd held her the very first time.

And, floating slowly to the front of his mind, as if his subconscious self knew he needed to see it...

Kelsey in a navy graduation gown and cap. The tassel kept floating into her eyes. Or maybe she was playing with it in her nervousness, as he watched from the bleachers in the high school gym. She was seated with her class of thirty in folding chairs lined up on the basketball court, in front of the moveable stage they'd erected for the event.

He hooted when she crossed the stage. She flushed a delicate pink, and he knew she'd heard him.

After the ceremony, he'd found her in a crowd of friends and family. It seemed almost everyone in Taylor Hills had shown up.

He scooped her up and twirled her in a circle. She'd giggled, her hair falling on his face.

He kissed her soundly when he put her down, not caring that they were in public.

"Where's your ma?" he asked, not wanting to get her in trouble on such an important date.

Kelsey's smile faded slightly. "She had to go back to the café. Everyone and their dog will want to eat out today to celebrate. She let me have the day off, though."

He knew the café was a point of contention between the two, knew that Kelsey hated working there and that her mom relied on her too much.

He followed her like a puppy toward the parking lot behind the gym. "Do you want to drive down to Dallas? I bet Uncle Pat knows a fancy restaurant, and we could call ahead for a reservation." He was so happy for her, proud to bursting and he knew he was rambling. "When we're married, we can do that every weekend. You deserve it."

He'd parked next to her car, in the back forty of the lot. Why had she parked back there anyway?

Her head was down as she turned to him. She was playing

with her keys, her hands almost hidden in the folds of the voluminous gown. "I think we should talk."

"Okay. Shoot." He'd had no idea what was coming. Had been so blindly in love.

She took a deep breath. "I think we should break up."

He laughed, sure she was joking. Until the downward tilt of her chin and the fact that she wasn't looking at him cut through his confident happiness. "What? Kels, what's going on?"

When she raised her face, tears stood in her eyes, but he also saw the determined set of her jaw. "Matt, you're a small-town guy, and I... I want more than Taylor Hills. I'm going somewhere with my life."

He already knew that.

"If this is about me taking a gap year—"

"It's not. I don't want a long-distance relationship, and I don't want to be together anymore."

He didn't know where this was coming from. "If you want me to come to Houston while you're in school, I will. I can find a job—"

"That's not what I want."

Her tone was final. He knew she wasn't going to change her mind. His stomach caved in on itself.

"You don't love me anymore?" he dared to ask.

Her eyes glittered as she stared at his face, but it was a hard glitter. Not tears. "Maybe I never did."

A sucker punch. H didn't know what to say to fix this, to make it right. He stood there like a dummy while she got in her car and drove off.

He'd stuck to the Triple H and avoided town until September, well after she'd left for university.

She hadn't come back. Hadn't changed her mind.

And the small-town boy had enlisted in the USAF. Partly to prove he could be more than what she'd thought of him. And partly to get away from the memories that plagued him in Taylor Hills.

He'd been heartbroken. Still hadn't understood what was it about him that wasn't good enough for her.

She'd walked out on him.

She'd walked away, and his entire life had changed because of it. He'd changed. Enlisted. Become an airman, a good one. He'd seen enough of the world to know that Taylor Hills was just fine, thank you very much. Seen enough to know that the grass was not greener over the horizon. He was a different man because of what Kelsey had done.

And he liked the man he'd become.

He didn't know what life would have looked like if Kelsey hadn't broken up with him, and he couldn't say for sure it would be better. Even with the roadside bomb, even with the amnesia, maybe this had been the better path. Maybe he and Kelsey had needed to separate to learn how much they truly meant to each other.

Yes, she'd walked out on him. But he could forgive her.

She wanted to be together now. Maybe she hadn't settled things with her dead ma, but that shouldn't keep them from being together.

By the time he'd sweated through the last of the pains, he figured he had most of his memory back. The mundane, the terrible, and the beautiful.

Dawn was lightening the horizon, and he couldn't wait any longer to tell Kelsey that he remembered.

And that he still wanted to be with her.

He showered the nasty sweat off. His hair was still damp when he pulled up to Katie's place. Kelsey's car wasn't in the drive. That gave him a little hesitation, but they'd cleaned out the old garage behind the house. Maybe she'd parked in there.

It was Katie's hangdog expression when she answered the door in an old bathrobe that told him first.

"She's gone?" he asked.

Katie nodded, gripping the doorframe, her own sorrow evident.

He reeled, returning to his truck as if in a trance. She'd left him. Again.

This time without a goodbye.

Chapter Eleven

A week after she'd left Taylor Hills, Kelsey stood in the center of her tiny efficiency apartment, hands on her hips.

She'd come home determined to find her way alone. Only to realize maybe she was more like her mother than she'd thought, because when she'd opened her closet to hang up some blouses, she'd nearly been toppled by a box wedged between two others. She'd ignored it for so long but... her closet was bursting with junk.

She'd ripped the boxes from the closet and began unloading the contents, tossing things across the surface of her bed. She was sure it was all trash, just like Mama's had been.

But it wasn't trash.

She'd unboxed all the paintings and sketches she'd done in her first two years of college. Before Professor Bernard's harsh criticism had humiliated her.

She'd spread them out across her apartment, feeling again the emotions she'd experienced as she completed each piece.

Back when Bernard had humiliated her, she'd stuffed them away with ruthless efficiency. She'd turned her entire focus to distance running and the Olympics. And she'd locked away all the feelings associated with them.

But her closet had exploded, and so had her once-hidden emotions.

There had been a piece portraying her mother, one hand cocked on her hip, the other on a coffeepot as she talked to a crowd of good ol' boys in the café. A close-up of Katie with a winsome smile. And several of Matt—with his horses, sitting on a rail fence, dancing in the moonlight, though Kelsey had purposely obscured her own features in that painting.

She'd been exhausted from her drive and the pain of abandoning Matt all over again, but she hadn't been able to look away from the paintings. Not for hours.

The next day she'd unearthed her easel and paints.

She'd made a trip to the local art store and come home to throw herself into a painting of herself, crossing the finish line at the Olympics.

That painting was followed by one of her mother outdoors on a quilt, something Kelsey remembered from a special childhood picnic they'd taken on one of Mama's rare days off. There could've been so many more of those, but it was what it was.

She painted one of Matt sitting on his tailgate with a grin, hints of red paint smeared across his cheeks and forehead.

Now, she sat on the floor, staring at the three paintings and what they represented for her life. The emotions that had spilled out on the canvas.

Something had clicked inside her, something that had been missing for a long time. Professor Bernard had shaken her confidence, made her question her talent and self-worth. He'd rattled her enough to make her her listen to the tapes she'd thought long-buried, the ones of her mother's words, her mother's lack of faith.

She didn't have to believe Bernard anymore. She didn't have to believe her Mama's words, either.

And she knew what she wanted to do.

A knock on her door brought her to her feet—the Chinese takeout she'd ordered a half hour ago.

When she opened the door, it wasn't a deliveryman.

Matt's muscled frame filled the doorway.

Conscious of the painting in the living room behind her and

what it said about what she felt for the man, she closed the door partially behind her.

"What are you doing here?" She crossed her arms over her middle.

He raised one brow. "You left without saying goodbye. Mind if I come in?"

He reached past her, as if he were about to slip inside.

"No! I mean, yes." She shifted to block him. "I mind." That painting...

He smiled, a dangerous, satisfied smile that made her stomach do a slow flip. "Fine." He propped one hand against the doorframe above her head and leaned close. "We can talk right here."

Too close.

She slipped out from the space between his body and the wall, backing through the door. "Come in then."

She did her best to angle her body between his view and the incriminating painting, moving quickly to turn it to face the wall. She left the other two paintings where they were.

Of course, he didn't miss anything, that brow arching again as he watched her.

He stood with feet braced apart, his presence making the tiny living area slash kitchen slash breakfast nook seem that much smaller.

He looked all around, taking in every detail of her life. The running shoes spilling out of her closet. The sticky notes that lined her fridge door, reminders of appointments and phone numbers for favorite take-out restaurants. The art supplies that covered her small kitchen table.

Was he ever going to speak? What was he doing here?

"I remembered," he said after a long silent wait. He looked right at her, and she could see it was true.

She swallowed.

"Everything."

She closed her eyes a moment, wishing she could sink into the floor. Here she'd been so hopeful...

But why had he come here? Surely not just to tell her he hated her.

"You remembered that I broke up with you? Broke your heart?"

"Broke both our hearts, if I'm guessing right." He stepped toward her, expression serious. "I also remembered that I didn't come after you."

She started to tremble.

He took another step forward. "You were right, back then. I was a boy. A man would've known to fight for the woman he loved."

She swallowed hard. Shook her head. "I—"

"You were scared. And we were both young. I can forgive you. If you can forgive me for letting you go."

He stopped right in front of her. "I'd like to see that painting you're hiding behind you."

This was her moment. She could keep running forever or...

She shored up her courage and stepped to the side. He squatted and reached out to turn the painting around. He propped it against the wall.

He looked at it for a long moment, finally straightening with his gaze still on the painting. "That's me, right?"

She reached to pinch him on the arm, but he intercepted her, turning at the same time so they faced each other. His hands rested on her waist.

"I figured out what I want to do with my life," she blurted to the collar of his shirt, too afraid to say it to his face. Not yet.

"Oh yeah?"

She nodded. "I want to do art therapy. Help children and young adults express themselves through art."

She looked up enough to see the twitch of his mouth.

"This a personal quest?" he asked.

She shrugged the tiniest bit. "Art always helped me express myself. Until I started second-guessing myself, and then I sort of... forgot. Started running away from my problems instead of solving them. Like with my mom. I think I... I think I could help kids not to do the same."

His smile broke through. "That sounds rewarding. I'm happy for you."

He brushed a kiss across her forehead. "If your paintings

express your emotions, you want to tell me what that picture of me means?"

Heat flared in her cheeks. Cocky man. She pushed slightly against his chest. "You know."

"Maybe. I'd still like to hear it."

She looked him full in the face, gathered all her courage. "I love you, Matt."

He pressed his lips to hers lightly. "I love you too. Never stopped."

It was so unbelievable that tears pricked her eyes. "Really?"

"Really. And I don't want to freak you out again"—he leaned back and made a pretense of checking whether she was wearing shoes. She was barefoot—"but I still think we should get married."

She laughed, albeit a little soggy. "If I do this art therapy thing, I'm going to have to finish my degree. Maybe have a second major or get my Masters." She'd have the money, thanks to Mama.

He shrugged, his brawny shoulders moving beneath her hands. "Whatever you need to do, I'll be there for you."

This time, she kissed him.

When they were both good and breathless, they broke apart.

"I can probably find a school closer to Taylor Hills," she told him.

"That's good, 'cause I just lost one of the cowboys, and the Triple H is depending on me."

She played with the collar of his shirt. "The ranch would be a beautiful place to get married...in the spring." She could bunk down with Katie until then.

His smile rivaled the sun. "Yeah? Is that a hint? Good thing I brought this."

He pulled back, reaching into his right hip pocket. Her breath caught as he pulled out something sparkly.

Then it felt as if she'd inhaled too many paint fumes; her mind spun as he sank to one knee. "Kels, I can't live without you. Please marry me and make my life whole."

She nodded, tears coming as he slipped the band on her finger. He gathered her in for another deep kiss and then let her loose to gaze at the ring.

"This is your grandma's ring," she said, realization falling over her. The trio of small diamonds in the middle of a plain gold band was familiar.

"Kinda fitting, since you'll be a Triple H bride and all."

A Triple H bride.

Matt's bride.

She itched—but not to run. To paint. To create because of the man who'd never stopped believing in their love, who'd never stopped believing in her.

A Triple H bride.

Yes, please.

Courting Carrie

Chapter One

Christmas cheer. He wasn't feeling it. This year, he felt more like Scrooge.

Trey Reynolds sat behind the wheel of his truck, parked on Taylor Hills's Main Street, and chomped on a ham sandwich that tasted about as *blah* as he felt.

Over the past two weeks, he'd seen the town transform into a Christmas wonderland. During previous Christmases, he'd worked the ranch—the Triple H, his home for eight years. But this holiday season, he had a firsthand view as the decorations appeared: green garlands strung with lights and twisted around every light pole, storefronts filled with Santas and elves, wreaths on doors and windows all along the small downtown.

After leaving the Triple H, he'd taken a temp job at the feed store. It would last him through the holiday season. Then, he'd have to get serious about hiring on at another ranch.

Preferably somewhere far away. Far enough that he could heal from his broken heart.

"Mr. Trey!"

A child's voice drew his gaze down the sidewalk to the short brunette in her bright red pea coat. She was waving wildly from the sidewalk. Scarlett Hale.

He waved back, then glanced past her, over her head and down the sidewalk to see if her mom was following and how much trouble he was going to be in because he'd let himself be seen.

But Carrie Hale was nowhere in sight. Not on the sidewalk or in the doorway of the small grocery store. He didn't spy her car parked along the street. Curious.

He opened the door and stepped onto the sidewalk as Scarlett started toward him.

Where was Carrie? It wasn't like the single mom to let Scarlett out of her sight.

The spiffy new jeans he wore chafed slightly, and he spared a mournful thought for his old, worn-in work jeans. But the feed store didn't appreciate the stained, frayed jeans, so he'd grudgingly plopped down hard-earned cash on a new pair. A chill seeped beneath the collar of his open jacket.

He caught the small torpedo of energy as seven-year-old Scarlett Hale launched herself at him. She smelled like kid shampoo, and he also picked up a whiff of sugar and cinnamon—like maybe she'd been in the bakery across the street?

"Hey kiddo. What's doing?"

She laughed when he tickled her chin, but he was quick to set her down, knowing her mom wanted more distance between them.

And because he loved Carrie, he was giving her what she wanted.

"Um...shopping."

The kid's vague answer set off alarms in his head. He started a slow meander back the direction Scarlett had come from. "From the sidewalk?"

The astute little girl sent him a sideways look but fell into step beside him. "Haven't ya ever heard of window shopping?"

"I have, I just didn't know little girls were allowed to window shop without their mommies."

She looked down at her feet, but not before he caught the guilt playing across her features.

That's about what he'd thought.

And right at that moment, a harried-looking Carrie ran out of the dress shop—not the bakery like he'd thought—pausing on the sidewalk as she frantically looked in all directions.

He saw the stark fear and intense relief hit when she caught sight of Scarlett beside him.

"There you are!" He heard the frantic note in her voice, but a glance down at Scarlett showed the girl was oblivious to her mom's panic.

"Why did you leave the store?" Carrie demanded. She knelt to Scarlett's level. "You know you're supposed to stay with me unless you get permission."

Scarlett ducked her chin. "I'm sorry, Mama. I saw Mr. Trey's truck, and I got so excited to see him."

Carrie slid an abbreviated look to him, her gaze not quite hitting his face.

He brushed off the sting of that, focusing on the girl at his side.

Scarlett reached up and placed her tiny hand into his meaty paw. "I gotta talk to Mr. Trey about something. It's important."

Now Carrie's gaze bounced off of him again, this time settling a little longer. There was a definite hint of death glare involved. "What do you need to talk to Mr. Trey about?" *That you can't tell me?* The subtext was clear.

Scarlett looked up at him, her pixie features serious. "It's sorta a secret."

"A secret." Carrie didn't sound happy about that at all.

"Please, Mama. It's important. *Veeeeery* important."

Carrie loved her daughter, it was evident in everything she did, and this was no exception. "All right, sweetie." But the glare she gave Trey told him she'd be following up to find out what exactly the secret was.

He shrugged, shoulders shifting beneath his jacket. He had no idea.

"If you want to keep shopping, I'll sit right out here with her." Trey jerked his thumb toward a bench just outside the dress shop, which, of course, was decorated with swags of greenery on its back and arms. "Unless it's too cold for her to be out here."

The girl had had an asthma attack almost a month ago, and he'd never forget seeing her tiny body in the hospital bed, white as the sheets beneath her.

Carrie gave him a look that was half exasperation, half reluctant appreciation.

"It's not cold today, Mr. Trey," Scarlett said.

Carrie still looked like she wanted to refuse. "It's pretty mild," she agreed with a grimace.

"You can watch us through the windows the whole time," he reassured her.

"Fine." Her word was uttered with little grace and a heavy sigh.

He sat on the bench, one arm stretched across the back, trying not to let the greenery poke his neck beneath his Stetson. The scent of pine seeped in, but even though he was seeing his two favorite girls in the world, he couldn't find cheer, not really. Best to just get through this, whatever it was.

Scarlett perched beside him, her legs swinging above the ground. She kept looking over her shoulder until she was satisfied her mom had disappeared inside the dress shop.

Trey was under no misapprehension that Carrie wasn't watching his every move through the storefront window.

He was also unbearably curious what Scarlett's big secret was.

"I need some help," Scarlett said. "With Mama's Christmas present."

Okay, this wasn't so bad. He didn't know what he'd been expecting, but he could probably find a way to help with a gift. His job search was taking longer than he'd expected, and maybe this distraction would help get him through the holiday season.

"What do you want to get her?"

"A husband."

He choked on his own saliva and had to cough past the burn in his throat. "What?"

"I've been watching other Mamas, you know, at my friends' houses sometimes and at church and like at the family fun night at school. Those Mamas that have husbands, they giggle a lot. And they get this special look in their eyes when they're looking at their husbands. Sorta a googly look."

A *googly* look.

She looked down at her swinging feet. "And...sometimes the husbands take their little girls to the daddies and daughters Christmas Eve dance or other special things like that."

His heart panged for the little girl who was watching so

closely to notice those things. Scarlett needed a daddy. And yes, he'd often thought Carrie needed someone to look after her. He'd wanted to be that man for both of them.

"So I thought maybe you could be Mama's husband."

That's when he really started to hurt. His insides burned worse than they had a few years back when he'd gotten gored by a longhorn cow.

"Scarlett, your mama and I..." He didn't know what was the right thing to say here. He still didn't know what had gone wrong between him and Carrie. They'd been dating, spending lots of time together, and then all of a sudden, she'd ended things. No matter the roses he'd sent her after or how many times he'd asked, she'd never spilled about what he'd done wrong.

"Honey, I wish I could be your daddy. I really do. But I can't be your mama's husband."

He hated her crestfallen look. Hated the serious little nod she gave. He especially hated that she'd seemed to expect his answer.

She turned that earnest, trusting gaze on him again. "Then, can you help me find a different husband for Mama for Christmas?"

And wasn't that a hit to his solar plexus, thinking about Carrie with someone else? Scarlett had no idea that she was kicking his butt in an internal boxing match she couldn't see.

He tried to put her off. "That sounds like a job for Santa Claus."

He expected her to light up with Christmas joy, but instead, her mouth settled into a tiny straight line, as if she were willing her lips not to tremble, and her head tilted downward.

"Santa's not real," she whispered.

Another ouch. Seven wasn't too old to still believe in Santa, was it? Shoot, he still wanted to believe sometimes.

He had to work at keeping his face neutral. "Who told you that?"

A small shrug, with her head still down. "Some boys in my class."

Who oughta be sent to the principal's office.

"*I* still believe in Santa," he said. Because sometimes you just had to believe in miracles, Christmas and otherwise. He'd seen miracles happen for other people, even if he'd never expect one for himself. "And I bet if you asked your mama, she'd tell you she believes in Santa, too."

Scarlett sent him a sideways look. Almost like she wanted to still believe but wasn't sure.

"When you go to see Santa at the community center"—where he showed up every year for two Saturdays in a row—"why don't you ask him for a husband for your mama?" Oh, he almost choked on the words.

And Scarlett sent him a sly glance. "I'll ask, but only if you promise to help me look for a good one."

He gave it some real thought, staring at his boots. Because he cared about Scarlett, and because the girl deserved a real daddy in her life, not the deadbeat who'd abandoned her and Carrie years ago.

It hurt like being gored all over again, but he nodded solemnly. "Okay."

She lit up like a Christmas tree. "You promise? Pinky swear."

He made the required promises, and she bounced off her seat and inside the store.

There was no way he could face Carrie right now—his face burned just thinking about telling her the promise Scarlett had extracted from him—so he waved to her through the window and high-tailed it back to his truck. Back to work. Coming over to Main Street to eat his lunch had been a mistake, but he'd been itching with the desire to move, to get out of the shop for a while. He missed his wide-open spaces.

Taking the job at the feed store was a tactical move. Every farmer and rancher around came through there. Surely *somebody* was looking for a cowhand.

Right now, he didn't even care about clocking back in. All he wanted was to hide from Carrie. If she wanted to know what Scarlett's secret was so badly, she was going to have to track him down.

"AND THEN HE ran off like his spurs were on fire." Carrie Hale sidled closer to the styling chair and the client she was giving a dye job. She pulled the small brush with its glob of hair dye through the strands of hair and then carefully folded the piece of foil until the hair was enclosed. It was the last one, thankfully. "There."

From the chair, her best friend and the town's veterinarian, Sarah Campbell, stared at her in the mirror, her nose slightly wrinkled. After years of dyeing and perming hair, Carrie had gone nose-blind to the scent of the dye.

"It was probably nothing," Sarah said.

With Trey Reynolds, it was never *nothing*. It'd been three days, and Carrie had been unable to focus on much besides the secret conversation her daughter had had with Carrie's ex-boyfriend.

Scarlett was *her* daughter. There should be no secrets, especially considering Scarlett was only seven.

"You're right," she agreed. "It's probably nothing. I don't want to think about Trey, anyway." That was pure truth.

"For someone you don't want to think about, we talk about him an awful lot."

She stuck her tongue out at her friend in the mirror before leading her across the room to the small seating area near the front window and caddy-corner to two seats with salon dryers. The window overlooked Main Street and was partially blocked by a curtain along the bottom half. The top half was left open for natural light to spill in.

Carrie visually checked on Velma Marrs, whose white-haired perm was setting in one of the heater chairs. The older woman was deep in a magazine.

The highlight on Sarah's head had been extensive and taken the better part of an hour, because her friend never took vacation days and tended to let her personal grooming slide. She'd only taken this afternoon off because her fiancé was coming to town later, and she hadn't seen the guy in a couple of months. And Carrie had begged her to do some highlights to cover the grays peeping through Sarah's dark locks.

Sarah looked to make sure Velma was under the heater and couldn't hear before she leaned in to Carrie. "I can't believe Matt let him quit."

"Let who quit?"

"Trey."

Sarah's statement didn't make sense, and Carrie flicked her own look at Velma before leaning close to where Sarah had sat. "What do you mean, Trey quit?"

Sarah's surprise was evident in her raised brows—ones that needed waxing. Carrie made a mental note to suggest it before she left the shop today. "When I was out there to drop off the barn cat we spayed, I saw him packing up his truck. Matt told me it was his last day. I thought you knew. I heard he'd taken a job at the feed store temporarily."

She hadn't known. And why hadn't her brother told her?

"How long ago was this?"

"Hmmm. Maybe three weeks? But you don't care, right?"

Carrie firmed her lips. Her friend was right. She shouldn't care. She left Sarah with her own magazine and headed back to her chair to sweep up the hair clippings and put away the dyeing supplies. Fuming, but only a little.

What happened out at the Triple H wasn't her business, but still...

Trey wasn't her business either, not since she'd broken things off.

But with the small-town grapevine active and crazy fast, how was it she hadn't heard about this?

Trey had quit.

It felt wrong. Very wrong. When they'd been together, he'd spoken frequently and fondly of the Triple H being home.

A man didn't leave his home, not unless he made a mistake like she had all those years ago. What was he thinking?

She kept her eye on the two timers as she swept the floor and reorganized the bottles at her station that always seemed to get out of place. She'd worked at the small salon—only three styling chairs—since she'd finished her stylist's license after high school. Back then, she'd had big dreams of moving on to bigger and better things.

Now she'd settled in to small town life. Sure, her salary and meager tips would never be enough to afford a European vacation, but she didn't need much. She had a mortgage on the bungalow two blocks from Scarlett's elementary school. She'd probably pay the house off by the time her first grandchild arrived. She was close to Matt and his fiancé Kelsey and got to speak to Gideon overseas every other week.

She didn't need to go home anymore.

The bell over the front door jangled a welcome as someone entered. She was the only stylist working this afternoon, so she turned to greet the next customer.

It was Zach Evans. They'd been a grade apart back in high school, and he worked at the small Taylor Hills bank as a manager or something. He'd never come into the salon for a haircut, at least not when she'd been working.

But he smiled, and after she checked the timer for Velma's perm, she motioned him into the chair and swung a cape around his shoulders.

"What brings you in today?" she asked as she aimed her water bottle at his hair. It was nice and thick. Just the very thinnest sprinkling of gray hairs. Felt like he used expensive salon shampoo, though he wasn't one of their usuals.

"Oh, you know." He motioned to his hair, the movement of his hand rattling the cape. He smoothed it over his thigh. "It's about time."

His hair wasn't that long. It had to have been cut less than a month ago, and she knew lots of cowboys—the whole gang at the Triple H—who only came in when it became necessary because their hair was getting in their eyes. Maybe Zach was more particular.

"You want it cut in the same style?" She smiled at him in the mirror, and he nodded.

She got out her electric clippers and a comb.

She'd learned that styling hair in a small town meant that most of her customers wanted to chat, even though she'd prefer to do her work without the distraction. She'd also learned that being friendly got her bigger tips, and business had been a little down lately. That was a bad thing with Christmas coming up.

So she worked up the best smile she could muster. "How've you been? Things busy at the bank this time of year?"

He started to nod and then thought better of it with her clippers at his neck. "Yeah, a little. Not as bad as tax time or harvest."

"Gotcha. Well, do you have any big plans for Christmas? Your parents moved away, didn't they?"

She kept her eyes on his hair. Almost halfway done now, this would be an easy one...

"Yeah, they're in Florida now. I go down every other Christmas, but this is my year to stay here."

She finished clipping the front of his head, only half aware that he was probably staring right at her stomach and those last fifteen pounds of baby weight that she'd been planning to lose since Scarlett had been born. He wasn't bad looking, she mused as she moved around to the back of his head and tilted his chin down so she could attack the line of hair above his collar. But the only man she'd sucked in her tummy for had been—

She cut off that line of thought just as she noticed his hands fidgeting on his knees. Was he nervous or something?

"Done," she said in her most chipper voice, unsnapping the salon cape. She grabbed a soft barber's brush and swiped away the stray hairs from the collar of his shirt.

He shifted nervously in the chair, meeting her gaze in the mirror. "Say... do you want to grab a cup of coffee sometime? Or maybe hot chocolate. You know, 'tis the season and everything."

It was so out of left field that she stared at him in open-mouthed shock for at least a second before she pulled herself together. "Oh, that's...nice. Thank you for asking, but, um...I don't think so."

Other than a blush high on his cheeks, he didn't seem fazed by her blundered rejection, only nodded and got up from the chair, paid and left.

The timer for Velma's perm dinged, and Carrie didn't have time to ponder the weirdness of Zach's request until she'd washed the dye out of Sarah's hair and got her settled back in the stylist's chair. Her friend stared at her, wide-eyed, in the mirror. "What was that?"

"I have no idea," Carrie said.

She wasn't the kind of girl guys randomly asked out. Everyone in town knew about Scarlett, knew she was a single mom. She wasn't ashamed of it, but it was baggage, and in her experience, the good guys didn't seem interested in baggage.

Except for Trey.

. . .

Dusk was falling as Sarah Campbell exited her veterinary clinic in a rush, her usual modus operandi. She needed to call the ram's owner and tell them the surgery had been a success. She'd put her phone on speaker and do it on the way—her truck was too old for Bluetooth technology.

First, she had to call James.

She took a deep breath of the chilly evening air, wrinkling her nose against the last vestiges of antiseptic smell that wanted to cling to her olfactory glands. Her truck door creaked as she wrenched it open. The truck was only two years old but already had almost two hundred thousand miles on it, thanks to the demands of her job.

Today's emergency call had come just as she'd been leaving Carrie's salon. She'd purposely kept her afternoon free of appointments, but when Jessie had called with news that one of their client's sheep had gotten run over by a tractor wheel, Sarah had gone into *rescue mode* and forgotten about everything else. As usual.

James answered his phone with a distracted, "Yeah?"

"Hey, honey!" she said in her cheeriest voice, holding the phone between her ear and shoulder as she shifted the truck into reverse.

"Sarah."

He was mad.

She exhaled a sigh. She'd ruined their evening together, one they'd been planning for several weeks. But she couldn't just let the ram die.

"I'm so sorry. Where are you?" she asked. "My house? I can be there in about ten minutes—"

"Slow down. What are you talking about?"

Through the connection, she could tell he'd gone from distraction to attention. But his question...

"Our date night?" she prompted. *The one we've been planning for weeks...*

He groaned. "Oh, no."

"You forgot," she whispered. She kicked the truck into park and slumped in the driver's seat of her pickup, suddenly drained from the adrenaline and intensity of the afternoon. At this time of night, the parking lot was empty except for Jessie's truck, and no one cared that she was half-in and half-out of the parking spot.

"Sarah, I'm sorry."

"It's okay. I just..." She didn't want to sound petulant. James was working hard toward a partnership in the Austin firm where he was an attorney. He was doing it for them. "Actually, I just got out of an emergency surgery. A ram got run over and suffered from internal bleeding—"

"You can tell me all about it later, babe. I'm right in the middle of a deposition, and I've got to go."

"Okay—"

She looked down at her phone. Had he hung up on her? She tapped the screen. It showed the call's duration and that it had ended, but it was impossible to tell whether the call had dropped or if he'd hung up on her. No, he wouldn't have, even if he'd been in the middle of something important.

They loved each other. They were getting married next summer.

And she could forgive him for being a slave to his job, right? She'd joined the country practice as partner two years ago, and she barely had time to eat, herself.

Since James wasn't in town waiting on her—was, in fact, a good eight hours away—she climbed out of her truck and returned to the clinic.

Her assistant Jessie looked up from their back office computer, where she was no doubt writing up the report from the surgery where she'd acted as nurse.

"He cancelled?"

Sarah shrugged off the slight judgment in her coworker's statement. "Turns out I don't need you to stay and observe the patient. Go on home to Rex."

"You need a vacation," the very pregnant Jessie muttered, but she didn't protest as Sarah nudged her out from in front of the computer.

Sarah barely registered her leaving as she input every detail she could remember from the surgery. Her professors had lectured often on how important it was to record every detail.

Sometimes one tiny factor could affect an animal's recovery, and it was important to have all the data at hand.

Almost an hour later—after she'd raided the fridge in the tiny break room and scarfed down a questionable piece of left-over quiche—she returned to the large surgery room to check on the ram.

He was still sleeping off the anesthetic.

She moved closer, cautiously. Out of habit, she plugged her stethoscope into her ears and listened to his breathing and heartbeat.

He was resting, which was what she wanted. She eyed the bandages he wore over his hip and leg. No blood was showing through, and she wouldn't check beneath the bandages until the morning.

As she stood, she looked around the large surgical room. She loved this country practice, loved the fact that they had a surgery room for her large-animal patients.

What would it be like when she moved to Austin and began to practice there? This year was slipping away—it was almost Christmas. Next summer would soon be upon her.

Anxiety twisted in her stomach.

James was pressing her to change her specialty to small animals. Certainly it was more lucrative because she could see more patients in a day—often her house calls to farms and ranches ate up time. But she didn't love working with small animals. Maybe that would change, in time.

James was in Austin. That was the important thing, wasn't it?

So far, she hadn't had any luck finding a replacement for herself, but she remained determined to do so. She knew what it felt like to be abandoned, and she wasn't going to do that to the three other vets she now counted as friends.

<h1 style="text-align:center">Chapter Two</h1>

BY THE TIME CARRIE HAD HELPED WITH SCARLETT'S homework—why did first graders have to do so much reading, anyway?—fed them both dinner, gotten Scarlett in bed, delivered a necessary cup of water, cleaned up the day's dishes, and laid out clothes for both of them for tomorrow, she'd run out of procrastination.

It was late, but not that late, so, standing in the kitchen in her bare feet, she dialed Trey's cell.

"'lo?"

Hearing his voice over the phone hit low in her belly. She'd forgotten about that. Or maybe blocked it.

She took a deep breath. "It's Carrie." She sat down at the table, careful of her suddenly weak knees.

"Yeah, I know."

Of course he did. "I thought you might've..."

"Erased you from my phone?" *And my life?* His silent question judged her.

She knew he hadn't. Just two months ago, he'd shown up at the hospital when Scarlett had had an asthma attack.

She played with the half-burned candle in the center of the tabletop, squeezed her eyes closed. She knew he was a good guy. It just couldn't matter.

"I'd like to know what Scarlett said to you last Saturday."

He was silent for long enough that her gaze had wandered and she noticed the crumbs in the corner of the room. Then, "It's about a Christmas gift for you. She swore me to secrecy, or I'd tell you more."

That was a relief. It wasn't anything sinister. Maybe she shouldn't, but she trusted that he was telling her the truth.

"Can't you give me a hint? Should I be expecting anything in particular?"

There was an awkwardness in this pause. "I couldn't say."

Silence descended between them. She stood and paced to the kitchen sink. Outside, it was dark, but the tree in her yard blocked most of the stars from view.

The silence hurt. Before, when they'd been together, they'd filled hours upon hours with conversation.

All of that was gone now.

She gripped the sink, her knuckles turning white. The floor was cold against her bare feet, and the chill seeped to the top of her head. She should've brought a sweater from her room.

Finally, he asked, "Was there anything else?"

She should leave it alone, but she blurted out, "Did you really quit your job at the Triple H?"

He sighed softly. "Yeah."

"Because of what happened with us?"

"No," his retort came sharply. "Never that."

"Then what? You loved working there."

There was a mumble that she couldn't make out, one that sounded like *love you more*. But when he spoke, it was, "With Matt home now, I'm not needed there."

She doubted that. Trey had been a part of the Triple H for years, working with her brother Gideon and the foreman Nate. Recently, Gideon had relocated overseas with his wife Alessandra, a European princess, and left Nate with more responsibility. She'd always been jealous of their brotherhood, the camaraderie all the cowboys shared.

Trey was an integral part of that. She knew he didn't have close family ties; the Triple H had been his family. Why would he give that up?

"Are you going to move away?"

She couldn't imagine him being gone.

"I'm sure I'll be fine wherever I land."

He would.

But would she survive without Trey in her life?

TREY TURNED off his phone and stuffed his device in his pocket.

Nate was lying flat on his back on the barn floor beneath an old tractor, tinkering with a wrench. He stuck out his head long enough to give Trey a look, complete with raised brows.

"You didn't tell her, did you?" Nate slid back beneath the tractor, a clang of metal echoing in the barn.

"He didn't tell her," Chase agreed. The other cowboy reclined on a stack of hay bales, chewing on a single straw. His hat rested on one knee.

Winter was always a slower season for the ranch, allowing more time to maintain the equipment and make repairs to the buildings, if needed.

Which left Matt Hale more time to spend with his fiancé, Kelsey, and left the foreman and cowhand with some downtime to razz Trey. He had an evening shift at the feed store tonight, and Nate had been bugging him to come and get the cats.

The two barn kittens were maybe three months old, and Trey'd gotten attached to them. So had Scarlett, but Carrie had said she couldn't take both. Scarlett loved those kittens, and he'd promised her he'd find them a good home. The hotel manager had taken pity on him and was allowing him to have them in his room, provided he paid for any damages. Surely someone in town wanted to put two rowdy kittens under the Christmas tree. Right now the kittens were frolicking in one of the empty stalls nearby.

He shouldn't have stopped to chat with the cowboys, but he'd missed their company. Not their ribbing.

"She already has enough negative feelings about this place," Trey said, crossing his arms over his chest. "She doesn't need to think she's the reason I'm leaving."

"She *is* the reason you're leaving," Chase said.

Trey shrugged. "She's not all of it."

The other cowboy raised his brows until they disappeared into his shaggy hairline.

"You've been chasing her long enough." Nate's voice was muffled from beneath the tractor. Metal clanged again. "It's time. Just wish you didn't have to leave."

It would be too hard to stay at the Triple H and watch Carrie move on with someone else. And if he was part of the reason she didn't want anything to do with the ranch, he couldn't stand that.

"Her brothers need to get her back out here," Trey said. "This place is in her blood, even if she doesn't think so."

Chase chewed on his piece of hay some more. "She's stubborn."

Not so. She'd been hurt in the past, hurt a lot. Somehow, she hid it from everyone but Trey.

"You want me to go in and get a haircut?" Chase asked with a slow grin. "Ask her out, too?"

Trey's stomach rolled over, but he forced a smile. "If you want to." He never should've told the cowboys about Scarlett's request or his idea, but they knew him better than anyone else. They were like brothers.

He was going to miss them.

Nate pushed out from beneath the tractor and set the wrench on the dirt floor at his side. He rested his arms on his bent knees. "It's not too late to change your mind."

Trey nodded. "I'm stubborn too. This is the right thing for both of us."

Now if only he could believe his own words.

Chapter Three

A WEEK AFTER MAKING HIS PROMISE TO SCARLETT, Trey had a cardboard box of two scuffling kittens next to him in the cab of his truck. He felt bad leaving them cooped up in the motel room all day—and his wallet was feeling the burn as they'd destroyed two sets of curtains.

He'd made arrangements with his boss at the feed store to put them in a small crate and hang out with them near the store's front doors today, so hopefully someone would decide to take them home.

He passed Carrie's little hybrid, parked in her regular spot in front of the salon. That was one thing about living in town. He always knew where she was, because he could always spot her car in the town full of pickups.

His phone buzzed in his hip pocket, and he pulled into a spot on Main Street to answer. The kittens yowled when the motion of his truck stopped.

"This is Trey."

"It's Johnnie Miller."

"What can I do for ya, Mrs. Mayor?"

"I'll cut right to the chase. My regular Santa just called in sick, and I'm desperate. I heard you might be looking to pick up some temporary work, and I need you. Taylor Hills needs you."

He had to chuckle at her desperation. "I'll do it, Ms. Johnnie. Where and when do you need me?"

"Can you be at the community center in fifteen minutes?"

He glanced at the cats who'd gone silent. One orange-and-white paw was jutting out of the corner of the box, grasping and clawing at the cardboard. He hated to drop them back at the motel, especially considering what they might destroy in his absence.

"Can I make it twenty?" he asked.

She paused. "You'll have a line of children out the door."

He rang off and only paused a moment before dialing Carrie. "I need a favor," he said when she picked up. "It's for the kids," he rushed on before she could hang up on him.

Five minutes later, he was in her driveway, walking up to her front door with that cardboard box beneath his arm.

"Please tell me this isn't the Christmas gift," she said in a mock-whisper, eyeing the box curiously. She was in her sock feet on her front stoop, a knee-length knitted sweater wrapped around her, her arms crossed over her chest. Seeing her, he got that same horse-kick straight to the gut, just like always.

"It's not." No, he was still working on Scarlett's *husband gift*. So far his plan was failing. Just thinking about that made him want to grimace, so he focused on the here and now.

"Thanks for keeping them for a couple of hours." Hopefully they would be so distracted by Scarlett that they wouldn't destroy any of Carrie's curtains. Or her couch. Or anything else.

"Scarlett will be thrilled. I hadn't told her yet." She glanced over her shoulder. "I'm a little surprised you brought them with you to the motel."

He shrugged, rolling his shoulders beneath his coat. "I promised Scarlett I'd find them a good home. Just because I left the Triple H doesn't mean I'm backing out on that."

Her gaze rested on him for moments too long. He wondered what she was looking for, what she saw. A cowboy without a spread to work? Or something else?

He passed the box into her arms. Got a kick out of her expression of surprise when the kittens shifted inside, still angling to get out.

"Speaking of, Nate said you hadn't been out to the place recently. The ranch misses you."

She snorted, shifting the box in her arms. "The ranch doesn't have human emotions."

"You sure about that? The land and the property change based on who touches them, who puts time into them. And you're a third owner."

Her lips tightened into a frown, lines around her mouth showing her distress. "I doubt my absence for all these years has had that big an effect on the place. Gideon and Matt run things just fine."

He shifted his feet. "Might run even better with you out there, actively involved."

And when her frown deepened, he knew he'd said enough. He nodded, letting his hat tilt down to cover his eyes from her. "Thanks again."

He was turning to get back in his truck when she spoke. "I can't believe the mayor roped you in to playing...you know who."

He hadn't told her about Scarlett's doubt about the man in red and white, but he shrugged again. "It's just an afternoon, and a lot of kids will be disappointed if no one shows."

He looked back to see that same speculative gaze on her face again.

"You sure you're okay?" he asked.

"I think so. You're coming back to get them later, right?"

He thought about teasing her, but it didn't feel right, not with all the tension still between them. "I'll be back for them."

CARRIE SHOULD'VE KNOWN BETTER than to agree when Trey had called to ask for her help. His statements about the Triple H had hit some hidden, soft place inside of her, reminding her of her Uncle Pat and his ultimatum. Plus, seeing the loyal cowboy in town was like seeing a fish out of water. He belonged on the Triple H.

And then there were the kittens.

Tom and Jerry, the two kittens, had hopped out of the box in Carrie's living room and given her identical snooty looks before going straight to Scarlett and rubbing their faces all over her.

Scarlett was in heaven. She was in love with the kittens, had begged all afternoon to keep them.

Carrie had kept with the firm *nos*, but her daughter was stubborn. She'd angled for them to nap with her, even though she hadn't napped in ages. When Carrie had gone to check on her—a quiet little girl was often a little girl getting in to trouble—she'd found Scarlett curled around one of her stuffed animals, the two kittens stretched out on the bed beside her.

That had lasted all of ten minutes. While Scar had slept, the two kittens had batted at the Christmas stockings hung from the brick fireplace mantle, ripped up part of the carpet in one corner of the living room, and knocked over a potted plant, spilling dirt across the floor.

At least they hadn't tried to use it for a litter box or attempted to climb her decorated Christmas tree. Small blessings.

Now evening was falling, the earlier winter sunset one of Carrie's least favorite parts of the season. She heard Trey's truck in the drive and went to the front door while Scarlett played on the couch with the orange-and-white kitten.

She'd opened the heavy wooden front door and flipped on the porch light. It flickered and the bulb went out with a pop. She sighed.

She pushed open the screen door and stepped onto the stoop. It was cool through her socks; the chilly night air enveloped her.

The neighbors had strung colored twinkle lights across the lower line of their roof, and that offered a bit of illumination, barely enough to see that the man who passed through the rectangle of light thrown from the open living room window was not Trey.

It was Rob.

She went hot and then cold. A shiver that had nothing to do with the air slithered down her spine.

"You're not supposed to be here."

But her weak words didn't stop him.

Her heart thudded in her ears. She was frozen. She couldn't

breathe as fear rushed to take the place of the oxygen in her lungs.

Time seemed to slow as he crossed toward her.

He glanced to the side, and she could imagine his view through the window—Scarlett playing on the sofa, in plain sight.

And the knowledge that her daughter was just inside galvanized Carrie.

She yanked the screen door open, stepped inside, and slammed it behind her, latching it quickly. She knew how powerful he could be—hadn't she worn the bruises to prove it? —and quickly pushed the oak door closed as well.

"Scarlett, baby, go into your room," she ordered.

"Why?"

Of all the times for her daughter to decide to question her. Fear rose up in her throat, making her voice quake. "Now, Scar. Leave the kitties."

Scarlett must've understood the urgency in her voice, because she hopped off the couch and ran into the hall that led to her room.

Memories poured over Carrie as she leaned against the door. Rob's fists pounding into her flesh. He'd cracked one of the bones in her cheeks.

"Aw, c'mon Carrie," he said from outside. "I'm clean. I just wanna see you."

She didn't know whether that was true or not, and she didn't care. "Go away. I'm calling the cops."

She fingered the lock, checking that she'd really thrown it. And then she couldn't remember whether she'd locked the back door, the one in the kitchen, when she'd taken out the trash earlier.

Panic had her running, her sock feet slapping hard against the wood floors and then linoleum. She slid the last two feet and saw that it was locked, thank God.

Rob pounded on the screen, and she could only pray that Scarlett had closed her bedroom door and maybe even turned on the television. She didn't want Scarlett to hear.

Memories buzzed. She scooted down, her back against the wood and her knees pressed to her chest. She bent her head to meet her knees and wrapped her arms around her head. A memory assaulted her.

They'd been divorced for three and a half years. Scarlett had just had her third birthday. Uncle Pat was dead. Carrie's grief was still new, and she'd stupidly opened the door to Rob.

He'd stunk like alcohol and stale sweat, and she'd known letting him in was a mistake, but it was too late. When she'd asked him to leave, he'd thrown the first punch.

She'd screamed for help—Scarlett was in the house!—and that had infuriated him. When she'd fallen to the floor, he'd kicked her. She'd curled into a ball, and his kick bounced off her thigh, the blow radiating pain up and down her leg.

Stupid. So stupid. She'd let this monster into her house. What if he went after Scarlett next?

But thankfully, Scar had hidden in her closet, buried in stuffed animals. Rob had signed away his parental rights at her birth. The restraining order and police report Carrie had filed after the attack should have been enough to keep him from ever having a chance to get a judge to allow him access to her daughter.

But no piece of paper could control that temper.

If he was angry enough, would he break into their house?

Someone pounded on the door at her back, and she yelped.

She stood, shaking. Spied her cell phone where she'd left it on the kitchen table earlier.

"I'm calling the police," she shouted through the closed portal.

Then, "Carrie? What's going on?"

Trey's voice.

Trey.

Her hands were shaking as she threw the bolt. The knob twisted in her hand—he must be turning it from outside.

And then the door was open with a blast of icy air, and she fell into his arms.

"Honey, it's cold out. What're—"

He shifted the both of them inside; she made it difficult for him as she clung.

She knew she shouldn't. It might give him the wrong idea.

But she desperately needed to feel safe, and locked in Trey's arms, she was.

TREY HAD no idea what was wrong, but obviously something had happened here since he'd dropped off the kittens four hours ago. Carrie hadn't answered the front door, apparently hadn't even heard his knock, so he'd come around to the back.

Carrie was sniffling, her face pressed against his neck, trembling in his arms.

None of that was like her. She was the strongest woman he knew. He couldn't think of one time he'd seen her cry, except maybe at Pat's funeral.

To say it disturbed him was an understatement. But he wasn't getting any answers out of her until she calmed down.

The kittens came into the kitchen with twin *meows* and began winding around his ankles. They were probably looking for their dinner.

He hadn't been inside her house since they'd broken up, and the place smelled like her. Warm, spicy, *home*. It hurt to be inside, but it would hurt worse if she kicked him out now, if she didn't let him fix whatever was wrong.

After the storm had passed, Carrie gulped a few breaths of air, though she made no move to extricate herself from his arms.

Holding her was both wonderful and painful.

"What happened?" he asked when it seemed the worst of her emotion was past.

But before she could answer, Scarlett rushed out from the darkened hallway. "Trey, Trey!"

Now Carrie pushed away from him, quickly wiping her eyes as Scarlett burst into the room, crying noisily.

She didn't head for her mom, but for Trey, who scooped her up into his arms and held her on his hip. The child sobbed into the shoulder of his shirt. It probably smelled gross. He'd sweated through the white T-shirt worn beneath the used Santa suit. His chin and jaw were abraded from the fake white beard.

Unlike her mama, who wanted to hold her fears close, Scarlett talked as she sobbed.

"A b-b-bad man c-c-came to the d-d-door, but mama told him to g-g-go away."

His gaze went sharply to Carrie, who'd turned her back, maybe so Scarlett wouldn't see her tears. She glanced over her shoulder, her red-rimmed eyes a horse-kick in the gut.

She shook her head slightly. She didn't want to talk about it in front of Scarlett. Was it her ex? Who else could've frightened her so badly?

He turned his attention back to Scarlett as she went on.

"And I didn't get to finish playing with the k-kitties because Mama sent me to my r-room."

Scarlett's outburst had slowed to the occasional sniffle as she spoke.

"Well, you don't have to worry about that. I've got a bucket of chicken out in the truck. The kitties and I will stay awhile, and you can keep on playing."

He didn't phrase it as a question, didn't leave room for Carrie to refuse, though she sent him a sharp glance. He'd figured on scarfing down the chicken on the way to his evening shift at the feed store, but he'd have to call the owner and beg off for the night. No way was he leaving when someone had come to the door, leaving both girls upset. Even if he wasn't wanted.

Scarlett brightened considerably, and he set her on her feet.

"I'll be right back," he said.

And miracle of miracles, Carrie nodded. She must be really scared if she was willing to put up with him for the evening.

He ran out to his truck and grabbed the paper bucket and the bag that held the side dishes. But he made time for the phone call to his boss and a quick detour to the neighbor's house before he returned to Carrie's place.

"When's school get out for break?" he asked as he delivered the bucket of chicken to the table.

Carrie grabbed three plates.

"Friday is our last day for two whole weeks!" Scarlett bounced across the floor, going to a drawer and fishing out spoons for the mashed potatoes.

He and Carrie crossed paths as he went to the upper cabinet near the fridge, found the glasses where they'd been last time he was here, and took down three.

It was all so domestic that his gut started to hurt. What was he doing here? He should've called Matt to come over. Her brother could handle this.

But he didn't leave.

Scarlett was all smiles and giggles as they ate, though she winked at him twice. Maybe thinking about her Christmas secret for her mom?

Carrie was quiet and contemplative and left most of the conversation to him. That was fine for now, but she had to know he wasn't leaving until he got some answers.

He helped with cleanup as Carrie got Scarlett ready for bed, dumping all the paper and Styrofoam containers into one big bag. He took out her trash, which was maybe presumptuous of him, but he didn't care that much. He didn't want to think about her going out in the dark to do it herself.

There were some used cereal bowls and two cups on the counter, and the girls were taking their sweet time—maybe Carrie thought she'd get rid of him if she out-waited him—so he dumped some soap and ran hot water into the sink.

He was scrubbing the last cup when Scarlett ran back into the room. "Trey, Trey! Can you come tuck me in? Mama said it was okay."

Carrie stood in the hallway, silent.

"Sure, kiddo. Let me rinse this." He finished with the cup and pulled the stopper out of the sink. He dried his hands on a towel quickly before he padded down the hallway behind the girls.

He'd been in Scarlett's room a couple of times, but the bright pink walls and profusion of stuffed animals on the bed always took him aback for a split second.

"We ran outta books, so we've got to go to the library, but mama said you could tell me a story, if you wanted, or just listen to my prayers. She said not to pressure you into anything, but I didn't really know what that meant, so she said just leave it up to you what you want to do. So... do you want to tell me a story?"

He sat down on the bed beside her, laughing a little at her chatter. He'd always admired how she could fill any length of silence with her voice. He'd missed hearing about her days in kindergarten—first grade now, he realized. He'd already missed months of Scar-stories. He hated this distance. And soon, he'd be out of her life completely.

"I don't mind telling a story."

Carrie stood in the doorway, watching as he spun a made-up yarn about a boy who'd gone to visit a department store Santa and gotten lost in Elf Town. Scarlett helped him fill in details like the reindeer barn kittens and striped socks that the elves wore.

Her eyes were getting heavy, but he didn't want to leave without talking about it.

He put his large hand over her smaller one. "Kiddo, you know you're safe, right?"

She went quiet, part of the light that was Scarlett dimming behind her eyes. She nodded slowly. "Yeah."

"You still scared about what happened earlier?"

She squinted up at him. Shrugged her narrow shoulders.

"I get scared sometimes," he confessed. Like when Carrie had thrown herself into his arms earlier.

"You do? But you're a brave 'ol cowboy."

He had to smile at her blind faith in him. It was a lot to live up to.

"I do. But do you know what helps? If I'm scared, I tell a friend."

He purposely didn't look at Carrie in the doorway, but he could feel hot emotion coming off of her.

"So if you feel scared, it's okay to tell your mama. Or me. Or your Uncle Matt."

"Or my teacher, Mrs. Gray?" He saw her mind whirling as she got into it.

"Sure. You've got a bunch of grown ups around who love you lots." Him included. "And who'll do anything to keep you safe."

He leaned in and bussed her forehead with a kiss, then got up. The soft smile on her face as she hugged her raggedy stuffed bear made him feel all fuzzy inside, like he'd done something good.

And he took that feeling with him as he went back into the living room to face off with Carrie.

He'd need all the goodness he could get right now to hold onto his patience.

. . .

CARRIE WAS EXHAUSTED, both physically and emotionally.

The last thing she wanted was to argue with Trey. She went to the front door to open it for him, praying he would take a hint and just leave, but when she looked behind her, he wasn't there.

She turned around, one hand still on the knob, to see he'd settled in on the sofa, right in the middle seat with his legs stretched out in front of him beneath the coffee table and both arms extended along the back of the couch. If she sat on either side of him, he'd be in her space.

She growled internally.

"I'm really tired, so..." she hinted, but he only nodded.

"Me too." It wasn't often she saw him without a smile, but he wasn't smiling now. "One hundred and twenty-seven kids. I didn't even know we had that many kids in our elementary school, but that's how many little rascals climbed all over me today. I'd really like to hit the hay, but I don't feel right about leaving until you tell me whether the bad man who scared you and Scarlett was your ex-husband."

Just hearing him say it made her go hot and cold again, like when she'd first glimpsed Rob on the sidewalk outside.

Across the room, the black-and-white kitten batted at an ornament on a lower branch of the tree, making a bell jingle. The sound usually comforted, but tonight felt harsh.

Her hand fell away from the doorknob. She should've known he wouldn't make this easy on her.

Trey's posture changed, as he went from relaxed—had he just been pretending?—to concerned. He leaned forward, put his elbows on his knees.

She hated the way it felt as if he could see inside of her.

"Did you call the police? Because last I heard, you had a restraining order filed against him."

She was cold again, and she wrapped her arms around her waist. She crossed to the wooden rocking chair that had once belonged to her grandma and sunk down into it. What usually made her feel safe was broken, violated. And it didn't matter that Rob hadn't made it inside the house. He'd been here.

Disrupted her safe space. Only it wasn't safe. Probably never had been.

Oblivious to the human tension, the orange-and-white kitten strutted into the room with its tail held high and jumped up onto her coffee table, walking right up to Trey and then butting him in the chin.

He idly rubbed along its back, but his gaze never left Carrie's face as he waited for her to answer.

"It expired," she whispered. "I didn't file again, because I hadn't seen or heard from him since that night."

There'd been no reason for him to come back into her life. She didn't have the kind of money he'd been looking for then, and she didn't have it now, either.

"Any particular reason you didn't call your brother? Or one of the other hands?" He was such a conundrum. His voice was deceptively quiet and calm, but she'd felt the tension in him when she'd clung to him earlier.

"Or me?" He burst up from the couch, startling the kitten into jumping off the table with a disgruntled yowl. "I know you aren't interested in having me in your life, but—" He cursed. She'd never heard him do that before. "I woulda been here in three minutes, even if I'd had to wear the Santa suit."

He was breathing hard, emotion riding him.

She just felt numb.

His hands hung at his sides, not even clenched into fists. She knew he'd never hurt her, not like Rob had.

She shook her head slightly, breaking the moment. "I just...freaked out. Thank God he left, because if he'd broken down the door... I don't know, I just couldn't get off the floor. I started thinking about...remembering what'd happened before, and I just spiraled down..."

He pulled her out of her chair and cupped her jaw with both hands. "He's never going to hurt you like that again."

For one terrifying moment, she thought he was going to kiss her. And if he did, she would be so lost...

But he didn't, just stared down at her. The intensity shining from his eyes made her want to trust so bad...

But she sniffled, and a single tear ran down her cheek.

"You can't promise that," she whispered.

He smiled a feral smile. "Sure I can. Even if it means I have to sleep in my truck in your driveway."

She shook her head, dislodging his hands. He stepped back, allowing her space to breathe. "You can't. Think what people would say."

"I couldn't care less. Whatever it takes to keep you and Scarlet safe." He held out his hand to her. He must've picked up her cell from the kitchen table; now he extended it to her. "Call the precinct."

Her hackles came up. She really hated it when he ordered her around, but in this case, he was right.

She sat back down in the chair, and did what he'd asked. The officer on duty took down a report that her ex had been on her property, and that while she didn't have a valid protective order against him, it had scared her. She was put on hold, and then the captain came on, a man who'd been a friend of her Uncle Pat's for years. He told her they'd send a patrol car down her street several times a day and at night, until Rob left town.

She hung up feeling slightly reassured.

Trey had listened to her side of the conversation, and she was glad to see he now had his coat on and one kitten tucked under each arm like twin footballs. He was tall and solid and ready to leave and for one micro-second, she wished he would stay.

"You could always relocate out at the Triple H for a little while," he said. "Nobody'd get to you out there."

The thought caused an instant bloom of hope before she quashed it quickly. She was a big girl. She'd stay in her own house.

She shook her head. He smiled with half his mouth, like he'd expected that answer.

"You sure you don't want me to sit outside? It's not like I've got to be up with the rooster tomorrow morning. I don't have to be at the feed store until noon."

The reminder that he no longer belonged at the Triple H was a blow, but she shook it off. She had to be strong for Scarlett, for herself.

"I'm sure." She stood, ready to show him the door, just like earlier.

But he didn't walk straight to the door. He came to her

instead, standing close enough that she had to tilt her chin up to look him in the face. One of the kittens struggled in his big hand, getting one claw stuck in the shoulder of her sweater.

"If you get scared, call somebody," he said quietly. "Your brother, the cops, your friend Sarah."

It was so like what he'd told Scarlett earlier that more tears threatened, but she blinked them back. Watching him comfort her daughter had done something to her. That was all, that was the real reason for her tears.

"And... I might've snuck over to Mrs. Cherry's house earlier and told her you'd had some trouble. She'll be looking out for you too."

He ducked out the front door, squirming kittens in hand, before he could see the roll of her eyes.

She should be mad. Mrs. Cherry was her next-door neighbor, a kindly older lady who also happened to be a busybody. She'd probably be watching out her windows day and night to see if Rob would come back.

Carrie should be mad, but actually, she felt a little warmer inside because of what he'd done.

"Lock your door," he called back to her without looking.

She did, leaning against the inside of the door and listening to him fire up his truck and then drive off.

Maybe it wasn't wrong to lean on Trey, just for this one night.

Chapter Four

A week later, Carrie was experiencing the pre-holiday slowdown. There hadn't been many clients in today. A cold front had come in, the local weathermen forecasting an ice storm overnight.

She hadn't seen any hint of her ex-husband, but she had seen way too many of the single men in town. A total of five guys had randomly asked her out after getting their hair cut in her chair. She couldn't figure it.

Today's bachelor—number six—was one Joe Bob Rivers, a dairy farmer from across town who smelled like manure. She settled him in her chair thinking about the moment when she could wash her hands after he left. Even so, she refused to give a paying customer a bad cut and, after she'd finished, was eyeing the line of hair around his ear, attempting to judge whether she'd cut one shorter than the other.

She had a tickle in her throat and cleared it. "Are you spending the holiday with your sister?" Scarlett had had his sister for her kindergarten teacher last year.

"Yep. She'll roast a turkey, and I'll bring the mashed potatoes."

"That's nice." She snipped a stray hair behind his left ear. She was looking closely and saw a line of pink creep up from the collar of his shirt as he flushed. Oh, please. Not again.

"Would you... would you think about goin' to a movie with me sometime?"

It was a good thing she was done with the cut, because her temper flared, and she slammed the scissors down on the counter. "What is it with all the eligible men in town suddenly asking me out?" She propped her hands on her hips and faced the man still in the stylist's cape.

"Ah..." he stammered.

She probably shouldn't have asked the questions. She'd managed to keep her temper through five others. But now that the question was out there, she wanted an answer. She waited.

His face reddened even more. "I—"

She tapped her toe.

He exhaled noisily. "I saw Trey Reynolds at the feed store earlier in the week, and he insisted I come in here and ask you on a date."

Trey.

She felt blindsided. She'd never imagined that Trey would do something like this to her. He must've asked each of those five other guys to come in, too. Six gullible guys! Why? Why would he think she needed or wanted a date? After all they'd been through, didn't he know better?

Did he feel sorry for her?

"I think we're done here," she said. She whipped the cape off of his neck, carefully folding it, paying attention to what her hands were doing as her face burned.

He stood, hesitated, gripping the back of her stylist's chair. "So that's a...no?"

"It's a no."

He turned tail and left, which was a blessing because she didn't have an ounce of patience left.

Trey!

Cassandra, one of the other stylists, blew into the shop on a gust of freezing air. It was almost three o'clock—Carrie's quitting time—and Cassandra would take over the afternoon shift.

Carrie was still hot all over, steaming from the inside out, and when the gust of cold air blew against her overheated skin, she started shivering. And couldn't stop. Her bones ached suddenly. But she couldn't get sick. She had a little girl to take care of. And a man to ream.

"Hun, you don't look so good," Cassandra said with a pop of her gum. Good thing the shop was empty.

Carrie raised her gaze to the mirror to see that she was indeed pale, with huge red blotches on both cheeks. She raised the back of her wrist to her forehead. "I don't have time to get sick. I still have Christmas shopping to do."

Cassandra didn't laugh at her lame joke. In fact, she looked concerned. "There's a nasty flu going around the elementary school. Maybe Scarlett brought it home."

She shook her head, though now her head was starting to feel as if it was stuffed with cotton. "She hasn't been sick."

"Doesn't mean she didn't bring a germ home for you."

Minutes later, Carrie sat in her car in its parking spot on Main Street, trying to rally. Didn't she have some Tylenol in her purse? She rifled through the contents of the bag and found a small pill bottle that seemed right. She popped three, hoping the medicine would kill this nasty fever.

She felt worse as she drove to the elementary school to pick up her daughter. She parked in the lot, head lolling against the steering wheel as she tried to find the energy to walk to the doors and claim her daughter. Her eyes fell on the pill bottle that had fallen into the console and not back into the purse. Xanax. She didn't have a script, but Cassandra had pushed the pills on her earlier in the week, when Carrie had been complaining about her nerves, her fear that Rob would return.

She knew better than to take pills not prescribed by her doctor. Why had she kept them? She should've tossed them. Now as her head spun and she drowsed off, she knew this had been one giant mistake.

A blast of cold air roused her from a fevered daydream about her brother Gideon's royal wedding. She pried her eyes open to see Scarlett slipping into the car. The door almost slammed shut on the girl's leg, blasted by icy wind.

"Are you okay, Mama? My teacher waited at the door, but all the other kids already got picked up and she let me walk across the parking lot because it's pretty empty..."

Scarlett kept going, but the fuzz in Carrie's ears got louder.

She lifted her wobbly head off the steering wheel long enough to see that most of the cars had vacated the lot. She waved at Scarlett's teacher, watching from the sidewalk just in front of the double doors. The woman seemed happy enough to duck back inside and out of the freezing wind.

Carrie could do this. She just needed to stop her eyes from crossing, and then she could drive home, make Scarlett an afternoon snack, and curl up on the couch with a blanket to ride this out. Surely she'd be better by morning.

No.

She couldn't do all that.

She wanted to cry just thinking about it.

She refused to put her daughter's life in danger because she was too proud to ask for help.

"Baby, I think I'm sick." That's what she said, but what emerged from her mouth was a garbled mess. "I think I need some help." Again, her words were a mumble with no distinguishable syllables.

Her body went limp, her head lolling on the steering wheel as she watched Scarlett dig through the mess of napkins in the center console before she found Carrie's phone.

There. Scarlett would know to call someone for help. Even if her daughter dialed 911, the town was small enough that they'd know it wasn't a real emergency, and someone would come and help her get home.

"Uncle Matt...? Oh, it's your recording. ... Mama is sick. I'll call Trey next."

That was a good idea. She wanted to talk to Trey about...about something. His number was still saved in her Favorites. Scarlett would reach him...

Stubborn woman.

Trey's heart was in his throat, but he kept up his "calm and collected" act as he balanced his cell phone between his shoulder and ear and drove at the same time.

The slate-gray skies had begun to intermittently spit, which meant he didn't have much time for this rescue mission before the weather got really dicey.

Luckily, he'd already been in his truck and only a few minutes away from the elementary school when Scarlett had called.

"Is your mama still awake?" he asked the girl.

Scarlett was so brave, not breaking down in tears like many little kids might've when they saw their mom faint, or whatever had happened before Scarlett had dialed him.

"Kinda," she said now. "Her eyes are a little open, and she keeps trying to talk, but I can't understand her. Her cheeks are red and I touched her forehead and she's really hot."

He'd considered asking her to hang up so he could call an ambulance, but with the weather bad and turning worse, the rescue crews would already be working, and it might be faster for him to take Carrie to the ER than wait on an ambulance.

He hoped it was the right thing to do.

He'd been shocked to get the phone call, still wasn't sure why Scarlett had called him. Did she know his number, or had she just found it in Carrie's contacts list?

His truck slid on the ice as he pulled into the elementary school parking lot. Carrie's car was there, along with three others. Had everyone just drove off, not seeing the woman slumped over her steering wheel? Had they all been so worried about the weather that they'd just rushed past her without seeing?

He threw his truck into park and got out, immediately getting a blast of cold air where his coat was unzipped.

He opened the driver's side door, worried when Carrie slumped toward him, her body almost totally limp. Scarlett watched wide-eyed in the passenger seat.

He braced himself and let Carrie rest against him. Her head lolled in the crook of his neck, and Scarlett was right. She was burning up. He could feel it through the layers he wore.

"I found this," Scarlett said. She held up a pill bottle. "I don't think it's Tylenol. Do you think she took some? I don't know what KKSS... KKSS. Argh. It's spelled X-A-N-A-X."

He looked at the bottle. Why would Carrie have taken that? He didn't know she was on an anti-anxiety med. He'd have to figure it out later, or maybe her doctor could. She was so feverish that he was worried.

"Climb over, kiddo," he said to a worried-looking Scarlett. "Grab your mom's phone. We're going to the hospital."

He hooked one arm behind Carrie's back, the other beneath her legs, and lifted her.

She mumbled something as they emerged from the shelter of her car into the icy wind. He battled the passenger door of his truck, grunting as the wind tried to slam it on him.

While Scarlet circled to the driver's side, he settled Carrie in the seat, carefully belting her in. Because of the way he had to lean over her, her mouth was close to his ear, and he heard her whispered, "No hospital."

He moved back to look at her face. Her glassy-eyed stare was almost as worrying as the fever.

"You're burning up and Scarlett said you were talking nonsense."

"Just the flu," she whispered. "Rest. That's all. Took the wrong pills. Thought they were Tylenol."

He got that she didn't want to go to the hospital. When they'd dated, she'd once confessed that she hated the place. Always reminded her of when that snake Rob had beat her up. He'd also once seen a bill he shouldn't have and knew her insurance was terrible and wouldn't cover all the costs if she were hospitalized. With Scarlett having to go in overnight recently for an asthma attack... She was probably worrying about the money, too.

But if she was in danger...

"I'll take you home for one hour," he said. "One hour. If your fever doesn't come down some, then it's the ER for you."

And he didn't promise that he wouldn't call her family doctor.

Chapter Five

Carrie's fever did come down.

A call to her family physician had provided some answers. The Xanax explained the drowsiness and slurred speech. Her doctor had told him to watch for shallow breathing, but that didn't seem to be an issue for Carrie. He'd watch her carefully until that stuff was out of her system.

She rested on the living room couch, curled beneath a well-loved quilt, while he made grilled cheese sandwiches and chicken noodle soup for Scarlett's supper. He had very early memories of his grandpa making the same meal. Being in Carrie's home again reminded him that *this* was what he'd wanted all along.

Another two weeks, and he'd be gone. He'd been offered a job on a big spread near Grapevine and would head out just after the new year.

After he'd called the doctor, he'd called Matt, sure she'd want her brother here instead of him. Except he hadn't counted on the roads already being iced over. Or that Matt was out in the fields hunting down a couple of missing cows. By the time Matt got back, it would be dangerous to drive in from the Triple H, dangerous and unnecessary, when Trey was already here.

Next, he called the motel, and the kind manager assured him she'd check in on the kittens before she went home for the night.

He poured a bowl of soup and fixed a half sandwich for

Carrie, then set them both on a tray. He left Scarlett at the kitchen table.

In the living room, he froze when he saw her. She must have been feeling slightly better, because she glared at him. "You're not supposed to be here."

"You're welcome," he said, ignoring her words and setting the tray on the coffee table in front of her.

"I'm mad at you."

Maybe it was the fever talking. He didn't know what it was, but he couldn't help smiling at her petulant statement.

"Joe Bob came in to my shop today."

Uh oh. He froze halfway back to the kitchen. And maybe he should've kept on going, because his stopping could have been seen as an admission of guilt.

"He said you'd sent him and some other guys to come in and get their hair cut."

And judging by the glare that was singeing the hair on the back of his head, Joe Bob had spilled all of it.

"And to ask me out."

He glanced into the kitchen, where Scarlett sat poring over a chapter book that was probably above her pay grade. He turned back to the steaming woman on the couch.

She was mad, but he was afraid she'd see through him, to the feelings he couldn't seem to get rid of.

"Can we talk about this later?" he asked, with a nudge of his chin toward the child.

Carrie's eyebrows came together. A moment passed before she said, "Fine. But I'm not letting you off the hook."

Her threat might've carried more weight if her eyes hadn't been drooping closed in exhaustion. He figured the thing she needed most right now was sleep.

He joined Scarlett in the kitchen, sitting down in one of the chairs, and stretched his legs out. "You got homework, kid?"

"Nope. I finished it all during quiet time in class this afternoon."

It'd been a long time since he'd been in first grade. "What's quiet time?"

"It's right before recess. We get thirty minutes to work on

class work we haven't finished for the day or, if we're done, then we can work on our homework. I'm almost always done."

He didn't doubt it. Scarlett was one of the smartest kids he knew. Got it from her mama. It was no wonder the woman had figured out his plan. It hadn't been that great of a plan to start with.

He glanced in at Carrie. It appeared she'd drifted off, judging by the even rise and fall of her breathing.

"Mama was s'pposed to make Christmas cookies with me this afternoon. We do it every year for my school teacher and my Bible class teacher and the principal, and we even save some for Uncle Matt and the Triple H cowboys, but you already know that..."

She ran out of steam long enough for him to say, "I'm not very good at baking cookies."

She squinted at him. "You can read, can't ya?"

"Well, yeah."

"Then I'll show ya Mama's recipe book, and we'll be good to go!" She beamed. How could he say no? He figured he could replace whatever ingredients they used, and Carrie and Scarlett could redo the cookies when she was feeling better.

Ice pellets battered the window as he washed up at the sink. Scarlett rummaged beneath the cabinets, coming up with plastic mixing bowls, several spoons, measuring cups, cookie cutters and who knew what else. She spread all of it across the kitchen counter, and he knew he was in for trouble. If they used all that stuff, he would be up half the night washing dishes.

But the joy shining on Scarlett's face would be worth it. He just didn't know if his heart would survive.

TWO HOURS LATER, they had a pile of sugar cookies made. One batch was burnt black, and they'd scraped that into the trash can first thing. The next batch was brown and a little crunchy, but not too bad. Batches three and four had been better.

Scarlett had set about decorating, but he hadn't known how to work the little piping dealies, and there were blotches of icing all over the countertops.

But the girl who was covered in flour and had a smudge of icing across her nose was shining with joy. That made it all worth it.

She had her tongue sticking out the corner of her mouth in concentration as she worked on the last two man-shaped cookies.

She didn't look up as she spoke. "The Daddy-Daughter dance is on Christmas Eve. D'ya think Mama's"—she glanced over her shoulder toward the darkened living room, lowered her voice—"*husband* will be ready by then?"

With the show of temper Carrie'd shown earlier, it was clear his plan had failed. He'd hoped—sort of—that there might be a spark of attraction for one of the men who'd asked her out. It wouldn't take long for someone to fall for Carrie. She was sweet and spunky and independent. It wasn't like he could force her into a marriage, but things would progress if one of the guys in town would just get their heads on straight...

Except now Carrie had things figured out. And there was only a week left until the holiday.

"I don't know, kiddo." He tried to draw a beard on the Santa-guy he was supposed to be decorating. His big hands weren't made for the detail work, and Santa ended up looking more like one of the seven dwarfs. "Sometimes Santa doesn't work as fast as we want. Especially when it's something big." How could he explain the progression of dating, falling in love, marriage...?

Especially when her mom wasn't cooperating. He could only imagine how badly she was going to ream him when she found out what he'd agreed to.

He'd been thinking of Scarlett, and of Carrie, but she might not see it that way.

"Maybe the kids in my class are right. Maybe Santa's not real." She said the words matter-of-fairly, still focused on her cookie art.

He could still remember when he'd found out. He'd been six, and his mom had just died. He'd been heartbroken.

He didn't want that for her. How could he fix this?

She went on. "Last year, I asked Santa for another pony at the community center. I even wrote two letters."

He hadn't heard this story before, from her or from Carrie. "And I didn't get one."

He set aside his icing and moved the cookie man onto the wax paper they'd set out for drying. "You have lots of horses, out at the Triple H. What about Peppermint?"

She shook her head slightly. "Peppermint is really Uncle Matt's. Not mine. I want one that's really *really* mine. One that I could see every day."

He grabbed a washrag from the drawer beside the sink and started wiping up their mess. "It'd be kinda hard to have a horse here in town. Even if you could talk your mama into letting it sleep in your bedroom, there's not much grass in the backyard for it to eat."

She giggled. "No, that wouldn't work at all. But my school friends would think it was cool."

"Did you talk to your mom about last year's Christmas wish?" He asked the question as casually as possible.

Scarlett finished her last cookie and ducked her head. "A little."

He could imagine how that'd gone. He'd never been able to understand why Carrie wouldn't move back to the Triple H. The property was hers, too. And he figured Matt would love having her around. Gideon would, too. Not that he was there very often.

Scarlett put her icing packet on the counter and hopped off the chair. "It's probably time for my bath and to get ready for bed."

He hadn't been watching the clock. He glanced and saw it was almost eight.

"Do you need help?" *Say no. Say no.*

"Mama showed me how to take a shower by myself."

"Okay." He got up, thinking he'd better check on Carrie before he hit the deep cleaning.

She turned back at the door. "Trey, do you think you could take me to the Daddy-Daughter dance?"

Oh no. He thought she'd moved on from the dance.

"I don't know, kiddo. Your mama might not like that very much."

She tilted her chin and turned those big baby blues on him. "Couldja ask her?"

Oh, come on, kid.

"Sure."

"Thanks!" She skipped down the hallway and disappeared into the bathroom.

He leaned his hip against the counter, stretched his neck back to stare at the ceiling. How did he get himself into these things?

Obviously, he had a problem saying no, especially when it came to Scarlett. He couldn't help it. He and Carrie had circled around each other for years, with him working at the Triple H, but it hadn't been until Gideon's princess had arrived in town that very first time that Trey'd gotten up the courage to do something about it. They'd gotten real close, real fast, and he'd fallen in love with the both of them. Carrie and Scarlett.

Maybe that was why he was here tonight. Why he hadn't been able to move on yet. Because he was a fool.

He found Carrie sound asleep on the couch. He touched her forehead. Her fever was up again. Her doctor had thought she could ride it out, but Trey couldn't help but worry.

He padded back to the kitchen to get some more Tylenol and refresh her glass of water, glancing at the Christmas tree in the corner on his way. The first thing Scarlett had done when she'd gotten home was plug in the lights. In the darkened living room, the colors beckoned him.

He stood for a long time, staring at the colorful lights on the tree and listening to the sound of Scarlett singing loudly and off-key in the shower.

And wished.

CARRIE WAS HOT ALL OVER. She'd kicked off her blanket and taken more Tylenol, but nothing worked. She'd meant to tell off Trey for something.... But she couldn't remember. He'd brought her some soup, forced a few spoonfuls of it down. That was good.

So what was she mad about?

"Hey." She heard his voice from far off. Had she conjured him just by thinking about him? "Carrie. Wake up."

His touch was cool against her cheek, and she leaned into it.

"Open your eyes," he demanded.

"Bossy," she mumbled. But it felt important, so she pried her eyes open.

He perched on the coffee table in front of her holding a water cup with a straw in it. He held it out toward her. "Drink."

She did, the water cold enough to elicit a shiver as it slid down her overheated throat.

"Is Scarlett in bed?" She had no sense of time. The room had been dark from the storm outside when she'd fallen asleep. It could be the middle of the night, for all she knew. The tree lights were still on, lighting the room with dim, colorful lights.

"Yeah, for a couple hours now."

That long?

She blinked sleepily, felt like she was trying to come awake through a fog. "Are you going then?"

His mouth tipped. "You anxious to get rid of me?"

In her state, she couldn't work out whether he was teasing or not. "I...don't know."

"One, you're pretty sick, and I'm not leaving until I'm sure you're okay or your brother can get to town."

Oh. The roads.

"Two," he said with a nod, maybe following her line of thought. "I'm pretty sure my truck's frozen to your driveway."

"Oh." She took another drink. Her stomach gurgled.

Of course he heard. "You want something to eat? Some crackers?"

"If it's not too much trouble."

He disappeared into the kitchen and returned with a box. He also brought a cool, damp washcloth for her to lay across the back of her neck. It was heavenly.

This time, he settled next to her on the couch. He was quiet while she downed a few crackers.

When she was finished, he reached for her. "Let me rub your shoulders. You're all tensed up..."

She should protest, but any argument died on her lips as his fingers prodded achy muscles, sore from fever.

It felt so good.

She didn't mean to, but she leaned in to his touch. "I'm supposed to be mad at you," she said, mostly to remind herself. "But I can't remember why."

He chuckled. "I'm sure you will."

Her head lolled back. "You're good with Scarlett."

She'd been listening in on their conversation while they'd been baking and making noise in the kitchen.

"Maybe too good. She wants you to be her daddy."

She hadn't meant to say that, but there was no taking the words back.

His fingers prodded a knot at the base of her skull, and she sighed.

"For a long time, that's what I wanted too," he said quietly.

They sat in silence. He continued to massage her, his hands moving to her shoulders.

"I'm not going to start liking you again just because of a neck rub." Again? Right. Her feelings for him had never gone away. That had never been the problem.

But her words had opened some kind of door between them.

"You never did tell me," he said, "what it was that I did that scared you off."

She never meant to. Except in her fevered state, her mouth was already moving. "You're so protective that it scares me sometimes."

His hands stilled on her shoulders.

"Rob spent so much time making me think he was trying to protect me, but really he was isolating me from my family and friends, people who cared about me. Then he could do whatever he wanted to me to keep me there."

They sat frozen, his hands still on her shoulders, as if he didn't dare move. She couldn't believe what she was confessing. She'd never opened up to him about her relationship with her ex before. Maybe it was the fever making her so talkative.

"Is that how you think I'd be, if we got married?" he asked. His voice was dangerously low, and she didn't have the energy to face him.

"No. I don't know. Last fall, when you told me not to drive on that rainy day, it felt like... it just reminded me that when you're in a relationship with someone, you give them some control over you."

He was quiet for a long time. She finally shifted, turning slightly, so she could see his face.

"Was it really so bad, leaning on me tonight? Letting me help with Scarlett? Having someone to watch your back when you're sick?"

There was something in his voice. A depth of emotion. A question, one that put a pit in her stomach.

What he was offering was everything she'd wanted for so long...someone to lean on.

She whispered, "It's scary. Too scary."

Or maybe she was a coward. Maybe it was as simple as that.

Rob would've gotten mad. Would've cajoled and tried to convince her she was wrong. But Trey didn't do any of that.

His arm curled around her shoulders, and she leaned into him. Another thing she shouldn't do, but she felt so out of control tonight.

And he was a rock. Steady and dependable, and she needed to lean, just for a minute.

She rested against him, his skin cool against hers. She'd move away in a minute.

Just a minute...

Chapter Six

IT WAS INSANELY EARLY WHEN TREY WOKE WITH A crick in his neck. He was still on ranch time, because the sun wasn't up yet.

The tree lights were still shining, and Carrie was still curled up against his side. She felt slightly cooler, though he'd sweated through his shirt where she'd pressed against his side.

It felt like the perfect place for her. But her words from the night before returned.

He didn't know where to go from here. She couldn't—didn't want to—trust that their relationship would work, and after what her ex had done to her, he couldn't blame her.

He sat there, afraid to move for fear of waking her, half dozing and still wishing that things might be different between them.

The sound of an interior door opening roused him. He doubted Carrie would want Scarlett to see them curled up together on the couch. The girl already had enough ideas.

He started edging away from Carrie, and she moved, her head lolling to the opposite side. And then a quieter sound, one that didn't belong, had him sitting up quick.

Wheezing. Shallow, difficult breathing.

He bolted upright, shaking Carrie's shoulder. "Wake up."

Scarlett came down the hallway, one hand trailing along the

wall. Her face was pale, and it was obvious she was struggling for each breath.

"Where's her inhaler?" he demanded.

Carrie still looked like she was in a fog, but coming alert quickly. "There's one in the kitchen. The drawer next to the fridge."

He raced in there, adrenaline waking him faster than caffeine ever could. He heard Carrie's voice speaking softly to the girl, couldn't make out the words as he yanked the drawer open, almost pulling it off its rollers.

Pencils. Kid scissors. Tape. *There.*

He grabbed the small inhaler and raced back to the living room. Carrie'd gotten Scarlett to sit next to her on the couch. Her mannerisms were calm and collected, but when she glanced at him, he saw the wildness in her eyes. She was freaking out, which told him this was a true emergency.

He brought the inhaler straight to Carrie. "Here we go, kiddo."

He sat on the opposite side as Carrie helped spray the stuff into Scarlett's mouth. It broke his heart listening to the girl working to inhale. Her breath was choppy, and she couldn't seem to get her lungs full.

If this didn't work, what would he do? He remembered the image of Scarlet on that hospital bed not too long before. She'd had an inhaler that time, too, but it hadn't been enough. And now... He stood as nonchalantly as he could manage and crossed to the front window to peek outside. The sun was just coming up, illuminating a silvery, sparkly world. A dangerous world. Everything was covered in ice.

Icicles hung off the houses. His truck was covered, the windshield and windows so thick with it that he couldn't see through to the inside. The roads would be dangerous, maybe even deadly.

When he turned, Carrie was watching him.

He shook his head slightly. "Do you have one of those machines? The ones where it's a mask over her face?"

"A nebulizer," Carrie said. "In my bedroom."

He picked up Scarlett and carried her, not waiting for any kind of argument from Carrie. He got none.

He settled Scarlett on the bed while Carrie set up the machine, finally settling a plastic, clear mask over the girl's face.

"Do you want to watch a movie, honey?" She moved a lock of hair off the girl's forehead.

Scarlett nodded.

He jerked his thumb toward the door. "I'm gonna run out to my pickup." And turn it on, de-ice it. Just in case they needed to be ready to go to the hospital.

He pulled his boots and coat on in the kitchen and then headed out. The ice was about an inch thick, and he was praying the hardest he had in a while that that nebulizer thingie would work, because he hated to think what the roads must look like. The safest thing for every person in town would be staying inside with the ice this bad, and it wasn't going to warm up until late this afternoon.

By the time he got back inside, his fingers and toes and nose were numb from cold.

Carrie met him in the living room.

"I left the truck running." She could've probably seen him through the front window, and even now he could see exhaust rising from the tailpipe like steam.

Her cheeks still had a slight flush to them, and he didn't imagine she felt that well. Her hair was tousled adorably. In another circumstance, he might pull her into his arms and hold her close.

But he was a good boy and kept his hands to himself.

"I think the nebulizer is doing the trick," she said, hugging herself. "I still want to watch her for a few minutes to make sure we're past the worst of it, but I think the attack is easing off."

Relief crashed into him, and he nodded tightly, holding all that emotion close because he didn't want to scare her again. Not when he didn't have any place to go today except his ice-cold truck if she asked him to leave.

"Was there—?" He had to clear his throat when his voice broke. Embarrassing. "Did I miss some medicine I was supposed to give her last night, or...?"

She shook her head. Her eyes were softer than he'd seen them in a long while and again, he resisted the urge to pull her close.

"Sometimes when the weather gets really cold quickly, it causes an attack. I think we caught it early enough this time that we shouldn't need a hospital trip."

"Good. Good. Great."

He got a head rush so bad that he sat down at the kitchen table so he didn't do something foolish, like faint dead away. He put his head in his hands.

Not his fault. Nothing he could've done.

But he'd been so scared when he'd seen Scarlett struggling for breath... He still felt the squeeze in his heart. What if she hadn't been able to get out of bed? What if the nebulizer wasn't enough?

What if, what if...?

He felt a light touch on his shoulder and turned his head slightly to see that Carrie had padded into the kitchen.

It was probably the first time she'd voluntarily touched him since she'd decided they weren't going to be together anymore.

She didn't say anything, just stood there a minute with her hand on his shoulder, before she left with a softly murmured, "I'm going to go check on her."

Maybe it was a good thing she'd broken things off. He didn't know if he was cut out to be a dad, not when something like this happened.

A COUPLE OF HOURS LATER, Carrie cuddled in her bed with Scarlett. Scar's attack had happened so early that it still wasn't even mid-morning yet. Trey was still here. She knew, because she heard him puttering around somewhere else in the house. Maybe the kitchen. But he'd seemed content to check on them sporadically, letting her and Scarlett rest, drowse and watch cartoon princess movies.

Logically, she knew he cared about Scarlett. But seeing how upset he'd been when Scarlett had had the asthma attack earlier... He really loved her daughter. It had been evident in his urgency, his willingness to brave the treacherous roads if need be.

But mostly in the way he'd been so relieved that he'd had to sit down in her kitchen. If she wasn't mistaken, his eyes had gone wet before he'd hid his face in his hands.

He loved Scarlett.

And if he loved her baby that much... he must've loved her too, before she'd pushed him away.

Somebody willing to risk life and limb for her daughter was somebody worthy. He'd been nothing but trustworthy, nothing but tender and kind to both of them. It had been her own fears that had ruined things.

But after this morning, she was rethinking everything.

The movie ended with a happily ever after as only a Disney princess could have, and Scarlett shifted in the bed, her small body rustling the covers as she stretched. "I'm getting hungry."

"Me too, Peanut." She started to sit up, but Scarlett seemed reluctant to move as she lay there, tracing patterns in the quilt.

"Mama?"

"Yeah, baby?"

"Is Santa real?"

Dread pulsed through her, along with the fuzzy memory of overhearing Trey and Scarlett talking about this last night while she'd drowsed on the couch. She'd really hoped to have another year before she'd have to explain the truth about the man in red to her daughter.

"Well...what do you think?"

Head down, Scarlett shrugged.

"Maybe there's not a man who visits every single kid in one night, but I believe in Christmas miracles, so that sorta means I believe in Santa, right?"

Scarlett squinted up at her. "Trey said he believes in Christmas miracles, too."

Of course he would. The man was kindhearted to a fault. He probably *made* Christmas miracles.

And then Scarlett subject-hopped like only a six-year old could. "Do you think the bad man will come back?"

Rob. Carrie hoped not. With the local police patrolling her street more often than usual, she could only hope whatever had brought him here was over, and he'd left town.

"I don't know, baby. Do you know who that was?" Another thing she dreaded having to explain to her daughter.

Scarlett nodded slowly. "It was my bio-biorogical dad."

"Biological. We don't talk about him very much, but—"

"Cause he's a bad man," Scarlett interrupted.

"Well, yes." And because she was ashamed of the way she'd fallen for him. Still.

"He hurt you."

A hot knot in her throat, Carrie nodded. "You were little—"

"I hid in my closet. But I saw some."

Carrie's breath froze in her chest. She reached out and touched Scarlett's arm. "You can remember that?"

Scarlett nodded. "I was hugging Oreo. He kept me safe." Maybe that was part of the reason her girl was so attached to the stuffed bear. "There was a tiny crack in the closet door and I could see some into the hall."

Carrie swallowed hard. Scarlett had never mentioned this before. She'd taken her daughter to a therapist after the attack, and as far as she knew, Scarlett had never mentioned it to the therapist either. Was she bringing it up now because Rob had shown up again? She hated to think that her daughter had seen her helpless, had seen Rob attacking her.

"After Rob did that, the police told him he can't come near us anymore." It was a simplified explanation of what had happened with the court and the protective order.

"So how come he came here the other night?" Scarlett asked.

"I don't know. I called the police, and they're watching out for us."

"And so is Trey. He won't let anything happen to us."

That knot in her throat wasn't going away any time soon. "Honey, you know that Trey isn't... that he's just our friend, right? He took care of us last night, but he doesn't live here."

"He could. If you got married to him."

Oh, the simplicity of children.

And wouldn't Carrie like that? She'd been able to pretend she didn't have feelings for Trey, but all those lies were stripped away now. Now that he'd come to her rescue. Now that he'd come to Scarlett's rescue. But her feelings didn't seem to matter anymore. Trey'd been trying to set her up with someone else. Had actually gotten other men to ask her out. She didn't know why, hadn't worked that one out yet. But it proved that she'd rejected him one time too many. Trey would never want her back now. "That's not going to happen," she said softly.

. . .

THAT'S NOT GOING to happen.

Carrie's words played over and over in Trey's memory as the day wore on. No matter what he'd wished and hoped for, Carrie didn't see him in her future.

That's' what he got for eavesdropping.

Maybe it was a good thing he was leaving for Grapevine.

He needed distance, but he didn't get it as Carrie and Scarlett emerged from the master bedroom. He made omelets for breakfast and tried to pretend nothing was wrong.

He couldn't wait to escape, but the temps hadn't gotten above thirty yet, and it would be taking his life in his hands to drive out there, even only a couple of miles to the motel.

The early morning had taken its toll on them all, and Scarlett was drooping and cranky by lunchtime.

Carrie took her in to get her to lie down. He picked up his keys from the kitchen table, flicking them around in his palm and wondering if he dared get out of here. He'd scraped his truck windows clean earlier, after all.

He'd though Carrie might nap with Scarlett. He could tell she still wasn't feeling well, but she joined him in the kitchen and started to make a cup of tea. "You want some?"

"No. Thank you."

A few minutes passed in silence as she pulled out the sugar and added it to the hot liquid. "I remembered what it was I'm supposed to be mad at you about." She stood with her back to the counter, holding her cup in front of her.

He also noticed she only said she was *supposed to be* mad, not that she *was* mad.

"Why did you send all those guys into the shop for haircuts?"

He nodded to the hallway. "She really asleep?"

When Carrie nodded, he told her about Scarlett's request for a husband for her mom for Christmas.

Carrie looked at him in disbelief. "And you agreed to this plan?"

Yeah, it seemed dumb now. His face was hot. "You can't say no to her, either," he argued.

She laughed. "Sure I can. If I said yes to everything she

wanted, I'd be living in a rainbow-colored zoo with seventeen lizards trying to eat the twenty hamsters. She's seven. She doesn't always know what's best."

He stayed silent, not sure how best to extricate himself from this conversation. He figured he was going to have to give up on Scarlett's plan now.

His silence made the smile on Carrie's face fade. Her knuckles whitened on her mug. "I've got it now. Scarlett doesn't know what's best for me, but you do. Is that right?"

He shook his head, her words from earlier still ringing in his ears.

"Do you think I picked random guys?" he asked. "All of those men were good guys who would've done right by you. And believe me, I didn't enjoy one minute of trying to fix you up." Even thinking about it now gave him heartburn. "But if I'm not good enough for you, maybe one of them is."

"It was never about that—" She broke off, eyes flashing. "I just can't believe you'd try to pick me out a husband."

He shrugged. "Sorta seems like God made us all to be part of a pair. Family works better when there's a mom and a dad. So yeah, I want you to have the best, and yeah, I think that means you having a real family." Then his temper flared, and words he'd meant to keep to himself flew out. "But I don't want it to be some other guy."

She set her cup down and stepped toward him, and he was hot enough under the collar that he didn't back down when she stepped even closer.

She poked him with her index finger, but he clasped her hand in his.

And used it to tug her closer.

It was stupid. He was stupid, but that didn't stop him as he kissed her.

All the emotions he'd tried to hide—of the past twenty-four hours, maybe the past week, or maybe ever since the breakup—came out in his kiss. The knife of fear he'd felt when Scarlett couldn't breathe. The warmth he'd felt when Carrie'd leaned into him on the couch. The hot anger that she still didn't want him.

Her kiss said otherwise as she clung to his shoulders and pressed even closer.

He couldn't do this to himself.

He gently pushed her away. And stepped out into the icy world.

Chapter Seven

"WHAT ARE YOU DOING OUT HERE? WHERE'S THE squirt?"

Carrie stood in the Triple H's kitchen staring out the window above the sink. She acknowledged Matt's entrance with a nod but kept her eyes focused out the window on the barn in the distance. It'd been too lonely at home by herself, so she'd used the chance to bring out her groceries for tomorrow's Christmas feast.

"Your niece talked Trey into taking her to the Daddy-Daughter dance. And somehow, she also talked me into letting her."

Matt chuckled. "I'm not surprised. She's got a way of bringing you around to her way of thinking."

"I'm going to have to get a lot tougher before she turns into a teenager."

He set about making a pot of coffee. "So are you and Trey back together?"

She sighed. "No." After the kiss he'd laid on her in her kitchen, she hadn't seen him until today. She knew he was working extra holiday hours at the feed store, but even when he'd been available, he'd avoided her.

The single men parading through her shop had also dried up. Thank God.

After seeing how well he'd taken care of Scarlett and how worried he'd been, she'd been unable to *unsee* how much Trey loved her daughter. And the feelings she had for him, the ones that had never gone away, had rushed to the forefront in full force.

She loved him. And he was leaving.

She'd heard through the town gossip chain that he'd taken a job near Grapevine that would start right after the holiday.

She'd done what she'd intended. She'd driven him away. For good.

And the stupid thing was, she didn't want him to go.

"You two girls coming out for Christmas supper tomorrow?"

"Of course. I hope Kelsey likes your gift." He'd begged for Carrie's help, and they'd spent an afternoon at one of the ritzy Dallas shopping malls finding the perfect outfit.

"You and Scar could spend the night here if you wanted. Wake up on Christmas morning at the ranch. She might like that."

Her stomach pinched at the suggestion. "I don't think so."

He was silent for a moment, then, "You really don't feel like the Triple H is your home, do you?"

Oh, she did. It was just...

He shook his head. "I didn't believe him..." he muttered to himself. Then, louder, "Why not?"

She avoided his gaze. "It's personal."

"And I'm your brother." He leaned his shoulder against hers in solidarity.

She might as well spill it all. "Pat never liked Rob. When I told Pat we were getting married, he tried to talk me out of it. He told me if I left to run away with Rob, that I couldn't come back home."

Matt was silent, serious. "And you believed him?"

She shrugged, a sad smile coming. "I thought it was a bluff, but... Pat was so quick to move my boxes of stuff to Rob's place. He and I made up later, but I never really felt welcome out here while he was alive."

Matt put his hand on her shoulder. "Pat loved you. Even if he made a mistake, he left you a third of the Triple H. Gideon and I want you to know it *is* your home."

Tears made her eyes hot as she shook her head. "It doesn't feel that way."

"It *is* that way," he insisted. "In fact, I kinda think you and Scar should move out here."

She shook her head with a teary laugh. "And what, Scarlett can ride the early bus to school every day, like we did?"

"Maybe. We've got plenty of hands to cart her to school if you want her to have a ride."

She shook her head. "It's not just that... I don't..."

She couldn't say it.

"Belong?" he guessed. "That's a lie you've let yourself believe. You belong here as much as I do. When we were little, you'd ride more than I would. This land is in your blood."

Again she shook her head. "I can't, not now—" *Not without Trey.*

The place just felt empty without him.

"You could ask him to stay," he said. "He still loves you."

Her breath caught at the thought. He'd said he wasn't leaving the Triple H because of her, but he'd always known she didn't feel like this was her home. Had he thought it was because of him?

She'd barely acknowledged to herself that her feelings had never died. That *she* still loved *him.*

Could he really still have feelings for her, when she'd been so hot and so cold?

Her cell phone buzzed from her pocket. Then Matt's did.

They shared a worried glance.

"It's the sheriff's office," he said. He answered it. "Hale."

He was grabbing his keys and motioning her to follow him before he said another word.

Trey had never felt as out of place as he did right now.

And he loved every minute of it.

He kept nodding to friends and acquaintances, all of them looking like they were choking with ties and suit coats. Every single one was accompanied by a little girl dolled up like a princess.

He felt a huge amount of pride at having Scarlett on his arm in her deep green velvety dress and with her hair in some kind of intricate braid.

Scarlett looked up at him, beaming, as they took a turn around the dance floor, her standing on his shoes.

He wasn't much of a dancer, but she didn't seem to notice.

Something huge and hot had settled into his chest cavity when he'd picked her up at Carrie's earlier.

This might be the last time he spent with her. He was leaving for his new job just after the holiday.

He'd be out of Carrie's way, out of both of their lives.

After what he'd overheard last week, he had to believe Carrie was done with him. That, and the fact that she hadn't made any effort to reach out to him after they'd parted ways.

He was just having trouble getting his heart to accept it.

"Can we have some more punch?" Scarlett asked as the music ended.

"Sure, kiddo." She'd done all right with the red stuff earlier, no spills, so he figured it was okay.

"D'you wanna say hi to Santa?" he asked on their way across the hotel ballroom that'd been turned into a winter wonderland. He didn't recognize the yahoo they'd wrangled into the Santa suit this time, but he had to admit it made for a cute photo op.

She angled a look up at him. "Are you still leaving for Grapevine?"

"Yeah."

"Then no, I don't want to talk to Santa right now."

He wanted to chuckle at her adamancy, but another part of him was sad. During the three-course tea-slash-dinner that'd been served earlier, he'd explained to her why he was moving and where.

She'd nodded in that serious way she had, not crying like he'd thought she might.

They were on the edge of the dance floor when he had a sense that something was out of place. He was already holding Scarlett's hand and tightened his grip on her as he glanced around.

Somebody in the entrance, caddy-corner to the punch bowl, was causing a ruckus. He was in jeans and a ripped brown coat, not dressed for the event. He looked like he hadn't shaved in days.

Trey didn't know what was going on as he tried to hustle Scarlett farther from the door.

"Sir, you don't have a ticket." One of the organizers, a woman, was attempting to block the man from coming farther into the ballroom. "And this is a Daddy-Daughter dance."

"My daughter's in there."

At the sound of the shout, Scarlett froze, and since they were still connected, he had to stop too.

"What's the matter?" He looked down at her, but she'd gone pale and wide-eyed, staring at the stranger.

Suddenly, her hand was squeezing his tightly.

"That's the bad man," she whispered.

Her father?

Trey had never met him, but he felt Scarlett's fear and knew Carrie wouldn't want the man anywhere near her daughter. He looked around for help.

"That's her. Right there! Scarlett!" The shout came as Rob broke away from the organizer lady.

Trey scooped Scarlett into his arms and walked calmly toward Randy Quaid, the police captain who'd already left his daughter at their table and was heading their way. Jim McClellan, a firefighter, had done the same, walking behind the policeman.

"You can't keep my daughter from me!" Rob called out.

Since his arms were full of little girl, he jerked his head toward the man making a beeline across the dance floor. "That's Carrie Hale's ex-husband, and she and Scarlett have a protective order against him."

Trey was man enough to take on Rob, even if the guy was a good thirty pounds heavier. And there was a huge part of him that wanted to tell him a thing or two about beating up helpless women. But his first priority was Scarlett's safety.

So he would let the right people handle it.

"I've got you, kiddo. No one's gonna get close to you on my watch."

And she looked up at him so trustingly that that huge knot in his chest lit on fire.

. . .

"Can't you go any faster?" Carrie asked.

"I'm fifteen over the speed limit already," Matt responded.

Maybe it was a good thing he'd shoved her into the passenger seat of his truck. If she'd been driving, she'd probably have been going a hundred.

The call that had hit both of their phones was from one of the organizers of the dance, letting them know that she'd seen Rob trying to get in.

And Carrie was freaking out.

"Trey's not going to let anything happen to her," Matt said, the picture of calmness.

But she couldn't stop thinking about Rob and how strong he was.

One of Matt's hands came to rest over hers where she gripped the console. "He's not going to let anything happen to her," he repeated. "He loves her."

And then the memory that surfaced was of Trey at her kitchen table, head in hands, so relieved Scarlet was okay that he was in tears. Someone that loved her little girl that much wouldn't let Rob anywhere near her.

She'd been so wrong. About Trey, about everything.

Would he give her a chance to make it right?

Carrie was out of the truck before Matt shoved it into park.

"Wait up!" he called, but she couldn't.

There was a police car with lights on sitting at the curb, and as she was running to the doors, out came Randy Quaid in a dark blue suit, along with a uniformed officer. They were both escorting Rob out of the building in handcuffs.

Randy had a scrape across his cheek.

Rob was yanking against the cuffs and the men.

She stopped, hanging back in the shadows in hopes he wouldn't see her. She didn't want to argue with him, not right now, not when she was so worried about her baby.

When the two officers had him in the backseat of the patrol car, she rushed forward toward the doors.

Behind her, she heard Matt stop to talk to Randy.

"I'm not hurt," said the officer. "But he will be, for assaulting an officer."

Inside, red and green balloons and streamers covered the ballroom. Soft music still played, but no one was dancing. The men and little girls were clustered in small groups, all talking.

And there was Scarlett, pulling Trey by the hand toward her. "Mama, Mama!"

Trey's eyes were soft and apologetic as they neared.

Scarlett threw herself at Carrie's legs, and she accepted the hug, patting the girl's back. "The bad man came, but Trey didn't let him get to me!"

Matt came up behind them and clasped Trey's hand, slapping his other arm. "You did good."

"I didn't do anything," Trey said with a shake of his head. His eyes hadn't left Carrie. "Got McClellan involved immediately."

Smart man. If he'd thrown a punch or even let Scarlett down, there was a chance Rob could've grabbed her up and made a run for it.

Everything that'd been whirling through her head since earlier today suddenly crystallized, and she knew she couldn't let this man go.

"C'mere, squirt." Matt grabbed Scarlett up in a hug, making her squeal and laugh, and leaving Carrie and Trey semi-alone, if you didn't count the curious faces all around the ballroom. Right now, she couldn't care less about the people watching.

"Thank you for taking care of my baby," she whispered. If she spoke any louder, she'd burst into tears.

He nodded.

And she dared to ask for it all.

"Would you...would you take me home for Christmas?"

"Sure. I took off my jacket back at our table." His tie had come loose. "Let me grab it and my keys, and I'll drive you to your house."

"Not my house," she said, holding his gaze. "Take me home. To the Triple H."

Chapter Eight

CHASE SAT IN THE BARN WITH THE FOALING MARE. Christmas Eve, and here was his celebration.

It wasn't a baby Jesus or anything, but this foal was important to him. He'd spent a good chunk of his savings on the mare last year, and she was a keeper, a gentle soul with lovely lines.

He leaned his head back against the stall as the familiar scents of hay and horses washed over him.

His phone buzzed at his hip and he took it out. The screen was too bright against his eyes, which had grown used to the darkened barn.

It was a text from Sarah. The local large animal vet and a friend from high school who he'd recently reconnected with.

Sarah: How's the mama-to-be doing?

He couldn't help smiling at the question. Sarah was a workaholic. She loved her job, and it showed, considering it was almost midnight and she was still checking on a patient.

Chase: It's still early. She's too calm for anything much to be happening.

He knew there wasn't anything he could do to rush this.

Chase: I thought you were at some fancy party? Thought you'd be out past your bedtime.

He knew vets got called out at all hours of the night, knew she usually was in bed before ten because of that.

The party was for her hotshot attorney fiancé, some shindig their law firm put on every Christmas Eve.

Sarah: I'm hiding out in the bathroom. These other wives and girlfriends are like barracudas.

Merry Christmas to her.

Although their friendship had fizzled the years she'd been away at vet school, it had rekindled over the summer and fall, when she'd been called out to the Triple H at different times.

He was a little worried about her relationship. Her fiancé didn't treat her right, as far as Chase was concerned. The man expected her to give up her life, her thriving vet practice here, to move to Austin when they got married.

And she'd agreed.

Chase knew she'd had a hard time during her childhood. Didn't know all the details, but they'd both been locals, and he'd heard gossip back then about her lowlife mom. And then she'd gone into foster care, into a group home during her teen years. Both she and her sister Kayla, who was also back in town, now owned a farm nearby.

Chase: Your gift's waiting for you when you get back.

Sarah: Please tell me it's not a bouquet of pencils.

The memory of the prank he'd pulled on her back in their sophomore year made him grin. On her birthday, he'd sent bouquets of number two pencils tied off with ribbon to each of her classrooms.

Chase: Not even close.

Cowboys didn't make all that much, and without an education, he didn't have many options. He loved being out in the open, loved the animals. So since he was short on cash, he'd had to use his hands. He'd crafted her a bird feeder out of weathered metal. He'd installed it earlier this afternoon, complete with a big red bow on top.

She'd once confessed to him—the night of senior prom when they'd both ended up in a greasy spoon diner instead of at the dance—that she'd often wished she could be a bird and fly away. Did she even remember that? He'd never forget it.

Chase: Merry Christmas.

Sarah: You too.

. . .

CARRIE JOINED Trey in the darkened living room in the ranch house, where he sat on the floor in front of the unlit Christmas tree. She sat next to him and sucked in a breath of pine needles and man, only able to see shadows.

Matt was around, though he'd retired early to give her privacy. His fiancé Kelsey would join them in the morning. Carrie'd tucked Scarlett into her childhood double bed and would join the little girl there later. Tonight, after the scare they'd both had, Carrie needed to snuggle all night.

Nervous anticipation skittered along her nerve endings, lighting the hope that Matt's words from earlier were true.

"What're you doing?" Carrie whispered now, their knees bumping in the dark.

"Just listening," he returned, his voice a low murmur.

She strained her ears, trying to listen too. Texas wind rattled the windowpanes, and far off, there was the low of a cow. Around them, the old farmhouse settled and creaked.

These were the sounds of her childhood.

Did he miss being on the Triple H?

Finally, he shifted beside her, their elbows brushing as his back came to rest against the sofa, legs stretched out in front of him.

He broke the silence. "You asked me to stay for a while. What'd ya want to talk about?"

She didn't know if she could do this, but she jumped anyway.

"Matt said you'd stay on at the Triple H if I asked you, so I'm asking."

"I took that job in Grapevine."

Was he purposely misunderstanding what she was asking?

Her whole body was shaking. Anticipation? Fear of rejection? Probably both.

"I think you'll find more opportunities for advancement here," she said, heart in her throat. "Like all the way to partner."

There was a beat of silence.

Her pulse thundered as he moved—away from her. There was a soft snick, and the tree lights went on. She blinked against the sudden brightness.

"Sorry 'bout that." He didn't sound sorry at all, but he was sitting down next to her again. "The dark was real romantic, but I think I'd rather see your face right about now. What exactly are you saying?"

She breathed in deep and went for broke. "I'm sorry for being so cowardly before. You've done nothing but prove your love for Scarlett...and for me." She swallowed hard, tears pricking her eyes. "And I threw it away. Can you forgive me?"

It was one of the hardest things she'd ever had to do, but she looked him right in the eye.

And read the softness and, yes, the love there.

"Of course I can," he said in his quiet, steady way. He cupped her jaw in his big hand and leaned in for a kiss, which she was more than happy to oblige him with.

The side-by-side angle was awkward, and he didn't seem intent on moving anytime soon. His arm came around her shoulders and settled her in more closely against him. That was fine with her.

"I know what happened tonight scared you," he started.

She shook her head. "This isn't about that. It's about everything. You being there for Scarlett. And for me, all this time. Even the guys you chose to send into the shop to ask me out. There wasn't a loser in the bunch of them."

"You deserve better than that."

"See?" She picked at the hem of her jeans. "I never stopped loving you, you know?"

His voice got a catch in it. "No, I didn't know." And he tipped her face up again for his kiss.

When they were both appropriately breathless and he'd whispered that he'd never stopped loving her either, she laid her head against his shoulder.

"So if you decide to stay on at the Triple H, I'm thinking maybe you could make partner by summer."

"You think so?" He sounded amused.

"If you still want—?"

"I want." He pressed a kiss to her temple. "Merry Christmas to me."

· · ·

THE NEXT MORNING, it was still so early, and they'd had so much excitement last night, that Scarlett hadn't woken yet to attack the pile of gifts beneath the tree.

Trey sat in a wooden kitchen chair as Carrie swung an old towel around his neck. She'd dunked his head beneath the faucet, and he was chilled from that. She wielded silver scissors and a black comb.

He'd told her he needed a haircut before the obligatory Christmas morning photos commenced. But that wasn't the real reason. He'd gotten his Christmas miracle after all, and he wanted to seal the deal.

The wall-mounted phone rang, and she stepped away to answer it before it woke Scarlett. He knew their time was short —kids always woke energetic on Christmas morning.

"Yes, this is Carrie. Yes." There was a long pause. "Oh. Okay." She sounded choked up. "Yes, thank you."

She hung up and rested one hip against the counter, turning to face him. "That was the police department. Apparently, Rob had an Arizona warrant out for his arrest. The officer didn't say what the charges were, but that they were pretty serious and he doubted Rob was getting out of them, since he'd jumped bail as well. So, it looks like I don't have to worry about him right now."

"Ever," he said, doing his best to convey his seriousness with his eyes.

She lit up, a smile spreading across her face. She rejoined him at the chair, lifting the comb and scissors.

He shifted in the chair, his prize hidden beneath his palms.

"Sit still," she warned. "You're as bad as a little kid, and I don't want you to have a chunk cut out of the top of your head."

He couldn't stop grinning. He'd gone to bed and been unable to sleep, buzzing with hope and anticipation.

Carrie loved him. And unless he was sorely mistaken, she wanted to get married.

She came around to trim the front of his hair, her mouth pursed in concentration the same way Scarlett's did.

Her eyes flicked down from his hairline to his face, and her lips twitched. "What's so funny?"

"Just can't seem to stop smiling this morning. Merry Christmas."

He'd meant to be more polished, but he opened his hands, and her glance flicked down to the black jeweler's box he held.

Her scissors and comb lowered. "What's that?"

"Christmas gift. I've had it since last year, and I figure it's about time to get rid of it."

He took the scissors and comb from her and set them away as she took the box with shaking hands.

"Carrie, I couldn't love you and Scarlett any more. Please, will you marry me?"

She glanced up at him, and her eyes were wet. "Are you trying to do better than my proposal from last night?"

He laughed, his hands coming to her hips. "No way. Just wanted to make sure I do this right."

He pulled her onto his lap.

"Oh, you're doing it right." She took the diamond solitaire out of the ring box and slid it on her ring finger before sliding her arms around his neck.

He kissed her, losing himself in the feel of her in his arms. He was as content as he'd ever been until Scarlett ran into the room, shrieking.

"You're *kissing*! Uncle Matt, they're *kissing*!"

Carrie broke their embrace with a laugh, pushing out of Trey's arms and off his lap.

Her ring winked in the light as she moved, and ever observant, Scarlett caught that too. "A *ring*? Uncle Matt!"

Scarlett ran out of the kitchen and into the living area, shrieking with joy.

Trey winced. "Is she gonna do that every time we have big news?"

"Of course. Don't get up. I'm not letting you go with half a haircut."

He was pretty sure that while they were kissing, she'd mussed it up so that no one would be able to tell, but he sat obediently in the chair, unable to wipe the smile off his face.

He was proud that she wore the same kind of goofy smile every time she passed into his line of sight.

Matt stood in the doorway, leaning his shoulder against the jamb and smiling at them. "I guess you worked things out."

Scarlett ducked under his arm and danced circles around them. "Santa's real," she sang. "Real, real, real."

He winked at her.

She stopped short, propping her hands on her hips. "Now what about a baby brother or sister?"

Stealing Sarah

Prologue

"Shh."

Something was wrong.

A frisson of fear crawled up Sarah Campbell's spine as she turned the lock on her front door. She fumbled the black medical bag between her hands.

It wasn't dawn yet, and shadows abounded. Her porch light had gone out last week, and she hadn't replaced the bulb yet.

Had she heard a voice? She strained her ears.

Everything was silent. Even the Texas wind that usually rattled her eaves had stilled. Cold seeped into her skin through the coat, and she'd stuffed her gloves in her back pockets.

Maybe it was remnants of the nightmare. She usually didn't love being awakened in the middle of the night, but she hadn't been sorry when her cell phone had clattered on the nightstand, pushing away those dream images. The specifics had fled with sleep, but she could well remember the terror she'd felt.

No reason to be afraid. She was just still spooked from the dream, right?

With a horse in labor and the colt turned breech, she didn't have the luxury of giving in to silly fears. Or going back to bed.

She stepped off the stoop, and her feet crunched in the dead winter grass.

A hulking shadow separated from the corner of her house and lunged toward her.

She dropped her leather bag. Screamed. An arm snaked around her waist from behind, and a hand clamped over her mouth before more than a half-second of sound had emerged.

A bright light—a flashlight?—shone in her eyes. She blinked against it even as her eyes watered. She tried to see past it, to see who was behind the light.

"This her?" A male voice growled in her ear.

She struggled. Her elbow connected with flesh somewhere behind her, eliciting a grunt.

The iron bands of his arms around her didn't give.

"It's her." A male voice from behind the flashlight said. The light clicked off, but the brightness remained burned into her retinas. She couldn't see his face in the darkness that remained.

Her mind scrambled to process what was happening, how she could get out of this.

Her phone. It was stuck in the hip pocket of her jeans. If she could just maneuver her arm around, she could—

Rough hands patted her down and then her chance was gone because the man not holding her had stripped her of her phone. She heard it hit the driveway pavement and then a crunch as he stomped on it. No!

Her phone was gone.

Okay. She tried to breathe, tried not to panic as the hand over her mouth made it increasingly difficult.

Think it through. Who would miss her?

She hadn't spoken to her fiancé James in thirty-six hours. He was working a huge case and wouldn't even register something was wrong if he didn't hear from her this morning.

The call that had woken her had been from the answering service that handled the clinic's after-hours emergencies. If she didn't show at her client's barn, they would call back. If they couldn't get her, they'd have to call one of the other vets.

The clinic opened in two hours. If she didn't check in by nine, they'd know something was wrong. Could she survive that long?

The man with his arms around her loosened his grip slightly, barely enough for her to move. "Where's her bag?" His breath was hot on her head and stunk of halitosis.

The other guy bent, and she heard him rifling inside her medical bag.

Her chest started to burn.

She struggled harder, tried to bite the hand over her mouth, tried to shriek or scream or anything.

There was a scrape of metal against glass, and she hoped he wouldn't break her stethoscope, one of the thermometers, or the ophthalmoscope. What was he looking for?

"There's nothing here," the crook growled. Then he got in her face. "Where's the drugs? The pain pills? Ketamine? I know you keep it on you."

Drugs? That's what this attack was about? Heart pounding, she struggled against the hand over her mouth. Now that her eyes had adjusted somewhat to the dark, she could see the creep in front of her—the cell-phone smasher—was wearing a ski mask. She could see a mustache where the mouth hole was, but nothing else.

Ski-mask looked at the brute holding her. "She can't tell me with your hand over her mouth."

"Oh. Right."

He removed his hand, and she gulped in a burning breath of icy air.

There was a small metal safe in her covered pickup bed. Controlled substances were state-regulated, and she could only carry a small supply. Even that had to be locked up.

She doubted the guys attacking her would care about the details.

"I don't have any," she lied. "They're all at the clinic."

Ski-mask backhanded her. Pain exploded in her cheek, sending stars dancing in front of her eyes. The force of the blow knocked the breath from her chest. She stumbled on the sidewalk, almost went down to her knees, but the hand at her waist caught her.

"Don't lie to us!"

She sucked in a breath, tried to rally a scream. Her neighbor Wanda was an early riser. If Sarah could just—

This time the hand that clapped over her mouth didn't allow any room to breathe at all. Her lungs ached for air.

"What about the truck?" asked the man holding her.

Her head spun as they shoved her down the tiny sidewalk to her truck parked in the driveway, a darker blob in the dark morning, equidistant between her house and Wanda's.

She couldn't think. Panic shook her limbs. A breath. She needed air. She tried struggling again, but she was suffocating. Weak.

Were they going to kill her?

"Keys," one voice said, as if from a far distance.

"Where are they—" The voice faded out as her conscious wavered.

"Where are they?" This time the shout in her face roused her. Still, the hand was clamped over her face.

She shook her head, eyes watering uncontrollably.

And then they clocked her on the head. Once. Twice. Pain radiated through her skull, down her spine.

Everything went black.

Chapter One

FOUR WEEKS LATER

SARAH TAPPED AWAY AT THE KEYBOARD, INPUTTING A report on the one-month-old colt she'd seen earlier this morning at the Bar-None ranch just outside of town.

The day had been cold, made worse by dry north winds, so she was thankful to be indoors, but her eyes crossed from staring at the computer screen for so long. She'd been at this all afternoon.

She took off the reading glasses she used to work on the computer and raised her gaze from the screen to the good-sized window across the room that overlooked the parking lot and behind that, the empty field that belonged to old man Murphy. The last of the light was seeping past the horizon, leaving the nearly-empty lot dark.

She let her eyes unfocus and remembered the two-hundred-pound colt frolicking around its mother, breath puffing out in the cold, crisp air.

Those moments observing a healthy animal were what made her job worth the long, unpredictable hours, too much time spent driving between calls, and sometimes having to work in bad conditions.

A pair of headlights turned into the lot, flashing into her window momentarily as the vehicle pulled up next to her truck.

Memories flashed behind her eyes. Blood rushed through her veins. Her adrenaline pumped.

She went to the window and closed the blinds against the darkness and whoever had just pulled up.

There was nothing wrong. No attack coming, even if her body insisted there were.

It wasn't happening again.

Probably one of the other vets had forgotten something in his office.

She forced her breaths to even out. Beeps from the hallway outside her office indicated the alarm system being deactivated. Then came the sound of the back door opening and closing.

Two barks sounded from the indoor kennels, one low and gruff and one high-pitched.

It was late. What would they think about her being in the office?

She glanced around to make sure nothing was out of place. The leather sofa beneath the window was free of its usual mish-mash of vet implements, the ever-present stethoscope stowed in her bag for once. Everything else in the messy office appeared normal.

Her last check was that her long-sleeved sweater covered the scratch on her wrists. The bruises left by her assailants had faded, but one deep cut was taking its time to heal properly.

"Sarah?" That was Jessie's voice. Her assistant, who was supposed to be on maternity leave.

Sarah's breath whooshed out, and the tension left in a rush, making her bones feel like jelly.

She'd only seen her friend once since the baby had been born, and it appeared Jessie had slimmed down a considerable amount. A long, floaty dress almost reached the floor, and with her mahogany hair down around her shoulders, she looked beautiful. Or maybe it was because Sarah usually saw her in scrubs. During house-calls, Sarah's normal uniform was jeans and work boots, her hair tied back.

Jessie looked lovely, and very, very tired.

"What're you doing here?" Sarah leaned one hip against her desk.

"What are *you* still doing here?" her fiery assistant returned. Jessie propped one hand on her hip. "We talked about this before I went on maternity leave. You're working too much."

That kind of sass wouldn't be appropriate in another clinic, but Jessie had come on board six weeks after Sarah had hired on at the small-town clinic, and they'd just clicked. When Jessie was around, she usually kept Sarah from becoming the job.

Unfortunately, Jessie couldn't fix what was wrong with her.

Sarah shrugged and gestured with the glasses she still held to the piles of file folders threatening to avalanche off her desk. "I've got a lot to do."

It was a lame excuse and Jessie knew it. Unfortunately, she also knew Sarah and her work habits. Jessie stepped into the room and glanced at the top folder. "Did you pull these from one of the filing cabinets?"

In other words, were they open files or closed?

Jessie looked up with a challenge in her gaze.

Sarah tried not to wince. "Okay, so I'm working on a project I probably don't need—"

"One of the office staff can go through those old files."

"So can I." Sarah owned a quarter of the practice. She didn't have to explain herself to Jessie, her employee.

Even if Jessie was one of a few friends Sarah could claim.

They stared at each other. This was something Sarah wouldn't—couldn't—back down on. Not tonight.

Finally Jessie nodded slowly. "Okay. But how about you work on this tomorrow? I haven't been out of the house in two weeks, and the girls and I want to take you out for a night on the town."

Sarah scrunched her nose. "You don't need to worry about me. What girls?"

"Mostly your sister and me."

Sarah couldn't imagine what kind of girls' night out they had planned in Taylor Hills. The sidewalks rolled up at nine around here. "Why didn't you just call me?" Then it would've been easier to say no.

Maybe they'd worked together too long. Jessie seemed to read her mind as she smirked and reached over to Sarah's phone, where it lay face-down on the desk. She picked it up and flashed the screen at Sarah. Six missed calls.

Sarah sighed.

"I figured the only way to break you out of this quicksand"—she gestured to the piles on Sarah's desk—"was to bring you a rope myself."

It was a nice gesture, but Sarah wasn't interested. Not tonight. She started to shake her head.

Jessie's face fell. Her expression turned serious. "Okay..." She looked to the side for brief seconds and then back at Sarah. "It was supposed to be a secret but..."

"What's a secret?" Sarah almost barked the words. Surprises were not her favorite thing, not since the attack, anyway.

"Kayla planned this big birthday bash. A surprise party for you. I'm supposed to get you there."

Of course Sarah's sister would do something over the top. They'd both spent years in foster care, and sometimes they'd even missed birthdays completely. Now that Kayla was an adult, she could throw whatever huge parties she wanted.

"It's the big three-oh," Jessie said. But instead of excitement, her voice was more pleading. She rubbed a hand at her lower back. "Look, she started planning this all the way back before Thanksgiving. After—"

Sarah cut off that line with a glare.

Jessie waved her hand, glossing over what Sarah didn't want to mention. "After everything, I told her you probably weren't going to want a big party. Cate did too, but you know Kayla."

It was impossible to talk Sarah's sister out of something she'd set her mind to. Their sister-of-the-heart, Cate, was much more sensitive than her blunt persona put off, and Sarah knew that if Cate hadn't been able to get through to Kayla, no one would.

"What if I don't show up?" The one niggling hope that maybe she could not go died as Jessie shook her head.

"Then you'd have a living room full of your closest friends and your business partners wondering why and worrying about you." *Even more than they already are,* she seemed to say silently.

Or maybe that was just Sarah's imagination. It'd been over-active since that weekend.

"Fine." She grumbled the word, but Jessie lit up. "Just let me check on the big Newfie before we leave."

She would go and get it over with.

CHASE FORD STOOD in the kitchen doorway of Kayla Campbell's ranch-style house as the birthday girl came through the front door to shouts of "Surprise!" from her friends.

He saw the wince she tried to hide beneath her faked shocked reaction. Obviously, Jessie had told her. Probably a good thing, considering.

Sarah looked tired. More than the exhaustion, shadows chased behind her hazel eyes. That was no doubt the reason Kayla had insisted on this shindig on one of the coldest nights they'd had so far this new year. Even Sarah's hair, in a braid, seemed limp and pale. Maybe it was the lighting in the room. Or maybe not.

The attack was still haunting Sarah. And none of them knew what to do about it.

It was certainly giving him recurring nightmares. He'd been on an errand at the feed store when he'd overheard someone talking about an attack on the "pretty lady vet." He'd been worried enough to interrupt their conversation and found out that it'd happened two days before. He was barely Sarah's friend —high school didn't count—so of course nobody had thought to notify him, but two days was enough time for the story to burn like wildfire through their little town. Taylor Hills had experienced petty theft and some drug use, sure, but something like this... Sarah had been attacked in her own front yard by two unknown guys, badly beaten, and left for dead. They'd emptied the small safe in her truck of all the drugs inside. So far, they hadn't been apprehended.

No one had found her for hours, not until the older lady who lived next door had ventured out in the cold to take out the trash. Sarah had suffered from exposure and near hypothermia.

Now, her scrapes and bruises had healed. But he could tell she was still suffering. Still having nightmares? He didn't know.

He knew it could've been so much worse. Thank God she was alive. He was sure he hadn't offered that many frantic prayers since Gideon Hale's princess-wife had nearly been assassinated over a year ago.

All the drama had clarified one important thing for him.

He was in love with Sarah.

He hadn't meant for it to happen. He wasn't even on her radar. She was engaged to someone else, for crying out loud.

He'd had a huge unrequited crush on her during high school but never done anything about it. Even then, she'd been out of his league. After she'd left for college, they'd lost touch. They'd reconnected as friends last summer, and while he had thought it was only their friendship that had deepened, he'd been wrong.

His feelings were a tangled knot. And he was desperate to keep them a secret. There was no reason for her to know he cared about her, not with the way things were.

And that's why he slipped unobtrusively back into the kitchen on the pretense of checking on the cake. Kayla had wrangled him into being a part of this birthday gig two months ago.

And of course he wanted to be here for Sarah. Just not too visible in a room of her successful friends. His jeans and boots pegged him as a lowly cowboy, not like the slacks and button-up shirts her partners wore or the trendy clothes her girlfriends were in. He'd long ago left behind the kind of people who cared about the *in* styles, and he'd thought he didn't care about that stuff at all.

But he didn't like the way his clothes reflected his life, proved he didn't belong in this circle, either. Back when he'd chosen to leave it all behind, including the education he could've had, he'd never thought he might fall for someone like Sarah. And now it was too late to be the kind of guy she'd want.

Her sister Kayla was an entrepreneur was working to start a no-kill dog rescue. The property she'd bought was close to the Triple H ranch, where he'd worked since his early twenties, but the house and barn were obviously too much for one person and falling down around her. What was a young, single woman going to do out here? He didn't know.

Kayla had only invited him because of his history with Sarah. He'd known Kayla then, too. A town this small, everyone knew everyone.

He definitely didn't belong in this crowd of intelligent people, but he could bear it for an hour or so. For Sarah.

Where was Hero anyway? Somewhere in the last year he'd given her absent fiancé the nickname, only in his own skull. Hero didn't deserve her. Why couldn't she see that he was one of the chumps Chase had purposely turned his life around not to be?

It wasn't his business, no matter how much he wished differently.

AFTER AN HOUR OF FORCED SMILES, Sarah was about done. She'd opened gifts—some of them gag gifts like the box of Depends. Not all, though. Her sister had given her a beautiful silver charm bracelet; another friend had gifted her a year of free oil changes and tune ups. That was a great gift, especially with how rough Sarah was on her truck.

She was worn out. Sleepless nights and long days, often out in the cold weather had worn her out. She was ready to leave.

A niggling feeling wormed its way to her consciousness.

Where was James? She'd had the fleeting thought when Jessie had mentioned the party that he would be here. It *was* a milestone birthday. Had Kayla invited him? Her sister and James didn't get along, but surely Kayla wouldn't have left him out.

She excused herself for a bathroom break, sneaking out the door in Kayla's master bedroom to the back patio outside. Just a few minutes, then she'd return to the party. She figured she had to eat at least one piece of cake before she could escape.

It was dark and cold enough that her breath puffed out in front of her, and she had fleeting thoughts of *that morning*. She forced herself to recognize what was real. The moon was almost full and bright against the sky filled with stars. An owl hooted— maybe from Kayla's barn—and a whippoorwill called. In a distant pasture, a cow lowed. Just across the patio was the kitchen door.

This was not the same. She was safe here.

She wrapped her arms around her middle. She only had her sweater to protect her from the cool air.

Her phone buzzed from her pocket. Seriously, couldn't Kayla give her five minutes?

But it was James's name who lit up the screen.

She forced a cheerful note into her voice. "Hey!"

"Sarah, we need to talk." He sounded resigned, and unease filtered through her.

Perhaps he was tired from a long day in the office. His law practice often required eighty-hour weeks.

She wasn't one to talk, not with the hours she worked.

"If you're going to sing me the birthday song, I'll brace myself," she teased.

"It's your birthday? Of course it is," he mumbled.

Her heart thudded painfully and she swallowed hard. He'd forgotten her birthday completely? This was so much worse than him simply not showing up at the party.

She knew there'd been a disconnect between them lately. Even before the attack, there'd been something off. She'd thought that after the wedding in June, when she would move to Austin to be with him, it would go away. They'd grow closer, the way she'd dreamed they would since they'd met in college.

"Look, I'm sorry for the rotten timing, but I can't go on like this anymore." His words were cold through the phone line. Kind of like how she imagined him when prosecuting a case in front of a judge and jury. "I was going to do this last month, but then you'd had that scare."

A scare.

Yes, she'd certainly been frightened. Terrorized, even. She could've died. She wouldn't call it a scare.

"We both know this isn't working," he said flatly.

She'd thought she had time to fix things. "But, the wedding—"

"Sarah, there's not going to be a wedding."

"You're br-breaking it off," she stammered, the inane statement falling from her lips as she struggled to understand. "Tonight?"

"Sarah, it's time we let go."

Let go. Just like that.

She took the phone away from her ear. Stared at the dark screen.

He'd hung up.

He'd broken up with her on her birthday.

She wasn't shaking. Shouldn't she be crying or something?

All she felt was numb. Was numbness one of the stages of grief? Suddenly, she couldn't remember.

A man's throat cleared from nearby, and she jumped, whirling, her fingers scrabbling on the phone's surface as she tried to dial for help.

"Hey, birthday girl. It's just me."

She struggled to regulate her breathing, to calm the blood from rushing in her ears, the itch in her feet to run.

It was Chase. Just Chase. Her friend.

He was backlit by the kitchen light streaming out the back door behind him. She hadn't heard the door open. Had he been standing there the whole time?

Had she been so caught up in her own little world that she hadn't noticed him when she'd come outside?

How much had he heard? Everything, probably.

Enough to know she was pathetic.

"You're gonna freeze out here if you stay too long."

Was it cold? Her sense of cold had fled when that base survival instinct had taken over.

There was motion behind him. He said something over his shoulder that she didn't get all of but that sounded like, "she's on the patio."

More motion, a whisper, and then he stepped forward, holding something. The door remained open behind him.

He lifted up an afghan she recognized from the back of her sister's couch. She'd given it to Kayla two years ago for Christmas. Purchased it from one of her clients, who raised Alpacas and made yarn from their wool. Sarah was not remotely crafty.

He wrapped it around her, securing it over her shoulders, and she knew a moment of warmth, the scent of man and horse. Then he stepped back, shoving his hands into his jeans pockets.

"You okay?"

"Sure. Yeah." She jutted her chin up. Nothing to see here. She was fine.

She couldn't see his eyes, backlit as he was. She didn't have to see to know—he'd overheard.

He was just too nice to say anything. She hated that he'd seen her in this weak moment.

The cowboy hadn't been a close friend back in high school. Back then, she hadn't known how to protect herself, how to hide her feelings. She was a little afraid of what he might see on her face right now.

She didn't want to talk about James, and she really didn't want to talk about the Other Thing, so she pushed the afghan off her shoulders and straightened them. "I just needed a second to catch my breath. Let's do cake!"

He was practically vibrating with tension as she walked past him into the kitchen, forgoing a route back through Kayla's bedroom.

He held his silence. Not a skill that many men had.

The bright lights of the kitchen were blinding. She managed to focus on Kayla and Jessie, who watched her troop back inside. They both looked slightly anxious.

As if maybe they expected her to burst into tears or...something. She didn't know what. She hadn't cried in the hospital last month. Or later, alone at home. She was fine.

Her phone buzzed again. She considered tossing it down the garbage disposal. Probably would have, too, if she hadn't just finished uploading all her contacts after— Nope, not thinking about that. Not thinking about James, either. Or talking to him.

But when she glanced at the screen, it was the emergency call center associated with the practice. A frisson of unease went through her, but she took the call, turning her back on too many curious gazes.

"Doctor Campbell," she answered.

She absorbed the information the operator gave her. A rancher needed an exam on his daughter's prized 4H sheep on the other side of town. She agreed to take the call and rang off.

She had to go. Her duty to her clients demanded it.

Except, it was nighttime. And just the thought of going on a night call sent a shiver down her spine. She straightened her shoulders and turned to her sister and her friends. "I have to go."

"I'll go with you," Jessie said quickly. Her assistant's eyes were too sharp. Had she seen Sarah's momentary hesitation?

Jessie's husband stood in the doorway, holding a tiny bundle on his shoulder. The baby squalled, almost on cue. "No way," he said.

"I'll handle it," Sarah said firmly. She hated that they felt like they had to coddle her. But there was also a small part of her that wanted to curl up on her sister's couch and let someone else handle this.

She couldn't. She'd been a vet for five years. With the rancher on hand, examining one sheep was well within Sarah's capability.

It didn't stop her heart from pounding. Adrenaline rushed through her veins.

Jessie looked like she would protest, her jaw cocked mulishly as she looked over her shoulder to her husband.

"I'll go," came an unexpected voice from behind her. Chase. "I'm about partied out."

She turned on him. "That is really unnecessary."

He shrugged easily. "It's not calving season yet. I'm not needed at the Triple H, and it isn't like I've got a hot date waiting for me." He winced a little after the words had left his mouth. Maybe he hadn't wanted to admit that.

"Thanks, but I'll be fine. You've never assisted a vet before." When she turned, ready to find her coat and get moving, she caught both Kayla and Jessie making silent hand gestures and mouthing words to Chase. Now they both clasped their hands, manufacturing wide-eyed, utterly unconvincing looks of innocence.

"Oh, come *on*, you guys," Sarah protested. "I'm a grown woman. I don't need a babysitter." Plus, he'd just witnessed her most humiliating moment to date.

"He's not a babysitter," Jessie offered helpfully. "He's a cowboy."

Sarah shot a look over her shoulder to the man who stood immovable as a big bull, silent and watchful.

"No one said you needed a babysitter." Kayla linked her arm through Sarah's. "But it never hurts to have a friend."

A friend.

The soft thought brought immediate, unexpected tears, and Sarah blinked quickly, hoping no one had noticed.

"Fine," she agreed.

Only because it was dark. Not because she needed a friend.

Chapter Two

Kayla cleaned up the last of the paper plates and plastic cups, tossing them into a black plastic bag. Her movements were brisk and forceful. It was a poor one, but tossing the trash was at least some kind of outlet for her worry.

Something had happened when her sister had been on the phone during the party. Sarah had been on edge before she'd disappeared for her "bathroom break." Kayla had watched Sarah's tension grow as the party went on, but whoever she'd been talking to had only increased Sarah's unease. When she'd returned, Sarah's had reminded Kayla too much of their childhood.

She and Sarah had both grown up in foster care, then ultimately a group home. They both had attachment issues. Kayla held out hope that Sarah's engagement was *it* for her, even if she didn't particularly like James. He was too snooty for his own good.

And then it had been impossible not to notice Sarah's reaction to the after-hours house call she'd agreed to make. She was nervous, even if she hid it well.

Her house had cleared out quickly after Sarah's departure. It was a weeknight, and her friends had jobs. Jessie and Herb had the new baby.

It just seemed too quiet. Not the life she'd always dreamed of during her growing-up years.

Bando's nails clicked against the linoleum kitchen floor with a soft *snick, snick, snick* as her Border Collie mix wandered around that room, slurping up every crumb he could find.

Her sister needed a dog.

Sarah threw herself into her work, seeking comfort there, but what Kayla had found worked best to comfort was her furry best friend.

"Sixty seconds, and then we're going out to the barn," she told the dog.

He wagged his tail so hard his whole body wiggled.

Maybe some people might judge her for talking to her dog as if he could understand, but she judged those people right back. They'd obviously never been loved by the right animal.

She'd bent to pick up the last couple of of red plastic cups, half-hidden behind an end table, when she spotted yet another crack in the plaster on the wall.

She groaned, and Bando came over to sniff at the corner. He gave one wag when he didn't find anything malicious and wandered off.

Her house was in desperate need of repair. She wasn't a builder, didn't know how to fix cracked walls, replace broken bathroom tiles, or remodel the butter-yellow eighties-style kitchen. And she didn't have the money to hire it out.

Sarah was too polite to suggest that maybe Kayla had made a mistake buying this place. She'd come out to visit Sarah from her city apartment and fallen in love with the land. And no wonder the place was on the market for cheap—because of the disrepair in the house and barn. It would be perfect for the dog rescue she'd dreamed of since she was a little girl.

She just had to find some money first.

She shrugged into her fleece-lined jean jacket and tugged on her work boots. Bando bounced at her feet, and she laughed as she pushed open the door. She grabbed a flashlight from the shelf near the door before shutting it behind her.

The bitter cold stole her breath, and she hurried across the yard to the barn several hundred yards down the drive. She could've driven, but this mini-walk would give Bando time to do his nightly business and stretch his legs. And she loved being outdoors. The group home where she and Sarah had ended up by her tenth birthday had had strict rules about outside time.

The barn was the whole reason she'd bought this property. It was two stories high and had horse stalls down both sides. With a little TLC, she could really build something here.

She almost wrenched her shoulder out of socket pulling open the large double door. Getting some WD-40 on that was one of her first orders of business.

Inside, the musty, unused smell made her nose twitch. Wind whistled through cracks in the walls.

A pile of two-by-fours took up a lot of the free space. She'd demoed several stalls herself, leaving a huge open area for the large pen she imagined, a place for the pack of dogs she'd rescue. There was plenty of room along the far wall for individual pens. She shivered as she listened to the old heating unit chug away. She hoped the building wouldn't require a new furnace.

This whole thing had been one huge risk. Sarah wasn't the only one with issues from their childhood. Making this jump had probably been the hardest decision Kayla had ever made. Hopefully not one of the dumbest.

Bando bounced around the interior of the barn, sniffing to his heart's content. She'd done quite a bit of cleanup in those first few days here, making sure there were no stray nails, no hidden farm implements that a dog could hurt itself on.

She hoped no skunks had decided to hole up here for the winter. That would be a recipe for disaster.

She was peripherally aware of Bando as she perused the space. It was too late after Sarah's party to do any real work out here tonight, but she could dream.

Imagining the place full, imagining all the good she could do and all the dogs she could help, kept her going when she started drowning in doubt.

Which was all the time.

In her mind's eye, she saw a black lab mix romping through the as of yet unbuilt pens with his best buddy, a rotty mix. They were the two types of dogs that were hardest to get adopted. She wasn't afraid of hard cases. She'd fight for her dogs to the bitter end.

She *was* going to accomplish this. Maybe it would make up for the empty house. Who needed a man when she would have her dogs?

Bando barked, and this time she twisted to look at him. That was a different bark than before. An alert.

"What is it, boy?" She picked through the dirt-packed floor toward the far corner, where Bando stared and pawed at something.

She came up behind him, looking over his shoulder. "What is that...?"

Bando whined, scratching at the edge of the mound of straw she hadn't thrown out when she'd been cleaning.

There was an empty circular space in the hay, as if a medium-sized animal had curled up there at some point. Probably more than once.

"Back, boy."

Bando obeyed Kayla's stern command. He sat behind her feet. She didn't want him injured. It was likely that whatever had hidden out here had heard them coming and burrowed deeper in the hay. It could be poised to attack right this second.

The thought had her stepping back.

Minutes of stomping around the hay and tromping all over the barn hadn't turned up any clues.

What, or who, had been in her barn?

"YOU DON'T HAVE TO STAY," were the first words out of Sarah's mouth when Chase got out of his truck after following her to the Clemson ranch.

If he wasn't mistaken, the wind had picked up and he tucked his chin into the collar of his Carhartt jacket.

"Jessie'll have my hide if I abandon you now."

Her lips made the slightest twitch at that.

It was true. Her assistant was a pit bull. Even on maternity leave.

But that wasn't the real reason. He'd seen the sheen of tears in Sarah's eyes back in her sister's kitchen. And right now her shoulders were unnaturally stiff. She was acting like everything was normal, but she had to be a little nervous.

Sarah went to the camper shell on the back of her truck and opened it to pull out a black leather bag from behind the tailgate. Her doctor's bag, even though it seemed so old-fashioned.

He knew better than to offer to carry it for her. She was independent enough to get offended, and he was already on thin ice. She'd only allowed him to tag along because her friends had insisted.

"The operator said the rancher was out in the barn," Sarah said. Her chin had a stubborn lilt to it, all signs of hurt erased from her expression. Brave girl.

What was Hero thinking, letting her go? Guy was an idiot.

Chase fell into step beside her, their boots crunching in the dead winter grass. The barn was set back from the house, and the tracks were rutted and muddy after the rain they'd had the last two days. She was smart not to try to drive it.

A motion-sensor light from a corner of the barn roof lighted their way, that and the moonlight. The fields were silent around them.

"I guess you overheard my phone call," she said, breaking the quiet.

"Didn't mean to." He hadn't been eavesdropping. Kayla had asked him to open the back door and let some air flow through the house, and Sarah hadn't seemed to notice him as she'd crept outside at the same time. He'd only heard her side of the conversation, but it was enough.

She sighed softly.

"I was wondering why James hadn't shown up," he said. "Didn't realize it was something like that."

She swallowed hard. Maybe he should just drop it, but she'd brought it up. "I'm going to call him back tomorrow. We've had our differences, but..."

She loved him?

That was what Chase expected to hear, but it wasn't what she said.

"I can change," she muttered softly. "Be more of what he wants. I just have to convince him of it."

He barely kept himself from scoffing. If Hero couldn't see what a jewel he had, it shouldn't be up to Sarah to convince him. Chase opened his mouth to protest but thought better of it. She was hurting and he doubted anything he could say right now would make her feel better. She'd been quiet and serious back in high school, more lighthearted as he'd gotten to know her last year. How could someone as smart as Sarah have problems with self-image?

As they approached the open barn door, a figure appeared in the doorway.

Sarah tensed beside him, just the slightest amount, and it made him glad that he'd come along.

It wasn't a rancher who appeared. It was a preteen girl.

"Amanda." Surprise was audible in Sarah's voice. "Where's your dad?"

The girl sniffled but quickly wiped her face with the back of one hand. Her chin came up and the movement reminded him immediately of Sarah.

"He's not here right now," the girl said. "But something's wrong with Mallory—my sheep—and he said it would be okay if I called you. Mom's inside."

Sarah approached the girl, and he saw the compassion cross her features. She reached out to pat the girl's shoulder. "We'll get her looked at." Gone was any sign of residual fear. She was a consummate professional.

The barn was warm and well taken care of, but none of the other stalls—six in all—were in use. It was awfully cold to have horses running loose on the property.

Amanda had her ewe in a large, open stall, and had hung work lights from each side of the stall to illuminate the area.

"Tell me what's been going on." Sarah entered the pen, and the sheep skittered away. Its wool was clean, and it didn't look to be in any distress.

The girl's worry was obvious as she hopped into the pen with Sarah. With both of them in there, Chase figured he'd better go in too.

The sheep edged away from Sarah, and Amanda went at it from the other direction.

"She's never been this skittish," Amanda said. The sheep darted between her and Sarah. Chase attempted a block but he was to slow. It was going to be like that, huh?

"She's been off her food," Amanda went on. "And really

lethargic. She's been out in the pasture during the day, but I pulled her in here so you could see her."

Chase would get her still, so Sarah could have a look.

Three minutes later, he was sweating through his shirt beneath his coat. This was getting a little embarrassing, being bested by a sheep. Sarah had shed her coat and sweater, leaving her in a T-shirt. He caught a glimpse of a scratch on one arm that hadn't healed completely yet. Seeing it made acid churn in his gut.

The three of them finally found a way to use their bodies to corner the sheep. Amanda held its head and he used his legs to pin it to the wall as Sarah moved around the two of them to examine the animal.

Sarah's shoulder nudged his thigh as she reached beneath the sheep to palpitate its stomach.

"Glad to have me here now?" he asked her in a low voice.

She shot him a glance over her shoulder, and he winked. She shook her head slightly. Though her face was turned toward what she was doing, he imagined the eye roll.

"Has she been... erm, visited by a ram?" Sarah asked. "Around Thanksgiving?"

Amanda scrunched up her face as if thinking. "Maybe." Her head tilted away, hiding her face behind the curtain of her hair. "My mom and I went to visit my grandma in Pennsylvania. We were gone for five days. When we got back, our neighbor said Mallory had broken through the fence. I don't know if she was in with his herd."

Sarah nodded to herself. "It seems like she must've been, because your ewe here is pregnant. I'd like to do an ultrasound to make sure."

Sarah straightened and turned to Chase. "Can you hold her here?"

He nodded. Probably.

"I'll be right back." Sarah hopped the stall wall and disappeared.

"That's pretty exciting," he said to the girl. "You're gonna have a lamb."

Amanda's expression wasn't joyful, like he expected. She was biting her lip and wouldn't look him in the eye. "I guess." But she didn't sound excited at all.

Sarah returned with a bulky machine that she set down in the hay near his boot. She fired it up, prodding the wand against the sheep's stomach.

"Amanda, can you see the screen?"

The girl stepped near Sarah.

Sarah held the wand against the doe's stomach with one hand and pointed at the screen with the other. "Here's a little hoof...the skull." She was quiet for a moment. "And here's the second lamb."

Again, he expected a different reaction than what the preteen was showing. Her lips pinched in a tight white line. "Twins?"

"Twins," Sarah confirmed. "If she hasn't been eating enough and is acting lethargic, it could be toxemia. She's not getting enough nutrients."

Amanda was quiet. He saw the tremble of her bottom lip and the quick blink, as if she were trying to hold back tears. "That's bad, right?"

"We have some things we can try," Sarah said, her voice even and reassuring. She started to pack up the machine, nodding to him that he could let the sheep go.

He did, and the animal skittered away.

"I'm estimating she's got about six weeks left before these lambs are born, and we'll want to watch and make sure we take care of her."

He and Amanda moved to the edge of the pen. Sarah was quick to follow, toting her machine and her bag.

"I'll give you some propylene glycol. Your dad can drench her two or three times a day. Something else that works is yogurt diluted with water. The bacteria from the yogurt will stimulate the rumen. If she doesn't go back on her food in a day or two, I want your dad to call me, okay?"

"Um—" Amanda's eyes skittered off to one side.

"I'll call your dad first thing in the morning to let him know—"

"No!" Amanda's outburst shocked Sarah into silence, but the girl quickly continued. "I can tell him."

Sarah's glance slid to his, then back to the girl.

"I'll plan to come back out in a couple of days and check on her. In the meantime, you and your dad will want to make sure you're documenting any change in her behavior or diet."

Amanda nodded gravely. "But what about...? When the babies are born...sometimes doesn't one of the twins get abandoned by its mama?"

Sarah nodded. "Sometimes. Sometimes, the mom sheep accepts both of them. If not, we'll try for a surrogate mother, or the twin might have to be bottle-fed. It'll be okay. Don't fret."

Amanda's frown remained, tiny lines fanning around her eyes.

"We'll walk back up to the house with you," Sarah said. "Make sure you get inside."

Amanda shrugged, her eyes shifting away, but she bore their company as they trudged back to the ranch house.

"Did you have a good Christmas?" he asked when the quiet became awkward.

Amanda shrugged. "It was okay."

He tried again. "You'll probably want to tell all your friends about the new baby lambs."

Again, the girl shrugged, her face tucked into her coat. They reached the ranch house, and she slipped inside the back door with a short wave.

He followed Sarah to her truck, lugging the ultrasound machine.

"That seem a little weird to you?" he asked.

She took the machine from him, stowing it in her perfectly organized truck bed. "There's definitely something going on. I'll call her dad in the morning."

"Even though she didn't want you to?"

Sarah shrugged. "Dad's paying the bills, right?"

He supposed that was true. The preteen couldn't foot the bill for vet care, so it made sense that Sarah would follow up with the rancher to determine a solution for care.

Sarah shut the tailgate and reached up for the camper shell, closing it as well.

"I'm following you home," he said.

She frowned. "Not necessary. Thanks for coming with me, assistant-boy."

"It's non-negotiable." He didn't want to think about her going inside alone. The police hadn't yet caught the guys who'd attacked her.

Her frown deepened. He didn't know what the big deal was, but she was obviously unhappy with that thought. Maybe she wanted to be alone to think about Hero some more.

"Fine."

He didn't appreciate her tone, but he figured she'd had a lousy night, and it was her birthday. He let the attitude go.

His headlights illuminated the rough dirt roads and the back of her truck as he followed her back to her little bungalow.

She wanted Hero. Because the other guy was an attorney? Whatever the reason, she and the big shot lawyer had clicked.

For the first time, Chase questioned whether he should've tried harder to fit in with his family. He'd wanted something different. Mostly, he'd wanted not to turn into his dad, who still worked sixty-hour weeks and had no plans to retire soon.

But if working a job like that would've won him a girl like Sarah...

He got out of the truck when she hit the driveway, but he stayed back while she approached her front door. She went inside with only a little wave.

He climbed back in his truck and sat for long moments, wishing things were different. Maybe he should feel some kind of hope. Now that Hero had broken things off, Sarah was available, but he figured she still loved the guy.

And anyway, how could he stand up to Hero? James was a high-powered attorney with a college education and smarts that Chase could never live up to. That was the kind of guy Sarah wanted, and Chase would never be that.

But he could still be her friend.

Chapter Three

Early Monday morning, Sarah sat at her desk and perused her schedule. She had three appointments out of town this afternoon, but... hadn't there been one this morning too?

She checked her leather bag for the essentials, adding some more gauze bandages to replace what she'd used on a late-evening Saturday call, and made her way to the break room. She needed a cup of coffee. Or two.

Along the way, she couldn't help ducking in to the kennel area. One of the technicians was cleaning cages and looked up at her entrance.

"Hey, Dr. Campbell. You back to visit the stray?"

"Morning, Ian." She stopped in front of the largest kennel, where the huge, black dog raised its head from its paws. A slow wag of its tail rattled the wire side of the cage.

The Newfoundland mix had been found by a farmer wandering along a road close to town. One of its feet had been broken, and its ribs had been showing. The dog had obviously been abandoned.

They'd healed the foot and put out flyers, hoping to either find the dog's owner or someone to adopt it.

They'd had no luck. She worried because a big dog like this was a big commitment, a lot to manage. And it was an adult, not a puppy. The practice wouldn't feed the dog indefinitely. Something about the dog drew her, and she found herself visiting it a little too often. Not smart to get attached.

"Thanks, Ian," she said, and continued to the break room.

Two of the three other partners were there, sipping coffee. As was Jessie, who looked at Sarah slightly guiltily. Her assistant wore street clothes.

The back of Sarah's neck tingled with warning. "What's going on? Aren't you supposed to be on maternity leave?"

"Jessie came to us with some concerns," Dr. Brown said in his usual matter-of-fact way. "About the extra hours you're working since she's been on maternity leave. Above and beyond the occasional night or weekend house call."

"Are you joking?" Sarah asked.

The serious expressions told her they weren't. A sense of betrayal roiled in Sarah's gut.

She straightened her shoulders and fought against the urge to clench her hands into fists. "There's no issue."

Dr. Everly, the only other woman in the practice, stepped forward, reaching out to put a hand on Sarah's shoulder. "We don't want you to burn yourself out. You came back to work so quickly after..." She fumbled over her words. "After the event. We all thought perhaps you'd want to take more time. Or work half time. There's no reason to push yourself so hard."

Sarah hadn't been able to stand sitting at home alone. The silence that had surrounded her had allowed too much space for memories and those had been so vivid and frightening...

"I didn't—don't need time off."

"What about that call last week? The early-morning one I had to take when you bailed?"

Sarah's face burned. "That was an isolated event. I woke up nauseated." She'd made it all the way to the door, coat on and medical bag in hand, but hadn't been able to turn the handle. She hadn't been able to face the darkness without Jessie by her side.

Dr. Everly's kind eyes didn't waver. But Sarah had the sense that she knew what had happened.

"I love this job," Sarah said. Her words were a reminder to herself. She *did* love this job. "And I'm fine."

It was just that even the thought of making house calls before dawn and after dark sent tendrils of fear through her.

"Your passion for the job is not in question," Dr. Brown said.

"Sarah." Dr. Everly's tone was a little more compassionate than their male counterpart's. "We know you've been through a lot—"

"But we can't disappoint our clients, or worse, risk losing an animal," Dr. Brown interrupted. "And we should've made arrangements sooner. It's a security risk, one we hadn't taken into account until now. You need an assistant."

"I don't expect any special treatment." Sarah slashed one hand through the air. She hadn't required an assistant all the time before Jessie's leave. "I'm fine."

She had to stop saying fine, or they'd think something was wrong.

"We've made a decision," Dr. Everly said. "It's not up for debate."

More heat boiled into Sarah's face. "I thought I was an equal partner in this practice."

"You are." Dr. Brown put down his coffee mug. "But you're not going out on calls alone. Not with the two criminals who kidnapped you still on the loose. We've hired a temporary replacement for Jessie until her leave is over."

Now Sarah propped her hand on her hip. They'd done this behind her back, blindsided her. No warning. No question about how she'd feel about it. She hated knowing she was being handled with kid gloves. She didn't want anyone thinking she couldn't handle the job. She just had to overcome this... this stupid fear. She'd gone head-to-head with angry bulls. She could wrestle her own paranoia. Couldn't she?

"It's not up for discussion," Dr. Everly said. The fact that the usually laid-back surgeon was being so firm told Sarah there wasn't a chance of changing their minds.

She shrugged. "Fine. Who's the loser you got to follow me around?"

A throat cleared from behind her, and she whirled to find Chase standing the doorway in work boots, jeans, and Stetson.

"No way." She shook her head. "You already have a job." And had recently been witness to her humiliating breakup.

"It's the slow season," he said in his calm, slow drawl. "Matt's home for good. Nate doesn't mind me taking a break for a few weeks."

A glance at her partners had them nodding, expressions still deadly serious. Jessie still looked guilty. Sarah would forgive her eventually, but for now the feeling of being blind-sided held.

"Fine."

There it was again, that word.

That impossible word.

"ARE you really going to give me the silent treatment for the next three weeks?" Chase asked late in the afternoon.

He sat in the passenger seat of Sarah's pickup as she drove down a bumpy, rutted dirt road. They were halfway between Taylor Hills and the outskirts of Dallas. He hadn't realized her house calls took her so far out of town.

He was fed up with Sarah's silence. They'd gone the last thirty minutes without talking. She'd been polite but distant in front of her clients and given him a cold shoulder when they'd been alone.

And he was tired of it.

"I don't need a babysitter," she muttered, her hands tightening on the steering wheel.

"Nobody said you did," he returned. "Would you call Jessie your babysitter?"

"I don't want to talk about Jessie." The frown lines around her mouth deepened.

He knew she had to feel bad about being called out in front of her partners, but he'd overheard some of Jessie's concern that Sarah was working long hours, into the night. That she might be scared to go out to see clients when it was dark. Not that he could blame her.

"Look," she said, "I know we've been friends, and I'm sure you took the job because you feel sorry for me, or—"

"I don't." He felt a lot of things for her, but pity wasn't one of them. "We didn't know each other all that well in high school, but I won't feed you a load of manure. Your partners hired me to help you out. You can sit there and endure it or maybe we can try to have some fun between calls."

She slid a glance to him, but he couldn't read her.

"I know I'm not as well-educated as the folks you're used to hanging around—I dropped out of college after my third semester—but I'm here."

He felt curiosity and something else radiating off of her. "It's not about you, Chase. I don't want my partners to question my abilities."

Oh.

"I don't think they are," he said quietly, seriously. "I think they're trying to look out for you the best way they know how to right now."

Her hands fisted on the wheel again, and her teeth were gritted when she spoke. "I wish they didn't have to do that."

"So do I."

She couldn't know how much he meant it. He hated seeing her afraid, hated that she might be scared to leave her house in the dark of morning.

He wanted to help her.

All she had to do was let him in.

THE NEXT AFTERNOON, Sarah slid behind the wheel, cranking the key to start the truck as Chase got in on the passenger side.

She yanked the gear shaft, and the transmission protested.

"Easy, Tiger," he said. He fumbled with his seatbelt buckle as her tires hit a rut on the dirt drive.

"No time for taking it easy," she said. "There's a horse with breathing distress. The farmer was calling it heaves, which could mean anything from an asthma attack to something worse."

He groaned.

"What?"

He'd been surprisingly easy to work with. His easy-going nature was pleasant, and his occasional quips made her laugh at surprising times. He was great with her clients, a steady presence that they appreciated. All in all, he was just overall likable. He hadn't complained once.

He laid one hand over his heart, drawing her eyes momentarily to his broad chest. "While my heart appreciates your dedication to your work," his hand moved to his stomach. "My belly is grumbling for some sustenance."

She laughed. "Well, you're out of luck for now. I might have a stick of gum in the glove box."

He pulled a face, but that didn't stop him from rooting around in the compartment until he pulled out a pack of gum. He offered her a piece, but she shook her head. He unwrapped and popped a piece in his mouth.

"You skip lunch often?" he asked.

She shrugged, letting one hand fall into her lap as she steered with the other. She clenched and unclenched her fist, trying to work some warmth back into her extremity. Her heater was slow to warm up. She couldn't wait for spring, when higher temps would make working outdoors slightly more palatable.

"So that's a yes," he said.

"When the day calls for it."

He settled back into his seat, one arm resting along the passenger window.

"Missing your ranch job yet?" she asked.

"No. Being your assistant is interesting. Seeing you work with the patients from this side of the table is... enlightening."

Heat flared in her face. "I'm sure you're bored out of your mind."

"Not even close. You've always treated us at the Triple H with professionalism, but I never realized how much you cared about the animals."

She rolled her shoulders. Tight already, from sleeping on her office couch.

"Like just now," he went on. "You spent a few extra minutes calming that llama before you examined it. I think it was the way you touched its face..."

She hadn't realized he'd been watching so closely. She wasn't embarrassed. "I guess... It's always been easier for me to relate to animals than to humans. They don't lie, they'll always show you what's wrong if you have the patience to find out."

She could always understand animals, but sometimes the human dynamic went over her head.

His head tilted toward the window, his Stetson casting shadows over his eyes. "Humans don't always tell the truth, do they?"

"No." No, they didn't. "Kayla and I once had a foster family that claimed they were going to adopt the both of us, but then they got pregnant, and we were thrown right back into the system. And...I don't know why I just told you that."

Maybe having him ride along with her *wasn't* a good idea. He was too easy to talk to, if she let her guard down.

"I'm sorry. To have the hope of a forever home ripped away..."

She lifted one shoulder. "It is what it is. God got Kayla and me through those rough years"—by the skin of their teeth—"and we're both better for it now." Maybe scarred, but scars proved character, right?

Her phone buzzed in the console, and a glance showed her sister's name lighting up the screen.

"You want to pull over and answer it?" the cowboy asked.

"No. It's Kayla, and she just wants to talk about—" *James.* Sarah cleared her throat. "I'll call her back later."

The cowboy was silent for a beat. Then another.

"I'm okay with the breakup," she said in a rush. "I mean, I'm still upset, but I'm getting over it."

There was a slight hesitation before he said, "Good for you." And that was it.

She'd tried to call James a few days ago, to get some closure. She'd known things weren't as they should've been. He'd been the one to insist she take the job at the Taylor Hills clinic. He'd agreed that a separation of two or three years while he worked his way up the ladder at the law firm wouldn't be anything. But the distance between them had grown and grown...

As evidenced by the fact that he hadn't realized how the attack had affected her. Maybe he had noticed, but been too busy to care.

She'd thought—hoped—everything would be fine once the wedding happened and she was back in Austin.

Was there someone else? Or had he just grown tired of the disconnect between them?

Would she really have been happy in Austin? Working with

small animals instead of the horses, cows, sheep, and even alpacas that she loved?

She didn't know anymore.

THE NEXT DAY, Sarah worked the both of them through lunch again.

This time Chase was prepared.

He'd just watched her wrestle a breech calf into the world, and, as far as he was concerned, she was a miracle worker. And she had to be hungry.

He buckled up and reached beneath his seat to the miniature cooler he'd stored there this morning.

He unloaded two hoagies that he'd made, wrapped in white butcher paper that crunched beneath his fingers. Two tubs of pasta salad came next. He put Sarah's in the cupholder. Two bottles of water rested at the bottom of the cooler, and he pulled those out, too. They were still cold.

"What's all this?" she asked with a curious glance as she pulled onto the county road.

"Decided to pack lunch, since you're such a slave driver, you won't let us stop."

She laughed at his petulant complaint. "You didn't have to make me one."

"Someone has to take care of you." The words popped out before he'd really thought them through. He'd been hiding his true feelings from her for weeks—he couldn't afford to slip up now. "Or you'll get so skinny you'll blow away in this Texas wind."

A gust blew against her truck as if to punctuate his statement, and she laughed, shaking her head. "Yeah, right."

Thank goodness she let his statement go.

He focused on unwrapping the paper from the top of her sandwich before handing it to her.

"I *am* starved," she admitted, taking it. "Thank you."

She took a bite as he unwrapped his own sandwich.

"This is really good," she said before taking another bite. She swallowed. "Where'd you learn to craft a sandwich like this?"

"A man's gotta learn important life skills when he's batching it." He took a swig of his water. "Sandwiches are my specialty when it's my turn to cook for the ranch hands. The trick with these is the correct meat to cheese ratio, and the tomatoes. Roma is the best, but you can do regular ones if they're fresh." He held up the sandwich to illustrate the meat and cheese ratio. "I also make a mean meatball sandwich. Oh, and there's a turkey and dressing and cranberry sauce hoagie that the hands love around Thanksgiving."

She hummed. Then tilted her head. "How come you're still a bachelor? Some woman never snatched you up?"

That was a story he didn't really want to tell, but she had shared a little about her background yesterday, so he felt obliged to return the favor.

"I was on the cusp of getting engaged, back in college. But when I decided to drop out, she broke up with me. I guess she wanted someone who could finish what he started." It was a joke, and one corner of Sarah's mouth turned up.

Really, Penelope had wanted someone who was going to provide a comfortable, stable life for her. Someone who was going to work himself to an early grave working long hours in an office, trapped in a metal and glass urban landscape.

"I haven't dated much since then." He'd been too afraid of getting close to someone, perhaps another someone who had bigger plans for his life than he did.

Sarah took a few more bites. Then, "Once before, you mentioned that you'd dropped out of college. I'm curious as to why."

"My dad had a heart attack."

"Oh, no. I'm so sorry."

He shrugged, looking out the window at the passing landscape. Someone else's ranch, grassy fields stretching to the horizon, broken only by a line of trees that must surround a creek, snaking across the plain. Two horses, a mare and colt, raced through the field, their manes and tails flying behind them like flags. You couldn't see something like that in the city.

"He's okay. He made some changes to his diet, gets more exercise now." But the biggest stressor in his dad's life was still there—his job. "I had this...moment, I guess. He was still in the hospital, I was visiting him, and he kept talking about wanting to get back to the office. His department was in the middle of this big project. I just looked at him, a guy working seventy-hour weeks, and for what? I realized that if I stayed in school, got a business degree, I was going to end up in a job I hated somewhere with a life I hated. I didn't want that."

He tilted his head toward the fields surrounding them. "Do you ever just stop and take a look around when you're out on these calls?"

She nodded slowly. "When I can."

"I do. I'll be working the herd or mending fences, and I'll just look up and... I love it out here, you know? The sky as big as you can imagine. The animals working the land right along with you. It's in my blood, I guess."

He flushed. He'd said too much. Now she'd think he was some sort of cuckoo tree hugger or something.

But when he dared glance at her, she gave him a soft, contemplative look.

And he wondered if maybe she understood, when no one else in his life ever had.

Chapter Four

THREE WEEKS LATER

Sarah woke to the buzz of her phone, its screen glaring light against the early-morning darkness. Much like it had *that morning*.

She sat up from the couch in her office, swiped her hair out of her face, and attempted to come fully awake.

Heart pounding her out of her groggy state, she answered, taking down the information about a cow having a difficult breech birth.

After she hung up, she took several moments to steady her breathing.

She swung her legs over the side of the cool leather couch in her office, reaching for her work boots.

She dialed Chase, tucking her phone between her ear and shoulder. The line connected, and she didn't wait for his hello.

"I've got an emergency call south of town. Can you meet me?" She rattled off an intersection, the best way she'd found to give directions for out-of-town visits.

There was a pause, one long enough that she took her phone away from her ear to see whether it was still connected.

"I'll do you one better," he said finally. "I'm already outside the clinic."

Adrenaline surged, throwing her heart up into her throat.

She hung up on him.

She sat with her hands on her knees, staring at the floor. She hadn't told *anyone* she was living out of her office.

Who did he think he was? It wasn't any of his business if she slept in her office or at home.

He wasn't her keeper, even if their friendship had bloomed these past few weeks.

She was a grown woman who could do what she wanted. She straightened her shoulders and ran a hand through her hair before she tied it off with a band from her wrist.

She splashed her face with water in the employees' restroom. The dark circles beneath her eyes could be attributed to the early morning calls. Maybe.

It would have to do. She shrugged on her coat and threw a woolen scarf around her neck as she walked down the hall.

She disarmed the alarm and slipped out to the parking lot, re-arming the system once she was outside.

The sun was just barely peeking over the horizon.

And a cowboy leaned against her car, his ankles and arms crossed. It was a deceptively casual pose.

"We've got a mama cow in distress," she said dismissively. "Are you coming or not?"

She reached past his broad body for the door handle, but he didn't move. She stared at the sleeve of his coat. She tried to give herself the same pep talk she'd given inside. *It's none of his business.*

"We don't have time for this." Her breath puffed out in front of her face. She didn't owe him any explanation for why she was staying in her office when her little bungalow was less than ten minutes away.

He moved slightly, and she exhaled a small sigh of relief.

Too quickly, because he didn't move away. His hand came up to cup her elbow.

"We're not done," he said. "Not by a long shot."

She swallowed.

His voice was intense, his breath stirring the fine hairs at her temple and sending a shiver down her spine.

He moved away, rounding the front of the truck as she

climbing into the driver's side. His truck was parked on the other side of hers and he paused momentarily to retrieve something. When he got in, the strong scent of coffee preceded him and he held two Styrofoam cups, juggling them as she backed out of the parking spot.

"What're you doing in town so early, anyway?" she asked.

The wheel froze her fingertips as she turned out of the lot. He played with the controls for the heater, and she wished again for a vehicle with heated seats.

"Couple of Triple H cows decided to calve in the night. I figured I'd stop by the coffee shop early. Then I passed the clinic on the way and saw your truck there."

Ah. "So...coffee?"

He pressed a warm mug into her palm. "I was *very* early. Had time to stop and see if your truck had moved."

"Oh, Chase. You're the best."

He snorted, and she shot a glance that way to see him staring into his own mug, clasped in one big hand.

She was grateful for the reprieve. She didn't want to face off about why she couldn't sleep in her own bed. She didn't even want to think about it.

Thirty minutes later, she was shoulder-deep in a cow's hind end, reaching with the tips of her fingers to try and grasp the breech calf's hoof. The barn was poorly insulated—there was a two-foot hole knocked in the wall behind her—and freezing air swirled around her, chilling her to the bone.

If she couldn't turn the calf, things were about to go from bad to worse. She was worried, and when she worried, she babbled.

Chase stood nearby, holding the pair of forceps the farmer didn't want her to use.

"*This* is probably why James lost interest," she muttered.

She stretched her fingers forward until a contraction in the cow's uterus froze her motion and squeezed all the feeling out of her arm.

"All his good stories are about courtroom drama," she went on through gritted teeth. "And mine are about helping cows give birth. I'm all about blood and gore. I'm all the rage at Austin office parties."

He didn't laugh or chide that she should quit complaining. He watched her with those intense eyes.

The contraction eased, and she was able to push her hand forward just an inch more and... there!

She grasped they calf's hoof and held on through another contraction. Then she was able to tug with just the right amount of pressure.

A few moments later, the baby bovine slid to the hay-strewn floor.

Sarah moved back, Chase helping her up with a hand beneath her elbow. Her leg had been bent at an awkward angle, and when she stood, feeling rushed to her extremity. She stumbled and landed against his chest.

For the first time, she realized the breadth of him, the strength he harnessed in all those muscles.

He looked down at her. "Your stories are about miracles," he said quietly.

Looking up at him, her heart did a funny little lurch, and she quickly pushed away with her clean hand. "Watch out, I'm likely to slime you."

"I've been slimed before. Doesn't scare me."

He let her go, and she busied herself washing up at the pump outside, shivering in the icy wind. He'd already packed up her bag by the time she'd ducked back into the barn. The new bull was suckling noisily, already dried with whorls in his fur from the cleaning the mama cow must've given him.

The farmer watched with his chest puffed out in pride, as if he'd been the one to birth the calf.

And she had to smile. Farmers and cows, she could relate to.

When she glanced at Chase again, he was watching too, wearing a soft smile that matched hers. His eyes shifted to her. Something almost tangible hovered in the air between them before she bent down in a pretense of checking her bag.

When they got in the truck, she was still shivering. Before she could buckle up, Chase shouldered out of his heavy coat and threw it over her shoulders.

"Oh. That's—"

"Necessary," he said unapologetically. "Your lips are blue."

The coat smelled like him, even over the scents of blood and fluid that still filled her senses.

They went straight to a scheduled stop. They were vaccinating a small herd of goats when Sarah began to get uncomfortable. It was as if a switch had flipped inside her.

She couldn't *not* notice the strength in Chase's hands as he held a nanny steady. The way the afternoon sunlight glinted off his blond eyebrows and the way his eyes flashed with determination when a hard head butted him in the thigh.

She'd known Chase was male all the way back to high school, when everyone had been overly-aware of the opposite sex. Back then, Sarah had never seen him as more than a friend.

Until now. Where was this insane attraction coming from?

And what did it mean about her former relationship with James? If she'd really been in love with him, wouldn't she still be hung up on him?

Was it possible she'd been in love with the *idea* of James, not the reality? She'd lived through a childhood of neglect and loneliness. She'd done her best to be strong and provide love for Kayla, but there'd been no one to love *her*. And then James had come along and swept her off her feet, promising security and family. She'd been so eager to be a part of a pair that she hadn't noticed that they didn't fit...

She didn't want to notice Chase. He was a good friend. One she didn't want to risk losing if she were to act on her attraction.

She had issues. She couldn't even sleep in her own home. Since she'd been little, she'd craved security, and starting a new relationship was just asking for trouble.

But none of her reasoning kept her from being aware of his presence at every move.

THEY DIDN'T MAKE it back to the office by suppertime.

They'd loaded up from a house call out past the county line and his stomach was gurgling again when her phone rang.

He was going to crack a joke about Sarah's work habits when she rang off with the call service, but before he could even get a word out, her shoulders slumped. It was slight, but he still noticed.

"What's wrong?" he asked quietly.

She only shook her head, her hands gripping the wheel until her knuckles were white. "We have to take this call."

He nodded.

He expected to pull off the road and drive up to a barn, but all his expectations were blown out of the water when they turned down a dirt road and viewed the scene.

Two sections of fence were down along the road. An older model truck was in the ditch, one tire blown out and the front fender crushed. Another truck was parked over the center line behind it all.

In the middle of the road, an injured horse lay on its side.

It was bad. He might not have a degree, but he'd worked with horses for years and even without seeing Sarah's tight expression, he knew. The horse wouldn't make it.

Darkness was falling, and Sarah left her headlights on, illuminating the scene as they got out of the truck and approached. A man who must have been the horse's owner stood near the horse, face drawn. In the ditch, two teen girls stood holding onto each other, crying quietly. The ones who'd caused the accident? At least they looked uninjured.

One of the horse's front legs was crushed from the shoulder down. Blood flecked the foam at its mouth.

There was nothing to be done but to put the animal down.

And yet Sarah knelt beside it, used her stethoscope to listen to its vital signs, ran her hand along its neck in a calming manner.

Chase stood by helplessly, holding her bag.

The headlights sparkled on tears standing in the rancher's eyes.

Sarah's compassion shone through as she spoke to the rancher in low tones. The man didn't walk away, let her do all the hard work. Instead, he knelt next to the horse's head as Sarah administered an injection. The rancher wiped his eyes.

Chase had his own ball of emotion strangling his chest. He'd worked with his horse, Calypso, for seven years now. They were friends. Understood each other. If this had happened to his horse, he sure wouldn't be as composed as the rancher.

Sarah was professional and sympathetic the entire time. He

felt helpless as she packed up her things, made a call to someone who would pick up the animal.

Chase he met her at the tailgate. "I'll drive," he said, not leaving her another option. He'd never driven her truck before. She hadn't let him and he hadn't pushed, but he could see how shaken she was.

She gave him the keys without comment, rode silently back to the clinic, staring out the window the whole time. The tablet she usually made notes on lay abandoned on her lap.

He'd been planning to confront her about sleeping at her office—he was worried about her—but not now. Not when she was heartsick.

When he pulled into the lot, there were still two trucks there, even though it was after hours and the clinic was closed. All four of the vets worked long hours.

He trailed her inside, letting her disappear into her office. He helped with some final cleanup in the kennels. Then the other vet and the secretary left, shooting him curious looks. The place went dark without them there. Only Sarah's light and the hall light remained.

He couldn't just leave her alone. Not knowing that she was too scared to go home.

An hour passed while he stared at a sitcom in the break room without really watching it. His stomach grumbled again.

He'd thought Sarah might come looking for some food but she never did, so he heated up a mishmash of leftovers from the fridge and headed to her office.

She barely glanced his way, head tilted low on her elbow, face turned toward the open file folder on her desk, though he had the sense she wasn't reading it. Her shoulders were low, her posture conveying brokenness. She'd known he was waiting on her.

"Can we please not do this right now?"

He hated the defeated tone in her voice.

"I don't know about you, but I get grumpy when my blood sugar falls too low."

Her head came up, and she registered the floppy paper plates he held, one in each hand.

He jerked his chin toward the couch. "Take a break and sit with me."

She hesitated. Finally, she stood and headed his way. Maybe the scent of microwave pizza did all the convincing.

They settled in, her shoulder bumping his as she tucked one leg beneath her. She'd changed out of the blood-stained jeans she'd worn earlier.

"Extra saucy or big air bubble?" He offered her the choice of plates. The two slices of pizza that had been left in the box were obviously the losers of the pie.

"Bubble, of course." One corner of her mouth ticked up, but as she bit into the pizza and chewed, her gaze went unfocused, and the miniature smile disappeared.

"Don't forget your veggies," he said.

She looked down at the plate, where a glob of coleslaw slowly spread and someone's leftover green bean casserole congealed. He won another of those short-lived smiles.

He didn't know how to take away the pain of what she'd had to do earlier. He doubted he could, but at least he could sit here. Offer her his shoulder, if she needed it.

"I think that casserole has been in the fridge since *last* Christmas," she said softly.

If she wanted to joke around, he'd joke around. He lifted his plate to sniff at the portion he'd put there. "No way. It's supposed to smell like that."

She tilted a glance his way, long enough for him to see the shadows still chasing each other behind her eyes.

"You know Jessie's like the fridge police. She caught me once stealing a Coke and gave me the what for."

"Then it's a good thing she's still on maternity leave and I'll be long gone before she has a chance to kick my butt for stealing this..." He raised his plate. Crinkled his nose when he couldn't quite identify the other blob. "...some kind of casserole. You don't think I'll get sick from this, do you?"

Chapter Five

THE SKY OUTSIDE SARAH'S WINDOW WAS DARK, AND all but the questionable pumpkin pie had disappeared from their plates. She'd never had such a weird dinner.

She needed to get rid of the cowboy. After losing the gelding this afternoon... There'd been nothing she could do. She'd easily seen that before she'd even gotten out of her truck. And now she had no emotional energy left to argue with him.

The silence as they'd scarfed down their stolen food had been companionable, and she hated to break it.

"I'm not going home." She kept her eyes on her plate as she said the words, idly scraping her fork through the nasty pie and drawing designs in it.

She was so tired...exhausted to the bone, but she didn't want to close her eyes, because when she did, she'd either think about the gelding's lifeless body or those moments when her attacker's hand had closed over her face.

He shrugged, the movement breaking the runaway train of her thoughts. Somehow they'd shifted closer to each other as they'd eaten, and the movement nudged her shoulder.

"I didn't think you would," he said quietly.

Not angry, like James would've been that she wasn't bending to his will. He'd always had a need to be right. Would've told her she was being ridiculous, ordered her outside and into his car.

He'd never have shown the patience and friendship that Chase was showing right now.

What had she ever seen in that jerk anyway?

The cowboy beside her made no move to get up. His steady presence reminded her again that he wasn't just an assistant, he was a man. A handsome man who she was attracted to. Best to get him out of here now.

She pushed herself up until she stood, threw the used paper plate in the trash can near her desk, and turned to face him.

He hadn't moved. He sat with relaxed grace, his boots on the floor in front of him, feet crossed at the ankles as if he hadn't a care in the world. That made one of them.

"So...I'll see you in the morning?"

Her gaze skittered away under the intensity of his stare. "I didn't think you'd go home tonight," he said quietly, evenly, "but I didn't say I would either."

That was completely unnecessary, and a ball of panic lodged itself in her throat. Good thing, too. Otherwise she'd tell him off.

What if she had the nightmare again? What if she cried out in her sleep?

He stood, left his plate on the couch as he came to her. He didn't touch her, but she had to tip her head up to look into his face.

"Sarah, if you're scared enough that you can't sleep in your own bed, how could you think I'd let you stay here alone?"

"I don't want—" *that*. But she couldn't quite say the word.

She did want somebody to care enough to notice. She wanted somebody to be a shoulder to lean on. Someone to depend on.

She'd just never expected it to be this cowboy.

Her eyes filled with tears, and his hands cupped her elbows. He held her gently, still inches between their bodies. He didn't tug her closer, didn't let her escape. He was just there.

It was she who leaned in, who closed the distance between them. She buried her face against his broad chest as the tears came full force.

She rested her hands against his chest, and his arms curled around her back.

It should've been awkward. She was only a month out from

her breakup with James, the man she'd thought she would marry. Had that even been a real relationship?

This should've been awkward, but it wasn't.

He let her cry, and she didn't worry about him judging her or knowing her secret. All her pent-up emotions let loose like a tsunami.

When she was spent, he kept on holding her. Maybe he was just being nice because of the way she clung to his shoulders, but for the moment, she didn't care. He was here, and he was Chase, and she needed him.

It was okay to need someone, wasn't it?

Her thoughts whirled again, exhaustion loosing the emotions she usually kept so well hidden.

Chase set her back slightly. He dug in his back pocket and came up with a handkerchief, which he offered.

She mopped up her face. That was...really old-fashioned. And kind of romantic.

She didn't want to think about Chase and romance.

She clutched the thin, white cloth between her fingers and let her eyes sweep toward the floor. "Thanks for...that."

He was still close, and when he raised his hand, her chin followed the motion up. He tucked a piece of hair behind her ear. "Get some rest."

But then something seemed to stall him out. Instead of his hand falling away, his thumb brushed her cheek. And then he was leaning closer—or maybe she was—and his lips were brushing hers.

Once, twice... unconsciously, she made a little noise in her throat, and maybe he took that for permission. Or maybe she scooted closer. Suddenly, instead of a soft brush of lips, they were sharing a full-on lip lock.

Somewhere along the way, her arms had wrapped around his neck. One of his hands was buried in her hair.

His nose pressed against her cheek and their chins brushed and he tasted delicious—

And then it was over. He stepped away, his arms falling away from her, one hand coming up to rub the back of his head.

She felt off-balance and stunned and gripped her desk with one hand to keep herself upright.

"Night," he said. He reached up with that same hand, as if he would tip his hat, but he wasn't wearing a hat and his hand fell away awkwardly.

At least she wasn't the only one discombobulated.

He disappeared out into the hall, his boots clicking against the tile floor.

But then his footsteps stopped. "I'm not leaving," he called back.

She didn't know what to feel now.

"Night," she whispered to her empty office.

HE SHOULDN'T HAVE DONE that.

Chase reclined on the uncomfortable plaid loveseat in the clinic's breakroom. This sofa wasn't made for stretching out, and so he had both feet planted on the floor, reclining as best he could.

He knew two of the other vets had couches in their offices, but it felt like intruding to go in there and sleep without an invitation.

And he definitely couldn't go back in to Sarah's office.

Not with his heart still pounding out of his chest.

Something had changed between them tonight. He'd seen a vulnerable side of Sarah that she didn't show anyone else.

In all the years he'd known her, he'd never seen her cry.

He knew that traumatic events caused people to act in a way they normally wouldn't. No doubt that's why she hadn't made a more rational decision about her sleeping quarters, like staying at her sister's place.

She might be making excuses to herself, like she didn't want to inconvenience Kayla, but sleeping in her office for all these weeks?

And how had no one else noticed? Jessie was nosy enough that she'd normally be all over this. Except she'd probably been caught up in last-minute things before her baby was born and then she'd been on maternity leave. Sarah hid it well. Heck, he hadn't even noticed it for weeks, and he'd been with her every day.

And now he was thinking himself in circles instead of focusing on the huge elephant in the room.

He'd kissed Sarah.

And it wasn't some little peck, either. He'd really laid one on her.

He hadn't intended to kiss her, but the tear tracks still wet on her cheeks and the vulnerability shining in her eyes... he hadn't been able to help himself.

Maybe she'd still had some grief to burn, because she'd kissed him back, and...wow.

Hero had been an idiot to give her up.

Thinking about the other man finally stilled his whirring thoughts. Sarah was getting over a bad breakup. She'd thought she was going to marry Hero.

She was vulnerable, she'd just been through a serious of traumatic events.

He couldn't take advantage of that. Sarah needed a friend. Subtract his personal inadequacies from the equation completely.

He couldn't act on his feelings.

The question was, could he be that friend without his feelings getting in the way?

Chapter Six

THINGS WEREN'T AS AWKWARD AS SARAH EXPECTED the next morning. Chase had disappeared sometime in the early hours before the other partners arrived at the practice.

She knew he'd stayed all night, because at one point she'd woken to use the restroom and gotten a glimpse of him stretched out on the tiny breakroom sofa, limp and snoring softly.

She didn't get why he'd done that for her. Sleeping here, so she'd feel the extra layer of security. The office had an alarm, and not being at home usually helped her sleep better, but her nights had still been long and difficult. Knowing he was here had made her feel safe.

He'd greeted her with a friendly smile when he'd arrived bright and early. And made no mention of the kiss when they'd been alone.

She didn't know what to make of it.

There'd been another call from Amanda about her pregnant ewe, and since Sarah had the morning open, she headed that way. She'd left a message for the rancher after Amanda's initial call, but she hadn't heard from the man since.

Amanda was at the barn, which threw up a red flag for Sarah. It was a school day.

"Morning," Chase greeted her in his easy drawl as they spilled from the pickup.

"You're not in school?" Sarah asked.

The girl's expression was closed off. "My mom said I could stay home—that she'd take me to town after you'd visited."

"Nice," Chase said to the girl. In a lower voice as he met Sarah at the back of the truck, he said, "My mom never would've let me."

"None of my foster moms would've either."

The group mother had been run so ragged by the mix of twelve kids, ten and up, that she'd rarely let them have any extra-curricular activities. It just hadn't been feasible. Sarah would've loved to raise a sheep in 4H. Kayla snuck pets into the home until she'd get found out.

Things had been pretty bad back then, but look at them now.

The ewe was in its pen again, and again she made it difficult to get close enough to examine her. Her vitals were fine.

"Has she been eating better?" Sarah asked, looking up at the girl even as she palpitated the ewe's belly. The twin lambs seemed to be the right size.

"She hasn't been off her feed again, but she's been real lazy."

Sarah wiped her hands on the thighs of her jeans. "Every-thing seems to be in working order."

But storm clouds remained on the girl's brow, in her scrunched eyebrows. "Can you tell me again what happens if she abandons one of the twins?"

Sarah began packing up her instruments. "It's a big if. She might accept both of them."

Amanda lowered her chin. "I was reading online..."

Sarah stopped her there. "You can't trust everything online. A lot of it is junk. But you can trust me."

She exited the pen, Chase right behind her. "*If* mama aban-dons one of the sheep, we'll help you take care of it."

Some of the anxiety cleared from Amanda's face, but a tiny bit remained.

"Don't worry," Chase said. "Your dad'll help too."

Amanda's face clouded over again, and Sarah shot the man beside her a look.

He was silent until they were near the truck. Amanda was

already on the way up the porch steps to join her mom, who stood there wearing a coat.

"You shouldn't say something like that," Sarah said. "If the rancher doesn't want to help..." She couldn't forget the shadows behind the girl's eyes. Something was going on.

He shrugged slightly. "Why wouldn't he help his daughter?"

She shook her head. "You never know. Sometimes they don't want the trouble or expense of caring for an extra animal."

Besides...

"Something's off," he said, echoing her thoughts.

"Yeah. I don't know what. I left a message last time. And the practice's billing department hasn't told me anything about him refusing payment. I'll have to be more thorough this time."

She'd get it figured out.

"C'MON, I'm stealing you away."

Sarah's head had been bent over her desk. She looked up, and Chase saw the words register, saw her flinch.

"Sorry—"

She sliced one hand through the air. "Don't apologize. I know what you meant."

Didn't mean he shouldn't have been watching his mouth.

He rubbed one hand at the back of his neck, dislodging his hat. He settled it with the other hand.

She stood and stretched, both hands above her head. It was Saturday afternoon, two and a half days after he'd kissed her, and he had no idea how long she'd been sitting there. She'd told him she had plans Saturday morning, but where was she going to hang out all weekend, if she was staying at the vet clinic?

Maybe he shouldn't have come. He hadn't kissed her again. Their relationship was in a weird place. He couldn't put his finger on it, but she looked at him differently. Watched him sometimes, when she thought he wasn't looking.

"What's up?" she asked. Her head tilted.

"It's a surprise."

Her eyes narrowed slightly, but she followed him out of the building and to his truck.

They arrived on the Triple H a bit later. She'd been pensive, staring out the window almost the entire time.

She turned her head toward him. "No offense, but I've seen my share of patients this week."

He shook his head, enjoying her slight consternation. "It's not a house call. And doctor Everly is on-call this weekend, remember?"

That didn't mean Sarah wouldn't get called by ranchers who had her number on speed dial. And if the other doctor had a double-whammy of an emergency, she'd be first on the answering service's list.

He bobbled his cell phone on his knee—even though he technically wasn't supposed to text and drive, he was in the ranch's driveway—and texted that they'd arrived.

She stared at him curiously as he drove up the bumpy lane all the way to the barn.

"You don't want me to go riding, do you?" She was still fishing.

He jerked his thumb toward the barn. "Get out of the truck."

She did, a little reluctantly. Cold air swirled around them, and he sucked in a deep breath.

It was home. The unique combination of scents and sounds that was the Triple H.

As they passed, one of the horses stuck its head over the corral railing and shook its head, snorting in welcome. He took her elbow as they neared the barn. "It's way too cold to go for a pleasure ride," he said. "But I'll take you up on the offer later this spring."

The words popped out before he'd realized what he'd said, and he wished he could call them back. That was presumptuous. And they were just friends.

But there was a softness in her eyes when she looked at him.

Inside the barn, the open area between the tack room and the horse's stalls that lined one wall had been swept clean. It was also covered in several yards of thick, blue workout mats.

"What is this?" she turned to him with a frown, her brows drawn.

"Personal self-defense class."

His old boss, Gideon Hale, traipsed into the barn behind them, bringing a rush of cold air. He closed the outside door.

"Gideon. Good to see you. It's been a while." Sarah shook the man's hand. Gideon's gold wedding band glinted in the light as he took off his leather gloves. The man was married to a princess of some small, European country that Chase had never heard of until the princess had arrived on their doorstep some two years ago now.

Gideon shucked his winter coat, but Sarah was shaking her head. "This really isn't necessary. I don't need self-defense lessons—"

"Everybody could use some information about how to take care of themselves," Chase argued.

Gideon shot him an intense look he couldn't decipher.

Sarah still shook her head, her arms wrapped around her middle. "This isn't—"

Gideon cleared his throat, silencing the both of them. He leveled his gaze on Sarah. "I haven't been in the country, but Chase told me some of what happened. After a premeditated attack like that...two men against one woman...you're lucky to be alive."

She shivered, and it was Chase's turn to glare at Gideon. Did he have to bring up that night? And did he have to be so callous about it?

But Gideon totally ignored him.

"The best you can do in a risky situation—like being a woman entering or leaving a residence after dark—is be aware of your surroundings and know some moves that might help you get away. It's still not a guarantee. But then, I know you know this because of your job—there aren't any guarantees in life, are there?"

She shook her head, slightly subdued.

"I'm here, and I'm willing to give you some pointers on how to protect yourself. And it means you get to beat up on this guy." He jerked his thumb at Chase. "You game?"

She answered with only the slightest hesitation. "Okay. Yes."

At Gideon's bidding, she and Chase stripped out of their coats. They both wore long-sleeved T-shirts with their jeans. It was chilly in the building, but not uncomfortable. Presumably they were going to get warm exercising anyway.

Gideon ran them through several different drills. Some that would be appropriate if a man came at her from the front, then from the side.

After a bit of practice finding her balance, Chase suddenly found himself on his back on the mat, trying to catch his breath. His shoulder ached a little from where she'd just yanked it to make him fall.

"Good," Gideon said.

Chase pushed to his feet, rubbing his backside.

"Did you feel how your weight, with momentum, changed everything?" Gideon asked Sarah. She nodded, deadly serious.

He'd hoped this might loosen her up a little, make her less nervous to be by herself. He couldn't erase the physical and emotional memory of what had happened in her own front yard, but he'd hoped to give her some sense of security. But she hadn't cracked one smile since they'd come in here. She vibrated with nerves.

"Your assailant got you from behind, didn't he?" Gideon asked.

Chase felt Sarah's tension rise by a notch. She nodded, silent.

"Now that you're warmed up, let's practice what you can do if that ever happens again."

He was still a yard away but saw Sarah pale.

"Why don't we take a break?" Chase asked, hoping to diffuse the tension that had just ratcheted up. Maybe this hadn't been such a great idea after all.

He hadn't meant for Gideon to stomp on her hot buttons.

"I don't need a break." But her voice was nearly a monotone, and she didn't look at him as she edged closer.

She turned so her back was to him, but he saw the quick tremble of her lips.

He didn't touch her, didn't raise his hands from where they remained at his sides. "We don't have to do this," he said quietly, not caring whether Gideon heard him.

The barn was silent except for her harsh breaths.

"I think I..." Her voice trailed off, then returned stronger. "I have to do this."

Gideon asked her what she remembered about how the man had grabbed her. She answered, and he put Chase's hands in that same position, one at her waist and one over her nose and mouth.

She was shaking so hard, he didn't know if he could do this. Act like her attacker? All he wanted to do was comfort her.

She inhaled a trembling breath, and he could feel the tension radiating off her. She was barely holding on to her composure. He'd have let go if not for the slight shake of Gideon's head. The other man was watching her face, and whatever he saw there... maybe it was a blessing that Chase couldn't see from behind.

They went through several rounds of practice. First, Gideon had her stomp on his instep—which *did* hurt every time, even through his work boots—and pretend to jam her elbow into his solar plexus, and once at his nose. Every time she did it, Sarah got stronger. Her spine straightened. Her breathing evened out.

"You're pulling punches," Gideon said. "It's hard—we can't really practice at full strength. Don't want to hurt our guy."

Sarah threw a look over her shoulder at him. Her eyes were dry but red-rimmed.

And he said the stupidest thing he could think of. "If you want to try it for real, I can take it."

His foot was mostly numb anyway.

Sarah started to shake her head.

"Do it," he said. "Gid, tell her."

The other man shrugged, raising his hands at both sides as if he wanted to stay out of it.

Sarah was starting to move away, and he got stupid. He just went after her, one hand at her waist and the other around the bottom half of her face, like they'd been practicing.

And a split-second later, he hit one knee, his foot crying out in pain and blood splatter from his nose dripping down his shirt.

Sarah said a curse word he'd never heard from her before.

He put pressure on his nose with one hand, bracing against his knee with the other. He still felt off balance, as if his brain were sloshing around inside his skull. He tried to say, *I'm fine,* but what emerged was, "I'b fide."

And she looked like she was going to cry again.

Gideon got there first, helping Chase straighten up. "Is it broken?"

He started to shake his head but thought better of moving it. Might make the headache worse. "Do't fink so."

"Have you ever broken your nose before?" And Sarah was there, hip-checking Gideon out of the way and reaching up for his face. She displaced his hand and pressed her thumbs against both sides of his nose.

"Ow!" He jerked away, putting pressure back on with his hand.

"It's not broken," she confirmed.

"Are you an MD now?" he groused at her.

"I'm sorry, okay?"

He shook his head, and yeah it did make him see stars. "I'm not. Sorry. That you did that."

Her eyes softened, held.

He clamped his lips shut, determined to stop while he was ahead. Sort of ahead.

Chapter Seven

Sarah sat on the floor in the kennel room, her back to the wall. Only three kennels were occupied, two basset hounds in for boarding and the long-timer, the huge black Newfie.

They'd had flyers out for weeks, and no one had adopted him. Being in a cage, with only occasional walks outside, was no way to live. If only Kelsey's no-kill rescue was up and running…

Beyond the walls of this interior room, evening was falling, the time when normal people went to their safe little homes. The time when husbands and wives shared stories about their days. The time when teenagers practiced their sports and children bent over their homework and babies had baths.

While she sat alone in her workplace.

This couldn't continue.

Chase found her there. He sat next to her on the cold tile, his arms resting over his bent knees. He leaned his head back against the wall.

"I didn't mean for this afternoon to turn out the way it did," he said. He still sounded congested, like he was stuffed up from a cold, and she was hit with another pang of guilt. She hadn't meant to hit him that hard.

"I meant…" He exhaled softly. "I don't know what I thought it would accomplish. Give you some confidence, maybe."

She kept staring at the dogs. "It was thoughtful." He just probably hadn't planned for it to bring back visceral, frightening memories.

She wanted him to leave, wanted him to stay. Wanted to feel safe again. "I thought I was going to die." The words surprised her when she uttered them. She hadn't told a soul how she'd felt. The facts—nothing more. Nothing deeper. But Chase sat silent, and she couldn't help herself. "They were so violent... They hit me so hard..."

She hadn't been able to look in the mirror for days, always shocked and frightened anew at the bruising on her face.

His hand closed over hers on the floor. She hadn't realized how cold she was until his warmth enclosed her.

She blinked against the horrifying flashes of memory. Her wrists itched. At one point, she'd scraped all the skin off trying to erase the memory of that's man's hands on her. It was healed now, barely.

He still had hold of her hand, so she reached across her midsection and closed her fingers around her wrist, trying to forget.

His hand shifted. She thought he was letting go of her, but the warmth of his touch moved from her palm up her wrist. His fingers slid beneath hers. Not worrying the skin like she would've, but gently brushing against it.

"I haven't talked about it—with anybody," she whispered. *Until now.*

The cowboy didn't move. "When I was ten, our house got broken into." His voice was low and steady like the thrumming of a train along the tracks. Soothing. "We were coming home from somewhere—I don't remember now—and it was dark. I opened the front door, not realizing anything was wrong. And saw the couch cushions on the floor, ripped. The back door slammed—whoever it was had still been in the house when I went in."

His thumb continued rubbing gentle circles on her wrist as he spoke.

"For a long time, I tried to make sense of it. Why would somebody break in to our house? Steal our stuff? How did we become targets? Just out of convenience? Or just bad luck?"

His head tilted toward her. "When it's something traumatic like what you've been through, I don't know if you ever make sense of it."

She'd shifted closer to him, and now her cheek was close enough that if she leaned, she'd bump against him.

She did it, resting her cheek against the hollow between his shoulder and pec. "Will I ever sleep through the night again?"

He gave her wrist a squeeze. "Probably one morning you'll wake up and realize you slept through. Then it'll be two nights in a row. And then a week. Then a month. You'll never forget what happened, but the memories will sting a little less."

"It sounds nice," she whispered.

"Have you talked to your doctor about some meds to help you sleep?"

"No. I've tried them before, during vet school, and I didn't like how they affected me."

Maybe she needed to sell her house. Get away from the physical memory of stepping off her stoop and onto the sidewalk.

Or maybe she just needed to suck it up.

"I'm going home tonight," she said.

She felt his stillness beside her. "Good for you. If you want me to sleep on your couch a couple of nights, until you get settled..."

Now she moved away from him, pushing off of the floor. "Thank you. But I think I need to do this on my own."

He stood too. "Okay. You gonna go *Jessie* on me if I go with you, check the place out, make sure things are okay before I go back to the Triple H?"

Looking up at him, she couldn't think of anything she wanted more. "That would be nice." Then she broke into a smile. "I'm going to have to tell her you turned her into a verb."

He winced slightly, but smiled. And then he headed for the door while she remained where she was.

He looked over his shoulder. "What're you doing?"

"I think it's time to do something about this guy, don't you?" She moved toward the Newfie's cage. He looked up at her with those big, dreamy eyes, made that slow tail thump.

"You're not going to put him down...?"

She unlatched the cage, and the dog looked up at her as if

asking what she wanted him to do. So polite. She lifted one of the slip leashes from the wall hook and secured it around his neck. She patted her thigh, and he took one cautious step out of the kennel. Then another, and then he sat in front of her, looking up at her with curious eyes.

She touched his head, fingered the silky, long ears.

She turned to Chase. "I'm taking him home."

The dog's tail thumped against the floor as if he knew the word.

She held Chase's gaze. "I think it's time I opened my heart to some new opportunities."

And she didn't just mean the dog.

CHASE SAT in his truck down the street from Sarah's house as the night deepened around him.

She'd insisted he go home, and he would. He just wanted to stay for a while...for himself.

She'd humored him as he'd walked the perimeter of her house with a flashlight and scoped out her backyard with its 6-foot paneled fence. Her new dog had trailed him the entire time, snuffling his way around the yard.

The big Newfie was Mr. Laid-Back. He seemed to tiptoe around the property, almost as if he was afraid Sarah was going to change her mind and take him back to the kennel at the clinic. Chase felt a little silly, attributing human thoughts to the dog.

Sarah had done the walk-through of the interior of her house alone. It had been cool and quiet inside, smelling slightly musty, like after you'd gone on a two-week vacation. That would clear up soon enough.

Everything was normal, but Sarah's anxiety was almost visible. She was jittery and quieter than usual.

He'd talked her into playing a movie. A romantic comedy that he normally would've stayed far away from. They'd snuggled up on the couch, his arm around her shoulders. The big dog had lain across their feet, and he'd finally felt her relax a little.

Until the credits had rolled.

When she'd shown him the door, obviously ready to turn in for the night, he'd wanted to shake her out of the fear she was trying to hide. So he'd kissed her in the doorway, cold air seeping around him, a reminder so he wouldn't get too carried away.

It didn't work that well, but she pulled back when a cold nose nudged his hand, which he'd rested at her waist. That dog was *tall*.

He'd whispered goodnight, climbed in his truck, and driven down the street a little ways.

The kiss they'd shared, the second, had been just as good as the first. And she hadn't pushed him away. He hadn't meant for it to happen, but his heart was starting to hope.

Hope was dangerous.

Sarah had pulled herself up from nothing, gone to college and vet school. She was passionate about the career she'd thrown herself into. He'd done the opposite, choosing the land and a low-paying career that he loved instead of pursuing education and a traditional job.

Was he crazy to even think that someone like him could end up with someone like her?

Chapter Eight

Sarah hadn't managed a full night of sleep, but she'd had a couple of good snatches of a few hours each. She woke refreshed.

Or maybe the euphoria she felt had more to do with Chase's good-night kiss.

He'd been delayed at the Triple H, and Amanda Newton had called again. Sarah was outside the vet clinic, closing the hatch after packing up her truck when her phone rang.

She didn't recognize the number.

"Dr. Campbell," she answered.

"This is Detective Owens over at the Taylor Hills PD. I wanted to let you know we'd made an arrest in your case. Two arrests."

Her knees went weak, and she clutched the tailgate to steady herself.

"That's good. Right?" Knowing the men who'd attacked her were still around somewhere had messed with her head. Surely now she could find some peace...

"We've been working hard to build a case that'll hold up in court. I think you can safely go to bed at night knowing they're off the streets. We've got them."

She was safe. Tears prickled, and she closed her eyes against them, against the emotion that was a tight knot in her chest.

She had to clear her throat twice before she could get the words out. "Thank you for letting me know."

He hung up, and she slipped her phone in her pocket, but she couldn't move yet. She gripped her truck for several more moments while she let the truth settle. The police had caught the bad guys. She'd begun to fear they'd never be caught—knew it was a long shot based on the little amount of information she'd been able to give them about her captors.

She was still shaking when her phone rang again. Her heart leapt. For one crazy second, she thought it would be Chase calling at just the right moment so she could tell him the news.

It wasn't. When she picked up, it was Amanda's father on the line.

"Mr. Newton. I'm glad to finally speak with you."

"I'm sorry it's taken me so long to call back."

"It's all right. I'm sure you know Amanda's been worrying about her ewe."

There was a silence. Too long.

"I'm not sure what Amanda told you, but her mother and I have separated."

"Oh." Sarah didn't know what to say to that. "I'm sorry to hear that."

"We're going to be selling the property. I don't know what's going to happen to Amanda's sheep, but—" His audible sigh came through the line.

"I can certainly keep my ear open for someone who might be willing to take on the ewe and lambs, or at the very least, let her board there."

"Thanks, that's very kind."

"Is it all right that I take care of the ewe until things are settled? Amanda is very worried about the birth and the babies."

"Yes, send me the bill." He rattled off an address, which she rapidly took down, and they ended the call.

Her earlier elation was dampened as she hung up with the man.

It was clear now why Amanda was overly concerned with one of the lambs being abandoned. If her parents were splitting, she was worrying about being abandoned *herself*.

Sarah remembered the heartbreaking grief when the family

she'd thought would be hers and Kayla's forever was suddenly torn from her.

And it was a stark reminder that relationships didn't last. What was she doing with Chase, when she hadn't been able to interest James? What would she do when Chase's interest waned?

KAYLA TOOK Bando for their usually nightly patrol. She'd been doing so since the night of Sarah's birthday party, and so far, she'd seen nothing else out of place. Except she and Bando'd been out of town for the past two nights, visiting a friend of Sarah's in Galveston who had given her some priceless advice on applying for grants. A grant could mean money for her rescue, money she desperately needed.

Something was off in the barn when she went in, though she couldn't put her finger on it. She tightened her grip on the Mag flashlight she held, prepared to use it as a club if an animal was in here.

She edged toward the back of the barn, where the little burrow had been that first night, though it had been empty since.

Was that a scuffle? She whirled toward one of the empty stalls but didn't see anything moving there.

There *was* something huddled in the hay. She approached while Bando issued a warning growl.

"Don't hurt her!" The voice was young, angry. "Get away, or I'll, I'll—"

Startled by the sudden outburst, Kayla backed away from the tiny dog lying in the hay.

A boy who couldn't have been more than ten rushed out of the nearby stall but slowed when the mama dog—a Chihuahua—issued a warning growl.

"Don't touch her," Kayla warned.

"Go away." The boy turned to Kayla and snarled. His hair was mussed, one knee of his jeans ripped. He was almost as scrawny as the dog. And as dirty. His jacket had stains on the fabric, and his face and hands had shadows that looked like they'd scrub right off in a tub. Not the shadows in his eyes, though. No soap and water would remove those.

"This is my barn, my property," she pointed out. "Where'd you come from anyway?"

He shot a glare over his shoulder. His lips were clamped shut.

"Have you been staying here?"

She raised an eyebrow at Bando. He'd gone forward to sniff the boy, who was still standing back from the mama dog. Bando snuffled his feet and hands. The boy looked like he wanted to ignore the dog, but there was no ignoring the crazy tail wag and happy body wiggle the border collie gave.

Big help he was. Where had Bando and that sniffer been while she'd had a trespasser on her property?

The boy bent over and scratched Bando's ears, though he kept a wary eye on Kayla. She recognized that wariness. Meanwhile, Bando panted happily.

That Bando had obviously given his seal of approval was evident, but Kayla wasn't going to be swayed so easily.

"Do you live around here?" she asked. The only neighbors she knew were an older woman her grandma's age and a wealthy rancher with high school kids. The Triple H wasn't too far, but she knew there were no kids his age living there. Who was this boy?

He didn't answer.

"What's your name?"

Still nothing.

There was an audible stomach gurgle, and it wasn't from her. The kid's head was down, and he made no acknowledgement, just kept rubbing the soft fur at the ruff of Bando's neck.

Who was this kid?

And why did he remind her with a visceral punch of her own childhood?

He sniffed, rubbed his nose with the grubby sleeve of his jean jacket. He hadn't given her any information, and she couldn't just leave him out here. This was her property, and she was responsible for what happened here.

She pulled her phone from the pocket of her coat. "If you won't tell me who you are, I guess I'll have to call the cops."

His face went white, and he started to back away. Bando, thinking it was some sort of game, starting jumping and barking around him.

"Hey, wait."

But he didn't wait. He threw one more look over his shoulder at the mama dog and bolted.

"Wait!"

Kayla started to follow, but the kid was fast, darting through the open doorway and out into the darkness.

Bando followed, playing a happy game of chase. He barked joyfully until Kayla cried out, "Bando!"

Then he returned to her, barking his joy.

By the time her feet hit the dirt outside the barn door, the kid had disappeared. She blew out a frustrated breath.

"That could've gone better," she told her dog, who just looked up at her with a wide, doggy smile and lolling tongue.

Their breaths puffed out like fog in the night air. She walked the perimeter of the barn, thinking maybe the kid had just hidden behind the building, but he was well and truly gone.

She tried to remember if she'd locked the back door of her house. There was hardly anything of value inside, but still...

She went back in the barn where the mama dog hadn't moved. "You need something to eat, don't you, girl?"

Bando barked, because he knew the word *eat* usually meant his bowl being filled.

"Not you," she said with a nudge of the dog's shoulder.

She had the sense of being watched as she walked back to her house, but no little boy jumped out at her. Not even a blade of grass moved, as if her land was holding its breath too.

Maybe she should call the cops, alert them...

But something made her wait.

She returned to the barn with a paper plate and an open can of wet dog food. She'd left Bando in the house, penned in the laundry room with a tall baby gate that he couldn't jump. He'd howled mournfully as she'd exited with the food. But he was rowdy, and she wanted to win the trust of the little dog or they'd get nowhere.

Out in the barn, the mama was appropriately wary until she got a scent of what Kayla carried. Then her nose began to twitch.

Kayla left the paper plate and bowl of water a few feet away from the Chihuahua and backed off. Mama dog left her puppies curled in a sleeping pile of fur and kept one eye on Kayla as she sniffed and crept closer.

She didn't let up with watching Kayla as she gulped down the food with huge greedy bites, her stomach quickly becoming distended. Kayla hadn't put much on there, not wanting to make the dog sick if she was starving.

Next the dog lapped up the water.

Kayla would have to get Sarah out here tomorrow to examine the poor thing, make sure they weren't dealing with other medical issues, only the near-starvation. And the puppies.

But what was she going to do about the boy...?

Mama dog went back to her puppies and curled around them with a satisfied doggy sigh. Kayla scooted away. She caught sight of something peeking out of one of the few stall doors.

She sidestepped to get a better look. There.

Inside the stall was a faded quilt with a tear on one side, along with an unopened can of baked beans, two candy bar wrappers, and what looked like a faded photograph.

This was the boy's stash.

Was someone in town missing a boy?

Chapter Nine

Jessie had been back from maternity leave for two days, and Chase had barely spoken to Sarah in that forty-eight hours. After spending hours on end in her company, the distance was disconcerting.

He couldn't help feeling as if she were building a wall between them. He couldn't explain it, but he felt it. She'd moved home...moved on? Didn't need his friendship anymore?

And he'd reverted to that high school kid he'd been, afraid to ask for what he really wanted.

She *had* told him that Amanda's ewe was about to lamb any day, and she'd also shared what she'd learned about Amanda's parents splitting. He felt for the girl. He prayed that her dad would stay involved.

Chase was trying to be patient. He knew Sarah was swamped with work. He didn't want her to feel as if he were nagging her to spend time with him.

But that wasn't what stopped him from approaching her, not really. No, his fears went deeper than that, all the way back to Taylor Hills high. Eventually, Sarah would remember that he wasn't like her other friends. He didn't have a fancy degree. He wasn't brilliant and didn't make a lot of money. He was just a cowboy.

A cowboy who missed her. Missed hearing her funny

comments about the animal's personalities. Missed her self-deprecating humor. Missed that glint in her eyes she got when she was staring at him sometimes.

It was Friday, and Nate had sent him to town for some two-by-fours for a repair to the main barn. Well, afraid or not, enough was enough. He bought lunch at the cafe—to go, of course—and camped out in the clinic's parking lot. He knew she'd stop by for Jessie's sake, if she could.

He'd parked in the back corner of the small lot, and he was rewarded when her truck pulled in after only half an hour. She and Jessie tumbled out, laughing about something. Even though it had only been forty-eight hours since he'd seen her, the sight of her hair flying out of its braid and her laughing eyes hit him hard.

He loved her. It wasn't going away.

He'd propped open his door and had one foot on the running board when someone else stepped out of a low-slung black sports car that he hadn't noticed until now, parked front and center, blocking the sidewalk.

Chase had never met him, but it had to be Hero. His hair was slicked back and his tan might've been fake, but the dude was good-looking for a city boy. He carried a huge bouquet of red roses. Definitely two dozen there. Expensive.

And all Chase could remember was how heartbroken Sarah had been when Hero had ended their engagement. The stricken look on her face had haunted him for several nights.

Hero approached Sarah, and she certainly looked surprised to see him. She waved Jessie on into the clinic. She tucked her hair behind her ear in that sweetly feminine way she had, and when she looked up at the other man, it sure seemed to Chase that her heart was in her eyes.

He couldn't watch.

If Hero was here to win her back, the huge bouquet would be about 24 sweet-smelling points in his favor. As would the fact that he and Sarah had been together for so long.

What was Chase, other than a good friend? A loser with a low-paying job, no education to speak of, no chance for a future of wealth and success.

Which way would the scales tip?

Yeah, he wasn't staying to watch.

Chase closed his door as quietly as he could and fired up the truck. With Sarah and Hero on the sidewalk outside the clinic, maybe she'd be too distracted to see him go.

Or maybe she wouldn't care.

He left without knowing what had happened, but he couldn't help but guess, and the images were painful as he headed out of town and back to the Triple H. He'd lost his appetite and left the two meals on the kitchen table. Someone would eat them.

In the barn, he picked up a shovel and started cleaning stalls. Shoveling manure was one of the most-avoided jobs on the ranch, but right now he felt like manure, and the work would keep him busy.

Late afternoon, he got a text from Sarah. A picture, no words, just her and Amanda squatting in the hay next to two baby lambs. So the mama'd finally had her babies.

He could only hope, for Amanda's sake, that she accepted both of them. He knew Sarah would stay on for a bit to do what she could.

He didn't respond to the text. Finding out that she was back with Hero would be too painful. He pocketed his phone and kept shoveling.

"Gotcha."

Kayla grabbed the back of the jean jacket before the kid could get more than a step ahead of her.

"Hey, let go!" he cried, but she didn't. She'd been expecting him to run—she knew from experience—and she held on.

It was dark in the barn, well past her usual bedtime. In her lunge to grab him, she'd dropped her phone, and the flashlight app was on. It must've fallen face-up, because light shined in her eyes but didn't really illuminate the boy she was trying to keep from running.

"Just wait a minute, Miles. I'm trying to help yo—"

He struggled, pulling his arms right out of the jacket, since she held onto the back. He scrambled for what must be the hole in the back wall of the barn, because she'd been expecting him to come through the double doors. She should've guessed they were too heavy for a boy his size to pull open.

She'd known he'd be back for his things. Had stayed up all night last night, but he hadn't showed then.

When you only had four possessions in the whole world, you didn't leave them behind. Of course, he had five, if you counted the dog.

He headed for the door, and she paused long enough to reach for her phone. Thank goodness he hadn't stepped on it. He was quick, because he'd almost disappeared already.

She raised the light to see him about to duck behind a stall to where the hole must be.

"You'll freeze out there without this," she called out. She couldn't imagine how he'd kept warm the night before.

He hesitated, but it was enough.

"I've got grilled cheese and soup up at the house. Piping hot. Milk and cookies for dessert." That stopped him.

"You said you'd call the cops." His back was still to her, but he'd frozen in place.

"I won't call the cops," she promised. "I've got a warm bed and plenty of blankets, and you can see Bando. And your Chihuahua."

He didn't ask after the dog, but fairly radiated with wanting to.

"Did you name her?" she asked. "I haven't named the puppies yet." She'd taken the Chihuahua and pups up to the house in a cardboard box, where the mama had given her the cold shoulder, only eating and sleeping. Kayla couldn't wait to get her in the bath but wouldn't push the animal to accept what she wasn't ready for.

"You've been taking good care of her," Kayla said. She wanted to ask, *but who's been taking care of you?* The answer was obvious. He had.

He turned, shielding his eyes from the light with one hand. "How'd you know my name?"

"I found your stash." She bit her lip. "I was a foster kid— actually me and my sister both were—and I knew you'd come back for your stuff. That picture—you don't leave something important like that behind." She'd carried a wallet-sized photo of their family from before their parents had died. She still had it tucked away in a shoebox.

He looked at her from the side, a wary glance. But she knew she'd won.

She held out the photo. And he carefully made his way toward her to take it.

Chapter Ten

It was more than a half hour before sunrise when Kayla was awakened by Bando's soft woof.

She sat up from where she'd been sleeping on the living room sofa with a throw covering her legs. She slapped the light switch on the wall, illuminating the boy creeping toward the kitchen and the back door.

Bando jumped off the couch, where he'd been lying across her feet. He bounced, ready to go for the day even at the early hour. Crazy dog.

Miles threw up one hand over his eyes. "What're you doing?" he demanded gruffly.

He looked about like she'd expected, carrying his shoes and his belongings bundled in a sweatshirt, which he held against his stomach.

"What are *you* doing?" she returned, even though it was pretty obvious. So obvious that he didn't answer. *Leaving.*

She stood, and he looked wary, like he might bolt for the door anyway.

"Chill," she said. "I knew you were gonna try to sneak out. I thought maybe we could have breakfast first."

He shifted his sock feet.

"I'm not going to grab you and tie you up or anything," she

said. "It's just bacon and eggs." Or cold cereal if she managed to burn the food. She wasn't the world's best cook.

He hesitated. She'd known the food would tempt him. Last night he'd shoveled down the three PB&J sandwiches she'd made for him, plus two full glasses of whole milk. No doubt he was thinking about when his next meal would be. She couldn't forget that lone can of baked beans.

"Fine. But then I'm leaving."

It'd been late when they'd come in last night, and she'd tried her best to prod some information out of him as she'd settled him in the guest bedroom, to no avail. He'd stood with his back to the wall next to the door, arms crossed over his chest, silent and watchful as she'd made the bed.

He was a tough nut to crack, but something about him drew her—maybe his obvious love for the little Chihuahua—and she wanted to help.

Now she shuffled into the kitchen, covering her mouth to stifle a huge yawn that cracked her jaw.

"How come you're not married?" he asked, slumping into a seat at the table.

Yeah, that's the first question she wanted to get asked at oh-dark-hundred in the morning, before she'd had even one sip of coffee.

She punched the button on the machine as his question made her remember a nineteen-year old with dark scruff across his chin and an irrepressible smile.

She blinked the painful memory away. "Because."

She twisted the knob to turn on the stove and crossed to the fridge to pull out eggs, a package of bacon, and what was left of a pint of orange juice.

Bando's nails clicked on the floor as he crossed to the doggie door and slipped outside.

"Can I have some coffee?" Miles asked.

"No." She set a glass and the juice on the table in front of him.

He shrugged and reached for the juice.

She got the bacon sizzling in one half of a skillet and whipped together some eggs in a plastic bowl before she added them to the skillet to scramble.

The bacon popped, and she'd swear she heard a sniff of appreciation from behind her, but when she turned to glance over her shoulder, the boy was staring out the darkened window.

"Where are you from?" she asked. "Taylor Hills?" She doubted it. She hadn't seen a missing persons poster or heard of a search.

"Why'd you buy this place?" he said. "It's pretty far out of town for a girl to live. By herself."

"I'm building a dog rescue." This was an easy answer. "I'm going to save dogs from all over, dogs people don't want anymore. I'll rehabilitate them if they need help, then I'm going to get them adopted."

A quick glance showed he was thinking on her words, and the softening in his eyes told her that maybe he'd appreciated that answer.

Across the room, the Chihuahua rested in the basket where she'd curled up with her puppies. She looked up, surveyed the space, and then laid her chin on the edge of the basket. It was tiring being a mom. At least that's what Kayla had heard. Her mom had died before imparting much motherly wisdom.

She was chasing one dream, but it hurt too much to think about the dreams she'd turned away from seven years ago. Along with the man.

At the counter, she plated the slightly runny eggs and the bacon that was slightly too crunchy. The toast she scrapped completely, as it was burnt black.

Standing here, she had a view out the window and saw headlights turn into the drive, still a ways from the house.

She turned quickly to the table, hoping her body was enough to block Miles from seeing, and hoping the food provided enough distraction for the next few moments.

It seemed to work, because he didn't look up until the social worker opened the screen door and slipped inside.

She hadn't seen such an accusing glare since she'd once borrowed Sarah's Louis Vuitton handbag. "You ratted me out."

She wanted to explain but doubted he'd listen. "I only promised not to call the cops," she said softly.

He was gone minutes later, back into the system she'd hated

so much. His baleful glare followed her in her memories all day long.

TWO DAYS LATER, late on a cold and rainy Sunday afternoon, Chase delivered a bull the Triple H had sold to a farmer not far from Amanda's ranch, and on a whim, he decided to stop and check in.

He saw movement in the open barn doors and headed that way instead of up to the house.

Inside, he found a teary Amanda and her mom.

Her mom saw him first and came to meet him as he stepped into the barn.

"The ewe rejected one of the lambs," she said quietly. "And we can't keep it. It's hard enough just trying to keep our normal routine." She looked a little tearful herself.

Amanda sniffed loudly, wiping her nose with the sleeve of her sweatshirt.

"Did Sarah leave some formula, just in case?" He kept his voice low, but the girl standing several feet away still heard.

"Yeah, but mom won't let me keep the lamb!" Amanda burst out. She shot a teary glare at her mother.

With her red-rimmed, exhausted eyes, Mom looked like she was about to burst into tears too, and he did *not* want that. "It's too much, with everything... Feedings every two hours?"

He nodded. He got it, he really did.

He wanted to help, wanted to ease their pain somewhat, but the words that popped out of his mouth were a surprise, even to him.

"I'll take her home with me. Raise her up until I can find a 4H kid to take her on."

THREE DAYS after James's visit, Sarah drove out to the Triple H. Three days of complete radio silence from Chase.

She missed his emoji-filled texts.

She'd been so distracted by James's arrival and flustered by his profession of undying love that she hadn't noticed anything else. But when she'd gone into the clinic after getting rid of

James, Jessie had asked, "Was that Chase I saw in the back of the parking lot?"

She'd barely registered a truck leaving the lot, hadn't seen if it was Chase. But after days of hearing nothing from him, she'd known Jessie must have been right.

She'd wanted to find him to explain, but two late-night calls in a row had ruined those plans. There was no way she was taking James back. She might be stubborn, but not stubborn enough to stay with a man who'd treated her so shabbily. Not when the real deal was right in front of her.

Then today, Amanda's mom had called the clinic and tattled on Sarah's former assistant.

And Sarah knew she had to do something before she lost the best thing that had ever happened to her.

Now she checked in with the ranch house. It was suppertime, and everybody was clustered around the long dining room table. Everyone except for her cowboy.

The foreman directed her to the barn.

Inside, she found Chase sitting cross-legged in one of the horse stalls, holding a bottle while the tiny lamb sucked greedily.

He had two days' worth of scruff on his chin and looked shell-shocked and more than a little exhausted. She'd heard directly from Jessie that raising a baby could do that to you.

She stuck her head over the stall door. "Hey, cowboy."

Instead of the smile she'd hoped for, his gaze was wary as it lifted to her. "Sarah. What're you doing here?"

Well, that wasn't quite the greeting she'd expected.

"I heard I had a new patient out here. I thought I'd better—"

"Right. The lamb." His lips turned down in a frown, and he looked away from Sarah and back to the animal. The lamb sucked the last drops from the bottle.

Sarah opened the stall door and slipped inside. She squatted next to Chase, and the lamb knocked her knee with its head. She couldn't help a small smile as she quickly ran her hands over the animal, noting the little full belly and soft wool. The animal's eyes were clear and alert.

"She looks good." But when Sarah turned her smile on the cowboy, he ducked his head and stood up.

Sarah straightened, too. "Amanda's mom said you were

pretty empathetic about the situation, and she was impressed that you were willing to take on the lamb."

The woman's effusive praise had made Sarah jealous.

He remained silent. Scratched the back of his neck, knocking his hat loose. It fell into the straw at his feet, and Sarah snatched it up.

He reached for it, but she pulled it away, and finally, *finally*, his gaze flew to her face.

"Getting up to feed the lamb all hours of the night must be making you grumpy, because this isn't the greeting I was expecting."

He frowned. "Excuse me if I don't kiss you hello, since I'm fairly sure you're back with Hero and just haven't told me yet."

Hero? Oh. James. Her lips wanted to twitch at the nickname.

She slapped the hat against his chest instead, and he caught it before it fell in the straw again. She turned and stormed out of the stall.

He followed, leaving the lamb behind.

"I'm *not* back with James. As if I would take him back after everything—"

A firm grip on her elbow kept Sarah from getting any farther away.

Chase slowly reeled her in, turning her to face him. He tipped her chin up with his opposite hand.

"You didn't take him back?" His question was uttered with such disbelief, and the naked hope on his face bolstered her.

She put on her best stubborn face and raised her chin even higher. "As a matter of fact, I've discovered I wasn't in love with him after all. I'm in love with you, you big l—"

He cut her off with a sweet kiss, then moved to spread little kisses across her cheek and jaw. "I'm sorry," he whispered. "I love you, and I was so afraid..."

She pulled back to get a good look at his face. "Afraid that I'd forget the last two months?"

His shoulders shifted, his eyes cutting away. "Afraid you'd realize that I'm just a loser without an education. Hero's smart enough to keep you interested—"

It was her turn to shut him up with a kiss.

When she pulled away, he looked down at her with a heated gaze.

"He wasn't smart enough to keep me the first time," she said. "Or to make me fall in love with him. Not really."

Chase's gaze darkened. She pushed against his shoulders slightly. "Loving someone and being loved in return is far more valuable than a well-tailored suit and a high salary. Having a man with me, a man who cares about me, who sees me and hears me and *knows* me—that's worth far more than prestige and power in my book. And I love *you*."

He touched his forehead to hers. "I'll never get tired of hearing you say that."

He held her close and she reveled in the warmth of his embrace. "Then I'll never stop."

Epilogue

Nate O'Malley had been waiting for this phone call for nine and a half years.

He didn't recognize the number, but he did recognize Kayla's strident voice coming through the line.

"I just got off the phone with the courthouse," she blurted.

He couldn't help the broad smile that spread across his lips. She sounded *mad*.

"How is it possible that we're still married?"

Keeping Kayla

Chapter One

"I DON'T UNDERSTAND HOW THIS COULD'VE happened."

Nate O'Malley kept his back to the irate woman standing in the barn doorway as he unbuckled his horse's saddle. Casual as could be, that was him.

He could fake it, even if he didn't feel it.

The Triple H had been short on manpower ever since Dan had been arrested for embezzling ranch funds. He was currently serving the third year in a five-year prison sentence, something that Nate still felt guilty about. He should've known one of his cowboys was in financial trouble and desperate.

Another of the ranch hands, Chase, had recently won the heart of the local vet and was working half time with her as a vet tech. Which meant now that it was calving season, Nate's job as foreman required him to be out at all hours of the night whenever the cows needed him. He could hire—should hire. He had nobody else to blame for the fact that he'd been awake since four, was cold and cranky, and desperately needed a cup of coffee.

Well, he had been cranky until she'd shown up. Her temper tantrum was cheering him right up.

"You said you were going to take care of everything," Kayla Campbell said.

Just because his back was to her didn't mean he didn't know that she was standing with one hand propped on her hip, as sassy as she'd been at nineteen. He could picture her in his mind's eye, curly blonde hair tossing about her head like some crazy angel's halo. Her hazel eyes would be flashing fire.

His mouth kicked up in a smile just imagining it.

He flipped the saddle's leather strap out of its buckle, and the saddle loosened on the horse's back. His shoulder twanged from the cold as he lifted the saddle off the horse and deposited it on a nearby railing.

"Maybe I didn't want an annulment," he said calmly.

He heard her swift intake of air. It probably wasn't fair to provoke her, but old habits were hard to break, or so the cliché went. It was true for him, anyway. He liked the lightning that went off in her eyes, the way her lips would pinch in a frown that only he could elicit.

Besides, he wasn't even sure they were eligible to have the hasty Vegas marriage annulled.

"We *agreed*."

Oh, she was steamed now. He heard the stomp of her feet against the hard-packed dirt as she approached him.

"You told me what to do," he said, calm as could be. "I never agreed to it."

He patted the horse's rump, and it clomped off obediently toward its stall and the fresh grain waiting there. Nate knew the animal must be hungry after a morning of work—he sure was— and he'd follow soon enough to see the horse settled. He just had to deal with his sort-of wife first.

"You didn't disagree!" She was breathing hard. She reached out and grabbed his arm. She must've meant to spin him around —her temper was that hot—but he was already turning to face her, and the combination of movements threw her a little off-balance. She gripped his arm for balance.

As soon as she righted herself, she let him go as if he were hot as a branding iron, but not before his heart galloped, not before he felt the zing of her touch all the way down to his toes. A lot had changed in the decade since their annulment that wasn't, but the way he responded to her touch wasn't one of them.

Now that he was face-to-face with her and not picturing her

in his head, he saw she was way past mad and more like livid. Tears sparkled in her eyes. Seeing her emotion was like a horse kick to the gut. He couldn't breathe, but maybe that was a good thing, because the words that wanted to spew were dangerous.

He'd wanted to tell her for a long time, but he'd never imagined it like this. The words stuck in his throat. *I want to give this marriage thing a shot.*

Yeah, he could imagine how that would go over. Imagine her laughter. Or maybe she'd think he was crazy. They hadn't seen each other for nine years, hadn't spoken in over a decade.

When she'd moved back to Taylor Hills eighteen months ago, he'd felt a surge of hope that maybe his plan—his very long-term plan—could work.

He'd spent ten years working his butt off in hopes she'd notice. He'd given up his birthright and had a broken relationship with his dad to prove it.

"Don't you have anything to say, *Nathan*?" She used his full name the same way his dad always had when Nate had been in deep manure. It usually made him want to smile, but his thoughts were too much like a dust dervish to allow for any peaceful feelings right now.

The real kicker, his biggest secret, was the worst. *I think I'm still in love with you.*

She hadn't believed him back then. Why would she believe him now?

He needed a little more time. As if the decade hadn't been quite enough. Maybe he'd been fooling himself all along.

She closed her eyes, and when she re-opened them, where her tears had been, only fire was left. And determination.

"Never mind." Her shoulders straightened. "I don't know why I bothered coming out here."

She whirled and started out of the barn. He'd once been thankful for her impulsive decision-making, but right now, he needed a few seconds to gather his thoughts.

Too late.

"Kayla, wait!"

He started after her, but a whicker from Bluebell reminded him that he hadn't put the horse up. She was now wandering back toward him. Or maybe the open barn door.

He'd been foreman for five years. He was proud of the profits the ranch turned. Five years he'd been responsible for the livestock, for the operations, and for the four cowboys. He couldn't just walk away from that responsibility, even if his personal life was blowing up.

He put the horse away.

By the time his boots hit the gravel drive, she was gone, leaving only a cloud of red dust along the road.

He stood blinking in the harsh winter sunlight. He'd planned to eat something—his grumbling stomach reminded him that the granola bar he'd eaten at four a.m. had long worn off—and maybe catch a combat nap, but not now.

Kayla didn't live far. As the crow flew, her place was only a quarter mile away. After he checked in with the boss, Matt Hale, at the ranch house, he took off.

He didn't have a plan, but he was going.

He wasn't going to let Kayla get away a second time.

KAYLA CAMPBELL SWIPED at a stray tear as she turned her truck down the rutted dirt road toward home.

It was stupid to cry. Tears had never changed anything, a lesson she'd learned early in life.

She'd hoped that when she faced off with Nate, he'd tell her it was all a big joke. They weren't still married. The county courthouse had just misplaced their certificate of annulment—or whatever it would be—and she could go on with her life.

Ha.

It was all big joke after all. Her life was one big, cosmic joke. And the punch line was always on her.

It wasn't fair. Guys like Nate O'Malley walked around with everything handed to them. Born with a silver spoon in their mouths. It didn't help that he was movie-star handsome with blond curls that peeped beneath his hat and warm chocolate eyes that made you feel like you were the most important thing in his world—

She shook herself out of that dangerous thought.

People like Nate were given jobs just because they knew someone who knew someone.

While she'd had to claw her way out of poverty with her bare hands. She was still too close to losing everything, too close to the poverty that always felt like it was sniping at her heels like a rabid dog.

She slapped the steering wheel of her fifteen-year-old truck, but it didn't do anything other than make her palm sting.

Her thoughts went to Miles, the young boy she'd discovered in her barn four days ago. According to the social worker who'd picked him up, he was an orphan. He'd been living with an uncle who'd passed away, and then he'd been shifted into a group home. He'd run away, spent almost a week in her barn without her noticing, creeping in after her bedtime.

He was crafty, sneaky...and lonely. She'd seen herself in him. She'd long ago left behind the lost little orphan girl. But her memories remained.

She'd hoped to get an emergency foster placement. Maybe even something long-term. And then the social worker had called and asked about Kayla's *husband*. Kayla'd thought the stupid Vegas spur-of-the-moment wedding had been annulled years ago, but apparently, she'd been wrong.

The social worker would never place Miles with her now.

Her eyes smarted again, and she blinked furiously.

She wouldn't give up. Miles deserved better, just like she and Sarah had.

She almost missed it because of her misty eyes.

There'd been a slew of late-winter rains, and the ditch beside the road that led to her ranch had filled with water, mud, and debris. At one point, the ditch had widened where her neighbor's farm pond had overflowed. Barbed wire fence stretched across the water, but part of the fence was submerged and tangled with a felled tree. She saw movement. Was that an animal?

She slowed her truck, blinking away the moisture in her eyes and squinting. Were her eyes playing tricks on her?

There...yes. The animal was struggling, a black head above the water, but barely.

A dog. One in perilous danger.

She jammed the brakes, threw the truck into park, and jumped out. She shed her light coat and tossed it in the truck bed. Cold wind bit her skin through the sweatshirt and T-shirt both.

She slogged through the ankle-deep ditch further back and lost precious seconds when her sweatshirt caught on the barbed wire when she ducked beneath the fence.

She ran around the muddy edge of the pond, her boots squishing against moist, dead winter grass and sinking into the red mud. She spent another ten seconds pulling the boots off at the water's edge and wading along the fence line toward the dog. Its thrashing had grown weaker. In the time it had taken her to circle around, the dog had swum farther away.

She had no choice but to keep going. Maybe once she got to the dog, she could climb through the knot of protruding tree roots.

"Easy, boy."

She didn't know if the animal was a male or female, but it seemed like the right thing to say.

Mud and moss sucked at her feet with each step. Icy water covered her ankles first, then her calves, thighs, hips. This was deeper than it had looked from the pond's edge.

If the dog had been trapped for long, it might be hypothermic. She was already starting to shiver, and she'd been in the pond less than a minute.

When the icy water reached her chest, she started to worry. How could she drag a scared dog out of this if she could hardly keep her own head above water?

She brushed away the fears and rushed forward, shocked when her foot suddenly didn't find ground to stand on. She flailed, panicked, and barely kept her head above water as she reached to grab the nearest thing she could see. Thank goodness she missed—a barb from the wire fence wouldn't have helped a bit.

The water lapped at her chin and mouth. She stifled a gasp.

"I'm coming, fella." She hoped the dog couldn't hear the note of desperation in her voice. She didn't have a good relationship with deep water, another thing her childhood had taken from her.

Now that she was close, she could see the dog had a crude rope around its neck. The rope was tangled in the roots of the horizontal tree, and the dog seemed to be tangled up too, unable to get its feet on anything solid.

"How'd you get in this mess, huh?" she asked, trying to inject a note of calm in her voice. She should've brought something—shears or wire cutters, not that she had either of those in her truck.

She got close enough to touch the dog, but it was panicked and hit her with its front paws. The pressure dunked her beneath the water, submerging her into the inky iciness. The wire bent beneath her hand, but she held on and managed to drag herself back above the surface.

She might've shouted or gurgled, she didn't know which, only that a sound of true panic had escaped.

The dog whined, a similar sound of distress. She could hear its labored breathing above the sounds of their splashing.

She managed to get her arm—the one that wasn't clutching the wire strand for dear life—around its middle. She hugged the dog as close to her as she could, but the frightened animal still thrashed, making it hard for her to tell which direction was up.

This was a disaster, a dangerous one. If she'd been smart, she would've called someone for help, but it was too late now. She was afraid to leave the dog, afraid it wouldn't make it if she abandoned it.

But she was also afraid for her own life. Full body shivers wracked her, and her strength was quickly draining as she clung to both the wire and the dog.

"Kayla!"

She turned at the shout. That was Nate's voice.

She nearly cried, her relief was so deep, but she managed to swallow the hot knot that rose in her throat. Even with his presence, she'd need her wits to get out of this mess.

"I'm coming to you," he called out. His voice was near, but she couldn't move adequately to see where he was coming from.

Apparently, he'd approached from the closer side, the tree side. Within moments, he was lying flat on his belly on the felled tree, reaching through the mess of roots toward her.

His hand clasped hers on the wire, heat enclosing her frigid digits.

"You're freezing."

"Water's c-cold." Her teeth chattered, and she got a mouthful of mud just forcing the words out.

"And this guy's tangled up."

How funny that he assumed the same sex for the dog that she had. Wouldn't they both be surprised if *he* turned out to be a *she*?

She might be tipping over into hypothermia herself with the way her thoughts had started whirling.

"Don't let go," she breathed.

He squeezed her hand. "I won't."

He grunted as he stretched out, his other hand fighting through roots to where the rope was tangled.

The dog gave a mighty kick, which landed against her gut. Kayla's breath was thumped out of her lungs. She sank lower in the water, her grip slipping on the wire. Her hands were so cold.

"Water's d-deeper th-than I th-thought."

Maybe a little bit of her panic was seeping through in her words, because Nate stopped what he was doing and grabbed her hand with both of his. "You still can't swim?"

He'd once teased her about never taking lessons. She'd been too embarrassed to take them as an adult.

She was eye-level with his frown, saw the way his jaw firmed with determination.

This time, instead of trying to untangle the dog's rope, he reached for the animal's head with one hand—he still hadn't let go of her—and started working his hand between the rope and the dog's fur. Smart. If they couldn't untangle the rope, they could untangle the dog.

It was probably only the work of a few moments, but time seemed to slow as he pulled the entire collar off over the dog's head.

The dog must have sensed how close it was to freedom, because it gave a renewed surge of kicking, this time against her legs. The wire was biting into Kayla's hand now, and even with Nate's grip on her, she started to slip, sinking into the water.

And then Nate had somehow lifted the dog from her arm, using some kind of superhuman strength.

She couldn't feel her legs anymore but kicked anyway as she started to slip.

And then Nate leaned back down to her. He clasped both hands around her upper arms. With her arms in his grip, he fell onto his backside and with his momentum, pulled her out of the water. She slid against his muscled body, then slid off and landed in the cold mud on his opposite side. Dry land, sort of.

The chilly air bit her wet skin and set her teeth chattering.

"C'mon, we've got to get you warm." He pushed to his feet, mud smeared across his face and clothes. He helped her up and steadied her when her legs wobbled.

"I'm n-not l-leaving the d-dog."

He gave her one long look, followed her gaze to the lab who seemed to be recovering as it lay in the mud, sides heaving. The poor thing probably didn't have much strength left. Out of the water, Kayla could see its black fur was matted with burrs, and ribs were showing through the once-glossy coat.

"Fine." Nate picked up the dog, cradling it like a small child. The animal didn't struggle.

Kayla hobbled behind him toward the road, detouring quickly and avoiding his scowl as she retrieved her boots from the field.

He didn't let her get in her own truck, the pushy man.

That was fine, because as she collapsed into the passenger seat of his, the dog across her feet, she couldn't control her shaking limbs. No way could she have driven anywhere.

He cranked the heat, and warmth seeped through her chilled skin.

"Take this off." He pulled off her sweatshirt. Luckily she was wearing a T-shirt beneath. He wrapped a blanket that smelled suspiciously like horses around her shoulders.

"M-my house—"

"I know where it is." He gave her one last look before he threw the truck into gear.

Chapter Two

Nate still had adrenaline rushing through his system and was working hard to keep a rein on his temper as he pulled up to Kayla's run-down farmhouse. What had she been thinking to go into a dangerous situation like that? And into the water, when she couldn't swim? She could've drowned.

He glanced her way. Probably not hypothermia. Her color was good, and she seemed alert, though quiet.

He wanted to strangle her.

She *hadn't* been thinking, that much was clear. She'd seen an animal in danger and had jumped to the rescue. But who'd she figure on to rescue her? If he hadn't come along... No, he wouldn't think about that right now.

She stepped out of the truck as he rounded the front of the vehicle. She glanced at the interior of the truck—probably at the dog still lying across the floor—then back at Nate, biting her lip. A quick glance at the house.

He waited.

"Would you carry him inside for me?"

"That wasn't so hard, was it? Asking for help?"

She glared at him.

Maybe he shouldn't have said it, but the fear that was still running through him wouldn't let him stay quiet.

"Happy to." And if she thought he was going to drop off the dog and walk back out, she was sorely mistaken.

He brushed past her and carefully got the dog out of the car. It laid its head on Nate's shoulder. It was obviously exhausted and felt lighter than a dog its size should've. But it wasn't scared of him. Or maybe it was too tired to be scared.

She'd already climbed the porch steps and was opening the door—folks out here usually didn't bother locking things up. He followed her into the foyer of the ranch house.

He'd barely gotten over the threshold when another dog, this one a black-and-white Border Collie, ran into the room, its nails clicking and clattering on the scratched wood floors as it rushed Kayla. It took one sniff at her and beelined for Nate. He braced for impact, but the dog stopped short. It sniffed his boots and circled him before looking up and trying to get a sniff of the dog in his arms. At least Kayla's dog hadn't jumped on him.

Kayla disappeared down the hall, leaving him alone in the mostly-empty front hall with two canines. He hoped she was going to change into some dry clothes.

"Where do you want this one?" he called out. He wanted to put the dog down and make sure Kayla was all right. She wouldn't welcome a hug, but seeing her so frightened—he'd probably have nightmares of her white-faced terror in that water —made him long for an embrace.

"The kitchen." Her voice returned distant, maybe from a bedroom in the back of the house.

"The kitchen," he muttered. "Which is...?" He did a slow turn. Through a large, curved doorway, he could see a room with a light brown sofa and colorful throw pillows. A brick fireplace was unlit, and a dog bed lay empty on the floor. Dog toys were strewn everywhere. Several books and a pile of papers had been spread on the coffee table beside an open laptop.

The other side of the foyer opened to a hallway, which he assumed led to the bedrooms. If he had to guess, there'd be three bedrooms, based on the age of the house. He followed the third option, walked straight ahead, and got dumped into a sunny, open eat-in kitchen. She had a small round table and chairs in the nook that looked out toward the barn. The linoleum and appliances were butter yellow, clearly relics from the eighties. Nice.

She had a nice toaster and one of those single-cup coffee makers on the counter, but two small appliances didn't make up for the cracks in the sheetrock, peeling paint, or warped spot in the linoleum just in front of the dated fridge.

The whole place needed updating. Desperately. It was an awfully ambitious project for a single woman.

From the corner of the kitchen, he spied another dog, this one a Chihuahua in a flat cardboard box curled around little fluff balls. Puppies.

He started to shake his head. What was Kayla doing with all these dogs?

He set the lab mix on the tiled floor. He could still hear Kayla rustling around somewhere else in the house.

He looked down at the black-and-white dog, who'd sat at his feet and was staring up at him with an adoring doggie grin.

"I wish your mama would look at me like that," he mumbled.

A knock on the back door brought his head up and a sharp bark from the border collie. The dog went to the door, wagging its entire backside. Either whoever was on the other side of that door was a friend, or the dog was a horrible guard dog. Or both.

The nook window showed enough of the back stoop to see a woman standing there. He opened the door and hoped he wasn't stepping on Kayla's toes.

"Mornin'," he said. She wore a neat suit jacket and matching skirt with a red wool coat unbuttoned over them.

A noise behind him had him glancing back. Kayla entered the room, her arms full of a load of towels. "You don't have to stay—"

She stopped short, and her eyes widened as they darted from his face to the woman at the door. "Rachel. I wasn't expecting you."

"I came by to talk about the emergency placement."

Emergency placement for what?

Kayla shot him a sideways glance that had his mouth clamped shut.

Rachel nodded to him. "This must be your husband."

· · ·

Blood rushed from the top of Kayla's head into her toes, making her feel faint. What was the social worker doing here?

"This is—this is Nate." She couldn't force the word *husband* from her lips. Her hands were shaking and she quickly deposited the soiled towels on one of the kitchen chairs. Laundry could wait.

Was he going to deny it? He'd joked about not wanting an annulment.

He held Kayla's eye contact for a moment before he reached forward to shake Rachel's hand.

"It's nice to meet you," he drawled in his calm, easy way.

Rachel responded with a murmured greeting, her gaze not missing a thing. Not his dimpled smile, not the sparkle in his eyes, not his muscles shoulders.

Kayla wanted to strangle him. Even more when he settled closer to her, his shoulder almost brushing hers.

"I came by to drop the paperwork off so you can make corrections," Rachel said. She tapped a thick sheaf of papers against her opposite palm. "That is, if you still want to take Miles on."

Kayla's stomach plunged. "Of course I—we want him here."

Her face flamed, and this time, she couldn't look at Nate. Her ears were ringing as she waited for him to say, *who is Miles?*

But he didn't.

Rachel laid the pile of papers on the kitchen table—thank God Kayla'd cleared away her cereal bowl from this morning—and glanced around the kitchen. She'd only been here to pick up Miles before, and Kayla realized her first impression of the home might not be ideal.

She opened her mouth to say something about it, but Nate beat her to it.

"We've got a long list of repairs," Nate said easily. "Probably start with the floors and work our way up."

Her mouth snapped shut. She wanted to reprimand him for speaking for her, but he was playing the part of husband, wasn't he?

Rachel's eyes shifted to the dogs. Bando had wagged his way to sitting at her feet, his tail sweeping across the floor. Another thank God that he hadn't jumped on her in his enthusiasm to meet a new person.

"I'm starting a dog rescue," Kayla said quickly. "Most of the dogs will be housed in the barn, but I haven't got it cleaned up out there the way I want it yet. Bando is a house dog." If that was a deal-breaker, she didn't know what she'd do.

Rachel's expression showed some concern. "Will you have time to care for a little boy while you're busy with all these projects?"

"Of course." The words were out before she'd really thought about them. It didn't matter. She could vividly remember being about eight and needing help with a third-grade homework project. She'd stood for a long time in a darkened hallway, watching her foster mom sitting at the kitchen table reading a magazine. She'd known, somehow, that her request for help would be met with a sneer and a dismissal. And it had been.

The next time, she hadn't even bothered asking. Sarah had helped, though it had meant her big sister had had to stay awake long after lights-out, using a flashlight beneath the covers to finish her own homework.

If having Miles here meant Kayla stayed up late working on her grant proposals, so be it. She never wanted another kid to feel like she had all those years ago.

As soon as Rachel left, Nate turned on her. "You wanna tell me what that was about?"

Kayla winced as she looked away from Nate and the intensity of his curious gaze. She ignored the towels she'd abandoned to the kitchen chair when Rachel had shown up and bent to check on the Labrador—who was, in fact, a girl.

Nate's larger-than-life presence here, in her kitchen, discombobulated her. She felt that same feeling of panicked weightlessness as she had when she'd sunk beneath the pond water.

"Nothing that concerns you," she bit out. She just wanted him gone.

He squatted on the other side of the dog he'd helped rescue. Even with the Lab between them, he was still too close. She kept her gaze on the dog, but as she reached out to towel it off, Nate reached out and tugged the towel from her suddenly nerveless fingers.

"Seems like it does concern me. An hour ago, you were reading me the riot act over the fact that we're still hitched, but just now you were play-acting like we're happily married."

She winced again, squeezing her eyes closed. "Yeah. About that..." Unfortunately, closing her eyes didn't make Nate disappear. He was still there when she opened them.

She focused on the dog, but it had that Lab fur that shed water quickly—the animal was almost dry. So she stood up. Anything to get out of Nate's overwhelming proximity.

"Who's Miles?" There came the question she'd been expecting earlier.

"He's little boy. Not so little, I guess. He's ten. He's in foster care, and I applied to be an emergency home for him. The social worker called me to ask why I hadn't included my husband's information on all the forms."

Those words over the phone had knocked the wind right out of her and sent her spinning for days.

Now, just remembering that out-of-control feeling went through her, and the nervous energy pushed her toward the pantry. She opened the large tub that sat on the floor and scooped out some dog food into a dish. Not too much. She didn't want the hungry lab to make itself sick by overeating. She set the bowl of food in front of the dog. From the corner, the Chihuahua hadn't moved from her position guarding her pups. It'd been four days, and Kayla still hadn't earned her trust.

"I'll bet that ticked you off," Nate said quietly. He rose from his crouch and stood with his hands loose at his sides.

Knowing they still shared a connection had frightened her more than anything else. The swirl of hot emotion that had risen when she'd remembered their quickie Vegas ceremony and her certainty that Nate was the one for her—and the devastation she'd felt the next morning when she'd nosedived and crashed back to reality. She didn't want to go through that—any of it —again.

She turned away from him, afraid he would see the naked emotion in her face. Miles had become important to her in only a matter of days. She didn't want to share that with Nate.

"That doesn't matter." She couldn't afford to let their not-annulled marriage affect her fostering Miles. "Now I need to figure out what to do about Miles. About this situation." She should've nipped the whole thing in the bud. But somehow, when Rachel had been here, the words *we're not married* had stuck in her throat.

Rachel must've been completely green to miss the tension in the room. How had she not known something was going on?

Nausea roiled as she thought of calling the social worker back to tell her the truth. And then she remembered Miles, remembered his tattered jean jacket and that picture of him and what must be his older sister. His only belongings. Then remembered the vulnerability behind the stubborn tilt of his jaw that said he didn't need anyone.

She rubbed her hands—still cold from the icy water—over her face. "How do I get myself into these situations?"

She thought better of asking Nate that question and whirled to face him again. "Don't answer that."

He'd crossed his arms, and that muscle in his jaw ticked away. He was probably holding back some snide remark about her impulsiveness, the trait that had been the reason she'd ended up in the Vegas chapel in the first place.

"Why does helping that kid mean so much to you?"

She examined his face, looking for any trace of a sneer or flare of his nostrils that might indicate his thoughts, but his expression was carefully blank. He'd always been able to do that, hide behind a blank mask. It bothered her then and it bothered her now.

"I wouldn't expect you to understand." She would have to figure a way out of this disaster on her own. She hadn't done any research yet on what it would take to annul the marriage. Maybe there was a way to expedite it. Of course, then she'd be in a world of hot water explaining herself to Rachel and why she'd lied about being married.

An ache started behind her eyes, and she rubbed the thumb and forefinger of one hand into her eye sockets, trying to ease it. She wished Nate would just leave so she could think.

But when she opened her eyes, he was still there, still regarding her.

"I'll help you," he said.

She waited. There had to be a catch.

"If you ask me."

His words threw her for a tailspin—they were an echo of what she'd said to him ten years ago. *I'll marry you, if you ask me."*

She bit the immediate denial that rose on her tongue. She thought of Miles, thought of the many nights she'd spent scared and alone in the world. What would she have done without her sister? And here was Miles without anyone.

She gritted her teeth and swallowed the hard knot in her throat—and maybe a good dose of her pride too. "Will you help me, *Nathan*?"

Chapter Three

It wasn't quite dawn as Nate stood across from Matt Hale, a large oak desk between them in the Triple H ranch house office. Nate had just finished going over the list of cows that were due for calving over the next two weeks. They never had a guarantee of what date a cow would have her calf, of course—only the good Lord knew that—but the list showed which cows were expecting.

"I appreciate you granting me a few days off," Nate said. Calving season wasn't the ideal time to be away from the ranch, but everything had happened so quickly with Kayla that he was still reeling. He'd already stowed his duffel bag in his truck. Next stop, Kayla's place.

Matt looked up from the mess of papers on the desk—the accounts payable that Nate had gone over with him not fifteen minutes ago—and leveled a hard gaze at him. He hadn't said much until now.

"What the heck are you thinking?"

Nate blinked at his boss's unexpected words.

"We've known each other a long time. You've worked the Triple H for...what? Nine years? Been foreman for five, right? I've never seen you tied in knots like this."

His friend was right. Kayla had been gone from his life before he'd come to the Triple H as a twenty-year old. He'd spent the decade working hard, proving himself, but he'd planned to win her back. Just not for it to take so long.

"My relationship with Kayla has always been... complicated."

"What relationship?" Matt knocked on the desk with a closed fist. "This is the first I'm hearing of this. And it sounds crazy. You've been married for ten years, but you're separated, and you never see her. That's not a relationship. That's not even a pen pal."

Nate shrugged, trying not to let his boss's words get to him. "I messed things up between us. When we got married, she freaked out a little, and I didn't say the right things and... she got away. I was going through some stuff with my dad and..." He sighed, shrugged again. "I should've gone after her, done things differently."

Matt shifted his feet behind the desk. "Do you even hear what you're saying? *It's my fault, I didn't, I should have...*" His forehead creased with emotion. "It takes two people to build a relationship. Are you sure she even wants to be with you?"

The barb hit home. Especially after Kayla's efforts to push him away, keep her emotions to herself. Nate's instinctive reaction was to strike back, inflict a wound of his own. Matt understood that well enough. His fiancé Kelsey had broken his heart years ago, and they'd only recently made up and gotten engaged. It wasn't like Matt was the poster boy for healthy relationships, either.

Nate swallowed the urge to bite back.

"I've been in love with Kayla for a decade," he admitted. "For a while, I tried to ignore it, pretend we'd never happened, but... I never could."

Matt's frown only intensified, though he must have been able to relate to what Nate was saying.

"This thing with the foster kid is an open door, and I'm going to walk through it. I'm going to fight with everything I have. And if, at the end of it, I come away with a broken heart, well, at least I'll know I didn't leave anything on the table."

Matt only shook his head.

"Thanks again for the days off. I'll touch base about next week."

He left his boss in the office. He had a wife to see.

. . .

Kayla was too antsy to stay in the house. The social worker was supposed to arrive sometime before noon with Miles. No doubt the boy would be standoffish and sullen, unable to believe he'd get to stay for any length of time.

But that wasn't what had driven her out of the house. She could find a way to expel nervous energy in the barn and headed that way.

Nate was coming back today. He'd left yesterday after delivering a simple, *I'd be glad to* in response to her request for help.

She didn't know what to do with that. She'd thought things were settled between them long ago. Now his presence was stirring up all those old emotions.

As she crossed the yard, she found her left thumb rubbing the base of her ring finger, the motion entirely unconscious. She fisted her hand and flung her fingers open wide, snarling at the muscle memories that had caused the action.

She'd only worn Nate's ring, a simple silver band, for the one night, but she'd felt it for months after they'd walked away from each other that fateful morning. For that one night, she'd felt like she belonged, a feeling she'd ached for her whole life. Then it had been ripped away.

She whistled for Bando, knowing her border collie would abandon his romp in the nearby grassy field. She could only hope the lab mix would come with him. The lab had been cautious around Kayla but had taken to Bando immediately, following him around with an adoring look on her face.

Kayla recognized the happy-go-lucky personality beneath the caution. She'd spent years working with the city obedience club while Sarah had been in vet school. The lab mix had no training but was curious and intelligent.

Kayla pulled the barn door open with more force than was necessary, but she stopped short when confronted with Nate himself, who was several yards inside the building. He wore a red-and-black flannel shirt that brought out the bright blue of his eyes, Wranglers that were perfectly worn in, and of course his boots and Stetson.

"What are you doing here?" The words came out demanding, covering the shock and surprise of seeing him. Her memories of their time together were too raw, too close to the surface for politeness.

He strode over to her, put an arm around her waist, and kissed her cheek before she had time to react.

She jerked away from him, her head knocking his Stetson back on his forehead. Bando rushed in, jumping around his feet and barking joyously. The lab hung back in the doorway, tongue lolling but watchful.

Nate laughed at Bando's antics, the sound deep and warm. "At least someone's happy to see me." He knelt and gave the dog a good rubdown. Bando rewarded his effort by lying flat out on his back, begging for a belly rub. Nate complied but slanted a glance up at her. "If you jump away from me like that, Rachel and Miles will know something's not right."

She swallowed hard. She'd known that if they were going to pull off this farce she would have to be in close proximity to Nate, but she hadn't considered *touching*.

"Don't kiss me," she said. She wiped at her cheek as if she could erase the feeling of his lips there.

It didn't work.

She felt as if he'd branded her, left a remnant of his touch behind.

He raised one pointed eyebrow at her. "I make no guarantees."

She didn't want to think about what that meant, so she shot a pointed question right back at him. "What are you doing out here?"

He stood, and Bando wandered off and the black lab followed, sniffling and snuffling her way through the nooks and crannies of the barn.

"I was trying to picture how you're going to do it," Nate said as if this were the most normal thing in the world. "I'd heard about your dog rescue before yesterday. I guess you've already started with these"—he motioned to the dogs—"plus the puppies."

"Bando is mine. And these other guys just came along..." She didn't want to think about the fact that he'd been listening to town gossip about her. "But I'm not anywhere near operational yet."

It'd taken nearly all of what she'd scrimped and saved to purchase the property. She was looking into grants to see if she could get the capital she needed to get things into working order. She'd had a plan that included living in the tiny city apartment for another two years, socking away money from her daytime job as a bank teller supervisor and her nighttime waiting tables, but Sarah had moved back to Taylor Hills. Kayla's other roommate had been fine, but she'd missed her sister, the only family she had in the world.

And when the property came up for sale, it had seemed like a sign from God that she should do it.

Now she was struggling to know where to go from here. Not that she'd admit that to Nate.

"I plan to have a large open area where the dogs can have some freedom to move around and several runs on each side of the barn. I've already started tearing out some of the stalls."

"I can see that." He walked over to where she'd taken a sledgehammer to one of the wooden partitions on a day she'd particularly needed to work off some steam. He toed the part of the partition that was still attached to the barn wall. "Did you know you've got some rot in the wood? Probably termite damage, but you'd need someone to verify that for you. Might want to have someone come out and check the house, too."

She hadn't known, and his words threw a bucket of cold water on the pride that had straightened her shoulders.

"I was getting around to that." She'd experienced some prideful thoughts about her own strength when the old wood had splintered and crumbled beneath her sledgehammer.

"You're asking for trouble if you don't get the beams and joists looked at. If you're lucky, maybe you'll only have to replace part of the walls."

She couldn't afford to replace *any*. But did Nate know about that kind of thing? Maybe he was wrong.

The sound of a car engine offered a reprieve from the panic swirling through her gut, though it prompted a new sort of anxiety. What if Miles didn't like it here? Didn't like her?

Her feet stalled on the packed dirt barn floor. Was this

another mistake? Was her impulsiveness going to get her into trouble all over again?

It was too late to back out, because Nate was at her side, his hand warm at her lower back as he ushered her out into the cool sunshine to meet her new foster son.

NATE COULD FEEL Kayla's tension even without touching her. Maybe he should've waited for a better time to bring up the sorry state of her barn, but the damage was done now. He'd help her with the needed repairs, if she'd let him.

The social worker was standing beside her car, neat as a pin again in a navy-blue skirt suit this time. The boy beside her had his arms crossed and shoulders hunched. He wore a scowl. His jeans were old and faded, and the jean jacket he wore was ripped. One elbow had a hole in it, it was at least a size too small. He had a bruise along one cheekbone, as if he'd been in a brawl recently.

This was the Miles that Kayla wanted to foster?

Yesterday when she'd claimed he wouldn't understand her reasons for wanting to help the boy, he'd wanted to fire back that he was plenty smart enough to understand if she'd *tell him.*

But he'd known that letting his temper fly wouldn't solve anything. And maybe this whole situation was the burr under his saddle that he needed to make a change. He'd let things slide for way too long, thinking he had all the time in the world to make things right between them. Now it was time to claim what he wanted. And what he wanted was Kayla.

Who apparently wanted this little thug in her home.

"Hi, Miles." Her greeting was soft and welcoming, and Nate had a moment of fleeting jealousy. She certainly hadn't greeting him so warmly.

She got nothing in return until Rachel nudged the boy with her elbow. Even then, the boy offered no more than a mumble, which Nate couldn't make out.

"Have you eaten breakfast?" Kayla asked.

Miles stared sullenly at the ground. Yeah, real winner, this kid.

"We hit the drive-thru on our way out," Rachel said a little too brightly.

The whole conversation was starting to make Nate feel uncomfortable. And a little useless. "You got any bags for me to carry inside?"

Kayla stepped on his toe, maybe on purpose. What was that for?

But the social worker was shaking her head.

Now Miles finally looked up, but it was to glare at Nate. What was the kid's problem?

"He probably doesn't have much," Kayla whispered.

Oh. Well, it wouldn't be the first time Nate had put his foot in his mouth.

"The Chihuahua is in the kitchen with her puppies," Kayla said. "I haven't named her yet."

This statement caused a very subtle shift in the boy's expression, a tiny candle flame lit behind his eyes. But he still didn't say anything.

"You can go in and see her if you want." Kayla's voice was tender and, somehow, relaxed.

The boy shrugged, but he did stomp off up the porch steps and into the house. Nate hoped Kayla had locked up any valuables.

Nate watched him go as Kayla and Rachel exchanged a few more words. The social worker got in her car and backed down the driveway. So that was that.

Nate was unprepared when Kayla whirled on him. " You couldn't just keep your trap shut? Miles doesn't need any more reminders of his situation."

"Whoa." He raised both hands like the victim in a holdup. "I'm not the bad guy here. I didn't realize it was going to be a hot button for him." *Or for you.*

In high school, he'd been a year ahead. He'd known she and Sarah had lived in the county group home, but he'd been so self-absorbed that he hadn't really thought about what that meant. What had it been like for her to not have a single possession to her name? He couldn't fathom it.

Her eyes flashed as if she'd heard his thoughts, but he quickly went on.

"What other things I am not supposed to ask about? It's not like I've had a primer in foster kids, you know."

Rachel had mentioned something about classes they'd have to take if they wanted to make the fostering a permanent thing, but he hadn't given that much thought yet. He was just trying to get through today's land mines.

But Kayla... Kayla knew, from her own childhood. And maybe he'd just hit the tip of the iceberg in hers and Miles's reaction to his innocent question. He wanted to know more.

Kayla was staring at him like she didn't know him at all. He'd wanted a chance to prove he wasn't that nineteen-year-old kid who'd hurt her and lost the best thing that had ever happened to him, and now he'd gotten it.

"You're not getting rid of me," he reminded her quietly. "And I want to help with—with Miles." He'd almost said *the kid.* That wouldn't have helped his case any.

She looked at the house. "A lot of foster kids have abandonment issues."

Abandonment issues. She'd been the one to walk away from him, but had she felt like he'd abandoned her?

She wasn't looking at him, but pink crept into her cheeks.

"I don't know what happened to his parents, but Rachel said Miles was living with an uncle who passed away. He's probably got trust issues. Maybe even trauma. Some kids need counseling."

Trauma. Like abuse? "Were you ever—?"

Her eyes darted to him and away. She shook her head slightly. "No. I never—" She shrugged, and her body language shifted as her shoulders came up. She closed him off.

"You won't know what his buttons are until you push one of them. Sometimes you'll repeat something that wasn't an issue before, but the second time around he's thinking of the family he's lost and it just hurts. He'll react in anger, because it's too scary to show that he's frightened—"

She stopped suddenly, maybe realizing she'd said too much.

He wanted to reach for her. Wanted it so badly, but he knew he hadn't earned her trust.

So he only nodded and followed her into the house.

· · ·

KAYLA STEPPED INSIDE, aware of Nate following close behind. She'd said too much. She didn't like the assessing look she'd seen in his eyes.

She didn't need his pity, didn't want it. Her childhood had sucked, but it was over. There was no use lingering on the past.

Miles. He was the important one right now.

She found him in the kitchen, cross-legged on the floor with Bando sprawled across his lap, the dog panting happily. He hadn't gotten too close to the Chihuahua, and she watched cautiously from her basket.

It was Miles's open, happy expression that stopped her in her tracks.

He looked up and registered her standing in the doorway, and the joyful expression disappeared instantly. A scowl replaced it, and he nudged Bando off his lap. His eyes skipped away from her as he stood and pushed his hand into his pockets.

Bando approached, waggling all over. She bent to give the dog a rubdown. He kicked one back leg against the floor when she hit a ticklish spot on his side.

"Are you so excited to have someone new to love on you?" she spoke to the dog in a baby voice. "Sure you are."

When she straightened, the cowboy was looking at her with one raised eyebrow, and Miles was just plain staring.

Her cheeks flushed slightly. "He can understand me."

Nate's eyebrow hiked even higher, but he didn't say anything.

"You can pet Bando or his new friend any time you want," she told Miles. "But be careful around our mama. She's pretty protective of her pups, and she hasn't warmed up to me yet."

Miles shrugged, his gaze cutting to the side. "They're just dumb dogs," he mumbled.

She might've believed him, if she hadn't seen him loving on Bando moments ago.

Nate sighed.

But she knew this tactic too. Pretend nothing mattered. If your foster mom knew something was important to you, it could become leverage, or it could be taken away.

"You want to go check out your room? It's the same one as before, but I got a few new things..."

He shrugged, but she turned toward his bedroom and heard him obediently trudging down the hall behind her. Nate brought up the rear. She'd kind of expected him to return to the Triple H by now. She knew being foreman was a big job. Didn't he have things to do?

She paused in the hallway just outside the bedroom door, letting Miles go in ahead of her. She was too aware of Nate at her back, watching everything over her shoulder.

When Miles had stayed overnight the night she'd found him in her barn, she'd had only a mattress—not even a frame or box spring—with mismatched sheets and a pancake of a pillow that had followed her around for years. The walls had been bare. After all, she'd planned to sink any funds she could scrounge up into the rescue. Until Miles.

Yesterday, she'd driven almost an hour to the nearest big box discount store and spent precious money on a simple black bedframe and box spring, a plain navy comforter and sheet set, and two posters of MLB players. She didn't know whether he liked baseball or not, but he was a ten-year-old boy. It was a decent guess.

A chest of drawers and a small desk and chair for him to do his homework completed the room. Simple navy curtains framed the window that had been bare before.

He slowly rounded the bed, letting his hand drag across the comforter. He stopped to look out the window, which had a good view across the yard to the barn and the fields behind. It'd been dark before when she'd brought him in and when he'd tried to sneak out the next morning. This was probably the first time he was seeing the view from the window.

"Do you like it?" she asked

"It's fine." He set his backpack on the end of the bed.

"I think you mean, 'thank you,'" Nate said behind her.

Miles's head snapped up, a hard light entering his eyes.

She didn't have to glance over her shoulder to know Nate was leveling a stare at the boy.

Miles stared right back.

She turned to face Nate, drawing up short because he was *right there*. She put her palm against his chest, intending to nudge him back into the hall, but she got a shock of attraction, like static electricity.

He felt it too, because his surprised gaze shifted down to her.

She jerked her hand away, squeezing and releasing her fingers in a fist, trying to rid herself of the unsettling feeling.

With an effort, she dragged her thoughts back to the issue at hand. "He doesn't need to thank me," she said. She hadn't done any of it for a thank you.

A muscle twitched in Nate's cheek. "We'll have rules in our house. One of the rules will be basic politeness."

Rules. A logical part of her brain said Nate was right, but another part, a place buried deep inside, landed on a long-ago memory of *rules* and *punishment* for taking a snack to fill her empty, grumbling belly.

She had to work to get her jaw unclamped. "There's a time and place for all of that," she said quietly. "Let's just settle in for today. Maybe for a few days."

He opened his mouth, and she knew he would argue, but she wasn't bending on this. "Shouldn't you get back to the Triple H?"

Something passed over his expression before he hid it behind that carefully crafted blankness. Hurt, maybe?

She hated that he could hide like that.

"I took a few days off."

"But—it's calving season."

He cracked a smile at that, but it didn't reach all the way to his eyes. "As much as I appreciate you keeping up with my job..."

That hadn't been what she'd meant at all.

"...it's important for me to be here. My boss understood and gave me the time off. If there's an emergency, I'm close enough to lend a hand."

It's important for me to be here. Why did those words both excite and scare her?

"Fine," she bit out. "But let's table the politeness discussion for later." She called over her shoulder, "I'll make some turkey sandwiches for lunch." She hoped Miles would know to come to the kitchen in a bit.

She moved past Nate in the hallway, trying not to feel the

spark of attraction as their shoulders brushed, trying to ignore the confusing emotions he engendered.

Unfortunately, the memory of the intensity of his words didn't leave her all afternoon.

It's important for me to be here.

What did that mean?

THE AFTERNOON WAS WANING as Nate strode through Kayla's front hall, his duffel bag slung over one shoulder.

He passed Kayla and Miles in the kitchen and didn't miss the glare she shot him or her awareness of his bag. He didn't much care. If they were going to make this marriage look real, he couldn't sleep at the Triple H.

Although it would be a relief to escape the tension that hovered like a black cloud. Kayla had spent the afternoon avoiding him. Miles had mostly kept to his bedroom. Which left Nate at loose ends, something foreign to him. He'd spent more time in her barn, pinpointing where the worst of the termite damage was.

It wasn't as if Nate had *meant* to step on their hot buttons. He felt like an idiot, not knowing that Kayla had so many issues left over from her rotten childhood. And having Miles here seemed to amplify her emotions in some way.

But he was a stubborn guy. He wasn't giving up.

He returned to the kitchen, where Miles sat staring at the empty table's surface. Kayla was doing something—he wasn't sure it could be called cooking—on the stove. The scent of something overcooked and inedible emanated from the trashcan in the far corner. His nose twitched.

The border collie laid beneath the table, head on its paws but clearly watching to see if Kayla was going to drop anything. The Lab paced around and sometimes between her feet. The Chihuahua was still in its corner box.

Nate stopped behind Kayla. She tensed up, but with his bulk blocking her, the kid probably couldn't see that.

"Hi." He pressed a kiss to her temple, smiling at the reflection of her frown in the darkened window. He let her go before she whacked him with the spatula she held.

He stepped back toward the table and placed a comic book on the surface, then slid it over to Miles. Surely the kid couldn't resist Batman. Batman was classic.

The kid raised his eyes to Nate.

"It's for you. Batman was my favorite when I was a kid."

He and his dad had collected the comics together. They'd amassed a huge collection before he'd reached high school. He wondered if dad had thrown them all in the trash after their falling-out.

"Thanks," the kid muttered to the table. But he carefully opened the front flap of the comic. Nate couldn't help noticing his skinny arms and scraped knuckles.

Kayla was peering over her shoulder, but when she caught him looking back at her, she quickly turned back to the stove.

"Want me to feed the mutts?" he asked. He was chafing from all the inactivity today. At the Triple H, he'd be doing a final check of the day's tasks, reassigning things that hadn't gotten finished for the next day and making sure one of the guys was available to do an evening check of the herd.

"They aren't mutts," Kayla said over her shoulder.

He waited, watched as she almost tripped on the lab once more.

"Yeah, I guess," she said.

He didn't smile at the tiny victory, just went to the pantry where he'd seen her retrieve the dog food yesterday. The shelves were completely disorganized. Cans of vegetables and beans were mixed in with cereal boxes and half-empty bags of chips. A shelf in the middle held an incredible amount of junk food. Sugary cereal, Doritos, Oreos and more. She'd obviously raided the snack aisle of the grocery store. All for Miles, no doubt.

The sound of the scoop in the bowl brought both larger dogs to Nate's feet, and he had to shuffle step to avoid stepping on any paws. The little Chihuahua didn't move from her perch in the corner, though her ears perked.

He put the two large bowls on the floor, and the two big dogs began to chow down. Still the Chihuahua didn't move from her spot.

"Here, girl!" he said. He shook her bowl.

Nothing.

Kayla looked over her shoulder again. "She won't eat unless you leave the bowl and we all clear out of the room. I don't know what happened to her before I found her in the barn, but she's still pretty spooked."

He left the two bigger dogs to their food. He was peripherally aware of Miles, who was paying attention covertly but not raising his head from the comic. Kayla was sure he had abandonment issues. Did Miles think they were just going to kick him out if they didn't like him?

What a sad way to live. Nate hated it for the boy. His childhood had been fairly average—his dad's oil money hadn't come into play until Nate had been about ten—and he and his dad didn't have the best relationship now, but he couldn't imagine not having the security of knowing you were going to have a roof over your head.

Nate sat on the floor near the Chihuahua's box with his back against the doorjamb. He rested the small food bowl next to his thigh. The little dog growled at him but didn't bark a yappy bark like he might've expected. He ignored it, and she stopped after several seconds, but she kept giving him the side-eye.

Join the party, he thought. Kayla had been doing the same all day. He didn't know what she expected of him, but he was doing his best to keep things on an even-keel and not press anyone's hot buttons.

The puppies were tiny and crawled sleepily all over their mother. In another few weeks, they'd be getting into everything. Kayla needed to get her kennels up and running. He'd bring it up again later, maybe after Miles was in bed. No use getting into a fight in front of the boy, and he had a feeling Kayla was going to try to reject his help.

Nate kept his gaze on the dog, but spoke to the humans. "Want to play hooky tomorrow? We could all three go down to Dallas and do some shopping for school clothes. Maybe catch a movie or do something else fun."

He was watching close enough that he saw Miles go perfectly still at the table. Except for a nervous tap of his foot beneath the table, he showed no other reaction.

"It's supposed to be his first day at TH Elementary," Kayla

said with a concerned glance that encompassed both of them. At least she didn't seem peeved at his suggestion.

Miles's shoulders dropped just the slightest bit.

"Yeah, but it's a Friday," Nate cajoled. "One day isn't nearly enough to make new friends, so why don't we take a fun day, and he can start on Monday. What do you say, buddy?"

Miles shot him a scathing look. Okay, so he wasn't his buddy.

"I don't care," the kid mumbled.

Nate would disagree based on how hard the boy was trying to play it cool.

"I guess I could call the school and Rachel and make sure it's all right." Kayla turned back to the stove. She didn't see the slight rise of a tiny smile on Miles's mouth, but Nate did.

That was one minuscule victory. Dare he try for a second?

Kayla let the two bigger dogs outside to do their business.

"Here, girl." He spread some kernels of dog food across the tile, tempting the Chihuahua out of her box.

Nothing doing. She just stared at him.

"She won't come out of there," Kayla warned.

He pulled a face. "Pessimist."

She shrugged. "It's not on me if you get bit. I know you're going to stick your hand in there next."

Miles turned his head—apparently, Nate getting bit rated a full-on look—and watched.

Nate loaded a bit of food into his palm and held it out to the dog. How bad could a little bite hurt, anyway? She growled, but Nate didn't flinch or move his hand. He waited her out.

He was rewarded when her little tongue poked out, and she took several pieces from his palm.

He looked up, but Kayla's back was to him. Miles was watching, and Nate winked at the kid, but he just frowned and turned his face away.

When he looked back, the dog was turning its nose up and refusing anything further. But Nate had won two small victories this evening, and it buoyed him. He could win Kayla back. He knew it.

Chapter Four

Kayla was wrapped in an afghan sitting in the darkened living room when she felt, rather than saw, Nate enter from the hallway.

Somewhere along the line, she'd dozed off. Now, awareness of the man had her heart pounding and drawing her fully awake. The clock on the DVD player blinked 12:03, but she hadn't bothered to change it for daylight savings time. Eleven p.m. Why did it feel like the middle of the night?

Nate's presence exhausted her. That had to be it. She'd meant to stay up and work more on the grant proposal paperwork, but now...

The house was silent, except for the slight creak of the floor beneath Nate's sock feet.

She was purposely half-hidden among the throw pillows on the couch, but she wasn't that surprised when Nate came right to her. He'd retired to the master bedroom earlier. She had hoped he'd be sleeping by now.

No such luck.

"What're you doing?" he asked.

"Shh."

She couldn't see his face in the dark but imagined him frowning.

"What're you doing?" At least he'd whispered this time.

"Waiting."

"For what?"

"Miles is going to try to sneak out. Run away."

Now she could imagine confusion cresting his features. Of course, he might not show that emotion either, just hide it behind his blank face.

"I thought we were doing fine. We've planned a fun day for tomorrow. We had a good dinner, even if he was a little quiet."

Yeah, real good dinner. She'd burned the chicken breasts and they'd had to settle for grilled cheese. Smoky grilled cheese.

She couldn't expect him to understand, not if he'd never experienced life as a foster kid. "It's just that when you get used to bad things happening in your life, you don't depend on the good to stick around. A lot of times, you plan to leave before it gets turns bad, because the good never lasts."

She expected him to tell her she was being silly, but he didn't say anything for a long moment, and then, "That sounds...sad."

His voice held a note of compassion that she'd never heard from him before. It threatened to draw her in.

She didn't want his compassion.

She needed to keep distance between them or else she'd risk him playing with her heart all over again.

And she didn't want to think about her childhood. "I'm surprised you're awake," she whispered. "I thought cowboys went to bed with the sun in order to get up with the chickens."

He didn't laugh, just stood there in the darkness, immovable. It started to make her uncomfortable.

"If you aren't going back to bed, you'll need to sit down somewhere out of the way."

"You mean hide?"

"Yes," she said testily. The man made her irritable. Probably because she could so easily start liking him again.

She'd expected him to cross to the overstuffed chair, but he wedged himself to a seated position on the floor between the coffee table and sofa, which meant his muscled shoulder was pressed next to her thigh.

She tried to scoot away, but her couch wasn't that big, and there wasn't anywhere to go. The darkness and the need to keep their voices low made everything seem intimate.

"I thought maybe you were avoiding coming to bed because I was in your bedroom."

It had certainly made her more willing to do the stakeout knowing she could avoid Nate. Not that she was going to admit to it.

"I made a pallet on the floor," he admitted softly. "But if your collie becomes my snuggle buddy, we're going to have words."

They hadn't talked about sleeping arrangements, and making the pallet had been thoughtful. The spot behind her nose stung suspiciously.

He was silent for a long moment, and she almost dreaded whatever he was going to say next.

He drew in a deep breath, and she braced herself.

"Back when we were together, I was pretty self-absorbed. I knew you and Sarah had lived in the group home, but I didn't really give much thought to what that must've been like. I don't know if it would've changed anything that happened between us, but I should've been more considerate about your...background."

That spot behind her nose stung, and she blinked mightily. It was maybe the nicest thing he'd said to her since everything had fallen apart between them.

"It wouldn't have changed anything," she whispered.

For that one night, she'd been perfectly happy, felt like she belonged. But in the light of day, she'd known they weren't a good fit. How could she belong with someone like him?

His head lolled back on the couch cushion. His hair brushed her bare upper arm, and she shivered.

"I know I was a punk kid, but I was gone for you." The whispered admission, the tenderness in his voice, snuck in her heart. "So much that there hasn't been anyone else..."

His words sent her stomach swooping.

"It's really hard to survive on love alone," she said. "And your dad never would've—"

She heard a creak in the hallway. She gripped Nate's shoulder, and he went silent too. Had she imagined it?

No, there it was again. Moments later, she could make out a shadow creeping along the hallway toward the front door.

She reached for the tabletop lamp and flicked it on. The

yellow light illuminated the boy with his jean jacket on and his shoes clutched in his hands.

"Do we really have to do this again?" she asked Miles.

Miles stuck out his chin stubbornly. "You didn't want me then, so why should I stay now?"

His words were sullen and angry, but she knew the hurt behind them.

"I did want you to stay," she said quietly. "But it's important to do things by the book, so I had to notify Ms. Rachel."

Her words struck a chord of guilt in her at the deception she and Nate were pulling. It was for Miles's benefit, but what if they were found out and everything disintegrated? Would that be fair to Miles?

Nate looked at her and for once, she could read the emotion on his face. He was thinking the same thing.

But tonight wasn't the moment to fix the mess she'd gotten them all in.

"I want you here," she said.

"Me too."

Nate's solid statement surprised her, but the look of determination on his face was familiar. How many times during her childhood had she longed to hear words like those? For someone to *want her*.

Miles scowled but marched back to his room.

Nate yawned. "Are you staying out here all night? Or do you want to take turns?"

The thought of spending the night in the same room as Nate was dangerous to her equilibrium. She was letting him in far too much as it was.

"I'll stay. You go to bed." This way was better. Or at least that's what she told herself.

It was a long time before she fell asleep again.

NATE HAD MADE LESS progress in the last twenty-four hours than he'd hoped to. After those few moments in the dark of night where she'd opened up to him, Kayla'd given him the cold shoulder all morning.

Miles was using the silent treatment, and that little

Chihuahua had completely ignored Nate's overtures at breakfast.

Maybe he should just call it a day and go back to bed.

Instead, he found himself packing into the cab of his truck with Miles in the center seat and Kayla in the passenger side. This was going to be a long trip if neither of them wanted to talk.

He kept quiet all of fifteen minutes, about the time it took them to get to the freeway pointed toward Dallas.

"It's almost baseball season," he said, searching for any topic that might be safe. "The middle school still has a team, doesn't it?" This he directed to Kayla.

She nodded. "Sarah's practice got hit up for a sponsorship."

"Are you going to go out for the team?" he asked Miles.

Assuming, of course, that Nate and Kayla got things sorted with the system and the boy got to stay.

Miles shrugged, picking at a string on the knee of his jeans.

"Can you play?"

Another shrug. This was getting tiring. Couldn't the kid make one overture?

"Maybe that's what we do instead of hitting a movie," he said to Kayla over the boy's head. "Hit the batting cages instead. You played a mean game of softball your senior year."

Her eyes lit up, but her smile was cautious. "That was part of the mandatory PE curriculum. I haven't picked up a bat since. I'm sure I've lost any skill I might've had."

"Aw, c'mon." He tapped the steering wheel in time to the country song on the radio. "It'll be fun. I haven't played in years either. I bet it's like riding a bike. And we can teach Tiger here a thing or two."

NATE HAD BEEN a trooper for over two hours of shopping. Getting Miles to cooperate enough to try on any clothes was like leash-training a lazy poodle.

Even the carrot of stopping for ice cream after they were done had barely been any motivation.

She'd planned to make the purchases for Miles—trying not to think about the dwindling balance of her bank account—but

Nate had pulled out his wallet before she'd even had a chance. And he hadn't blinked at the cost of several pairs of jeans, a few shirts, and a new coat, hat and gloves for the boy.

It must be easy to spend the allowance he got from his old man. Oil money. But she wasn't going to complain, not when he was doing it for Miles.

Okay, she wasn't going to complain aloud. She couldn't seem to help it internally.

Nate had cajoled the both of them, and now they were here at a batting cage place he'd looked up on his phone in an industrial part of Dallas she hadn't visited before. Right now, she and Miles stood near the line of available cages while he scouted for a bat and paid the rental fee. It smelled like sweaty gym socks, but Miles didn't seem to mind.

The cage was empty, so she tangled her fingers into the chain length and turned to the boy beside her.

"So what's up?" she asked. "You've been awfully quiet all day."

He shrugged, watching one of the furthest cages where a college-aged kid swung. The bat cracked against a ball as it flew off toward the end of the cage.

"Nervous about school starting?" she asked. "TH Elementary is a good school." But she knew how hard it could be to make friends as the new kid.

His chin jutted upward, and he turned a cool glance on her. "What's up with you? Last I knew, you weren't married."

She'd forgotten about that. The night she'd found Miles in her barn and talked him into a warm meal, he'd asked why she wasn't married.

"It's complicated."

He scowled and averted his face. "Not that complicated to get that they'll take me away when they find out you lied to them."

"It's not a lie. We're really married."

But he was right. Things could get crazy-messy if she couldn't figure a way out of this mess.

"Did you tell Rachel?" she asked.

He shoved his hands in his jeans pockets. His shoulders were hunched beneath his ratty jacket. "Why would I?"

Nate arrived with a bat and two batting helmets in hand. His gaze bounced between her and Miles, and she knew he must've picked up on the tension between them, but he only tossed the smaller of the two helmets to Miles, who caught it awkwardly.

"You two ready to rumble?"

Miles remained silent, which left Kayla to force a smile and step into the batter's box. The unfamiliar helmet was heavy and angled over her eye. In the time she took to adjust it, one slow machine-pitched ball sailed over the plate.

"You missed," Miles said helpfully.

Her face warmed a little. "I didn't even have my bat raised."

Nate linked his fingers in the chain link, and his body language relaxed. She let her eyes skip away from the warmth in his gaze. "She'll get it this time. Just watch, Tiger."

Gosh. No pressure there. She cocked the bat, tensed her grip slightly. The machine *clanked,* and a softball soared toward her. She waited and waited and...swung.

The bat connected with a metallic noise, and energy raced down her arms as she swung through.

It was clearly a foul ball, but it had some good distance on it.

"Nice!" Nate shouted.

She glanced at the two males. Miles was staring at her with interest. "I guess that was okay—for a girl."

Nate winked at her. "It was more than okay. Too bad. I was hoping I'd have to come in there and give you some pointers on your form."

Her face flamed again. Nate could tease and flirt all he wanted, but she was going to hold strong. They weren't right for each other. And Miles had reminded her that they had to get things figured out with the social worker, for his sake.

She couldn't afford to let him down.

Chapter Five

KAYLA WAS STILL TRYING TO FIGURE OUT A SOLUTION
as they drove home.

They were on the freeway, only a mile from the Taylor Hills
exit, when Miles spoke for the first time in a half hour.

"What's that?" he asked, pointing to something off the road.

Nate slowed the truck before she'd even spotted the splotch
of red on the pavement off the shoulder of the road. Just beyond
it lay a small golden dog lying in a pool of blood.

Nate said, "It's probably—"

"It's moving!" Miles exclaimed.

Her insides tightened into a ball of anxiety, hurt, and fear.
She and Nate exchanged a quick glance as he slowed the truck
and came to a stop well past the animal.

"If it was hit on the highway, there's a good chance the dog is so
badly injured it won't make it," she said quietly. She knew it, but
knowing the reality didn't soothe the ache that came from seeing the
injured animal. Had the car that hit it even slowed or just kept going?

Miles's expression tightened, shadows chasing behind his
eyes. "Can we check on it? Please?"

The plea was the most open piece of communication he'd
offered since his arrival.

Nate recognized it, too, because he rested a big, gentle hand on the boy's shoulder. "It can be dangerous pulling off to the side of the road," he said. "Will you promise to stay in the truck and let me and Kayla check it out?"

Miles nodded gravely.

Kayla shoved open her door and climbed out as Nate shut off the truck and pocketed the keys on his way out the driver's side.

They hustled toward the injured dog.

"Injured animals are sensitive," she said. "It might be inclined to bite, and it's probably scared."

They drew near, and she could see one of its back legs was completely useless as it dragged itself along the ground. Blood was visible at the corners of its mouth.

She knelt just out of reach of bite, just in case. "Hey, there, baby."

She couldn't help that her eyes welled up with tears as the animal whined in pain. It panted heavily, in obvious distress.

"It's probably got internal bleeding," Nate said, concern in his voice. "Even if we can get it to the vet, it's not going to make it."

"You can't think like that." She swiped of fingers beneath her eyes. "Maybe it's not that bad."

"Honey, he can't move that leg."

She blinked hard again. "Can we get him in the truck?"

"I've got an old blanket in the cab."

He rushed away as she edged closer to the dog. He returned a moment later.

They wrapped it and put it in the truck bed, and all the while, the animal yelped and whined.

The sounds hit her right in the heart, and she had to wipe her face again as she stepped back from the vehicle. She pretended Nate couldn't see and thankfully, he did, too.

"We can't just leave it to slide around," she said, the thought just now occurring to her. There wasn't really room in the single cab for it to ride up front.

"You drive." He tossed her his keys, and she fumbled them but caught them before they hit the ground. "Call your sister on the way."

She well knew how a cowboy's truck was more than just a ride. Nate was handing over his keys, just like that?

It was probably because Sarah wouldn't know what to make of it if he called. That's what she told herself, anyway.

KAYLA TOUCHED the small golden dog, fondling its ear.

It was unresponsive, out from the anesthesia Sarah had administered upon her arrival. Sarah and Kayla had worked in the ranch house kitchen, which looked more like a surgical suite now than the room where she so often burned bacon and scrambled eggs. Nate had taken Miles and the dogs on a long walk, promising to stay away from the house until Kayla or Sarah gave him the all-clear.

"I'll need you to steady her, here. Tightly," Sarah instructed.

Kayla blinked back tears, knowing Sarah would kick her out if she broke down. She was thankful her sister had been on a house call near the Triple H and Kayla's property.

Sarah was a large-animal doctor. Dogs weren't her specialty, though she'd scrubbed in for surgeries with the partners at her vet practice when needed. She must've heard the desperation and fear in Kayla's voice, because she'd agreed to see the animal at Kayla's place instead of advising them to take it in to the practice. It was after hours, anyway, and the clinic would be closed.

"Once we get the joint back in place, I'll tape it up and put on a sling. Then we can look at some of the road rash."

Sarah's first order of business had been checking for internal bleeding. She hadn't found anything worrisome and thought the blood at the dog's mouth had perhaps been from a bitten tongue. The dislocated hip was still worrisome. If it didn't heal properly, the entire limb could be unusable.

Kayla held the dog steady as Sarah manipulated the leg with laser focus.

"You want to tell me what the Triple H foreman is doing hanging around you and Miles?"

Kayla could play dumb, but her sister was too smart for that. Plus, she was in enough hot water with the slight fib about her situation to the social worker. It had to be the truth for her sister.

"Do you remember—I think you were in your first year of vet school—when I took a long weekend trip to Vegas?"

Sarah grunted as she pulled the dog's leg with both hands. "Do I remember the weekend you disappeared and didn't tell me you'd been to Vegas until after the fact? The weekend I called the cops three times to file a missing persons report? *That* weekend?"

Heat flared into Kayla's cheeks. Sarah shifted, moving around the dog's body to attempt the limb at a different angle.

"Um... I might've done something really stupid that weekend."

Sarah didn't speak for several moments. "Stupid, like blowing an entire month's paycheck on blackjack? Or stupid, like getting married?"

Kayla's stomach swooped low. "Um, the second one. To Nate."

Sarah didn't stop what she was doing, but Kayla could feel her sister's energy change. Maybe it was a cop-out, telling her sister when she couldn't fully react. Too bad. Sarah fairly vibrated, but Kayla couldn't tell whether it was curiosity or anger that had her sister wired. Suddenly, the dog's hip and leg shifted, and the ball of the hip slid back into place with a click. Sarah palpitated the joint, her fingers pressing into fur and flesh.

"How in the heck did that happen?" Sarah asked. "You weren't even dating. Wait—I need to do an x-ray. But we're not done with this. Not by a long shot."

Sarah shooed Kayla out of the room while she operated the portable x-ray machine. Kayla stood in the living room, hands hanging uselessly by her sides. She and Sarah had always had a good relationship. Why was she so scared of Sarah finding out about her past mistake?

Sarah'd always been the smart one. The one with the plans. Plans that she executed with skillful precision.

Kayla was the screw up. Always had been.

When she called Kayla back into the room, the machine was off and resting on the floor and Sarah was taping up the hip.

"So...?" Sarah asked.

Kayla stood near the table and wished she could do something useful, something to focus her attention on. She shifted her feet. "Nate and I had been casual friends during my senior year. He was a year older."

Sarah nodded as if she remembered, her attention on the dog.

"But I'd always had a crush on him, and he did ask me out a few weeks before we took off that weekend. It was kind of a whirlwind. We saw each other every day and talked all night on the phone—twice. I thought I was in love, but..."

Sarah finished with the wrap and moved to examine a gash on the dog's shoulder, maybe where it had met the pavement when the car had hit it. She was silent for a long time. Did she think Kayla had been stupid for doing what she'd done?

Finally, Sarah spoke. "I can't believe Chase never mentioned it."

"No one knew." At least, she'd never told anyone. She hadn't asked Nate outright, but she had the sense he hadn't told anyone either.

"Well, that makes me feel slightly better," Sarah muttered. "Why didn't *you* ever tell me?"

Something hot and hard lodged in Kayla's throat. She cleared her throat. "I don't know. I was...ashamed at first. For having made this giant mistake." Her hand fluttered in the air. It was mostly true. There was a part of her, a huge part, that had secretly hoped Nate would care enough to come after her, to fight for her. She shrugged, pushing that thought into the deep recesses of her heart. "And then it was over. Or, it was supposed to be. Apparently, the marriage was never annulled. Legally, we're still married."

Chapter Six

LATER THAT NIGHT, KAYLA SAT ON THE FLOOR IN THE semi-dark kitchen with the injured dog by her side. The Chihuahua was curled up in her box with her pups, resting but not asleep.

The golden dog had come out of the anesthesia. and Sarah seemed happy with his immediate recovery. She'd given orders to keep the boy as immobile as possible for a week and suggested Kayla crate him at night.

But Kayla wanted to watch over him, at least for these first few hours. Nate and Miles had gone to bed around ten, but she couldn't face her pillow. Not yet.

Talking about what had happened between her and Nate a decade ago had brought everything back to the surface with startling clarity.

She could still vividly remember waking up in the Vegas hotel room. With Nate.

She'd been self-conscious in the light of day, aware of her bed-head and morning breath. She'd hurriedly dressed even as he was waking up. Awkward didn't begin to describe it.

And then there was the weight of his ring on her finger. A tangible connection to him.

He'd rolled over in the big bed and smiled a lazy, warm smile that had her stomach rolling over like a puppy begging for a belly scratch.

She was helpless against his charm, unable to respond with anything other than a silly answering smile. He crooked a finger, inviting her back to the bed, but she hesitated.

His phone rang, buzzing noisily from the nightstand, interrupting them with reality.

He picked it up and glanced quickly at the display. And was instantly distracted. "I have to take this."

He stood and wrapped the sheet around his lower half as he crossed the room, raising the phone to his ear. "Dad. What's up?" He lowered his voice, but the hotel room was small.

"No, I'm not on campus yet." He shot a quick glance her way and offered a smile that, for the first time since they'd begun their courtship, felt false. He turned his back to her, faced the window. "Classes don't start until Wednesday."

Her stomach swooped low, a warning. They hadn't talked through logistics. They'd been in Taylor Hills yesterday when he'd blurted, *Let's get married.*" Two plane tickets, a rented dress, and a licensed minister later, and here they were. In the whirlwind of excitement and the crazy high of wanting to belong to someone, she hadn't even thought about where they might live. She'd driven up to Taylor Hills for the weekend to visit a high school friend, and she'd been living with her sister Sarah in the city in a cheap apartment near Sarah's vet school. She hadn't planed to enroll in college and instead wanted to take a gap year and sock away money.

But reality was intruding. Nate's dad was paying for his college education. She'd only met the oil mogul twice, but she knew he was hard-nosed and had expectations of his son. Ones that likely didn't involve a hasty marriage or a dirt-poor wife with no connections.

"No, I'm not in Taylor Hills again." Nate's voice had gone low and had an edge of stubbornness in it that almost made him sound like a little kid doing something he knew was wrong.

"Why is it so important for you to know? ...Fine. I'm in Las Vegas. No, it's not a guy's weekend. No, I didn't do something stupid."

But the last words had the slightest inflection, as if he were lying...

And sudden fear shivered through her.

He hung up moments later and turned to toss the phone onto the bed. He gave her another of those false smiles. Tiny stress lines fanned out from the corners of his eyes.

"You're still under his thumb." She sat on the edge of the bed because her suddenly numb knees wanted to buckle.

"No, I'm not." His jaw clenched, though, and she heard that same little-kid stubborn tone in his voice. Denial.

"You'll do whatever he tells you to do. Or he'll what...cut your allowance?"

She suffered a tiny flare of jealousy. It must be nice to have enough money not to worry about expenses that exceeded a paycheck.

Nate's expression cooled. "I try to be respectful. He's paying for my schooling."

She hated not being able to read him. What was he feeling? What emotions was he hiding from her?

She really hated feeling like she could ruin things for him.

She knew how expensive college was. Sarah'd scraped by with scholarships and loans. But Kayla also knew it was more than that for Nate. Hadn't he mentioned before how his father had his life planned out for him? A college degree, join the family oil business, probably live wherever daddy told him to.

"What's he going to say when you tell him about me?" Her voice was weak as she forced the question out. "I notice you didn't tell him we got married."

His wince was slight, but it was there. "We'll figure it out."

We'll figure it out. It wasn't much to go on. She'd done an impulsive thing last night, and now she was good and scared about what was coming next.

"Am I supposed to move into your dorm room? Are you going to get a job?"

All the details she hadn't thought about when she'd been caught up in the blush of love.

He ran both hands through his hair. "I don't know."

"Is he going to cut you off because of me?"

"No." But he didn't sound sure. "I said, he doesn't run my life."

Nervous energy pushed her off the bed. "What if he tells you to annul the marriage?"

"He won't. Kayla, calm down. You're blowing things out of proportion."

She was nineteen and on her own. She'd always been on her own, and she desperately craved security. Craved the home she'd never had. Craved a man to love her, just her. For one bright, shining moment, she'd thought she'd found all of that.

But she wouldn't ruin his life to satisfy her cravings.

"We can't do this," she said.

"Honey, we already did."

His joke fell flat, and the half smile faded when she didn't respond.

"I think we *should* have it annulled." The words dropped from her lips before she'd really thought them through. Impulsiveness, meet impulsiveness. Her voice was shaking as badly as she was. "Maybe we can talk again when you've figured out how to make your own way in life."

Kayla started and woke up, her present circumstances as hard and cold as the floor where she sat. How had she dozed in the wake of her memories? She ran one hand along the dog's back. Still breathing, still asleep.

It was Kayla's heart that was pounding against her breastbone.

What a mistake the whole thing had been.

She'd gone back to Sarah's tiny city apartment to find her sister frantic that she'd been out of touch for two days.

She hadn't told Sarah or anyone else. Had assumed Nate filed the annulment paperwork after she'd demanded it.

She hadn't slept for three days, her focus on her silent phone.

He never called. Maybe she'd wounded his pride, or maybe he hadn't really loved her after all.

She still didn't know, and she had no idea why he was in her life now.

. . .

NATE STOOD in the darkened hallway outside the kitchen, hesitating because he was a chicken butt.

Only the bulb above the stove was on in the kitchen, but between the dim light and the moon shining through the window, it was enough for him to see Kayla sitting on the floor next to the dog, which was laid out on a folded blanket. The border collie and Lab had been banished to Miles's room for the night, but the Chihuahua remained, tucked in her basket with her sleeping pups.

He needed to make a decision. Go in there, or go to bed. Where he wouldn't sleep.

Because...

I thought I was in love with him...ashamed of making such a giant mistake.

Kayla's words from earlier reverberated through his skull, bouncing around until he had to grit his teeth against the pain of them.

He shouldn't be hurt. Hadn't she already said she believed their quickie wedding was a mistake? She'd said it that next morning, and several times when she'd driven out to the Triple H the other day to berate him.

There was a part of him that had hoped she'd been lying.

Maybe he was the one lying to himself, believing she might still have feelings for him in some dormant part of her heart.

That's what he got for eavesdropping—a whole lot of turmoil.

He might've shifted, or maybe the floorboard beneath his sock feet creaked, but she lifted her head. He didn't know if she could see into the hall, but maybe she was sensitive, like he was. He was certainly aware when she was near.

So he went in. Because he wasn't going to sleep anyway, even if he went to his makeshift pallet on the floor of her bedroom.

"How is he?" He settled on the floor beside her, his knees popping like an old man's, thanks to one too many spills from the back of a horse. The cabinet knob bit into his back and he adjusted slightly, his shoulder brushing hers.

The Chihuahua shifted in her basket, putting her chin on the edge. Her eyes were open, watchful.

Kayla looked down on the dog at her side. Her fingers

brushed over the dog's ear, a gentle touch. "He's sleeping. Sarah seemed confident that he'd be okay."

Emotion filled her voice, and he knew she must be exhausted, because she usually didn't like him to see how affected she was.

"Why don't you let me take a shift? Get a couple of hours sleep."

She leaned her head back against the cabinets. He could see the silhouette of her slender throat and the line of her jaw. "Maybe in a minute."

It was on the tip of his tongue to ask if she would ever forgive him for letting her go ten years ago.

He'd fallen hard for her. He could even pinpoint the exact moment. Maybe it was when she'd ordered a chocolate shake with an extra scoop of chocolate ice cream. He'd never forget that adorable hint of a smile. He'd been a goner.

His feelings hadn't changed in all this time.

He didn't know if he could win over Kayla tonight, but he'd packed a secret weapon to try to win the Chihuahua. He'd kept a piece of bacon from the burger he and Miles had grabbed in town earlier, and it was now crumbled in his pocket. He placed a tiny piece on the floor, halfway between himself and the dog's basket.

"She's not going to come to you," Kayla said.

"Maybe not." But he wasn't the kind of man to give up. And that thought crystallized in his skull.

He couldn't give up on the dog. And he wouldn't give up on Kayla.

And as long as she'd give him a chance, let him stay close, he wouldn't give up.

He left the bacon on the floor and rested his hand on the floor next to his thigh.

"I've been wanting to ask you something." He felt her tense beside him at his words. "It's nothing horrible."

"What?"

"What's behind your passion for the dogs? You're like a magnet for injured and abandoned ones..."

He heard her quiet breaths and wondered if she would answer.

"Growing up, I always wanted a pet. Did you have one?"

He smiled in the dark. "A German Shepherd. She would wait for me to get off the bus. Every day, even when it was freezing cold, even when it was snowing. She died my senior year of high school."

"I'm sorry." She was silent for a moment too long. "Sarah and I were bounced from foster home to foster home and then to the group home when I was eight. I would've given anything to have a dog to come home to."

It was the second time she'd spoken of her early years, and the difference between her childhood and his was stark. He'd taken for granted the stability, the simple things that she'd never had.

He settled his hand over hers. She startled but tried to cover it. She allowed his touch for only a moment before she gently disengaged their hands.

"When I was ten, I snuck every stray I could find into the group home. Sarah helped cover for me, but I took care of them. I always got found out. But it never stopped me from trying again."

He chuckled. "I can see that."

"When I was thirteen, I was walking home from school and found a cat that someone had starved and then dumped. It was so weak."

He was suddenly unsure whether he wanted to hear this story.

"I didn't sneak around this time. I took her straight to the Home Mom and begged her to let me help the cat. Just for a few days, and then I'd find it a new home. I just wanted her to live."

Kayla's voice trailed off. He wanted to touch her again, wanted to offer comfort, but she'd already moved away from him, and he was afraid to reach for her again. Afraid his touch would silence her story.

"She refused. She made me put the cat outdoors and wouldn't let me feed it or give it any water. The next morning, it was dead. I could've saved it, if I'd been allowed."

She didn't sniffle. Her voice was matter-of-fact as she recited the facts of her story. But obviously, it had made a huge impact on her.

He didn't know what to say, how to offer her comfort. Silence stretched.

He'd been teasing when he'd said the words. *You're like a magnet for injured and abandoned ones...* How many others had driven past the dog on the highway without stopping?

Kayla saw the needy animals. And she did something about it.

Back then, Kayla had longed to save her kitten, when it was she who'd needed rescuing herself. He'd had a chance to play the knight, to fight for her, that night in Vegas. And what had he done? Left her out in the cold.

At least she'd tried with her kitten. He'd done nothing.

Was it really any wonder she didn't want to believe his good intentions now?

When the silence was broken, it came from an unexpected direction. Soft clicks from tiny nails as the Chihuahua climbed out of her basket and crossed the floor, ever so slowly, toward that piece of bacon.

Kayla stilled beside him.

The Chihuahua licked the bacon off the floor and daintily chewed it up.

He moved slowly as he reached into his pocket and brought out more of the bacon crumbs.

The dog eyed him.

Nate laid out three more pieces, and the Chihuahua grabbed them up with increasing abandon.

He kept the remaining pieces on his palm, open and flat on the floor.

The Chihuahua sat back on her haunches, looking at him expectantly.

"C'mon, girl." He whispered the words as an encouragement, not to rush her. And he waited her out.

Seconds passed before the dog moved hesitantly forward. Nate didn't move an eyelash. The dog ate from his hand, its tongue tickling as it lapped up the bacon pieces. It even touched his palm with one tiny paw.

"Good girl," he breathed.

And then, to his surprise, the Chihuahua leaned against his

thigh. He risked reaching out, and it allowed him to run one finger over its head in a caress.

"I can't believe she's letting you pet her," Kayla whispered, though she too was perfectly still.

"What can I say? I'm a trustworthy guy."

Kayla snorted softly. He didn't look, but he had the sense that she was smiling.

The dog returned to her basket and curled among the sleeping pups.

Kayla sighed softly. He could only hope she was softening toward him as well.

She yawned so big, her jaw cracked.

"Why don't you let me take a shift?" he asked for the second time. "Catch a few hours of sleep."

"I will in a minute." But this time her voice was sleepy and slow.

And then her head drooped. Slowly, it lowered until it rested on his shoulder.

He barely breathed, not wanting to wreck the moment. He could feel each of her breaths soft against the skin at his neck.

He slowly wrapped his arm around her shoulders. Both dogs slept on. And Kayla relaxed against him, falling into a deep sleep.

Chapter Seven

THE INJURED DOG WAS MUCH IMPROVED THE NEXT morning, so much so that Kayla decided to crate it to keep it from bounding all around the house on three legs. She had a medium-sized metal crate, which she set up in the kitchen so the dog wouldn't feel lonely as it recovered.

Midmorning, she looked up from a pile of grant paperwork and realized it was entirely too quiet in the house. Where had Miles and Nate gone off to? A moment later, she realized the pounding she heard wasn't the headache she'd thought it was.

It was coming from outside.

A step onto the back porch oriented her. The sounds were coming from the direction of the barn, so she headed that way.

She wasn't sure she was ready to see Nate. Her feelings for him were a confusing mix of attraction, trust, and fear, fear that eventually, he'd figure out she wasn't worth the trouble and disappear from her life all over again.

She'd fallen asleep on him last night, snuggled into his shoulder. It hadn't lasted long—he'd woken her and sent her to bed, promising to stay awake with the injured animal through the night.

She'd managed to sleep in her own bed until the early hours, when she'd relieved him to watch over the dog again.

He'd said he was trustworthy. It had been in response to the little Chihuahua, but the simple statement had resonated with Kayla, touching something deep inside her. She'd slept peacefully, trusting him to take care of the dog.

Trusting him. It had seemed wise in the dead of night when her bed had beckoned her, but now, she wasn't sure what to think. Could Nate be trusted? Could anybody?

She followed the pounding to the barn, where the sounds of hammering were accompanied by wood splintering, boyish shouts, and dog barks. Was something wrong? She sped up, almost running by the time she hit the open door.

Inside, things were chaos.

The dogs were frolicking in the back, barking and play wrestling with each other. Nate watched Miles swing a small mallet at the outside barn wall. There was already a gaping hole there, jagged edges silhouetted against the bright outdoors. Splinters and wood chunks and sawdust covered the floor and ground outside, while dust and dirt hovered in a cloud.

She propped her hands on her hips. "What do you think you're doing?"

Miles and Nate turned toward her, both wearing matching infectious grins.

"We're demo-ing!" Miles crowed, holding the hammer above his head.

Nate was close enough to gently guide the boy's hand and the tool back down to a safe level at his side.

She leveled a look on Nate. "I don't remember agreeing to let you demolish my barn."

He winked at her. "I knew you wouldn't complain about free labor. I did a little more looking, identified the major problem areas. I think if you replace this one beam here"—he patted a huge wooden beam that extended to the ceiling—"you'll be golden. The termite damage isn't as extensive as we thought."

We, huh? As if he had a say in what happened in *her* barn. As if he'd been around, been involved. As if he'd cared a whit about her until four days ago. And anyway, what did he know? "Are you an exterminator, now?"

"No, but the barn at the Triple H had the same issues. We had ourselves a nice construction project last year."

He seemed proud of the fact that he'd knocked down her

barn wall, at ease with the destruction that surrounded him like a war zone.

"This isn't the Triple H. This is my property. And now, I've got to pay to replace that wall."

Nate shrugged casually. "I have some money saved up."

And that sent her temper into a tailspin. "I don't want your daddy's money, and I don't want you wrecking my life! I didn't even want you here in the first place!"

Miles stared, wide-eyed, as her temper spent itself.

She was left breathing hard, as if she'd run a sprint. Her heart was pounding, and the raw hurt on Nate's face made her want to call the words back. But she didn't. She turned and left the barn.

N ATE FELT NUMB ALL OVER.

The kid was still standing there, watching him. He tried to find some kind of balance in the maelstrom that was his emotion, tried to dredge up some kind of smile.

"I'm sorry you had to see that," he said.

Miles was quiet and pale, a contrast to the kid who'd been whooping and slamming that hammer into the wall a moment ago.

"It's—" he started, but Miles shook his head.

"Complicated, right? That's what Kayla said the other night."

The border collie scrambled close, and Nate did a quick visual check to ensure there were no rusty nails in the area before he bent to pet the dog. Miles followed suit and was soon knocked to his butt from the collie's mad scramble for affection.

The boy laughed, but it was short-lived as he looked up at Nate with shadowed eyes.

"Complicated is right," Nate agreed. "I've been in love with Kayla since I was twenty. I knew her from high school, but I was almost a college sophomore before she swept me off my feet."

Miles wrinkled his nose. Maybe that was too much information for the boy.

"I messed up back then—pushed her too fast, and she got scared. I'm trying not to do the same thing now."

Though obviously, his words, his attempts to help, had scared her again. How could he make her understand how invested he was in their relationship? He'd thought she would get it if he bought into the dog rescue, but he'd obviously misjudged.

"So...you're not giving up?" Miles asked tentatively.

"Not by a long shot, kid."

Because behind Kayla's parting shot, he'd seen her vulnerability.

KAYLA AVOIDED Nate while she and Miles spent a couple of hours watching over the injured dog and talking pets together. He was quiet, hesitant, but finally started to open up.

Sarah came out for a while to check on the dog, and then asked Kayla to follow her out to her truck.

"Everything's fine," Kayla said as Sarah tucked her black bag into the cab.

Sarah just raised her eyebrows.

Kayla prayed her sister wouldn't notice her bloodshot eyes. She wished she'd thought to put on some dark sunglasses before coming outside. After she'd yelled at Nate in the barn earlier, she'd retreated to her bedroom and cried her eyes out.

"It's just a lot," she told her sister when Sarah's pointed silence continued. "Miles's arrival, the injured dog, and Nate in the middle of it all."

Sarah touched Kayla's elbow. "Are you thinking maybe this could be something real? Something more than just a mistake you made one weekend ten years ago?"

Kayla shook her head tightly. "It's too late for us."

Sarah smiled wryly. "I wasn't expecting Chase when my life imploded, but he was just what I needed."

"This isn't like that." Her sister deserved love. The jerk she'd been engaged to hadn't appreciated Sarah or her heart for livestock, and the former Triple H hand that had won her heart was one of the rare good catches.

Sarah squeezed her arm. "We both have a hard time trusting," she said. "Comes with our awful childhoods. But every once in a while, when it's the right person...maybe it's okay to let someone in."

Kayla offered a tight smile because that seemed like what her sister expected. Sarah got in her truck and drove off, leaving Kayla standing alone in the drive.

Sarah didn't understand Kayla's history with Nate. He'd let her walk away once. Wouldn't he just do the same if things got difficult now?

That thought put a bitter, hot lump in her throat.

The house wasn't silent when she re-entered it. Voices echoed from the kitchen. Nate and Miles.

Afraid they were disturbing the dog, she strode down the hall to interrupt them. But the golden dog was lying quietly on its bed, watching.

Nate and Miles stood shoulder to shoulder at the counter, both their sleeves rolled to their elbows. It was impossible not to notice Nate's tanned, muscled forearms and Miles's skinny wrists.

"What do you think you're doing?"

The both startled and whirled toward her, Miles with a slightly-guilty look and Nate with an implacable smile.

Nate raised a zucchini to salute her. "Making supper."

"You don't have to do that."

Nate and Miles exchanged a loaded look.

"What?" she demanded.

Nate whispered something to Miles, who shook his head, eyes wide. "No way."

Nate turned to her and waved the zucchini. "We want to treat you tonight."

"It's really—"

"*Really*," he interrupted. "We can't take another night of burned grilled cheese."

She tensed as his words registered.

He grinned. "Don't get all up in arms. We appreciate your effort. Right, kid?"

She slid her attention to Miles. "Do you feel the same way?"

He averted his eyes and bit his lip. That was as obvious as if he'd said yes.

"Fine." She threw up her hands. "If you want to cook your own supper, you go ahead."

If they burned it, it was on them.

"Nuh-uh, don't leave," Nate said. "We've got a job for you."

She hesitated in the doorway. Nate abandoned his vegetable and cornered her. "Spend time with us," he said quietly. His arm snaked around her, his hand settled at her waist.

The contact sent a shockwave through her, but somehow her feet had become cemented to the floor.

He brushed a kiss at her temple. "Give me a chance," he breathed against her skin.

She danced away from him. "What's my job?"

He grinned again and pointed to a cutting board on the counter. "You're on chopping duty."

He blew kisses to the Chihuahua, and she gave an enthusiastic tail wag as he crossed back to the counter.

"What're you making?" she asked as she stood beside him and picked up the chopping knife.

"Ratatouille."

She wrinkled her nose, slanting a glance at his broad-shouldered frame. "Rat-a-what? Is that as bad as it sounds?"

His grin didn't fade as he shook his head. "I saw it on a kid's movie with Scarlett Hale once. I make it every once in a while, when it's my turn to cook for the cowhands."

"You have to cook for them?"

His attention was focused at the parchment paper he was spreading across the counter, but his words were just a hint too casual. "I earn my keep. I have since my twentieth birthday."

She sliced into the onion, the immediate pungent scent making her eyes smart and nose water. "What's that supposed to mean?"

He nodded to Miles, who stood at his other elbow. "Maybe we can postpone this conversation until later."

"If you two are cooking I'll just..." Miles jerked his thumb toward the hallway.

"No way," Nate said. "I need you in here, man, to help counter..." He nodded his head toward Kayla.

"Hey!"

But Miles grinned.

"I'm a little surprised you don't think cooking is a girl thing," Kayla said.

Nate winked. "Nothing girly about it. Lots of the best chefs are men. Plus, it's a great way to impress ladies. How're we doing with that?" This time, he tipped his head toward her, letting the too-long hair fall forward into his eyes. He wiggled his eyebrows at her.

Kayla couldn't help a giggle.

Behind Nate, Miles was still smiling.

"You're doing fine," she whispered.

And he was. More than fine.

MILES and the dogs all abed, Kayla wandered out to the barn. After their dinner—which hadn't been half-bad—Nate had done the dishes and then disappeared out the back door. Had he come out here? Why?

Night had fallen, and she had her arms crossed over her chest to keep her coat closed.

He was in cleaning up, tossing large chunks of the barn wall into a pile and smaller chunks into a trash barrel he must've dragged in from somewhere.

He glanced up as she stopped in the doorway. "Everything okay?"

"Yeah."

"I'll be back in a few. Just wanted to clean up a little out here."

That was kind of him, especially after she'd let her temper loose on him earlier.

"What did you mean earlier in the kitchen?"

He tossed a large chunk into the bucket; it landed with a loud *clang*. He dusted his leather gloves. "You were right."

She moved to help him lift a huge piece and carry it outside through the hole in the wall. "What do you mean?"

"The morning after we got married. You said I was under my dad's thumb. You were right."

Wow. That was unexpected. He must've read her disbelief in her expression, because he chuckled, though there was a slightly bitter tinge to the sound.

"After you walked out on me, I went back to school. What else was I going to do? But your words stuck in my head like a burr under a saddle. By mid-semester, I'd started counting all the things I'd wanted to do in the past that my dad had talked or manipulated me out of doing. We had a falling out at Christmas. I didn't go back to school."

She frowned. "I'm sorry."

He shrugged. "It would've happened eventually, I think. You just made me see it sooner."

"You still don't see him?"

"About once a year, at Christmas. My mom tries to smooth things over, but we pretty much don't talk. My younger brother Trevor is his golden boy, now."

It hurt to think of Nate, the outgoing, funny, steady man, losing out on a relationship with his father.

Nate straightened and looked at her. "So, you see, I don't get an allowance, and any money in my bank account is mine and mine alone. And if I want to help my wife get her business up and running, it's my decision, not anyone else's."

His quiet, determined words sank into a dry, desert place in her heart. But the soil was so arid that the water sank right through.

"We're not really married." She barely got the words out, low and quiet.

He didn't flinch. "We could be. We're married on paper and have been for a decade. And I...I care about you. About Miles. That kid is really special."

She swallowed hard. Could she stay married to Nate, for Miles's sake?

"I think we go together to visit Rachel first thing Monday morning, when Miles is in school, and come clean. Tell her that we're planning to stay together."

As easy as that.

Only it wasn't easy for her to imagine. What would their life together look like in two years? In ten? She'd never lived in one place that long, not in her entire life.

So many questions, objections, barraged her mind. She grabbed the easiest one. "What about your job? Don't you have to be on the Triple H constantly?"

He shrugged. "I can talk to Matt, but I already know what he'll say. Your place is close enough for me to take an occasional night shift when it's needed, to be available for emergencies when it's not the workday. It's only a two-minute commute."

Her chest felt tight, and her skin prickled all over.

He stepped closer, tugging off his gloves. He tossed them on a discarded board. "If you don't want me, say so." He reached out and touched the back of her wrist with one finger. "Is that it?" His voice was low. Dangerous.

She shook her head, unable to push words past the tightness in her throat.

His hand moved to slide around her waist. He was hot, his touch a brand against her lower back as he edged closer.

And she didn't stop him. His arm came entirely around her waist, and he used his opposite hand to tilt her chin up. He brushed her lips with a tender kiss, one that took her right back to the kiss he'd given her as the Vegas minister had pronounced them man and wife.

The bottom dropped out of her stomach as his hand moved to cup her jaw. He deepened the kiss. She was drowning in him, in the sensations that promised everything she'd ever wanted...

He ended the kiss with one last sweep of his lips against her cheek.

She realized she was squeezing the material of his shirt in both hands. She let go, attempting to smooth out the wrinkles she'd made.

"Remember?" he asked, his breath warming her temple.

She pushed lightly on his chest, and he let her go, his arm falling away from her waist.

"Attraction was never the problem between us."

His head tilted toward her, though he didn't reach for her again. "It's more than that. At least, for me."

His words were like helium inflating a balloon inside her. If she let go of the strings, she could fly away...

She wavered. Her heart wanted to trust what he was proposing. Trust that a marriage between them wouldn't implode, trust that they could work things out.

But hadn't life experience told her how dangerous believing could be? Taught her that she should protect herself at all costs?

"Let me win your heart, Kayla." His voice was sure and strong, the confident cowboy she'd grown to appreciate the past few days.

How could he ask that? Didn't he know he'd already won her heart?

<h1 style="text-align:center">Chapter Eight</h1>

Monday morning, Kayla was strung tightly with tension as she waited in the hallway of the social services building, Nate beside her.

The county building was sterile, cold. The old linoleum tile and bare white walls were cold and unwelcoming. Being here was bringing back horrid memories from her childhood.

She'd sat on those cold plastic chairs too many times, feet dangling, waiting to find out what foster house they were shipping her to next. Thankfully, Sarah had been by her side during those scary times in her early childhood.

But today, Nate's hand closed over hers. The warmth of his skin was a shock against her chilled fingers.

"You're freezing." He turned to her, took both of her hands in his and rubbed them.

She kept her eyes on the shoulder of his shirt.

But apparently, he didn't need to see her eyes.

"Stop freaking out," he said quietly.

She accepted the warmth of his hands, the way he drew her closer and tucked her into his chest.

"Nothing bad is happening today," he whispered into her hair.

"You can't know that," she whispered back. They hadn't told Miles what their plan was before they'd dropped him off at the elementary school, but he'd somehow read her tension. He'd walked into the building with shadows in his eyes. When she and Nate had left him, he'd sent one last look their way before disappearing into a classroom with the assistant principal.

If Rachel wasn't understanding, Miles could be ripped away from them. Today.

"Kayla? Nate?" Rachel greeted them with a smile, but her concern was palpable. She motioned them to enter a small room, one that Kayla remembered.

It was decorated differently now. Posters with inspirational sayings brightened the walls. An African violet on the corner of the desk brought a splash of color to the otherwise drab room.

"Are you having a problem with Miles?" Rachel asked. The *already* was implied.

"No." Nate shook his head while he waited for Kayla to sit in one of the chairs in front of Rachel's desk. He sat in the other, never releasing Kayla's hand.

"There's something we need to come clean about," he said. His shoulders were straight and confident.

She startled in her chair at his blunt words. She wanted to tell him to take them back. No doubt it was too late now.

Rachel's expression didn't reveal much, but her slight frown sent a shiver down Kayla's spine. This was a bad idea.

Nate squeezed her hand.

"Kayla and I got married in Las Vegas just over ten years ago. We were young, and I was stupid, and we went our separate ways soon after. We never legally ended the marriage."

He looked right at Kayla, and the intensity in his gaze had her heart responding against her will. "I never stopped loving her, though."

Her face burned with volcanic heat. She was completely unprepared for his confession. He didn't blink, didn't push, just kept looking at her with...love?

He squeezed her hand. "When Kayla filed for the emergency foster placement and discovered I'd never applied for the annulment, I saw it as a chance to find out whether she still had feelings for me. And then I realized how great of a kid Miles is. Kayla and I want to make a go of our marriage. And we want Miles to be a part of our family. We realize there are classes and certifications we'll have to take to make the foster placement permanent, and we'd like to look into adoption. But we didn't want our relationship status to be a problem."

LATER THAT AFTERNOON, Nate drove over to Kayla's place. Rachel hadn't given them a final answer, only listened to their story and said she'd have an answer for them later in the day.

He'd dropped Kayla off at home and gone to the Triple H. A few hours of moving cattle on horseback, and his muscles were sore, his heart longing to see his wife.

Kayla had been so quiet on the way home, even after his confession of love. He hadn't expected her to say it back. He knew she cared about him, but she didn't know if she'd call it love. With her background, he was more worried about scaring her off than anything else.

When he rolled into her driveway, he saw her walking in the far field with the two larger dogs. He went inside, stopped in the kitchen to check on the recovering dog, who lifted its chin from its paws. A couple more days, and he would be out running the fields with the others, Nate was sure of it.

The Chihuahua jumped out of her basket to greet him. Her pups were sleeping in the larger box Kayla'd prepared over the weekend to accommodate their growing, curious natures. He scooped up the mama and went to meet his wife.

He found her walking the fence line, the dogs running ahead and barking. Kayla's expression was troubled, but a small smile crossed her face when he came near and she spotted the dog tucked in his arm like a football.

"She let you pick her up."

He fell into step beside her. "I figure she needs a name. What about Squirt?"

Kayla laughed, a startled sound. "Absolutely not."

"C'mon, I think she likes it." He looked down, and the dog looked up, its mouth open in a smiling doggie pant.

"No. Besides, she'll need to find a home when the pups get a little bigger."

"You're not keeping her?"

Kayla slanted a look at him. "I can't keep them all. The point of a rescue is to find them good homes. Forever homes."

Forever homes. Like the one that Kayla had been dreaming about for her whole life.

He rubbed Squirt's head with the point of his chin, then set her down and let her run off with the collie and Lab. Then he turned to his wife.

"What if it's a special dog?" he asked. "And what if we want it to be part of our life forever? Like Squirt?"

For a moment in her gaze, he saw the uncertainty, then she glanced away. But he wasn't walking away from this.

"We won't let her sleep in the human bed," he said. "And Bando will have to get used to a pallet in the corner. They'll get along fine."

She cracked a small smile that quickly faded. "I don't...I don't know how everything's going to work out."

He clasped her hand. "Neither do I. Nobody else does, either. We can't see the future, but we can do our best to make it the future we want."

Her expression remained shuttered. "You make it sound so easy. But what if...what if we don't get to keep Miles? Then all of this"—he waved her hand through the air—"was for nothing. Without Miles, we can go back to our separate lives."

He shook his head, and her gaze lifted to meet his. "I can't do that. Can't go back to a life without you."

He used up the last vestiges of courage. "I meant what I said in Rachel's office earlier. I loved you back then—even if I did a bad job of proving it. And I still love you. I want to be in your life, even if we can't keep Miles right now."

Her eyes shimmered with moisture, and he found himself blinking back the same.

"We'll fight for him," he said quietly. "If they take him away. We'll take whatever classes they tell us to and hire a lawyer and get him back. He needs us. As does this crazy pack of dogs," he added after a flurry of barking and fur.

She sniffled and swiped at tears escaping down her cheek. "Really? Because everything you're saying sounds too good to be true."

"Really," he promised. "Even if I have to call my dad and ask for pulled strings."

She smiled a little at that. But it faded fast. "I don't know how to believe in forever. I've wanted it for so long—someone to lean on, to be there, a family of my own."

"I'm right here," he said. "If you'll have me. To have and to hold, remember? For better and worse."

"What you said earlier," she said. He saw her swallow. "That you..."

"Love you," he said quietly when she trailed off uncertainly. "Still. Always."

Her tears spilled over, and this time, he cupped her cheek and brushed them away with his thumb.

"I think... me too. I...love you. Still."

His heart pounded a crazy rhythm as the words made all his dreams come true. "Always?"

She nodded. "For always."

Joy overflowed, and he swept her up in a whirling, laughing hug that ended in a passionate kiss. Finally breaking away, he looked down on her with a wild grin.

Bando barked, tearing his attention away from the woman in his arms. A cloud of dust followed a car up the drive. A car he recognized from a week ago. Rachel.

He felt a full-body tremble go through Kayla and squeezed her closer. "We're in this together."

She nodded, but he didn't miss the little hitch in her breath. He kept hold of her hand as they trudged through the field toward the house.

Kayla whistled for Bando and kept the dogs close as they approached the car. Smart. They didn't need the animals to jump on the social worker.

Rachel waited next to her car. Her expression was inscrutable. Would she deliver bad news? He knew it would devastate Kayla if they couldn't keep Miles.

"Howdy." He greeted her with the best smile he could muster.

"I won't beat around the bush," Rachel said. "I've spent all day considering what you told me earlier."

He felt Kayla brace for the blow, knew she was holding her breath.

"I'm still frustrated that you chose to lie to me from the start."

That sounded like there might be a *but* coming...

"But I believe you're sincere about wanting to make your relationship work. And about your desire to provide a stable home for Miles."

Kayla's breath whooshed out in a silent exhale.

Hope surged through him. "We can keep fostering him?"

Rachel leveled a look on him, conveying her seriousness. "There will be extra home visits. I'll be keeping a *very* close eye on you."

He hugged Kayla to his side. "Fine by us."

Kayla looked up at him, her eyes shining. "Is the school day over yet?"

"Soon," he said. "Let's go get our boy."

Epilogue

"IS THERE SOMETHIN' YOU WANNA TELL ME?"

Kayla looked up from the brown paper grocery sack she was unloading. An apple fell from her suddenly nerveless fingers and rolled across the counter as she saw what Nate held between two fingers.

After six months with Miles in their house, things had settled into a rhythm. Nate worked the Triple H while Miles was in school and some nights when it couldn't be helped. The three of them had ripped out and rebuilt the barn until it was everything Kayla had dreamed of. Nate had helped with her grants—mostly by connecting her with a friend of his father's who'd given her invaluable advice.

Six months of real marriage had been...amazing. Oh, they'd had bumps along the way. Like when she'd discovered Nate's love of binge-watching horror flicks. Kayla couldn't stand them, and when Miles had begged to watch, they'd had a knock-down fight. But mostly...

Nate brought her flowers. They had a standing Friday-night date-night. They snuck kisses and held hands, and she'd never been so deliriously happy. She was even beginning to trust that it wasn't all going to fall down around her shoulders.

One thing that hadn't improved was her cooking. So Nate

and Miles had taken over the cooking duties for the family and left her to do the shopping.

They were all unloading the groceries together, and Nate had stumbled on the package she'd wanted to sneak into their bathroom before anyone saw.

The pink pregnancy test looked unbearably silly in his big hand.

Miles's eyes had gone huge and round. The boy who'd come out of his shell and often cracked up with laughter, especially when he and Nate were teasing her, had gone quiet.

Her face flamed but she tried for a casual shrug. "There's nothing to tell. Yet." She gave her husband a pointed look. "We talked about trying for a baby, so I bought a test on a whim. Hopefully, we'll need it soon. But not yet."

"Ah," her husband said.

What did that mean?

Was it her imagination, or did Nate look slightly disappointed?

The thought that he was ready to have a baby *now* was enough to set her heart pounding.

Miles's hand twitched, drawing her gaze even as he turned to stuff a gallon of milk in the fridge.

His face was carefully blank when he returned to the table. All that was left was a box of cereal. "May I be excused? Can I walk Millie?"

Kayla's rescue wasn't officially open yet, but they'd placed four dogs over the summer and now had a female Rottweiler mix that had been dumped on a farm road and found by Sarah on one of her calls. Miles had formed an attachment to the adolescent dog.

"Okay," Kayla agreed. "It's Nate's night to cook."

The boy hustled out the back door.

And Nate, perceptive as ever, raised his brows at her. "What was that? Another of those *foster kids moments, you won't understand*?"

He'd been an incredible partner dealing with the inevitable meltdowns with Miles—better than she'd ever dared to dream.

"If I had to guess, he's probably scared that if we have a baby, we won't want him anymore."

Nate's expression was open and concerned. "You want to have that talk with him that we've been putting off?"

It wasn't really a matter of *putting it off*. Rachel had explained obstacles, and they'd agreed to wait until some of those obstacles resolved. But, clearly they needed to talk with Miles now. She nodded.

They found him in the renovated barn, on his knees with a lap full of dog. His arms were around Millie's neck, and his face was buried in her fur.

Kayla's heart melted.

Nate's boot knocked against the floor, and Miles raised his head. He quickly stood, brushing his face with one hand. His eyes were red-rimmed.

"Hey, buddy. Can we talk for a minute before you guys go on your walk?"

Miles's expression closed off completely.

Nate reached down to pat the excited dog, accepting the swipe of Millie's tongue in a doggie kiss.

Oh, how she loved this man.

Nate straightened. "Kayla and I have loved having you be a part of our lives these past months."

She was watching close enough that she saw Miles physically brace himself for what was coming next. Tears pricked her eyes, but she furiously blinked them back.

"We've been talking with Rachel, and we want to move forward with adoption. There are some obstacles—there's apparently still some long-lost great aunt—"

She put a hand to Nate's forearm to stop him, because Miles's face had lit, and he wasn't listening any longer.

His eyes had widened, and she could feel him vibrating. "You want to—?" He gulped.

"Adopt you," she said softly, her voice hushed with tears.

She saw the tremble of his lips, which was quickly eclipsed by the giant grin that stretched across his face. "For real?"

"For real," Nate confirmed. "We love you, and we want you to be a part of our family forever."

This was what she'd wanted for so long, and now, with Miles and Nate, she had it. And maybe one day soon, a baby. Her forever family.

Melting Megan

Prologue

EARLY PAROLE.

Good behavior.

Lucky.

Dan Evans had always wanted to win big. For one shining moment on his twenty-first birthday, Lady Luck had smiled on him. He'd won five grand at a casino blackjack table.

And then he'd turned around and lost it all. In twenty minutes. But the high...

For a kid whose mom had walked out and left him with his grandpops, the high been addictive, because it had made a lot of dark memories fade, just a little.

He'd been seeking Lady Luck's elusive smile ever since.

There was nothing lucky about three years of good behavior or his early parole. While in prison, he'd worked his butt off, kept his nose clean, sucked up to the guards so much he'd begun to hate himself. When he'd waited in county for sentencing, he'd had nightmares about what prison would be like, terrible visions of what awaited him. The reality had been much worse.

Today, he was going... somewhere. He was getting out. Taking a bus that the prison had arranged to a halfway house, which they'd also arranged. They'd even lined him up a job. Probably sacking groceries or working construction. Whatever it was, he'd do it.

He couldn't court Lady Luck any more. He'd learned his lesson. He wasn't one of the lucky ones. Wasn't meant to be a winner.

No highs were high enough to make up for this. The only good thing in his life had been his job on the Triple H ranch. The other ranch hands had been like brothers. And when Dan had gotten in too deep, stolen ten grand, he'd lost the only people who'd ever cared about him.

Midmorning, the guard escorted him to the intake room, where a uniformed guard handed him a paper bag with his belongings.

He'd worn the orange jumpsuit for three years. His jeans and T-shirt felt foreign. His boots fit like they always had—but how could that be, when he wasn't the same man anymore?

He left behind the cold, cement-block walls and iron bars. The cocky, arrogant man he'd been when he entered prison had long since disappeared.

Outside, Dan squinted in the sunlight, not for the first time wishing for his Stetson to shade his eyes.

His boots clicked on the pavement. His heart thumped hard in his chest.

There was a cold chill in the late October air that cut through his T-shirt. He'd been convicted on a smoldering day in the middle of summer.

He stopped on the sidewalk. Stood there, unmoving. Because he could. Because no one shouted for him to keep moving or get back in line.

He was out. Free—sort of. He still had to meet with his parole officer and make arrangements for continuing meetings.

He'd toe the line, and he'd never forget what he owed to the Triple H.

He looked for the big bus he'd been told would meet him.

But what he saw was two cowboys exit their truck and stand on the sidewalk with their feet spread wide and their arms crossed.

Gideon and Matt Hale. Two of the owners of the Triple H ranch.

The men he'd stolen ten grand from.

He didn't shirk from what was coming. He walked right up to them, bracing for a punch. Or two.

He deserved it, after all.

Would it be Matt? He had the hotter temper of the two. But Gideon had been the one to discover Dan's theft.

He would never forget the look of betrayal on Gideon's face that morning years ago. What was he doing here now? Shouldn't he be in Europe with his wife? He'd come a long way for his revenge, apparently.

Both men were ex-military. This was going to hurt.

It was difficult to meet their eyes. Probably the most difficult thing he'd done since being jailed. The breeze carried a slight whiff of leather and horses, punching him with memories.

The brothers were unsmiling, their eyes hidden in the shadows thrown by their Stetsons. Again, Dan wished for his hat. What had happened to all his things? He'd left a room full of clothes and a computer behind when he'd been incarcerated. The Hales had probably trashed it all.

"Go ahead," he said when the silence became unbearable.

Gideon raised one eyebrow.

"You're here to collect, right? I don't have your ten K, so you'll have to take it out of my hide."

Matt's narrowed eyes slid to Gideon. "Guess he figured us right."

Gideon didn't crack a smile. "Guess he did."

"Well? Get it over with." He closed his eyes, bracing for the inevitable punch. Maybe they'd go for the midsection, not the face.

Nothing happened.

He cracked one eye open to see them staring at him.

"We aren't here for revenge," Gideon said. *Dummy.* The name he hadn't called Dan reverberated in the air, unspoken.

Dan stood straight. What were they here for, then?

He was too proud to ask.

"Come back to work at the Triple H," Matt said. He almost sounded... exasperated?

Dan knew his mouth must be hanging open. Catching flies, his grandpops would've said.

Surely he'd heard wrong.

But then Gideon shifted slightly. "We're offering you your job back."

Okay, so he hadn't misheard.

"Why?"

He couldn't imagine any scenario in which they'd want him back. Was this to punish him? Get him out to the Triple H and then tell him it'd all been a joke?

Or was there some other reason?

Neither one answered his question.

"You got a better offer?" Gideon asked.

He didn't. And all three of them knew it.

If he stuck it out, did he have a chance at paying back his enormous debt?

A throat cleared from nearby, and Dan turned to see his parole officer. Was the tiny kernel of hope he'd just experienced about to be quashed? Had Gideon and Matt even cleared it with the officer?

Apparently they had.

"The choice is yours," the officer said. "You should consider that returning to a place that contributed to your state of mind before is likely to be more difficult than starting fresh somewhere else."

In other words, the guilt could eat him alive.

But would there really be a fresh start if he walked away from the Triple H? At least on the ranch, he knew the score. The guys would watch his every move. The foreman, Nate, his former best friend, would never forgive him. He'd barely make more than minimum wage, plus room and board. He'd never make it out of the hole he'd dug himself.

But going back was the right thing to do. Even if it meant he'd never make it out of Taylor Hills.

And he was done courting Lady Luck. It was time to buckle down and do right.

For once in his sorry life.

Chapter One

EIGHTEEN MONTHS LATER

Megan Fuller, M.D. paused outside the exam room door, smoothing her white coat out of habit, patting her pocket to check that the stethoscope was still there. She pushed her glasses up on the bridge of her nose. They needed an adjustment. They'd been slipping all day.

Last patient.

Based on how her day was going, inside she could expect to find a crotchety grandpa or a talkative mom with a toddler. She hadn't had an appointment end on time all week.

She glanced at the patient chart in her hand, squinting at the tiny type. Dan Evans. Crotchety grandpa it was.

She only let herself breathe for a moment, then pasted on a smile, knocked softly, and opened the door.

A man looked up from where he sat on the exam table. But this was no grandpa.

He was shirtless, and his muscled shoulders stretched for miles. His abs were defined, and she pretended her quick perusal was simple professional interest even as heat suffused her cheeks.

"Hello. I'm Doctor Fuller," she said quickly.

He nodded, his chocolate eyes darting away, lashes a dark smudge against his cheekbones as he stared at the floor.

His jaw was hidden by two days of scruff, but he had an elegant nose that defied the ruggedness of his features. His hair was... a mess. It looked as if it'd been shorn, buzzed almost to his scalp, but was now growing out—that awkward stage in between two male hairstyles.

It did not detract from his appearance.

As she stepped into the room, she saw the cowboy hat atop his button-up shirt, both lying on the chair in the corner.

A cowboy.

She pushed back the instant flare of attraction—how anyone could not be attracted to the man was beyond her—and let her physician's eyes catalog. His tension was obvious in his grip on the exam table and the muscle ticking in his jaw. Had she offended him with the perusal she couldn't help? Should she apologize? Pretend it hadn't happened?

"To what do I owe the honor of your visit today?" she asked, hoping a bit of humor might ease them both into the appointment.

"Stitches."

He twisted his torso and gave her a glimpse of the gash across his ribs, beneath his arm.

"Uh-oh." She set the chart down on the counter and moved to the sink to scrub her hands, putting her back to him momentarily. "Please don't tell me you got it doing something reckless like bull riding."

He didn't respond.

She glanced over her shoulder to see his eyes cut away. As if he'd been watching her while her back was turned.

"Or a farm implement gone rogue?" She grabbed a paper towel from the dispenser and leaned her hips against the counter to dry her hands.

The cowboy didn't look up, didn't crack even a hint of a smile.

"I tried to butterfly it, but the bandages wouldn't hold." He spoke to the floor. As a former ER doctor from Houston, she was used to all different reactions from patients. From talkative to comatose, from patients handcuffed to the bed screaming obscenities, to laboring mothers. In Houston, the cowboy's reaction wouldn't have blipped her radar as unusual. But she'd taken over the family practice in Taylor Hills two weeks ago, and every single person she'd seen had chatted her ear off. From the grandmothers who detailed their entire medical histories, to the men in their mid-forties who questioned her credentials because she looked younger than her thirty-five years, they all wanted to talk.

Not the cowboy.

Fine. She needed to get home to Julianne and Brady anyway.

"Let's take a look." She stepped to the exam table, unable to douse her awareness of his muscled form.

Ignore it. Pretend he's a grandpa.

Her internal instructions didn't help. Especially when she touched the corded back and he startled.

"Sorry," she murmured. "Cold hands are a hazard of the profession."

She had to gently shift his muscled arm forward, out of her line of sight with another touch. He remained frozen, barely breathing.

Maybe the attraction zinging through her veins was one-sided. Maybe he was married, though she didn't see a ring on his finger.

The laceration wasn't deep, but she could see how the location would be difficult to treat without help. It was surrounded by a fading yellow bruise. Curving along his upper ribcage, every time he moved, the bandages would pull.

She stepped back, relieved for the momentary distance. "I can stitch you up, but you'll need to take it easy for several days."

He shook his head very slightly, still not looking at her.

"If you lift too much weight or haul... I don't know, bales of hay or a baby cow or something, you'll rip out the stitches, and we'll be right back here."

His gaze flicked to meet hers for the briefest second. Was that a hint of a smile playing at the corners of his lips? It disappeared too quickly to be sure.

"I'm serious."

His eyes were downcast again. "I can't afford time off."

"I can have the office phone your boss," she offered.

He immediately tensed up, shoulders rigid.

She glanced down at the counter, at his chart. "Oh. I have a sticky note here from Rene at the front desk. I think it says"— she squinted at the loopy handwriting—"you put down that you're a cash pay but normally the bills are sent to the... Triple H? I think she wanted me to find out if it was a mistake." She looked back up at the man.

His stare was hard, any hint of humor gone behind a blank mask. His eyes narrowed, his hands clenched. If she'd thought him tense before, she hadn't met tense. She figured any second, he'd vibrate right off the table.

"I'm a cash pay." The words were said with deadly seriousness. And then she saw his throat work as he swallowed. Looked away again. "I'm good for it. I can make installments."

Pride was a funny thing. So he didn't want this *Triple H* to pay for the appointment. He still held that tension in every line of his body. The charge would only be for an appointment and sutures. She didn't know the ins and outs of billing—that's what an office manager was for—but how much could it cost?

She cleared her throat, forcing false brightness. "I'll make sure she gets it billed correctly." She reached up to the upper cabinet, pulled out a syringe. "Let me just get a local to numb the—"

"That's not necessary."

She looked over her shoulder at him. "Are you sure? Most patients find the needle uncomfortable." *Uncomfortable* was an understatement. Most people freaked out just looking at the curved surgical needle.

"I'm sure."

"Okaaaay."

She assembled needle and thread and washed her hands again for good measure.

He kept his focus on the floor as she moved close to the table.

"Can you hold your arm away for me?" she asked quietly.

He obliged, holding the limb aloft.

Several inches below the laceration was a fading scar she hadn't noticed on the first pass. Farming must be more dangerous than she'd thought.

"You'll feel a stick," she warned.

But he didn't jump at the first prick of the needle. She couldn't even be sure he was breathing.

"Deep breath," she said.

And then his chest expanded beneath her hand.

She kept stitching. *Three. Four.*

"Tetanus can be dangerous," she said. "I'd recommend a booster—"

"I'm current." His words were bit off, but when she adjusted her stance and glanced up at his face, he showed nothing of the pain he must be feeling. Good poker face.

She refocused on her task. *Seven. Eight.*

"I didn't see it on your chart—"

"I'm current." This on an exhale, the words would've been a howl if they'd been louder than a puff of air.

"Almost done." She just needed to tie... her opposite hand brushed his back as she manipulated the needle, and this time he did jump—away from her touch.

"Sorry," she muttered. "Hold still."

He went back to not breathing, and she tried to stifle the nerves. He was clearly not attracted to her. What was her problem?

"It's been a long day," she said. "Packed with appointments. It seems like every person in Taylor Hills wants to meet the new doctor. We could do a church potluck or something, but they all just want to book appointments..."

She forced the rambling words to a stop, snipped the end of the thread, and found her hand shaking slightly.

"Okay, you're done."

He was already off the table, his broad back to her as he reached for his shirt.

She backed toward the door. She hadn't been this flustered since her residency.

She didn't get it. She'd treated plenty of men. Handsome men.

The cowboy had barely looked at her. What—twice? Obviously, the flare of attraction she'd felt had been only in her mind. He couldn't wait to get out of here.

And then, his head turned as he shrugged into his shirt. Not all the way, as if he didn't dare look at her square on. "Thanks."

She saluted with his chart, which was silly because he couldn't see her, and ducked out, closing the exam room door behind her.

She rubbed a hand over her face. She was exhausted. Long days and interrupted sleep had worn her clear out. That's what the problem was. This had been an anomaly.

Maybe she'd imagined the whole thing.

She'd go home, feed the kids dinner, and get to bed early.

Except it was summer. And Friday night.

The kids would be wired for the weekend. Not for the first time, she had the thought that she wasn't cut out for this life.

But it was hers now.

Lady Luck was right there. Beckoning him.

Daring him.

Dan looked away from the gas station's lottery ticket display. Even from across the room, it had power over him. He hated that.

He slurped his fountain drink, trying to divert his attention. He waited while the attendant checked out the woman at the counter while his drink sweated almost as much as he did.

He'd only left the ranch a few times since his release. The first time, he'd gone to pick up a load of feed, and the store owner had made it very clear he wasn't welcome. Taylor Hills had a long memory, and he could see judgment in folks' eyes. He was still the kid from the wrong side of the tracks. Still the screw-up.

Only worse now.

A screw up with a record.

He'd only come to town today for the stitches. He'd been driving back to the Triple H in Matt Hale's truck when he hadn't been able to resist the urge to stop off for a soft drink.

But he wasn't walking out of here with a lotto ticket. Even if the late afternoon sunlight was beaming down on the display like an angelic halo.

The woman leaned on the counter, chatting. Giving him a

clear view of the display beside her.

One lottery ticket wasn't real gambling.

At least that's what the little devil on his shoulder would have him believe.

One lottery ticket wouldn't do much to scratch the itch between his shoulder blades. But it would do something.

Make him forget the last hour spent in the doctor's office, even if only for a momentary gambler's high.

He'd expected Doc O'Leary. Eighties. Failing eyesight. He'd been patching Dan up since he'd been a toddler.

Instead, the door had opened and *she'd* walked in. Wavy brown hair in a ponytail down her back. The crisp white coat and smart black slacks. She'd looked like a big-city doctor, so different from Doc, who wore Wrangler jeans to the office.

And those dark-rimmed glasses that had only highlighted her intelligent hazel eyes, which sparkled with curiosity.

Shame had poured over him, hot and thick. Everybody in town knew his history.

He'd given up on hoping that a single soul in Taylor Hills might not know that he'd been incarcerated. And what he'd done to deserve it.

For one wild moment, he'd hoped *she* didn't know.

And then she'd brought up Rene, the office manager. He'd gone to high school with Rene. There was no way she hadn't told the doctor to steer clear of Dan.

The doctor had been professional and polite, and all he'd wanted to do was run out of there with his tail between his legs like a pup.

He was what he was. No chance of changing it now.

But the shame threatened to eat him alive.

Made the voices in his head, the ones that begged him to hit up the nearest casino, just buy *one lotto ticket*, that much louder.

He didn't dare, even if the cost was only a buck.

Because if he could justify a buck, he could justify five. And if he could justify five, what was twenty, or fifty or a Benjamin?

Every dollar he socked away in his meager savings account was a dollar toward paying back the enormous debt he owed the Hale family.

Today, his savings had shrunk from the doctor's visit.

What a disaster, on so many levels.

A bell above the door chimed, throwing him out of his scattered thoughts. Someone else was coming in to the gas station.

He grimaced, turning away to stare at the display of candy bars.

Now it would be even longer before he could get out of here. Unless he just left, just faced whoever had come in and their judgment.

That he deserved.

Crap.

"Please?" said one child.

"Yeah, me too," said another child. "I want one, too."

The two children continued to beg, talking over each other.

"A hot dog is not an adequate source of nutrition for your supper."

Goose pimples traveled up his arms as he recognized the female voice.

He glanced up at the mirror that ringed the ceiling. It was meant to deter shoplifting, but it gave him a blurred view of the good doctor and two kids. Hers?

Of course she was married. Somebody pretty and smart like that. Of course she was.

"I see that pout, young lady." The doctor sounded tired, worn out in the way he'd come to recognize in Nate, his boss and former best friend. Nate had two kids now.

"It's going to take forever to get home and for you to make dinner," a girl whined.

"I have my own money," said a boy. "From raking Mr. Owen's grass cuttings. I'm gonna get a Snickers Bar."

"You can buy it," the doctor said, "but that doesn't mean you can eat it for supper."

"Aw, man!"

Dan realized where he was standing—next to the candy rack —just as they came around the corner.

The doctor pulled up short, but the two kids were oblivious as they rushed the candy.

"Oh," she said. "Hello."

He saluted her with the Big Gulp. "Ma'am."

And had to force himself not to wince. Lame. He was so lame.

She didn't bother to hide her wince. "I didn't look that closely at your chart, but you can't be more than one or two years younger than I am. Megan will do."

Megan.

The boy of ten or eleven with dirty blond hair and hazel eyes like the doctor's looked up. Dan saw the measuring gaze he threw his way. Nothing to see here, kid. A peon next to your mom.

The girl was cute. She had dark hair and a splash of freckles across her nose. It was she who spoke, looking up from her Crunch bar. "Are you a real cowboy? Like from the rodeo?"

"Something like that." He'd been in his share of rodeos in his younger years, before he'd busted a knee and realized taking his chances in casinos wasn't as hard on his body.

"Are you riding in the rodeo tomorrow?" the girl pressed.

"No," Doctor Megan said.

He raised one brow at her. Couldn't help it.

"Not with..." She gestured to his ribs. "No way."

It was kinda cute that she thought she could tell him what to do.

"I'm not riding," he told the little girl.

And then, "You should come," he said. "To the rodeo."

Where had *that* come from? He hadn't meant to issue an invitation. The Triple H ranch rodeo was a new annual event, one that had come about during his incarceration. He'd be working with the stock behind the scenes.

Both kids lit up before he could rescind the invite.

"Bring your mom, too," he said lamely.

And both kids shut down.

"She is *not* our mom," the boy spat.

He caught a glimpse of pain as it crossed the doctor's expressive face before she masked it. She stepped forward and reached for the boy's shoulder, but he jerked away, stalking off to the endcap of beef jerky. His crossed arms and general body language revealed a big ol' chip on his shoulder.

That's what Dan got for sticking his nose into their business. He'd stepped right into a manure pile in their family dynamic.

"I'm sorry," he muttered.

He turned and approached the checkout counter, interrupting Mrs. Mallory, who'd been his fifth-grade teacher. He plunked a dollar on the counter for his soda pop.

Kept his shaking hand away from the lotto tickets.

And got outta there.

Chapter Two

MEGAN HAD AGREED TO THE RODEO. SHE REGRETTED it as she pulled her Subaru sedan off the two-lane farm road and onto a rutted two-track driveway. At least she thought it was supposed to be a driveway.

She felt like a pushover, because she'd given in after the 15,237th time Julianne had asked.

And partly because Brady hadn't asked.

He didn't ask for things, because he didn't trust her. At least, that's what she'd guessed over the last nine months since she'd been awarded custody of her nephew and niece.

She's not our mom.

Brady's quick temper at the gas station had made her want to curl up in a ball and weep all over again. For what he'd lost. What they'd all lost when her sister and brother-in-law had been in a fatal car accident. Emma and Riley were gone.

One phone call had changed Megan's life, and the kids' lives, too.

Months had passed, and they were still walking on eggshells around each other. Trying to figure out how to do life now.

Thus, the rodeo.

It couldn't be dangerous to *watch* the rodeo, right?

"This is so exciting," Julianne squealed from the backseat of Megan's sedan. At eight, everything was exciting.

As the car bumped and tilted over the rough off-road terrain, Megan could only pray she wasn't doing irreparable damage to the car. She squinted against the setting sun, trying to find a place to park. She was surrounded by trucks. Finally, she pulled off the rutted lane and parked between two huge farm trucks in the tall field grass.

Hot, humid Texas air and the smell of animal feces hit her as she stepped out of the sedan. The summer grass crunched beneath her sneakers.

Julianne and Brady jumped from the back seat.

"Guys," she warned before they could run off.

They both froze, their energy instantly diminishing. Brady wouldn't look at her.

"What are the rules?" she asked.

"Don't go off by ourselves," Julianne chirped.

"And?"

"Don't eat junk food...?" the girl asked tentatively.

Brady stared off in the distance, chin set at a mulish angle.

She addressed him. "Is there anything you want to add?"

He shot her a glare. "Don't run around. Don't talk to anyone. Don't have any fun."

Well, that was a bit of an exaggeration.

"You know why we have the rules," she reminded them both. "It's not about keeping you from having fun."

"It's about *protecting us*." His mocking emphasis on the last words didn't go unnoticed, but she let it go.

She followed as they navigated through the sea of trucks and trailers toward a metal-fenced arena, where red dust rose above everything else.

Things had been going well—as well as could be expected, under the circumstances—until the last few weeks. Brady wanted to argue over everything. Felt her rules were too confining.

She didn't know what to do. She knew Emma hadn't let the kids run wild. She was maybe a smidge more strict than Emma had been, but she was still learning her way here too. She'd been working her way through med school when her friends had been having babies. People with kids Julianne and Brady's age had gone through the baby stages, the terrible twos, the beginning of the elementary years.

They knew what they were doing, parenting-wise.

She didn't, no matter the number of parenting books she'd stacked on her nightstand, too tired to crack them open after a full day of work and evening of corralling the kids.

They joined the small crowd—all of whom seemed at home in boots and jeans and fancy cowboy hats. Megan bit her lip to hold back a warning as the kids clambered up the stairs of the bleachers, the shiny new boots she'd bought them upon their arrival in Taylor Hills ringing against the metal.

She scanned for three seats in the first or second rows, hoping that if they stayed low to the ground, it would mitigate any damage if the kids got excited and fell through. No dice.

The kids were already halfway up the bleachers, heading for the mostly-empty top row.

"Guys!"

But they either didn't hear her or were ignoring her.

Someone in the row next to her whooped, and she whipped around, expecting to see a bull rider or something dangerous come into the dirt-packed arena.

It was a tiny boy, no more than four, riding on the back of a... sheep?

The sheep was running around the arena, and the boy was jostled off after a few seconds. A booming announcer called out a time, and the crowd cheered.

Megan turned back to locate the kids, and her heart rate skyrocketed. Where were they?

Wait. There.

Behind a man with a huge ten-gallon hat. Of course on the top row. She moved to join them and sat down on the metal seat. Heat seeped through her jeans and into her skin.

Another sheep-riding little boy entered the arena. This time, the sheep headed directly for the fence and knocked the little boy into it.

Breath caught in her chest as the sheep kept going, but the little boy was caught by his belt and left hanging upside-down on the fence. His hat came off as his head knocked into the railing.

Was he hurt?

She was ready to jump up and rush for her car to get her medical bag when a lanky cowboy dressed as a clown sauntered across the arena and righted the boy. He set the kid on his feet and plopped his cowboy hat back on his head.

The boy waved and the crowd went wild.

Seriously?

These people were crazy.

And Julianne and Brady were cheering along with them.

Across the arena, several cowboys and cowgirls lined the arena fence. The men wore black felt hats while the women had on fancy sequined vests and white hats. Their hair was eighties-big, and Megan almost thought she could smell the Aqua Net from here.

She let her eyes scan for familiar faces. She was *not* looking for Dan—but she found him anyway, behind some kind of chute, out of the way of most of the action. From this distance, it was impossible to know whether he'd seen her or not.

She didn't know why she was drawn to him, other than the intense flare of attraction she'd experienced in the exam room.

And then he'd witnessed Brady's mini-meltdown at the gas station. Way to make a great impression on the guy.

Not that she had time for dating. She was a single mother now. And she had a thriving, busy practice.

She didn't have *time*.

Next, the announcer called for the clover leaf barrels.

"Is this for *girls*?" Julianne asked excitedly.

The ten-gallon-hat man turned and gave her a winning smile. "It sure is. Maybe next time, you'll be down there competing."

Julianne lit up like a firecracker. She turned her bright face on Megan. "Could I?"

"Oh, honey. You don't even know how to ride."

Julianne frowned.

When the first girl, who was about Brady's age, came flying out of the gate, low on her horse's back, Megan knew she'd been right to discourage Julianne.

At that speed, one slip from the saddle, and a little girl could have a traumatic brain injury.

They weren't even wearing helmets!

Megan fought the urge to cover her eyes as girl after girl raced out, looped their horses around three barrels, and then raced back through the gate.

It was like watching a scary movie. She couldn't look away.

THE THIRD ANNUAL Triple H spring rodeo was in full swing. Dan had no idea what he was doing.

Nate had put him in charge of manning the chute for the steers they'd use in the calf mugging and later for the big bulls. It was hot, and he'd been slobbered and snotted on by two steers already.

The gate clanged open, and he swatted the steer's rump, not that it needed any extra encouragement. It ran into the arena, and he closed the gate, then ushered in the next animal.

He needed to brush his teeth. He'd eaten a bushel of dust already and the night was young. The sun was barely setting. They hadn't kicked on the tall arena lights yet.

He was itching between his shoulder blades again. Had pulled his Stetson down low over his eyes. His ears were hot.

This many folks from town...

He felt the weight of several dozen stares. Knew they were all talking about him. Waiting for him to screw up again.

Maybe he would. But not tonight.

He wouldn't.

Even if he had to stay on the ranch twenty-four seven.

Fifteen minutes ago, he'd overheard one of the bull riders chatting it up with Nate. And heard, *"Why'd Hale hire him back on?"* He'd known they were talking about him.

Nate's *"No idea."* had stung more than Dan wanted to admit.

He'd been right about Nate. He would never forgive him. The foreman tolerated Dan but didn't speak to him if he didn't have to.

He'd screwed up their friendship.

He needed to think about something else.

Megan.

He'd seen the doctor show up with her charges almost an hour ago. They'd climbed onto the top of the bleachers.

For some reason, he couldn't seem to stop glancing her way. Unlike many of the folks in the crowd, she didn't seem to have visited the food truck that'd set up on the edge of the parking grounds. No sign of corn dogs or pretzels for her. Was she a health nut? Because of her profession?

His curiosity about the good doctor couldn't be a good thing. He needed to keep his head down and remember the vow he'd made to himself. Pay back the Hales and get out. Even if it took him ten years. Or thirty. He was determined to do it.

But he also couldn't help noticing the way the doctor kept covering her eyes. Like right now, as the kid in the arena roped his calf and jumped off his horse. A glance in the stands revealed the doctor with both hands cupping the sides of her eyes, hiding.

Seriously?

She was adorable.

Why had she come, if the rodeo freaked her out? Was it for the kids? The kids who weren't hers.

"Hey."

A female voice interrupted his musings, and, for one microsecond, his heart leapt as if it were the doctor.

It was Kelsey, his boss's very pregnant wife. At his elbow with a dripping, ice-cold bottled water.

"Thought you might need to wash down some of that dust you're eating."

Through the bars, he took it from her. "Thanks." And then because he couldn't help it, "Aren't you supposed to be resting?"

He didn't know details but had overheard enough to know that she was supposed to be on bed rest during this last part of her pregnancy.

Right now, she braced one hand on her lower back, looking slightly miserable in a maternity shirt and jeans and... flip flops?

She followed his gaze down but grimaced when she realized she couldn't see her feet. "I can't get my boots on any more," she admitted. "I wanted to watch Miles ride. He's up next, isn't he?"

Nate and Kayla's adopted son was roping for the first time tonight, and the whole spread was anxious on his behalf. Even Dan, though he wouldn't admit it.

Her eyes caught on something over his shoulder. He craned his neck to look. There was Matt, looking like thunder and heading for his wife, though still yards away.

"And it looks like I'm going right back into the house to lie down on the couch."

Dan looked back at her, saw the pout.

"It's boring. I can't see anything, even from the living room window."

"I'm sor—" He didn't get the words out before she went pale. One hand clutched her stomach. and she reached out and grabbed onto the outside of the chute.

"Hold up," he shouted to the guy working the chute's lever several feet away. He stepped onto the bottom railing of the chute and used his momentum to propel himself over the top. He was halfway over when he remembered the stitches. Remembered because he could feel them tearing apart.

He made it just in time as she fainted dead away.

He caught her, lifted her, and turned.

"Kelsey." Matt scooped her out of Dan's arms. His face was almost as white as his wife's had been, his eyes wide. "What should I do?"

Nate had seen the whole thing and joined them. "Want me to call an ambulance?"

"I don't—" Matt muttered.

"The doctor's here," Dan blurted.

Both Matt and Nate turned identical hard looks on him, and he almost wished he'd kept his mouth closed.

But he liked Kelsey. She didn't treat him like dirt.

"I saw her in the stands."

"Go get her," Matt ordered as he strode off toward the ranch house, his wife in his arms.

SOMETHING HAD HAPPENED, over by the chute where all the huge, scary animals kept coming from. A fight? Or something else? She'd seen Dan go up and over the metal chute in a move that would've been beautiful if she hadn't known about his injury.

The rodeo stalled out for several moments, and then Megan was shocked when a shrill whistle came from behind her.

Julianne nudged her. "Look."

Megan glanced over the railing behind them, down the dizzying one-story height, to see Dan there.

"Come down," he called. "We need your help."

What was going on?

Adrenaline pumping, she grabbed Julianne's sweaty hand. "Come on," she told Brady.

He grunted, looked like he wanted to refuse, but followed them down the bleachers. Their shoes clanged against the metal, rattling her. Dan met them at the bottom step, another good-looking cowboy behind him.

Dan was out of breath.

"Did you tear your stitches?" she blurted. She shouldn't have. HIPAA protected what he'd revealed in her office, but seeing so many kids and adults doing dangerous stunts in the arena had her on edge. And she'd seen him jump.

And her mouth just ran away with her.

"What? No."

The man behind him scowled. "What stitches?"

Dan ignored him, his focus on Megan. "My boss's wife just collapsed. She's pregnant. Can you come help her?"

Megan felt herself slip into physician mode. "Where?" Then, "I need my bag."

"I can get it for you." Dan almost looked surprised at his own offer. Was that a blush rising in his face? The arena lights and the shadows where they stood beside the bleachers made it hard to tell. She wished she had time to try and make sense of his reaction.

"Want to come with me? Show me your... car?" He addressed Brady, stumbling over the words a bit, as if he'd been going to say *mom* again but thought better of it.

The cowboy behind him muttered something under his breath. Dan must've heard it. His jaw went rigid, but he didn't say anything else.

"Sure. Okay." She dug in her hip pocket for the keys. "Remember where we parked?" she asked Brady.

He gave her a look only a pre-teen boy could pull off. "Duh."

She kept Julianne's hand. Couldn't help looking over her shoulder as she followed the unnamed cowboy toward a two-story ranch house set away from all the rodeo commotion.

Dan and Brady disappeared into the parking area. The man's shoulders were set and tense.

"I'm Nate. I run the Triple H," the cowboy barked, drawing her attention back. "You the new doc in town?"

"Megan Fuller." She was huffing as she tried to keep up with his long strides, Julianne practically running beside her. "This is my niece Julianne. And my nephew Brady went—"

"With Dan," Nate said flatly. "You wanna tell me about these stitches he has?"

"I can't," she said. "Patient privacy laws. I shouldn't have even mentioned... what I mentioned."

He nodded, the set of his face hard.

And then they reached the yard. The two-story house rose out of the shadows above them. It was lovely, an older-style farmhouse with the kind of wrap-around porch that invited you to sit and stay a while. Lights blazed from all the first-floor windows.

"C'mon in." The cowboy strode up the steps and across the porch. He pushed open the door. "It's me with the doc."

Megan tried to shake off her awareness of the tension that had flowed between the two cowboys. Even though curiosity stabbed her like an out-of-control scalpel. She didn't have time for curiosity. She had a patient inside.

Chapter Three

Nearly forty-five minutes later, Megan scrubbed her hands in the small half-bathroom.

The cold water was a shock to her system.

Who was the woman in the mirror? Wisps of hair had escaped the clasp at the back of her neck and framed her face. Her cheeks were flushed, probably from the exertion of hustling across the fields to the ranch house. Maybe from seeing Dan again. Her eyes were even sparkling a little, something she hadn't seen in the mirror since Emma's death.

Enough of that. Single moms didn't have time to gawk at themselves in the mirror. Time to gather up the kids and head home.

She couldn't help glancing around as she left the bathroom. Earlier, she'd been too concerned about Kelsey to care about her surroundings.

The Triple H ranch must do well for itself. The house was furnished just the way she would've done it. Warm and homey. Family pictures everywhere, including photos of a princess— Matt Hale's sister-in-law. Books scattered everywhere.

Why did the ranch house feel like home so effortlessly, when Megan had spent countless hours trying to transform the bungalow in town to a place where Julianne and Brady would feel comfortable? She didn't have the touch, apparently. Or maybe it was her they didn't feel at home with.

Kelsey had claimed the books as hers. She'd still been explaining her pre-eclampsia diagnosis when Dan and Brady had appeared, the boy clutching Megan's black medical bag to his middle.

Matt Hale had shown Brady to the office, where Julianne was already watching TV. Dan had disappeared, but Megan couldn't forget the concern in his eyes. Kelsey mattered to him. Were they related? Friends?

By the time she'd taken Kelsey's vitals and found the baby's heartbeat the old school way—by stethoscope—the pregnant woman had stabilized. Her blood pressure had been slightly up, but they'd called Kelsey's obstetrician on speakerphone, and the consensus was that a late-night visit to the ER would do more harm than good. Kelsey had promised to come in for an office visit first thing Monday morning.

Megan had excused herself to wash up, unable to block out Matt Hale's quiet dressing down of his wife.

Megan only hoped the woman would listen. Pre-eclampsia was nothing to joke about. It was dangerous for both mom and baby, and even though bed rest had to be difficult for someone as active as Kelsey—a runner and former Olympic champion—it was necessary.

Not wanting to interrupt, Megan exited the bathroom and tiptoed down the hall. Lights flickered, and flat noise came from under a door midway down the hall. Must be the office.

But only Julianne was inside, her eyes glued to the cartoon characters on the screen.

"Where's Brady?" Megan glanced back down the hall, but she hadn't passed him, and no lights had been on in other rooms.

Julianne's eyes went to the floor.

"Where is he?" Megan's heart started thundering against her breastbone. She'd set the rules for a reason.

"He really wanted to watch the rest of the rodeo," Julianne said in a small voice.

Panic spiked. There were so many things that could happen to a little boy by himself.

"Come with me right now." Megan knew her voice was betraying her anxiety.

Megan grabbed the girl's arm as they hit the back porch. The fields were dark for nearly a quarter of a mile until the arena lights flooded the action over there. So many places a boy could stumble and fall. Sprain his ankle. Get lost.

"The next time your brother does something stupid, you come and get me," she muttered.

Julianne's voice was still tiny. "But you said not to interrupt you."

She had said that. It hadn't even crossed her mind that Brady would leave the house. He didn't even know anybody here.

What was he thinking?

DAN HAD BEAT feet back to the rodeo. Not because he didn't want to be around Megan, but he knew Nate expected him back. Though there were plenty of cowboys around, this rodeo was the Triple H's responsibility.

One of the stock contractors had relieved him when the bronc busting started. The men were particular about their stock—with good reason, the rodeo association had rules to protect the animals—and wanted to ensure their expensive stock got into the arena all right.

Nate wasn't around to give him another job, and it'd gotten dark and crowded enough that Dan could hang around the shadowed side of the arena without causing a ruckus. He tried to relax into the feel of the metal railing beneath his hands. Loosen up his neck and gaze at the sky between competitors. The stars were out.

The aura surrounding the arena had changed. With the kids' competitions out of the way, the adult riders were all business. Even the crowd's cheers had changed, louder and more raucous as the night wore on.

He'd loved the roping competition when he'd been sixteen. Had thought it was going to be his winning ticket out of Taylor Hills.

Until Jimmy ditched him.

He still liked watching the cowboys working in pairs. Could

still remember the feel of the lasso, stiff in his palm, sailing out over his head. The high of winning.

He still hadn't shaken the uber-awareness of his surroundings that his time in prison had instilled in him. If someone accidentally brushed against him, he jumped a mile.

Which meant he caught the slight movements to his right as a kid-sized body sidled up to the arena fence.

Dan squinted into the shadows. Brady. The doc's... sort-of kid.

He'd been quiet when they'd fetched the doc's bag from probably the only sedan on the property earlier. It'd been as out of place as the doc in her slacks with her hair up behind her head.

It went to show how small Dan's world had become. Sequestered on the ranch all the time. By his own choice.

He didn't have enough distractions. He'd thought of little besides the pretty doctor since he'd seen her both in her office and at the gas station. That glimpse of pain that had crossed her features... it had hit some kind of old-fashioned dinner triangle inside him. He still felt the echo of it.

And now the kid had snuck out here. Dan didn't have to do much guesswork to figure out why the kid was hiding in the darkest shadows.

Dan's senses tingled again, and he turned his head the other direction. Miles, Nate's boy, sidled up on his opposite side.

"Hey," Miles greeted him.

"Nice ride," Dan said.

Miles was the other person, besides Kelsey, who didn't seem to hold Dan's crimes against him. Maybe because the two of them hadn't known Dan before. Nate and his wife Kayla had adopted the boy just last year, the paperwork coming through just about the same time their baby girl had been born.

"My rope slipped," Miles said. "I lost a good half second for our team."

Movement from his other side. Brady was edging closer. Was the boy trying to listen to their conversation?

Dan turned to look at him. "You met Miles O'Malley yet?"

Brady's eyes caught a reflection from some light behind Dan, shining and about the only thing he could see of the boy in the shadows.

His eyes narrowed. He seemed unsure whether to run off or join the conversation.

Apparently Miles rated high, because Brady stepped into the light. "That was you riding? And roping?"

Miles smiled. You'd never know the kid had been an orphan before. He had an easy manner, helped in his mom's dog rescue. Loved to talk maybe more than he loved dogs.

"Yeah, that was me. What's your name? You new in town?"

"We just moved here. I'm Brady."

The boys knocked fists. They were probably two years apart. Miles was older. Brady could do a lot worse for friends.

"How'd you learn how to do that stuff?" Brady almost bounced in excitement.

"My dad taught me to ride." The pride in Miles's voice was easy to hear.

And Dan couldn't help the pinch in his gut. Nate was a good dad. Had been a good friend, until Dan had thrown everything away. That itch between his shoulder blades started in bad.

Miles's gaze slide to Dan. "I think Scottie is going to quit, though. He wants to play football, and his dad said he couldn't rodeo and play sports."

"Bummer," Dan said.

There was a beat of quiet. The bell rang, and two adult riders flew out of the gate on their horses, making quick work of roping and tying off a steer.

Dan heard the intake of air from Brady. And then the quiet, "Do you think I could learn how to do that?"

"Sure, you could," Miles was quick to insert.

But Dan knew better than to assume. "If your mom... I mean the doctor... if the doctor agrees, there's lots of places around here that give riding lessons."

Brady locked his eyes on the action in the arena. His shoulders drooped.

"She's not my mom," he muttered. "She's my aunt. My parents died."

Oh. Poor kid.

Miles moved around Dan to stand next to Brady and put his

hand on the other boy's shoulder. "I'm sorry. My parents are gone, too."

The boy's compassion put a hot knot in Dan's throat. Adults could take notes from a kid like this, a kid with a good heart.

Then a strident voice rose above the rodeo noise. "Brady!"

Dan raised a brow at the kid, whose expression showed a mix of guilt and anger.

When Dan caught sight of the doctor, she looked frazzled and stressed. Her hair had completely escaped the knot, and her face was pale.

He raised his hand in a wave. When her eyes locked on him, he pointed down at his side.

Relief crossed her expressive face, but by the time she'd navigated through the crowd to them, she only looked stern. She had the little girl in tow.

"Brady! What was rule number one?"

She didn't reach out and hug him like Dan might've expected.

And the boy's shoulders tensed up immediately. He didn't answer her, just stuck his chin out toward the arena, jaw set.

Miles watched curiously.

He could almost see the doctor rallying her patience. "Brady, rule one."

Brady gritted his teeth stubbornly, still staring at the arena.

"You were supposed to stay with your sister," the doctor said. "It's not safe."

"It's all good folks here," Dan said, trying to reassure her.

She cut him an angry look. "That's not the point. What if one of those huge bulls had gotten out? He could've been trampled."

Okay, so she'd gone from *a little worried* to *the sky is falling*. There's no way the stock contractors or the ranch hands would let that happen. Plus, there were extra hands on horseback if some freak accident happened.

But Brady was having none of it.

And Dan could see the doctor's temper was about to snap.

He reached out and put his hand on the boy's shoulder. "Your aunt was worried about you. You have anything to say to her?"

Brady slid a glance at Miles. Dan thought he might refuse, but finally he mumbled, "I'm sorry."

But when Dan glanced back at the doctor, her eyes were fixed on him, not on the boy.

"You've pulled your stitches," she accused.

"No—" But when he looked down, a red stain was growing beneath his armpit. "There's a paramedic on call for the rodeo. I'll have him fix me up."

But she was already shaking her head. "Let's go back to the house."

MEGAN WAS STILL SHAKING from the rush of adrenaline and fear when they reached the ranch kitchen. She needed to calm down, or there was no way she'd be able to stitch up the cowboy.

Brady had just walked off. Barely apologized.

She'd been so *scared*.

"Sit down," she told Julianne and Brady, pointing to the small table jammed in a breakfast nook. A glance through the doorway showed a long picnic-style dining table, which would've given the kids more room, but right now, she wasn't letting Brady out of her sight.

Dan addressed Miles. "Why don't you get your friends some lemonade? Scarlett probably has some cookies hidden away." The doctor looked at the other boy now. Seemed she'd barely noticed him when she'd found them. He'd followed them back to the house, and Dan had introduced him as Nate's son.

Julianne lit up, but Brady muttered, "Cookies are against the rules," beneath his breath.

"It's fine," Megan said through gritted teeth.

Of the two of adults in the room, it was easy to see who was making more of an impression on the kids. Julianne was smiling at Dan and even Brady had a sparkle of interest in his eyes.

Megan just wanted to get out of here. But she couldn't let a patient suffer. She put her bag on the table and opened it.

Her hands were still shaking.

"Is there a bedroom or somewhere...?"

And then Dan was there, closer than she expected. Pressing a hot cup of coffee into her hands, their fingers tangling.

"You can stitch me up right here. There's plenty of light. Why don't you take a minute, first?"

The mug's warmth seeped into her. For a few seconds, she and Dan shared a connection. She took a deep breath and inhaled the scent of coffee and man, and some of her fear drained away.

She was caught in his gaze, in his touch. Warm and appreciative. A tether back to steady ground.

And then... more. An electric charge, an awareness zinged between them.

Abruptly, he broke away and stepped to the counter. He looked out the darkened window. He was pulling away. She'd felt him do the same in her office. What made him distance himself?

She leaned her hip against the counter, allowing a sense of calm to steal over her. Letting her mind stop spinning from visions of everything that could've happened to Brady but hadn't. Behind all of it, she continued to be aware of the man nearby.

"How long have you been riding?" Brady asked, voice low.

Miles answered in normal volume. "Not that long. When my mom and dad started fostering me, my dad taught me. They gave me Buster for my birthday last year."

"Really? You have your own horse?" Julianne asked the question, but when Megan glanced at the table, it was easy to see the jealousy streaked across Brady's face.

"I want to learn how to do clover barrels," Julianne chirped.

Megan winced. There was no way. As far as she was concerned, riding was dangerous and *racing* was twice as bad.

She took a big gulp of her coffee, burning the back of her throat. Enough.

She set the coffee mug down and went to the sink to scrub up. Dan saw her coming and moved out of the way.

Once she'd washed and dried, she moved back toward her bag on the counter while, silently, Dan unbuttoned his shirt and slipped his arm out to give her access to his injury. His miles of muscles affected her only for a millisecond this time, because she was prepared for it.

"Local?" she asked softly.

He shook his head.

He jumped when she touched him again, a brush of her hand against his lower back.

He inhaled on the first stitch, but remained perfectly still otherwise.

"At least you've only pulled half," she murmured.

"You're gonna have a wicked scar," Miles said from the table. He sounded far too excited for her taste. "Maybe it'll impress the ladies."

Julianne dissolved into giggles.

Megan frowned. "Some women aren't impressed with scars. Especially when they're stupidly earned. How'd you get this any way? From a bull?"

The back door banged shut.

"Dad!" Miles yelled.

Megan glanced up only for a second, noting the hard gaze that passed between Nate and Dan. Dan had tensed up beneath her hand, and whatever tenuous connection had been between them disappeared.

"The lady asked you a question," Nate said tightly. "How'd you get that?"

"Scraped against a nail while I was tearing out the fence in the west pasture."

Brady and Julianne had gone quiet, somehow sensing the tension between the adults.

"Try not to do any lifting or straining this time," she said.

"I couldn't let her fall," he murmured.

Megan knotted the last stitch. "Done."

Dan turned away from Nate, shrugging his shirt up over his shoulder. He looked at the floor as he buttoned up. "You can send me the bill," he said quietly.

"No charge."

His jaw worked.

Nate said something to the kids that she didn't hear.

Dan flicked a gaze over his shoulder at the other man.

Muttered something under his breath. Then, to her. "I pay my debts."

Over Dan's shoulder, she saw Nate shoot a hard gaze at the injured cowboy. What was going on between them?

Nate's son jumped up from the table, breaking the tension that had grown from uncomfortable to super-sized. "Are we heading home?"

"Sure." Nate's ease with his son was in direct contrast to his manner with Dan. "Better go check on your mom and the pups. Buster's all loaded up. We'll just stay and walk out with the good doctor."

Dan's tension seemed to ratchet up even higher, but he didn't say a word. He kept his eyes focused on the floor in front of him.

"Goodbye," she said.

He didn't answer, even as she walked out the door with the kids.

Chapter Four

Megan woke the next morning to whispers coming from down the hall.

She dragged herself out of bed, glancing at the clock on the way. Six-thirty.

Between checking on Kelsey and repairing Dan's stitches, she'd gotten the kids home to her little bungalow in Taylor Hills an hour later than the kids' normal bedtime.

So why were they up at the crack of dawn? She usually had to wake them up for church services.

She padded down the hall in bare feet, squinting against the early-morning light streaming in from the living room windows. It still felt like all that rodeo dust was soaked in her pores.

Sleep had been evasive. Her brain had decided to replay those frightening moments when she hadn't been able to find Brady. And then when she'd finally been able to fall asleep, she'd dreamed of Brady riding into a rodeo arena, Julianne on horseback behind him, racing around with wild war whoops.

She'd woken from the nightmare just as they'd fallen from the horses and broken their necks.

And then she'd locked herself in the tiny hall bathroom with her phone, knowing it was crazy, and looked up videos of all the varieties of riding accidents kids could have.

Ads had started popping up on the videos. For learning to

ride. She'd finally clicked on one, and the narrator's voice overlay had spoken of the fact that giving the kids the right training could prevent riding accidents.

She'd gone back to bed with that thought on her mind.

Now, she shuffled down the hall. Brady's door was cracked, and she peeked inside. Both kids were huddled on the bed with a sheaf of papers between them.

"Hey, guys." She moved into the room, trying to ignore the way Brady shuffled the papers so whatever they'd been looking at was now on the bottom. Maybe they needed a rule about keeping secrets.

She crawled onto the bed with them, tickling Julianne until the little girl squirmed and giggled. She ruffled Brady's hair and lounged back against the pillows.

"You guys are up early. Want to get donuts before church?"

Julianne clapped her hands together. Brady shrugged.

And her stomach pinched again. She and Brady had had a special relationship as aunt and nephew. Now, he wouldn't even look at her, his focus still on hiding whatever was buried beneath the scratch papers on his bed.

She wasn't one to mince words or pull punches. She reached beneath the pile of papers and drew out the bottom one. "What's this?"

Brady made a grab for it, but she tugged it just out of his reach. Stared down at it.

It was a map, a crudely drawn one, from their house to what appeared to be the Triple H ranch. And an arrow going beyond.

Brady's expression was both angry and defensive.

Megan looked from him back to the map. Had the two of them been planning to run away?

"Miles told us his ranch is right around the corner from where we were last night," Julianne blurted.

Brady's jaw was locked.

Megan stared at him. "Brady?"

He didn't answer, just stared out the window where dawn was brightening the edges.

Everything she'd seen last night flew through her brain at high speed.

"Look, I know things are tough right now. You miss your mom and dad. I do, too."

Julianne leaned into her shoulder, and Megan curled her arm around the girl. "We're a team now, right?"

Julianne bobbed a nod, but Brady stared at the bedspread, tracing a pattern with his forefinger.

"I like it here in Taylor Hills. Don't you?" Megan asked. They'd all needed a change from the city. The long hours her job had required had been too much, and every time they'd driven by a familiar place, it hurt too much.

"Yeah," Julianne said softly.

"The rules suck," Brady said, chin popping up defiantly.

Well. At least she knew how he really felt.

"I know things are different with me in charge, but the rules—"

"Mom and Dad didn't have so many rules."

"I'm not Emma." She tried to get the words out evenly, but a catch in her throat betrayed her emotion. She never would be.

But maybe for this moment, right now, she shouldn't be focusing on the rules.

"Could we call a truce?" she offered. "No more running away."

Brady still stared at the bedspread, but nodded slowly.

And Megan swallowed back her fears.

"Would you like to take riding lessons?" she asked.

Julianne bounced off the bed with the force of her enthusiasm.

And Brady looked straight at Megan. She couldn't miss the hope shining from his eyes.

SUNDAY AFTERNOON, Dan had one of the stock geldings tied off in the barn aisle and was picking and brushing its hooves, clearing them of dirt and small rocks, when a shadow fell over him.

He didn't have to look up to know it was Nate.

"Today's your day off. What d'you think you're doing?"

He kept his head down, concentrating on his task.

Nate waited him out. Dan knew he'd stand there all day if he had to. Stubborn cuss.

"There's always work to be done," he said evenly. "Even on a Sunday."

He didn't answer the unspoken question. *When are you gonna leave the ranch? When are you gonna mess up again?* He didn't ask what Nate was doing here. It was his day off, too, and Nate had proved to be a family man through and through in the months that Dan had been back on the spread.

"Finish up. We need to talk."

Nate stalked off leaving Dan bristling at his order. It was the work of a few minutes to put the old boy back in his stall, but Dan worked the latch as slowly as he could.

He couldn't avoid the coming confrontation forever. He met Nate outside the barn, the sun harsh on his shoulders, the scent of baking fields in his nostrils.

The other man stood with feet braced apart and arms crossed over his chest, a hard light in his eyes.

Dan kept his hands at his sides. Tried to appear unthreatening. He had to fight against the behaviors ingrained in him from his time in prison in order to look the other man in the face. In prison, insubordination earned you a blow from the guard's club.

But this wasn't prison and Nate wasn't his guard. Wasn't his friend, either. Only his boss.

"You wanna tell me why you hid that injury from me?" Nate asked. *What else are you hiding?*

"It didn't affect my work."

Maybe he should've mentioned it, but Dan didn't want to give the foreman any reason to think he was shirking his duties.

"That's not what the doc seemed to think. She said no lifting."

"I'm fine."

Again, Dad resisted the urge to lower his gaze. He hadn't done anything wrong. And he needed the manual labor to keep him busy. The more exhausted he was at night when he fell into bed, the less he felt the ever-present itch to gamble.

Not that he would admit it.

Nate's stare didn't waver. Finally, he said, "You're on light duty until further notice."

"No."

Dan couldn't help instinctively bracing for a blow after his near-instant refusal. He clamped his back teeth together when Nate's sharp eyes narrowed slightly. Had the other man noticed?

"It's not a request."

Dan ground his teeth. "So what'm I supposed to do? Sit around and knit a baby blanket for Kelsey?"

Nate didn't crack a smile, but Dan knew his friend... former friend... well enough to know he was gloating about something. It was the light in his eye.

"You're going to be giving riding lessons. To the good doc and her kids."

"No."

Nate didn't bother to argue about it. He turned toward the house, where his truck was parked. He called over his shoulder, "You don't like it, you can always leave."

Dan was left steaming in the sun.

Riding lessons? He was no teacher.

Seeing the doc again would cause more pain than pleasure.

He liked her.

Was Nate trying to punish him? Laughing all the way?

Nate had always known when he was sweet on a gal.

Fine. Dan would do it. He wouldn't quit. Wouldn't give his ex-friend the satisfaction.

He'd do the riding lessons. But he'd keep his distance from the pretty doc.

Chapter Five

Evening was falling as Dan checked the saddle cinch on Peanut, probably the tamest gelding on the Triple H. He'd already saddled Tad and AC, and they stood inside the corral next to the barn.

Their tails swished. Reading his nervous anticipation?

He'd showered while he'd waited, but he'd already sweated through his clean shirt in the humid afternoon air.

He waited.

Was always waiting. To get out. To be free. Really free.

Nate had kept a close watch on Dan all week. He'd been prevented from doing his part to load a bunch of steers for sale and hadn't been allowed to help with inoculating the heifers the ranch was keeping. He'd basically been sitting on his hands all week, grooming horses. There was only so much of that to be done.

The itch to gamble was worse than ever.

Or maybe the itch felt like fire because he was going to see the doctor again.

He wanted to see her. Even though he shouldn't.

Even the kids, Brady with the chip on his shoulder and the little girl, Julianne, who was as cute as a baby bunny.

He shouldn't want to see them. He knew he was only setting

himself for disappointment, knew that someone like her would never get involved with someone with his past.

But none of that stopped him from watching the drive with eagle eyes.

And there they were, the Subaru throwing up a trail of dust behind it as it came up the drive.

The doctor parked halfway between the house and barn and almost before the tires had stopped spinning, both back doors popped open and the kids jumped out. The little girl let out a wild war-whoop.

He grabbed the riding helmets he'd dug out of the barn tack room and met them near the car, holding his free hand up.

The kids skidded to a stop, their boots creating small puffs of dust.

"Hi, Dan!" Julianne chirped.

Brady jerked his chin.

"Hi, guys."

Dan waited for the doctor to join them. She wore jeans that were so stiff, they looked like the could stand up by themselves. Must be brand new.

"I was going to stop by the ranch house, but I didn't see any trucks outside. How's Kelsey? Do you know?"

"Last I heard, she'd seen her regular doc and the baby was fine. She's still on bed rest."

He'd been immeasurably relieved when Matt had shared the news.

"You ready to do this?" he asked.

The doc's smile faded.

He might've balked when Nate had given him orders for this, but he wouldn't do the job halfway. And step one was to help allay her fears. He couldn't forget how she'd cringed at the rodeo.

"Before we introduce ourselves to the horses, let's talk."

"Good," the doc said. "Rules."

Julianne looked at him wide-eyed.

Brady slid a glance to his aunt. The easy smile he'd arrived with faded.

"More like guidelines," Dan said. "Horses are a lot of fun.

They can be your best friend. They also have their own personalities. Do you know what a personality is?"

Julianne's head tipped to the side. "Is that like how I'm happy all the time and Brady is so grumpy all the time?"

Ouch. Rough words, but Brady *did* have an excuse, losing both of his parents.

The doctor rested one hand on Brady's shoulder. Maybe she was thinking the same thing. "That's kind of it. It's more like the way you"—she focused on Julianne—"make quick decisions. Quick friendships. And Brady"—she turned her focus to the boy—"likes to think about things. To make sure he understands how things work before he decides."

Dan had guessed right. The kids would match up well with the horses he'd chosen. The doc...? That would remain to be seen.

"The more time you spend with a horse," Dan said, "the more you get to know them. Just like your human friends. And when you know a horse, you can tell if something unusual is going on. A horse can feel sick. Or get a rock in its shoe—just like you. If you think something's wrong with your horse, you should tell an adult immediately."

Both kids nodded gravely.

"Let's talk a minute about personal space." Dan shifted the helmets in his hand. So far the doctor hadn't counted. "Do you like it if one of your friends puts their hand in your mouth? Or pokes you in the eye?"

"No!" Julianne laughed.

"So let's not do that to the horses, okay?"

The kids nodded solemnly.

"One more important thing about space. Don't walk directly behind a horse. Any horse. It's better to give a horse a lot of space or walk in front. A horse has really powerful legs, and it can't see you when you're behind it. Believe me, you don't want to be back there if the horse decides to kick."

There was the doc's frown. He hurried on.

"Horses have special diets. Don't feed them unless you have permission. You can bring a treat from home next time. For now..." He reached into his pocket and drew out the carrots he'd sliced up earlier. "Put a few in your pockets."

He handed some to each kid, who eagerly stuffed them in their jeans' pockets.

He extended two carrot sticks to the doc, and their fingers brushed when she took them. Her hair wisped around her face in the breeze. A sweet scent carried to him—her perfume? Or maybe shampoo. There was a smudge of ink on her jaw, and his fingers itched to wipe it away.

"I hate carrots," Julianne muttered.

Dan quickly shoved away the wave of attraction that hit him low in the belly. He couldn't get distracted. He cleared his throat. "Couple more things to discuss, then you can meet the horses."

Brady's eagerness had returned.

"Horses can get scared, just like you can. Don't run or shout or be wild maniacs when you're around them. Capice?"

There were those twin nods again.

"Do you think a horse speaks English?" he asked Julianne.

"Nu-uh."

He turned his gaze on Brady. "What about you?"

The boy considered, eyes slightly narrowed. "Maybe a few words. Like commands?"

"Yeah. Good. But the biggest way you're going to communicate with them is your body language. And your legs, once you get in the saddle."

Julianne's nose scrunched. "What's body language?"

"It's how you hold yourself, short stuff," he told her. He made a show of slouching down, shoulders hunched. "If you walk up to a horse looking like this, the horse might think you're scared or don't have very much confidence." He straightened, standing tall. "If you stand and walk like this, the horse will know you believe in yourself. You're the boss. You're strong and confident and ready to ride."

While he'd been talking, Brady's spine had straightened incrementally. Julianne was already there, but her chin was up. The child exuded joy.

"Y'all ready to do this?"

The kids opened their mouths as if they were going to cheer, but they quickly stifled it.

"Yeah," said Brady gruffly.

"All right. Here's your headwear." He handed the black riders' helmets to Brady and Julianne and then quickly plopped the third one in the doctor's hands.

Her eyes widened instantly. He saw the word *no* form on her lips. He took the helmet back, spun it in his hands, and placed it gently on her head.

"Yeah! Aunt Megan's going to ride!" Julianne did a little jig at his side.

He reached for the buckle that went beneath her chin. His fingers brushed the softness of her skin, and he froze.

Megan's hands came up, but his tangled fingers blocked her, preventing her from pulling the helmet off.

He got caught in her eyes. Bright and intelligent and scared.

He cleared his throat, trying to break free of her tractor beam but not quite able to do it. He kept his voice low. "You don't want them to be afraid, do you?"

He could feel the kids watching them, but he still couldn't look away. Waiting to see what their aunt would do. Chicken out? Or accept his dare?

THE COWBOY WAS PLAYING DIRTY.

There was no way she was getting on a horse. But she couldn't say no to a dare.

And he'd dared her good.

"Fine," she whispered through trembling lips.

He smiled, though it wasn't smug. In fact, it seemed almost as if he were... proud of her. He tapped beneath her chin with one finger.

One of the horses blew, and it seemed to startle him out of the moment. His eyes were shadowed as he backed away.

Megan buckled the helmet as she followed the trio to the corral and the three horses that waited there. When they'd driven up, she'd stupidly thought that he meant to ride with the kids.

Not her.

She'd wanted to call the whole thing off the entire drive out, but every time she'd glanced in the rearview mirror, she'd seen Brady's face. She hadn't seen this level of happiness since before Emma's death. Ever since she'd told them about the riding lessons, he'd been steadier at home. Maybe this was what they needed.

Even though she had serious reservations, she couldn't take this away from him. Surely the cowboy wouldn't put her kids in danger.

She'd been reassured when he'd handed out the helmets. Until he dropped one in her hand.

The corral had two rails and the cowboy ducked through the open middle, motioning for the kids to follow.

Megan hung back.

"Coming, doc?" Dan asked.

She sighed and slipped between the rails.

Up close, the horses were even bigger than she'd expected. They all had reins draped over the corral railing. Were they even tied off?

"This is Tad," Dan said to Brady. He rubbed the neck of a huge blond horse with a dark mane and socks. "He's a buckskin."

He was huge, almost twice Brady's height.

Megan wanted to call her nephew back. The words stuck in her throat as Brady held out one hand. The horse didn't move at first. Dan whispered something to Brady that she couldn't hear. The boy was as still as a statue.

Several moments passed. And then the horse took a cautious sniff of Brady's hand. She watched as Dan helped Brady feed the animal a carrot, gave him some additional instructions, and then took Julianne's hand in his big one to introduce her to Peanut.

"She's so pretty," Julianne whispered. The horse was white with big brown splotches. Or maybe brown with big white splotches.

"She's what's called a pinto."

Julianne wrinkled her nose. "Like the bean?"

"Just like that, kid."

The mare snuffled Julianne's T-shirt.

Before she was ready, the cowboy strode toward Megan.

His eyes took her measure, and apparently she wasn't telegraphing her terror adequately, because he took her elbow and walked her over to the huge brown beast that remained without a rider.

"Relax," he whispered. "What's the worst that could happen? You fall off. And get back on."

"Lots of things could happen if I fall off," she said. Were her teeth chattering? She eyed the horse standing still at the railing.

"A twisted ankle. Sprained ankle. Broken ankle. Sprained wrist. Broken wrist. Concussion. Spinal cord injury."

She tore her eyes from the horse and looked at the cowboy.

The corners of his mouth were twitching. She should probably be thankful he wasn't outright laughing. "That's quite a list."

"I wasn't done. I worked in an ER before we moved here."

Something shifted in his expression. She didn't know whether it was a good or bad reaction. He smiled, but it didn't quite reach his eyes—not like before.

"You got that carrot slice? Come and meet AC."

"Girl or boy?"

"He's a gelding."

He nudged her forward when her feet didn't want to move. Stayed at her side as they approached the horse's head. She could almost feel his big, warm body walking just behind her.

Dan took her hand in his, his warmth shocking against her ice-cold extremities. He put the carrot in her palm and raised it toward the horse.

"What if he bites me?" she whispered.

"He won't."

He was right. The horse lipped up the carrot with the gentlest *whuffle* she'd ever experienced.

Slowly, almost like they were dancing, Dan moved her hand to the horse's cheek. His palm covered her hand, pressing it into the horse's coat.

Her heart rushed in her ears.

It was maybe the most intimate experience she'd ever had. Dan was good at leading.

She couldn't resist turning her head, meeting his eyes.

He seemed to realize just how close he was standing because he quickly backed off.

"Ready to mount up? Doc goes first."

She wasn't ready at all, but he boosted her into the saddle anyway, taking time to adjust her stirrups.

She clutched the saddle horn. Why had she ever agreed to this?

"What does AC stand for?" Her voice sounded high and far away, as if she were having an out-of-body experience.

The cowboy grinned at her right knee. "I don't think you want to know."

She swallowed hard. "Tell me."

"Same thing AC stands for at your house."

Air Conditioner.

"Because he likes to be pampered?" she murmured.

"Nope." Another one of those grins. They were lethal in their potency.

He held up the two thin leather strips, offering them to her.

She couldn't pry her hands off the saddle horn, and he seemed to realize she was at the end of her abilities. He touched her knee even as he wheeled the horse away from the corral railing.

She left behind her balance and weaved left before it caught up again.

They were just plodding along. It could barely be called a walk.

He squeezed her knee, one point of comfort. "So you worked in the ER, doc?"

She breathed in noisily. "Four years, not including my residency."

"Did you like it?"

She took her eyes off AC's ears to look at the horizon as her memories helped with the answer. "Yes. There were quiet times, but mostly it kept me on my toes."

"Lots of different kinds of cases?"

"Yes." The sun was dipping behind the horizon, casting the sky with layers or orange, red, and pink.

"Bet it was a lot different than practicing in Taylor Hills."

"In some ways. There are a lot of good things about practicing here. And it was necessary."

The sudden lump in her throat surprised her, and she cut her gaze to the cowboy, who was gazing up at her. His Stetson shadowed his eyes, and she couldn't get a good read on him.

Once again, he was putting that careful distance between

them. He'd been doing it since they'd met. She still didn't know why. It didn't diminish her attraction, only added an air of mystery.

"You did good, Doc."

And she realized they'd turned a complete circle in the corral and were approaching the kids, waiting by their borrowed horses.

"Who's next?"

"You can call me Megan, you know."

Dan looked over his shoulder. The kids were on the outside of the corral, saying goodbye to their new best friends. Fast friends after only ninety minutes.

Dusk was falling.

He was hauling the last of the three saddles, plus bridle and blanket, back to the barn. He'd kind of hoped the doctor wouldn't feel as if she had to say goodbye and if he delayed long enough, she'd be gone when he exited the barn.

But she was following him. Jogging to eat up the distance between them.

Dread sat in his gut like a sinking weight.

He stopped and faced her, kept the saddle in his arms like a shield. He needed protection from her, from this attraction he felt for her. An hour and a half together, and he'd memorized the curve of her smile, the slight dimple in her right cheek. Now, fireflies twinkled behind her. They couldn't help noticing her, too.

"You keep calling me doc, but I'd like it if you called me Megan."

Her expression was so open that it made him ache to his bones. She didn't know about his incarceration. He didn't know for sure, but after about the fifth admiring glance she'd sent him tonight, he figured she couldn't.

He'd gotten too close.

"I don't think that's a good idea," he said.

She drew up short, several yards between them. "Why not?"

She didn't beat around the bush. One of the things he liked about her.

He gritted his teeth against the bile roiling in his throat. He didn't want to watch her face close down when she found out.

But like everything else since his release, he faced it head on. What else could he do?

"I'm a little surprised Rene or one of your other patients hasn't told you about me."

She looked perplexed, and he took a deep breath, one that rattled his insides. "I'm an ex-con. I spent three years in prison. For theft."

She flinched.

He hadn't thought his gut could fist any tighter.

His voice shook as he finished it. "You're better off staying as far away from me as possible."

Twilight was falling, and it was hard to read her expression. There was a beat of silence, then she spoke quietly. "If that's how you feel, why give us riding lessons at all?"

"My boss ordered me to do it." It was true, but it didn't explain the joy Dan had experienced being around the trio. He'd experienced more peace tonight than he had in years.

The itch had even disappeared for a time, though it was back now with a vengeance.

"I see." But there was something in her tone he didn't recognize. "Thank you for the lessons."

She turned and walked toward her car, calling for the kids.

He couldn't watch them leave, so he turned to take the last saddle to the barn.

He blamed the hay dust for the burn in his eyes.

Megan and those kids were special. And they'd just walked out of his life. Probably forever, now that she knew.

Chapter Six

Megan wasn't surprised that she found Julianne huddled beneath Brady's sheet with him, a flashlight shared between the two of them.

Tonight's riding lesson had been the highlight of their entire summer.

"Rules," she reminded them.

Brady only mocked her a little, and both kids complied.

Megan kissed both kids a final time and sent the girl back to her room. She confiscated the flashlight for good measure.

But when she settled into her own bed, neither the book on her bedside table nor the late-night TV show could hold her attention.

She'd showered, washed away the scents of the ranch. But not the memory of the cowboy.

I'm an ex-con.

She'd flinched away from Dan's words and the message they carried. She'd been shocked. Hadn't known what to say, what to do.

He didn't seem like a criminal. Didn't act sleazy or secretive.

Wouldn't someone who intended to continue in criminal pursuits keep it a secret instead of telling her outright?

Some of the things that had puzzled her had clicked into place. How he'd flinched from her touch. That his tetanus vaccination was current, though it hadn't been on his chart. The shadows in his eyes.

You'd better stay away from me.

But the barn light had been shining on his face from one side, and his expression had been almost... desperate.

There was a part of her that did want to protect the children. But she didn't think Dan was dangerous.

She was sure there were folks in town who'd be happy to gossip about him. She could find out whatever she wanted to know if she asked around. But that made *her* feel sleazy.

And anyway, whatever he'd done, he'd paid for. And it seemed as if the man needed a friend.

Which was ridiculous, wasn't it? He was a grown man. He had a steady job on the ranch. He was surrounded by cowboys.

But when she'd stitched him up for the second time there'd been plenty of tension between him and Nate.

He'd been kind to Brady and Julianne.

Challenged Megan to ride.

Had them laughing and comfortable in the saddle in an hour.

And he was an ex-con.

A KNOCK on Dan's door roused him.

It was dark outside.

He'd just been dropping off to sleep, but now his heart was pounding as if one of the prison guards had come to drag him from his cell.

Light from his nightstand clock glared in his eyes. He rubbed his face, trying to clear away the cobwebs.

Someone knocked again.

"Yeah?" His voice emerged rough.

"Call for you on the house phone." Matt's voice came through the door. "You can take it in the office if you want."

He kicked his legs out of the bed and opened the door. Matt was still standing there, a questioning look in his eyes.

Dan raised his brows, and the other man shrugged, turning to go upstairs. Which left Dan to pad down the hall to Matt's office.

Previously Gideon's office.

And the scene of Dan's crimes. He hadn't been in here since he'd returned to the Triple H.

He hesitated on the threshold, eyeing the phone lying off its receiver on the desk.

Who was it? One way to find out.

He slipped into the room and picked up the receiver. "'Lo?"

"Hi, Dan."

Her voice was warm and sweet through the line, and he had to close his eyes against the rush of emotion.

"Hi, Doc. What can I do for you?" He steeled himself for *we won't be continuing our lessons* or *we'll have to reschedule*.

"It's Megan."

Megan. Not *Dr. Fuller.*

A hot knot rose in his throat.

"I just wanted to call and confirm that Saturday still works for our next lesson."

Seriously?

"Are you sure you want to do that?" he asked, unable to keep the words in.

"Are you kidding? Julianne's already snuck into Brady's room twice tonight. They're pumped."

The kids. But what about her?

There was an awkward pause.

Then, "We're new in town," she said with a soft catch in her voice. "And we can use all the friends we can get. And I was thinking... maybe you could use a friend, too."

Friends.

He wanted that more than he'd let himself want anything since the sheriff had shown up at his door three and a half years ago.

And that scared him. He had a history of being a screw-up.

But he found himself saying, "Yeah," through a thick throat. "I could use a friend or three."

Chapter Seven

THE KIDS HAD TAKEN TO RIDING LIKE FLEAS TO A DOG.
A month after that first lesson and they were racing across the
fields.

Today Megan had taken the afternoon off from the clinic—
and relaxed her rules, just this once.

She was still working on trusting in the training, trusting the
horses like Dan seemed to.

If she blinked for too long, she could still see the imagined
images of Brady or Julianne falling from a galloping horse and
suffering irreparable harm.

Today Dan had surprised them by bringing Miles and Scarlett Markson—Carrie Hale's daughter—who was Julianne's age.
The two additions to the party had been saddled up and waiting
for them for Brady and Julianne's first long out-of-corral ride.

Now the four children were outpacing Dan and her badly,
but Dan seemed content to stay beside her.

She wouldn't say she'd made her peace with AC, but she
wasn't as afraid of the animal as she had been.

She liked the man much more than she should.

The surprise he'd planned for this afternoon ride was only
one example of his consideration.

"That was real nice of you to visit Kelsey," he said.

Megan smiled. "I always like to meet new patients. Emmalei

is adorable." Kelsey's delivery had been two weeks early, but mom and baby were healthy and back home on the ranch. Megan loved well-baby checkups, and since Kelsey and Matt were first-time parents, guessed she'd see them in the office frequently.

"It won't be long until you're giving her riding lessons."

He snorted.

"Did you visit in the hospital?" she asked.

He shook his head. "Had to hold down the fort here."

She couldn't remember a time he'd mentioned leaving the ranch, going to town or anywhere else.

Brady wheeled his horse away from the other three and started back toward them.

Her pulse spiked. Was something wrong?

She must've goosed AC by accident, because the horse picked up speed, making her bounce in the saddle.

"Whoa, there." The cowboy beside her didn't get ruffled at all but reached out with one long arm and snagged the horse's reins under its chin, drawing him back to a walk.

"AC wants to gallop," Dan said.

"Let him." Her heart was racing from the terrifying jolt. "I can wait here. You can pick me up on your way home. Or I'll walk."

He grinned, and her stomach flipped. "Then you'd miss the surprise." He patted one saddlebag.

"Another one?"

He only kept that grin in response.

Brady circled around and joined them, comfortable on his horse like she could only dream of being. "Miles said he still needs a roping partner for the rodeo next month. D'you think you could teach me, Dan?"

Dan's glance slid to her. "That depends on your aunt."

She lifted her hand that wasn't holding the reins, then immediately snatched the leather strap again. She wasn't quite ready for one-handed. "I'll think about it, okay?"

Brady's fist shot up into the air. "Yes!"

He nudged his horse to a smooth canter and caught up with the other children.

"Julianne will be next," she warned the cowboy. "Two days

ago, she'd wrangled three of my kitchen chairs into the living room and set up a barrel course for herself."

Dan watched Brady ride off, smiling. "I've started calling her Turbo. They're good kids."

"I wish I could take the credit," she said. Watching Brady, a wave of grief hit hard, and she had to blink back tears. Her voice was husky when she spoke. "He's a lot like his mom. Emma was... She never made a decision without considering every angle. When she made a joke, it was always so unexpected that you couldn't help laughing. Julianne is more like her dad."

"Were you and your sister close?"

She felt the weight of his gaze on her. Curious, compassionate. And warm.

"Yes. Our parents were... workaholics, I guess. Slaves to their practices. They were both surgeons. Emma was five years older and pretty much raised me."

"So you followed in the family business?" he asked quietly. "What about Emma? Was she a doctor too?"

"The only thing she ever wanted to be was a mom. And she was a good one."

A sniffle caught her by surprise. She passed a hand under her eyes. Laughed a little at her own silliness.

"I went to eight years of medical school. Passed my residency. But I don't know what kind of clothes to buy Julianne for when she starts school in the fall. Brady and I butt heads all the time. I don't know how to reach him anymore, now that I'm his guardian and not just his aunt."

Dan was riding so close that his knee bumped hers. "You're kidding, right? Anybody can see how much you love those kids. Like they were your own."

She looked at him. Fell into his eyes, just a little bit. Had to look away, because tears were still pricking her eyes. "I just feel so inadequate sometimes. I can't quit worrying that they'll get hit by a car while riding their bikes or fall down a manhole."

She caught the skeptical raise of his brow. Laughed a little at herself. "I know. In Taylor Hills?" She shook her head. "Some of the things I saw in the ER..."

She took in the idyllic scene, the backs of horses and children ahead. On this path, on this beautiful summer day, it was hard to believe there was such tragedy in the world.

"How did your sister die?"

She'd experienced enough tragedy to know it always hit when you least expected it. She swallowed hard. "She and Riley were in a car accident. A head-on collision with a drunk driver."

They'd been DOA. She'd read all the reports. The police report, the paramedics' report, the coroner's report. All of it. She'd had nightmares for weeks afterwards.

"Maybe..." Dan said, "maybe you've had a trauma too. Because of the way they died. The suddenness. And maybe in your heart, you know that those things you're afraid of are a little ridiculous. But the trauma is making everything seem so critically important."

She'd never considered that before.

"And maybe in a few months, or in a year, you'll start to worry less."

A silence fell between them, a comfortable one, as she thought about the cowboy's words. Was she projecting fatal accidents onto the kids because of Emma's accident?

"I kind of wondered if it was because I haven't gone through any of the things normal parents go through." She let her eyes track the kids' progress as they approached a farm pond flanked by trees. "I wasn't there when they took their first steps." She looked at Dan. "I haven't had any of those little milestones with the kids."

"You were there when they learned how to ride."

She looked up at him. He was right.

He reached out touched her knee. "Nobody expects you to be perfect at this parenting thing. Except maybe yourself."

DAN COULDN'T BELIEVE how strong Megan was.

The two of them caught up to the kids, and after everyone had watered their horses, they tied off the animals.

Earlier, he'd prepped wood for a campfire in a rock ring that the Hales and Marksons used for cookouts. Now, he brought out the graham crackers, chocolate bars, and marshmallows he'd stashed in his saddlebag. The kids' resounding cheer gave him a sense of joy he hadn't felt in years.

"Let me get the fire going," he said. The boys squatted near to watch while Megan and the girls went after the hand sanitizer she'd stashed in *her* saddlebag.

She was amazing.

And she didn't even know it.

She claimed she was an inadequate parent, but he'd seen her put the kids' needs first time and again.

Like leaving her ER job. She hadn't said as much, but he knew why she'd relocated to Taylor Hills. When her sister had died and left Megan custody of the kids, she'd given up the job she loved to take on family practice here. She could spend more time with the kids, have more of a life.

But she'd given up what she loved.

She'd faced her fear of riding in order to give the kids confidence for their lessons. She was a fair rider herself, would be even better when she loosened up a little.

As far as he was concerned, she had nothing to worry about.

Give her another year or so, and she'd meet a nice guy, get married, and add some kids of her own.

The thought of her dating and marrying burned in his gut like a red-hot branding iron. He liked her too much. In the month they'd spent time together on the ranch, she'd become the friend she'd promised.

He'd let his mind wander too much. His feelings had gone far beyond friendship.

He wanted to think it was because he was starved for companionship, being so isolated here on the ranch.

But it was probably the woman herself.

Now she and the girls approached. Megan squirted the boys' hands first, then approached Dan where he squatted near the fire. It was really too hot for a fire this early in the day, but he didn't want to be near the water when the mosquitos got busy at sundown.

She laid her hand on his shoulder.

He'd finally stopped flinching at her touch. But every touch she gifted him with made him crave more. He'd started dreaming about what it might be like to kiss her.

He was pitiful.

She squeezed his shoulder and held out the tiny bottle of sanitizer.

He couldn't help a quirk of his lips but allowed her to squirt a dollop onto his big palm. First time for everything.

The girls were sitting on a big log stripped of bark a few feet back from the fire, where they whispered and giggled about who knew what.

"Can we roast our marshmallows now?" Brady asked.

"Not yet," Miles answered before Dan could. "You gotta get the right amount of red-hot coals at the bottom. That's the best place to roast your mallow."

Dan chuckled at the kid's expert roasting advice.

Twenty minutes later, the kids were eating their first sticky s'mores and hamming it up. They were a good match. Miles and Brady. Scarlett and Julianne.

One thing he hadn't considered when hatching this plan was that it left him paired with Megan. Without the kids as a distraction, her focus slid to him.

And he wasn't sure he wanted to know what she saw.

He pushed up from the log he'd been leaning against. "I'm going to check the horses." He pointed a finger at Julianne. "Don't hog all the chocolate."

She giggled, marshmallow and chocolate sticky on her face.

He hadn't counted on Megan following him. Her boots crunching in the long, dry summer grasses gave her away.

"Thank you for this," she said.

"Yeah, sure." Wow, he was a real winner. S'mores and a campfire. High society. She was probably used to five-star restaurants. Not a loser who couldn't leave the ranch.

Even so, her eyes were warm, and he really wanted to reach out for her, so he rounded Tad and put the horse between them. The animal was slightly restless, tail twitching, and Dan needed to make sure there wasn't a burr under his saddle or rock in his hoof before it was time to wrap up and head home.

She peered at him over the horse's back. "Do you really think the kids could be ready for the Bar O rodeo? It's only a month away."

He shrugged. "Just because they compete doesn't mean they'll win. Doesn't hurt to teach them and let them have at it."

She bit her lip. "I don't know."

He raised his brows. She might be too protective for that, but he let the offer stand.

"Are you going to compete? I heard you used to be a skilled roper."

Her unexpected question hit him like a punch in the gut. He sucked in a breath. *Used to be.*

"No."

"Why not?" She never pulled her punches.

"No partner." He'd killed any chances of that long ago. "Plus, I don't... I prefer keeping to the Triple H."

She knew why. He saw it in her eyes, but she asked anyway. "Why?"

And he didn't back down from it, even though saying it made his face get hot. "Too many folks know me. Or used to know me. I don't like it when they stare. Talk behind their hands. It's just easier to stay here and work."

She frowned. "You made a mistake. And paid for it. What's the big deal?"

"Small towns have long memories."

And his screw-ups had been happening long before the theft.

"It seems kind of... lonely."

She had no idea. Matt and Kelsey had forgiven him, somehow. Carrie and Trey, too. But he interacted with Nate more often than with the others, and that relationship was a compound fracture. Too much to repair.

Except for his time with Megan and the kids, he mostly walked around in a state of perpetual loneliness. Nowadays, his horse knew more of his secrets than any human.

"We've never talked about your childhood. Did you grow up in Taylor Hills?" she asked.

He shrugged, not really wanting to get into it. But she'd told him about Emma and about her feelings of inadequacy. Friends reciprocated, right?

"Yeah," he said. "My mom ran off when I was little. Found a

winner of a husband and left me with my grandpops. We lived in a little tin can of a trailer on the poor side of town."

He cast his eyes down because it was too hard to look at her.

"I always wanted to get out, you know? My best friend in high school got a scholarship to a D1 school, and I was jealous. I haven't seen him in years."

Last Dan had heard, Jimmy was an accountant with a wife and two kids somewhere in Kansas.

He glanced over her head. The kids were horsing around but weren't too near the fire.

"Where do you want to go?" Smart girl, using the present tense. Somehow she knew his desire to leave was as strong as ever.

He pushed his hat back on his forehead and looked up at the sky, which was just starting to purple on the eastern horizon. "I don't know. Anywhere. If I could just get free—"

He cut himself off, but he'd already said too much.

Her head tilted to one side, her eyes curious. "What do you mean?"

He exhaled noisily. "The Hales took me back, but sometimes it feels..."

She shook her head. "The Hales?"

"That's who I stole from. Ten grand."

Her expression revealed her genuine surprise.

"Don't you gossip at all?" he asked, half exasperated. It would've been easier if she'd known.

"I like to make my own judgments." Her gaze was steady.

Fine. Make him lay it all out for her.

"I'm addicted to gambling," he explained slowly. "I got myself in a heap of trouble, and when I couldn't pay back what I owed, I stole it from the Hales' bank account. They found out. I went to prison."

"They let you come back to work for the ranch?"

He still couldn't quite believe it himself.

He exhaled noisily again. "They said the slate was wiped clean, but if it is, why do I feel like the guilt is suffocating me?"

Her eyes were luminous in the falling darkness.

He needed to douse the fire and get the kids out of here before the mosquitos carried them off.

"You're trying to pay them back," she said. "That's why you can't leave."

He bared his teeth in a semblance of a grin. Of course she'd figured it out. "That, and my parole's not up. Takes a long time to earn ten K on a cowboy's wage."

MEGAN SAW MORE than Dan probably wanted her to know. Yes, he was eaten up by guilt, and he'd admitted his weakness for gambling, but she also saw the man now fighting to do what was right.

Before she could figure out a way to put that into words, a cry rent the peaceful evening.

"Aunt Megan!" Julianne's shout had Megan whirling and running back toward the fire. Had someone fallen in?

Dan outpaced her.

But it wasn't a burn that they returned to.

Brady had both hands on his throat, face white, breathing noisily. His eyes were wide and frightened. His cheeks were pouched out.

"He's choking!" Megan cried to Dan.

As she went to Brady, she barely registered Miles standing slightly behind her nephew. Scarlett was crying softly.

Julianne sounded near tears. "We were pl-playing a game. Seeing who could fit the most marshmallows in our mouths."

"He just started grabbing his throat and breathing funny," Miles added.

Marshmallows. They could melt in your throat, couldn't they?

She didn't have her medical bag, none of her tools.

But she reacted anyway.

Megan used the fingers of one hand to pry open Brady's mouth. With the other hand, she swept her fingers through his mouth, clearing wet, white blobs of sugar, letting them fall to the ground. She cleared as much as she could reach, but when she let go, Brady still struggled for breath, bending at the waist.

His lips were turning blue.

Dan was there, his hands coming around Brady's midsection from the rear. The Heimlich. Yes. Two pumps of his strong arms and Brady hacked and then spit another white blob onto the ground.

And took a deep breath.

She steadied her nephew as he straightened. Color was rushing back into his face.

He was a big kid. Nearly a preteen. But his face crumpled.

She grabbed him in a hug, squeezing him tightly. Realized his head already reached her cheek.

She could've lost him, just that easily.

Tears blurred her vision. She saw Dan step away to hug both girls, calming them.

Brady pushed away from her. He sniffled loudly, his eyes red but no tears on his face.

Miles still stood nearby, white-faced. "I'm sorry, man. That was a stupid game."

"You should never play games that involve putting food in your mouth," she snapped. She meant the words for all of them, didn't mean for her fear to manifest in such an angry tone, but she couldn't help the emotions running through her as the adrenaline drained away.

She was shaking. And she couldn't stop.

She couldn't do this.

"Excuse me." She turned and ran. Past the horses. Out into the open field. Finally stopped when her tears stole her breath and her shaking legs wouldn't carry her any longer.

She buried her head in her hands.

She'd almost lost Brady. Like she'd lost Emma.

She heard footsteps in the long grass. No way to sneak up on anybody out here.

She knew it was Dan. Felt his hesitation.

And then he stepped nearer and drew her into his arms.

She clung to him. Wept against his chest. Poured out the intense fear from just moments ago, poured out the grief she kept bottled so she wouldn't scare the kids.

He held on to her. Strong and steady, a boulder unshaken by the tempest of her tears.

Finally her sobs subsided to the occasional hiccup.

"I can't do this," she said into his soggy shirt.

He moved back slightly, enough to cup both hands against

her cheeks. He wiped her tears away with his thumbs. "Do what?"

"Be a parent. I'm not cut out for it. All my training—I completely blanked on what I should do. *You* had to do the Heimlich."

His smile was small, and soft. "I'm glad I was here. But I know if you'd been alone, you'd have still managed."

Maybe.

"And," he continued, "I hate to break it to you, but you already are a parent. A good one. Even good parents get scared sometimes."

He was so near, and her emotions were still rioting.

She really wanted to kiss him.

He must've seen the desire in her face because his expression hardened even as his eyes went hot.

But he didn't break away.

He groaned. "Megan."

She already had her arms around his waist. It didn't take much of a tug to move him closer. She raised on tiptoe, but he held himself back.

Until he groaned again and claimed her lips.

His hands were gentle, his thumbs moving against her cheeks again. He tasted like s'mores and delicious man. One of his hands cupped the back of her head, his fingers slipping into the hair at her nape. He deepened the kiss, his nose pressing against her cheek.

She could drown in his kiss. So easily.

He broke the kiss so suddenly that she was dizzy. With hands on both her shoulders, he steadied her. Then he drew away as if touching her burned him.

His eyes... something was burning him up from the inside.

"We shouldn't... I shouldn't have done that," he said.

She flinched. He noticed.

"I told you once to stay away from me." He mashed his hat on his head. "That still goes." A breath, a moment when he could've taken the words back. "I'm going to round up the kids."

He stalked off, not looking back.

Chapter Eight

DAN DUNKED HIS HEAD IN THE ICE-COLD WATER streaming from the outside faucet behind the barn.

It washed away the field dust he'd accumulated on today's long ride, but did nothing for the ache burning inside him.

He turned the off spigot, blinked water away from his eyes and shook his head like a dog.

"You really gonna let her get away?"

He stumbled, sure his ears were playing tricks on him. When he focused against the harsh mid-afternoon sunlight, he caught sight of Nate standing a couple yards away, arms crossed like they'd been the day he'd confronted Dan outside the barn.

"What?"

Maybe if he pretended he hadn't heard, his boss would go away.

"I asked if you're going to let the best thing that's ever happened to you get away. Megan," Nate drawled, as if Dan were too slow to figure out what he meant.

Dan didn't want to talk about it. Not with Nate. Not with anyone.

He only shook his head.

But Nate wouldn't be deterred. "Somebody like her wanted to be with me, I'd be all over that. What's wrong with you?"

Dan gritted his teeth. "You've made it plenty clear you don't want anything to do with me. Why don't you leave it alone?"

Nate's expression shifted from disinterest to something sharper. He stepped closer. His hands came down and fisted at his sides. "*I* made it clear?"

Anger, guilt, frustration rose up to choke Dan. Somehow he still managed to grind out, "I wish you'd just take a swing at me. Get it over with. I know I ruined our friendship. You think I don't know that? You think I don't regret it every single day?"

Nate's expression changed again. He stepped closer, and Dan braced for a punch. It would hurt, but maybe it would take some of the edge off of missing Megan.

"I don't want to punch you, you big dope. I've been waiting for you to say sorry so I can tell you I forgive you."

What?

He had?

Dan was dumbfounded. "I'm sorry." His voice emerged rough.

"I forgive you. Dope."

Nate hauled him in, not for a punch but for a man-hug. One that Dan had never let himself hope for.

Nate shoved him as he pulled out of the hug. "About time, man."

Moisture burned in Dan's eyes but he blinked it away. He could only give Nate so much ammunition.

"Come for dinner tonight," Nate said. "Kayla will set you straight about the good doctor."

Dan shook his head. "I can't."

Nate's smile faded, and his eyes narrowed.

"It's... really hard for me to leave the Triple H. There's still a part of me... it's like an itch I can never scratch. A little devil sitting on my shoulder, telling me to drive past your house and hit up the nearest casino."

Nate clapped him on the shoulder. "Admitting it is one of the steps to recovery, man. Come for dinner, and then come home to the Triple H. I'll call and check up on you, if you want. You can't stay isolated out here forever."

That Nate had slipped right back into their years-long friendship felt right. An enormous gift Dan had never expected.

But—

"It won't do any good. Siccing Kayla on me. Megan is... too good for me."

Nate laughed outright. "Welcome to the club, man. You've met Kayla, right? And Kelsey? Sarah? Carrie? Every single one of those gals is too good for the likes of us. But they love us anyway."

Dan shook his head. "Not me. I'm not..."

Nate shoved his shoulder. "You've had this thing since we were kids. Not seeing your own worth. Maybe 'cause of your mom."

Dan gritted his teeth. He hated it that the entire town knew about his family's dirty laundry.

"Putting myself out there feels like... the biggest gamble of my life. If I tell her how I feel and she doesn't want me, I lose."

"Everything." Nate nodded, expression serious now. "Been there. But what if you don't take the risk? What if you lose the best thing that's ever happened to you?"

Dan didn't know how he could bear it. A week without Megan and he felt like a zombie, barely able to get through his days. He missed her with a visceral ache.

She'd kissed him back. He kept trying to tell himself he'd imagined it. Couldn't quite convince himself.

But her emotions had been high after Brady's near-choking episode.

What if it had been a heat-of-the-moment thing?

He loved her.

But what if she felt nothing for him?

Did he have the guts to find out?

Chapter Nine

THE BAR O RODEO WAS AS DUSTY AND DANGEROUS AS the Triple H rodeo had been.

At least this time, she felt a little prepared. She had the official Texas uniform on. Jeans and boots that'd been appropriately worn-in.

She was more than a little freaked out. Her kids were getting ready to head into that arena.

Over the past month, she'd seen Dan a handful of times. She'd taken him up on his offer to rodeo-train the kids. When she'd seen him, he'd been friendly and courteous. He'd never brought up the kiss.

She couldn't stop thinking about it. His tenderness. His need, communicated so clearly through his touch, a need he never allowed himself to speak aloud.

Or maybe she was fooling herself. Maybe it had just been a great kiss, easily forgotten to him.

"Aunt Megan, do you see Dan anywhere?" Julianne asked.

The three of them were wedged between a two horse trailers on the back side of the ranch rodeo grounds, a side of the rodeo Megan hadn't seen before.

Carrie and Scarlett Markson were unloading Peanut, a task Megan felt completely unsure about. Tad already stood nearby, tied to the trailer.

At Julianne's question, Brady looked up from where he'd been stroking the animal's neck.

Megan hated to dash their hope. "Remember, he never promised to come, you guys." She didn't want them to be disappointed. When she'd brought it up during their s'mores ride, he'd had valid reasons for not wanting to leave the Triple H.

As Scarlett led the pinto down the ramp, Brady sidled up to Julianne and whispered something Megan couldn't hear. Julianne lit up, sending a not-so-covert glance at Megan.

Those two. Thick as thieves, even after she'd given in and agreed to the rodeo.

She'd started seeing a therapist after her breakdown when Brady had nearly choked. Through counseling, she'd discovered that Dan had been right. She did have lingering effects from the trauma of losing Emma and Riley. She'd been working on calming techniques to help her focus on what was real when her mind wanted to spin off into what-ifs.

She'd also put the kids in a group grief-counseling session for children. Brady had balked at first, but she'd only agreed to let him compete in the rodeo if he attended.

His reluctant attendance had turned into quiet acceptance. The sessions had helped. The kids talked about their parents more. Talked about their grief.

And sharing had opened a new facet to their relationship with Megan, and for that she was thankful.

Maybe she would be able to make this parenting thing work.

She was studiously avoiding thinking about the upcoming teen years.

And the man who had changed everything for her had all but disappeared from her life.

She was in love with Dan. He saw what no one else did. When he saw a need, he took action. And he kissed like a dream.

But apparently, he didn't want her.

Megan slipped one arm over Julianne's shoulder, catching the top of the pink sequined vest that had been a gift from Scarlett. "You're going to do great tonight."

Julianne shrugged.

That was an unusually subdued reaction.

Megan squeezed her shoulders.

"What if I fall off?" Julianne asked in a tiny voice.

"You've only fallen off once," Megan reminded her. She'd nearly had a cardiac event, but Julianne had popped right back up, corral dirt smudging her face. "If you fall off, you get back on and try again."

"I see Miles!" Brady waved over his head.

Carrie and Scarlett finished tying Peanut to the side of the trailer.

Carrie's husband Trey lugged a saddle from the truck bed parked in front of the trailer. "About ready, Turbo?" Dan's nickname for Julianne had stuck.

Carrie moved next to Megan. "We'd better go get seats. You don't want a bad camera angle."

The kids had told Megan they wanted Trey and Scarlett and Miles to stick with them outside the arena until it was their respective turns.

Kissing their cheeks and going off with Carrie was maybe the hardest thing Megan had ever done.

Carrie threaded her arm through Megan's elbow as they made their way through the crowd.

"Proud of you, mama," Carrie murmured.

When she would've climbed the bleachers, Carrie tugged her to a pair of seats in the crowded second row.

Wedged in between an old-timer in a ten-gallon hat—the same guy from the Triple H rodeo?—and a mama who seemed to know every kid's name who was riding, Megan wasn't sure she'd ever forget the anticipation bubbling inside her. She checked her phone numerous times to make sure she had the video capture loaded and ready to go.

But in the middle of all the action, her words to Julianne kept bouncing around her brain.

If you fall off, you get back on and try again.

Had she given up too easily when Dan had pushed her away?

Through college, medical school, and practicing medicine, she hadn't had time to date. If she'd had more experience with men, she might've been able to tell if he'd been sincere when he'd told her he wanted her to stay away or if he'd just said it to protect her.

She had no idea.

Just a gut feeling that they were meant to be together.

The last sheep was ushered out of the arena, and the announcer boomed over the loudspeakers that the girls' clover-leaf barrels were next.

Megan's gut squeezed.

"I think I'm more nervous than Julianne," she whispered to Carrie.

The other woman chuckled. "No doubt. She'll do fine."

One little girl rode out and traced the course pattern. She wasn't that fast.

Another one. Faster.

And then Julianne was announced.

Megan held her breath as her niece rocketed out of the gate. Her mouth was puckered in concentration, and she focused on the course. She rounded the first barrel, urged Peanut for more speed, and approached the second. The horse's flank nudged the barrel. It rocked, and Megan held her breath. If it fell, a penalty would be added to Julianne's time.

Carrie clutched her hand in her lap, the one not holding the phone/camera.

The barrel steadied.

Julianne raced around the final barrel and out of the arena.

Megan jumped to her feet, clapping and whooping. Julianne had done it! And she hadn't fallen.

She probably looked like a crazy person—or just like one of the other parents—so she quickly sat back down. The pair of seats directly in front of her cleared.

A few more riders, and then Brady and Miles would ride in the junior pairs roping.

It seemed to take forever, now that Megan had had a hint of parental victory.

And then the boys were announced. A steer raced out of its pen, and Miles and Brady gave chase on horseback.

Brady would rope first. No one would've guessed he'd only been roping for a month as the rope swung in a beautiful loop over his head. He flicked his hand, and the rope snaked out and snagged on one of the steer's horns and the side of its neck. She saw Brady's slight grimace.

"He wanted both horns," Megan whispered to Carrie.

"Still counts," Carrie returned.

Miles's rope shot out of his hands and snagged the steer's back hooves and tightened. The boys turned their horses to face each other.

The bell rang.

Brady's fist shot into the air. A good ride for him, too. Their time wouldn't win, but it had been an admirable first effort.

Megan stood, ready to go behind the arena and find the kids. Julianne approached.

"We can't leave yet!" Julianne cried. "I want to watch the grown-up girls race."

"But—"

"Hey!" Brady followed his sister, face covered with a slight sheen of sweat and dust. "Can we watch for a while, Aunt Megan? Please?"

The two of them shared a look. Something was up.

But the fact that Brady was being polite instead of sarcastic won him points. She agreed halfheartedly.

It would be a long night. They'd have to load up and return the Triple H's horses before they could go home. She'd had a busy day in the practice, a spate of summer flu cases taking up her afternoon and nearly making her late to pick up the kids.

And she needed to think through this Dan thing some more.

The kids squeezed into the now-empty seats in the row in front of Megan and Carrie. As the night wore on, they accepted congratulations from friends and acquaintances and some of Megan's patients as they passed by.

The sun set, and the arena lights came on to flood the arena. Mosquitos came out for dinner.

Megan was ready to call it quits, but as the men's pairs roping was announced, Julianne was suddenly on the edge of her seat.

And then over the loudspeaker. "Folks, I'm gonna ask your patience. We've got a special request from one of tonight's riders."

A cowboy in a light blue shirt and black hat stood on the raised platform across the arena, where the announcer and rodeo judges had been sitting all evening.

From this distance, she couldn't tell... the man looked familiar. Was that Dan? Those broad shoulders seemed familiar.

And then his voice came over the loudspeaker. "Hi, everyone." He hesitated.

And her heart was suddenly pounding. What was he doing?

"I..." He cleared his throat, the sound coming through the speakers. There was a squeal, and she thought she saw him wince. "Sorry. Some of you know my story. And some of you don't care. The fact is, I want to ask for your forgiveness for what I did almost five years ago." He swept his hat off his head. Wiped his forearm across his forehead. "That's right. You." He pointed at a random person with the hat. Pointed at someone else. "And you, too. All of you." He cleared his throat again.

Her heart was in her throat for him.

"A lot of you had a hand in my raising up, and I didn't act like a cowboy from Taylor Hills should. I got what I deserved, but a, uh..." He paused, seemed stumble over the next word. "A friend reminded me that an apology goes a long way. So I want you to know that I'm sorry for what I did. That's all."

There was another ring in the microphone. Dan handed it back to the man who must have been the announcer.

There was a smattering of applause from the bleachers. More murmuring, as if people didn't know what to do with Dan's apology.

Dan had gotten up in front of the whole town and apologized. What the heck?

She needed to find him. Talk to him.

Hold him.

She was on her feet without realizing it.

"Aunt Megan, we have to stay and watch the team roping," Julianne blurted.

Brady's eyes were a little wild.

But Carrie's hand on Megan's arm was a shock.

"Sit down," the other woman said.

Megan gestured toward the platform, but Dan had disappeared. "I have to..."

Carrie shook her head, her wide eyes trying to communicate something. "Just wait."

Just wait.

What did that mean?

"I'm gonna throw up."

Nate slapped Dan's shoulder, making his queasy stomach protest even more loudly.

"You didn't eat any supper," Nate said cheerfully. "Nothing to upchuck."

Dan had been too nervous to eat. A nervous wreck all day.

Part one of his plan had gone off without a hitch. He'd made a fool of himself but apologized to everybody at the rodeo. Word would spread around town in a matter of hours.

But that wasn't the reason for the nerves he felt right now.

He and Nate were going into the arena.

And he was going to—

"We're next," Nate said with another of those slaps to Dan's back. He was going to be bruised tomorrow.

Dan glared at him as the other man mounted up on his midnight-black gelding.

Dan's gut heaved as he mounted his own horse, the bay he'd ridden the night he'd kissed Megan.

"How come you're not nervous?" he asked Nate. "You haven't roped in years."

Nate smiled widely. "Roped *competitively*. We use our lariats nearly every day on the ranch. Nothing to worry about."

Maybe for *him*.

The competition was fierce with cowboys from ten surrounding counties.

Dan heard the announcer read their names over the loudspeaker. A whoop from the front of the stands might've been Brady. Or Miles.

And then everything was white noise except for his heartbeat and the beat of his horse's hooves as he and Nate raced into the arena.

Nate's lasso shot out first, snagging both of the steer's horns.

Dan let his go only a fraction of a second later, tagging the back hooves. The steer froze.

And the crowd went wild.

They must've posted a good time.

Dan loosed his lasso as the rodeo clowns took over with the steer, releasing it and herding it out of the arena.

Heart causing an earthquake in his chest, he turned his horse not toward the exit but toward the fence in front of the crowd.

Searching... there. Megan was just behind Julianne and Brady, wedged in next to Carrie.

He sidled up his horse in front of her. Still a couple yard away, but close enough to see she was crying, tears making silver tracks down her cheeks.

His gut plunged.

But he wasn't a stranger to doing hard things. And he was going to do this.

He took off his hat.

Brady jumped out of his seat, Julianne following.

"C'mon, Aunt Megan," Brady whispered when she didn't move.

That seemed to galvanize her. She stood, though she looked a bit shaky, and climbed over the front bleacher to stand next to the arena fence, just in front of him.

He handed her his hat. She might not know it, but a man's hat was a personal thing. He was basically giving her his heart, there for everyone to see.

She took it, and he couldn't help the relieved grin that spread across his face. The way her eyes were shining up at him...

"What are you doing?" she whispered.

"Making a declaration."

Her face turned an adorable shade of pink.

"These folks have seen me make a lot of mistakes over the years. Some big ones. I think it's about time they see me do something right, for once."

Nate wolf-whistled from somewhere behind him. Dan's smile turned wry. There were good things and bad things about having his best friend back.

"Megan, you've got my heart. And I don't want it back."

Another silver tear slipped down her cheek. Her smile was tremulous. "I'll take care of it. Promise."

He reached out for her.

She glanced at the arena fence. At his horse. At the crowd

behind her. Somebody high up in the stands shouted, "Go for it!"

And he recognized the determined look that crossed her face.

She mashed his hat on her head and started climbing.

He edged his horse sideways to the fence and caught her as she wobbled on the top railing. Pulled her across the saddle onto his lap.

And kissed her.

The crowd went wild again, cheering and whistling.

"All right, already," called a voice, interrupting the moment. One of the rodeo clowns was right there, waving Dan's hat. He hadn't realized he'd knocked it off, lost in the intensity of their kiss.

"Can we get back to business here?" the clown asked. His grumpy voice was at odds with the wide red smile painted on his face.

Megan giggled, hiding her face against his shoulder.

He took his hat from the clown, put it on, and galloped across the arena's dirt floor.

His arm solidly around her waist, Megan wasn't in any danger, but she clung to his shoulders anyway.

Outside the arena, he rode among the cowboys lined up to take their turns, the throng of bull riders waiting for the last event of the night.

Found himself getting slaps on the shoulder or the boot—depending on whether the slapper was mounted or not.

And it felt good.

After so long being separated from the town, he was home.

He rode until they reached the maze of trucks and trailers, finally pulling up where it was quiet and shadowed.

Megan looked up at him, and he couldn't help himself. He cupped her cheek and kissed her again.

Her lips were soft and warm against his mouth. She tasted like heaven. Like his future.

His horse shifted beneath them, and she broke the kiss, appropriately breathless. "I don't suppose we could get down now?"

He couldn't help smiling. "I love you."

She'd been glancing at the ground, but now her gaze returned to his, soft and sure. "I love you, too, cowboy."

He felt his smile falter as the facts crowded in. "I gave it a good start tonight, but I have a lot more of a mess to clean up around here. And I... it'll probably take me years to pay back what I owe the Hales. I have to do it."

She nodded. "But you don't have to do it alone. Not anymore."

Hot moisture burned his eyes, and he hugged her close, burying his face in her hair.

He'd never be sure what caused Lady Luck to smile on him in such a big way, but he was never letting Megan go.

Copyright © 2023 by Lacy Williams

All rights reserved.

No part of this book may be reproduced in any form or by any electronic or mechanical means, including information storage and retrieval systems, without written permission from the author, except for the use of brief quotations in a book review.

www.ingramcontent.com/pod-product-compliance
Lightning Source LLC
Chambersburg PA
CBHW051159190726
48288CB00006B/1715